CW00750040

PENGUIN]
SELECTED SHO

Mulk Raj Anand was born in Peshawar in 1905 and educated at the universities of Punjab and London. After earning his PhD in Philosophy in 1929, Anand began writing for T.S. Eliot's magazine *Criterion* as well as books on cooking and art. Recognition came with the publication of his first two novels, *Untouchable* and *Coolie*. These were followed by a succession of novels, including his well-known trilogy *The Village* (1939), *Across the Black Waters* (1940) and *The Sword and the Sickle* (1942). By the time he returned to India in 1946, he was easily the best-known Indian writer abroad.

Making Bombay his home and centre of activity, Anand threw himself headlong into the cultural and social life of India. He founded and edited the fine arts magazine *Marg*, and has been the recipient of the Sahitya Akademi Award, several honorary doctorates and other distinctions. Anand died in Pune in September 2004.

Saros Cowasjee is Professor Emeritus of the University of Regina in Canada. His published works include the novels *Goodbye to Elsa* (1974) and *My Dear Maura* (2005), critical studies on Sean O'Casey and Mulk Raj Anand, and several anthologies of fiction, including *The Oxford Anthology of Raj Stories* (2001) and *The Mulk Raj Anand Omnibus* (2004). His latest is a collection of his own fiction writings, called *Strange Meeting and Other Stories*.

Selected Short Stories

MULK RAJ ANAND

Selected and edited, with an introduction, by
Saros Cowasjee

PENGUIN BOOKS

PENGUIN BOOKS
Published by the Penguin Group
Penguin Books India Pvt. Ltd, 11 Community Centre, Panchsheel Park, New Delhi
110 017, India
Penguin Group (USA) Inc., 375 Hudson Street, New York, New York 10014, USA
Penguin Group (Canada), 90 Eglinton Avenue East, Suite 700, Toronto M4P 2Y3
(a division of Pearson Penguin Canada Inc.)
Penguin Books Ltd, 80 Strand, London WC2R 0RL, England
Penguin Ireland, 25 St Stephen's Green, Dublin 2, Ireland (a division of Penguin
Books Ltd)
Penguin Group (Australia), 250 Camberwell Road, Camberwell, Victoria 3124,
Australia (a division of Pearson Australia Group Pty Ltd)
Penguin Group (NZ), cnr Airborne and Rosedale Roads, Albany, Auckland 1310,
New Zealand (a division of Pearson New Zealand Ltd)
Penguin Group (South Africa) (Pty) Ltd, 24 Sturdee Avenue, Rosebank, Johannesburg
2196, South Africa

Penguin Books Ltd, Registered Offices: 80 Strand, London WC2R 0RL, England

First published by Penguin Books India 2006

Copyright © Mulk Raj Anand 2006
Introduction copyright © Saros Cowasjee 2006

10 9 8 7 6 5 4 3 2 1

Stories in this volume earlier appeared in the following: *The Lost Child and Other
Stories* (1934), *The Barber's Trade Union and Other Stories* (1944), *The Tractor
and the Corn Goddess and Other Stories* (1947), *Reflections on the Golden Bed and
Other Stories* (1954), *The Power of Darkness and Other Stories* (1959), *Lajwanti
and Other Stories* (1966), and *Between Tears and Laughter* (1973).

ISBN-13: 9780143062103; ISBN-10: 0143062107

Typeset in Perpetua by Mantra Virtual Services, New Delhi
Printed at Pauls Press, New Delhi

CONTENTS

Introduction

Mulk Raj Anand has long lamented in letters to friends and literary critics that little or no attention has been paid to his short stories. There is some truth here, except that Mulk himself has contributed to this neglect. Many of his short fiction anthologies, like the novels he wrote after *Private Life of an Indian Prince* (1951), were handed over to a variety of Indian publishers and published literally without being edited. His aim was to help promote Indian publishing, but some of the publishers he turned to promoted neither the industry nor the author. The stories now being presented by Penguin are from the seven collections published during the author's lifetime. A good few of them are from *The Barber's Trade Union and Other Stories* (London, 1944) and these are being reproduced as they first appeared. But stories from the later volumes called for some editing, and here every care has been taken not to tamper with the author's style and purpose. Should readers find one or more of their favourites missing from this collection, the failure is mine. But I hope such failure will go to demonstrate how rich Anand's stories are, and how difficult it is to select a few and pass them on as the author's best.

Anand's first short story, 'The Lost Child', shared a fate similar to that of his first novel—*Untouchable* (1935). Like *Untouchable*, it received several rejections before it saw publication through the intervention of friends; like *Untouchable*, its popularity remains undiminished to this day. Based on the author's own childhood experience, it is almost perfect in execution. We constantly hear and read of the agony of parents searching for their lost ones. Here we witness the traumatic experience of a child who is separated from his parents at a village fair. With deft strokes Anand portrays the sudden grief that overcomes this once happy and carefree child. A stranger, who has rescued the boy from being trampled underfoot, offers him the very toys and sweets earlier refused to him by his parents. But the inconsolable child wants none of it now. 'I want my mother, I want my father,' is all that he asks for, between sobs. The milieu, with its gay, carefree crowd, adds poignancy to the child's sense of loss.

.   The story can be read at different levels. At its simplest it is about a child's natural fear of being left alone; at its most profound, it is a metaphor for the human condition. The child in the story epitomizes our individual cravings, desires, fears, but most of all our vulnerability and dependence on one another. Anand has said that a maxim by Guru Nanak—'We are all children lost in the world fair'—was reverberating in his mind when he wrote 'The Lost Child'. This provides the essence of the story. The nameless child is the proverbial 'everyman', and the village fair is a microcosm of our universe with its beauty, joy and pleasures, but underscored by pain and insecurity.

Many of the stories are modelled on Indian folk tales and fables on which Anand grew up from his early childhood. While accepting the ancient form of the folk tale with its poetic resources and 'fabulous character', Anand discards the folk tales' overt moral teaching in favour of European psychological realism. In doing so, he attempts to create a new kind of fable, which combines the verve and vitality of the former with the psychological insights of the contemporary period. In 'The Barber's Trade Union',[*] Chandu rightfully refuses to shave the village notables who, with their unkempt beards, soon become objects of public mockery. It is a story promoting trade unionism, but it does so without our being made aware of it. The playful nature of the narration is never sacrificed to its serious intent; in fact, the words 'trade unions' are used only once in the story and that too in the last line!

'Lullaby' and 'A Village Idyll' again go to show how Anand has taken the fable mode a step further to bring it closer to our own

---

[*]   This story first appeared in John Lehmann's *New Writing*, Autumn 1936, along with Orwell's 'Shooting an Elephant', and V.S. Pritchett's 'Sense of Humour'.

times. In the former, a mother sings a lullaby to her dying one-year-old child as she feeds jute to the machine. Her song (reminiscent of Blake's 'A cradle song') 'Sleep/Oh sleep/My baby sleep . . .' is juxtaposed with the only other sounds in the factory: 'The engine chuck-chucked; the leather belt khupp-khupped; the bolts jig-jugged; the plugs tik-tikked; . . .' The child dies, and with it the human song; only the jazz of the machine goes on unbroken. The story presents us the harsh reality of life as we witness it, while in 'A Village Idyll', the very opposite of what we see is in fact true. By fantasizing the love-making of the two youthful rustic lovers in idyllic surrounding, Mulk reminds the Indian reader of what he has known all along—the stifling puritanism of Indian village life.

To his tales of East–West encounter, Anand brings his long experience of England and the English. Failure to communicate is the main reason he offers for discord between the two peoples, and he goes on to point out that no meaningful communication is possible if one side is arrogant and race-and-colour conscious, whilst the other side is given to suspicion and fear. 'Professor Cheeta' is a moving portrayal of an old and sensitive Indian academic whose life revolves round the British Museum (now called the British Library) in London. The difficulties he encounters in his daily pursuits result as much from his own eccentric behaviour as they do from the unspoken racial prejudices against him. His death causes no distress to his British wife or his English acquaintances; the reader is the only mourner he has. 'The Gold Watch' is about a dispatch clerk in a British firm in India who is informed by his English master that he has got him a watch for a present. Though no words are exchanged between the two, the clerk surmises that the gift betokens early retirement—something he can ill-afford. The panic, the fear, and the confusion that overwhelm the clerk at the possible loss of his livelihood shows Anand's capacity to get beneath the skin of his characters as few writers can.

Anand's leftest leanings and his immense sympathy with the underdog have led some readers to surmise that he is less successful when dealing with the affluent—specifically the landed gentry. This is far from being the case where his short stories are concerned. But his mode of treatment differs, since the lapses of the rich, unlike the poverty of the poor, make good subject for satire. Through ridicule, exaggeration and laughter, very much in the manner of Swift, Anand satirizes, to put it in one word, the foibles of the feudal lords. And he does so without any malice or condescension, but often with telling effect. In 'The Signature', the author pokes fun at the Indian nobility's outdated and extravagent ways of welcoming a guest, which often leaves the guest—in this case a banker in search of the Nawab's signature—distraught. The Nawab emerges at the end as irresponsible, though as affable as ever. But not all feudal lords are irresponsible or retrogressive, the author tells us. In 'The Tractor and the Corn Goddess', a forward-looking zamindar imports a tractor to make life easier for his tenants. But his tenants will have none of it. They are aghast at this 'new monstrosity', which, as they see it, has 'desecrated' and 'raped' the Corn Goddess, namely, mother earth. Not till it is dismantled completely, to ensure that no evil spirit is lurking within it, do the villagers accept it. The story, like 'The Power of Darkness'*, is essentially one of conflict between modern technology and the old way of life with its religious sanctions.

The two most amusing stories in this group are 'A Pair of Mustachios' and 'The Maharaja and the Tortoise'. The former satirizes fatuous pride through the altercation between a crafty moneylender and a proud nobleman, Khan Azam Khan, now fallen on evil times. The Khan comes to pawn his wife's nose ring and turns furious on seeing the moneylender wearing a moustache in a style resembling his own—rather than one with the tips down, as befits his lowly status. An argument follows between the indignant Khan and the cunning moneylender who, with imperturbable calmness, soothes his adversary's ruffled pride. He promises to keep the tips of his moustache for ever down if the latter will, in return for the favour, pawn the rest

---

*   This story, as well as 'Little Chics', 'Poem of Pity' and 'The Dove and the Crow', mentioned later in the introduction, are not part of this collection.

of his worldly possessions. The Khan agrees and, twisting his upturned 'tiger moustache', walks away, thus disproving the old adage that pride goes before a fall.

'The Maharaja and the Tortoise' is equally hilarious, though it lacks the simplicity and directness of the previous story. Here, a wily Prime Minister persuades the opium-addicted Maharaja to get a tank constructed and filled with water from the holy Ganges so that oblations and prayers can be offered to facilitate his journey from this world to the next. While performing the religious ceremony with his feet in the water, a tortoise bites off the big toe of the Maharaja. Regal rage is at its height, and a royal decree is issued to fetch the culprit who will be tried by the Ruler himself—the Ruler assuming the roles of both plaintiff and prosecutor. The story reminds one of Flora Annie Steel's 'At the Great Durbar'. In this story, a Sikh farmer, whose crops have been destroyed by rats, sets out to seek the Viceroy to tell him why he cannot afford to pay the taxes. To make his case foolproof, he takes along a captured rat, for the law requires the presence of both plaintiff and defendant!

Two other stories in this collection carry the author's impish sense of humour still further. 'The Liar', included by Salmon Rushdie in *The Vintage Book of Indian Writing: 1947–1997* (1997), is unalloyed comedy, with no instructions to the reader but to delight himself. In fact it is not at all about lying, for the quick-witted shikari, though from the sweeper class, is a poet—a man of imagination—who uses his native genius for storytelling to find sustenance in a caste-conscious society. Even at times of undeniable despair, the poet in the shikari weaves a world of fantasy and bewitchment. Lying limp on a broken string bed, he recalls his last expedition, where the sahibs wasted hundreds of cartridges while he killed tigers and panthers galore. And that wasn't all, for he 'saw a monster, which had the body of a bear, the head of a reindeer, the feet of a goat, the tail of a wild bull . . .' He knew it to be a Nepalese princess whom he must rescue from the clutches of a magician and take home as his wife, but the sahibs spoilt it all with their volleys of rifle fire! What could one expect from sahibs?

'The Hangman's Strike' offers a sampling of Anand's comic satire at its funniest, and deadliest. When Buta, a professional hangman, sees millions of amateur hangmen of two World Wars being awarded medals and land for a job in which he obviously is more skilful, he goes on a sit-down strike for a raise in pay. Buta is sentenced to six months rigorous imprisonment for his aberration, it being argued that without a hangman on hand, the very foundations of law and order are undermined. Accidentally, the date of his release coincides with the release of some Congressites who had been jailed for non-cooperation. The jubilant crowd that comes to welcome the Congressites, mistakenly garlands Buta as well and hails him as a true Gandhian for adhering to the doctrine of ahimsa and abjuring his post of hangman! Beneath the vibrant humour, there is a serious message. The story, like Orwell's 'The Hanging', pleads for the sanctity of life, but without the slightest hint of propaganda.

Though Anand paints a wide section of humanity, perhaps the widest ever for an Indian writer, he is best known for his portrayal of the very poorest in India—be they peasants or city-dwellers. He is able to enter into their most intimate sensations and emotions and reveal them, as it were, in the raw. In this respect, 'Old Bapu' remains unsurpassed. It is the story of what passes through the mind of old Bapu, a decrepit outcast who trudges seven miles in sweltering heat for a road-repair job only to be told there are none available. Exhausted, he turns to quench his thirst at a pan-biri shop, but from here too he is asked to move on while he examines his shrivelled-up face in the shop's mirror. 'Oh, ja, ja, ahead,' said the pan-biri wallah. 'Don't break my glass by showing it your ugly, old face.'

Anand often interpolates English and Hindi words, as in the above quote, to bring authenticity and Indianness to his dialogue. Indian phrases and idioms are also translated into English to convey the nuances and inflections of Indian speech. In 'A Rumour', a story almost identical to 'Old Bapu' in its theme and treatment, we find literal translations such as 'illegally begotten', 'the son of a donkey', 'the sinews of an owl!'. 'A Promoter of Quarrels' is another story particularly rich in such translations. Here, two cowherd women exchange abuse with a deceitful confectioner to whom they come to sell their milk. Anand has a gift of handing out insults left and right in any quarrel he sets up for his characters, and the repartee between the more spirited among them has an astonishing sprinkling of Indian idioms and proverbs literally translated into English. Phonetic spelling of English words as used by the semi-literate Indians, such as 'Dipty Collator' in 'The Parrot in the Cage', is another effective device in Anand's repertoire to make his portrayals seem essentially Indian.

In Anand's fiction, both novels and short stories, people leave the village for the city in the hope of finding a better life. But none succeed, and few return home. As for the city-dweller, what the elephant-driver told Munoo in *Coolie* (1936) is even more applicable today: 'The bigger the city is, the more cruel it is to the sons of Adam.' In 'Things Have a Way of Working Out', Anand gives a frightening picture of the homeless searching for sleeping space on the pavements and porches of the rich in the rain-swept Bombay of the monsoons. The opening is a masterpiece of irony, where two young waifs from a village argue over the number of Cadillacs in Bombay as they hunt for a niche to spend the night. One of them wishes he were back in the village, to which the other retorts:

> Salé! You were always a coward and a coward you will remain in spite of your bragging! . . . You know that nothing can be done here without difficulties. But we should forget about our villages and towns, with their narrow lanes and wretched little hovels, full of rats. Why, we have electricity here, and filums and shops and motors and aeroplanes . . .'

What keeps the poor going are their illusions, no less than their courage, and Anand extracts every ounce of irony from the situations his characters find themselves in. Young or old, and despite all odds, his characters fight on till their last breath. Suicide is never a solution, and in the thirty-two stories in this book, there is only one that deals with suicide. The act is abortive and the heroine's last words are, 'There is no way out for me. I am condemned to live . . .'

In Anand's sympathies for the poor, women have a special place as their suffering is the greater, owing to Hindu religion and tradition, and the strictures of a hide-bound society. A young bride, whose life has become a torment in the absence of her husband, is the subject of 'Lajwanti'—the longest story in this collection. Pursued by the lewd advances of her brother-in-law, and continuously abused by her mother-in-law, Lajwanti flees to her father's home. But the father cannot offer her protection—and lectures her that the only place for a married woman is in her in-laws' home. 'And as for you,' he tells her, 'I will take you back to your parents-in-law's house. I shall fall at their feet and ask them to forgive you. The disgrace of your widowhood without your becoming a widow is unbearable.'

Lajwanti's isolation is complete. The caged maina she carries with her is symbolic of her own situation, and her attempts to converse with the bird reveal her desperate sense of loneliness. Loneliness is also recalled in another story, 'The Parrot in the Cage', which has the partitioning of India as its backdrop. Rukmani, an old woman, migrates from Lahore to Amritsar with her sole companion, a pet parrot, having lost everything else in the Partition riots. The dialogue between the two not only emphasizes the old woman's loneliness, but also shows the empathy that Anand sees between man and animals. In addition, 'The Parrot in the Cage' reveals Anand's distaste for violence, for it is free of the killing and bloodshed so often associated with Partition stories. The horror of the event is conveyed artistically by what is left unsaid, as in 'After the Storm' by Attia Hosain—a novelist for whom Anand had profound respect.

Mulk's great love of animals is an extention of his love and concern for the inarticulate poor: for Bapu in 'Old Bapu', Dhandu in 'A Rumour', Rukmani in 'The Parrot in the Cage', and Lajwanti in the story of the same name. Anand is the spokesperson of the defenseless, of all those who cannot fend for themselves, and animals especially fall into this category. Three of the five pieces in his 'Five Short Fables' are not so much fables as brilliantly realized depictions of a dove, a crow, a peacock and a cockerel; all results of his deep affection for life other than human. The animal kingdom's natural fear of 'the beast called man' is brought out in 'Little Chics'; and in the 'Poem of Pity' we see the nonchalant attitude of the average human towards the death of an animal—in this case a buffalo.

Anand's success with his animal stories lies in his uncanny ability to enter into the mental processes of animals and to make us aware of what they might be wondering without striking a false note. In the fable 'The Dove and the Crow', the dove's fears and responses, as portrayed by Anand, are completely within the bounds of credibility. But it is in 'A Dog's Life' that Anand reveals his immense power of observation by delving into the mind of a stray dog to imaginatively reconstruct its pain, its helplessness, and its dependence on man. The story is among the most autobiographical of his writings in so far as he examines candidly, and with an astonishing degree of honesty, his own responses to seeing the dog meet its end at the hands of a beggar:

> I tried to rationalize my turning away [from the dog] by thinking that, through the cruelty of the beggar, I had myself been freed from the unbearable responsibility of looking after the dog, of my hope for its life, which I had half wanted to save, if only I could find some way and means to do so, and which I did not want to save because, at the best, he would drag his hind legs about for the rest of his sordid existence.

Painful as is the plight of the dog, the story is a terrible indictment of poverty in India where a beggar sees in the dog 'a possible rival' for food, and brutally dispenses with his competitor with a blow of his staff.

Among other memorable stories in this volume are 'Duty', 'A Confession' and 'The Thief'. Anand excels in description of nature in his novels, though one sees very little of it in his short stories. 'Duty' is an exception with its masterly portrayal of the heat on a summer's day, with the sun itself becoming an antagonist in the human drama enacted on the arid plains of northern India. But the power of the story lies in its theme—that cruelty begets cruelty. Mangal Singh, a policeman on point-duty, starts dozing because of the intense afternoon heat. His superior appears on a bicycle and canes him for dereliction of duty; in turn, the policeman brutally beats up an innocent rustic who is unable to control his herd of donkeys:

> 'Oh, forgive, Sarkar, it is not my fault,' the man shouted in an angry, indignant voice while he rubbed his limbs and spread his hands to ward off more blows.
>
> 'You, son of a dog,' hissed Mangal Singh as he struck again and again, harder and harder as if he had gone mad, till his stave seemed to ring as a bamboo stick does when it is splitting into shreds.

In his defence of the peasant, Anand's anger is never wholly directed at the feudal classes whom he often considers as themselves being victims of circumstances. His ire is directed, almost unfailingly, at the oppressive Indian police, the wily and heartless moneylenders, and the greedy priests fattening themselves on the innocence and superstitions of an ignorant people. Offhand, I cannot think of a single Anand novel or story where a policeman or moneylender or priest is shown with any virtue in him.

'Mahadev and Parvati' is among Anand's strongest attacks on the priest class. A couple, on the verge of drifting apart, go on a pilgrimage to the Kumbh Fair in the hope of renewing their love. Here they fall foul of an evil priest and his tout who steal their wallet and then try to extract a huge sum of money from them. The couple finally make their escape (the husband with his arm round his wife), and the author tells us that the man 'had never felt so near her before . . .'

No discerning reader can miss the author's meaning. What brings people together is not religion but togetherness, their common suffering, and the necessity to stand beside one another and offer protection. Though himself an agnostic, Anand does not mock the simple faith of the poor in the existence of God; what he does censure is religion as exploited by the priests for their personal gain. Though Anand mellowed with the years, his view of the Hindu priest underwent little change after the publication of his first novel, *Untouchable*.

Anand's main forte has been to awaken us to the realities of life in India, which we already know but to which we have turned a blind eye. 'The Thief', somewhat unusual in Anand's writings, belongs to a different genre—one that explores the deep recesses of the human mind. The protagonist in this story feels an irresistible sexual attraction towards a dirty but shapely beggar woman who is nursing a starving child. Self-examination leads him to conclude that his lust for her, and his concern for her well-being, have their origins in a past misdeed— when he unjustly accused a beggar of theft and had him severely beaten. But more satisfying than the psychoanalysis is the twist in the story's ending. The protagonist's boy servant, who has been turned out for telling a lie (he did so only to save his master), now joins the concourse of beggars to offer protection to the woman his master coveted but lacked the courage to acknowledge. The author is tight-lipped about the theme of the story, but is he implying that true camaraderie exists only among the poor?

These stories are not without their flaws. Some readers might object to the stylistic opulence that one occasionally encounters in stories like 'Lajwanti'; others might wish that the author would get straight to his narrative without introductory remarks. There may, rightly, be other concerns as well. But artistry, honesty and compassion are not among them. And these are sufficient virtues to ensure Anand a place in the annals of the Indian short story.

Saros Cowasjee
University of Regina, Regina

The Lost Child

It was the festival of spring. From the wintry shades of narrow lanes and alleys emerged a gaily clad humanity, thick as a swarm of bright-coloured rabbits issuing from a warren. They entered the flooded sea of sparkling silver sunshine outside the city gates and sped towards the fair. Some walked, some rode on horses, others sat, being carried in bamboo and bullock-carts. One little boy ran between his parent's legs, brimming over with life and laughter. The joyous morning gave greetings and unashamed invitations to all to come away into the fields, full of flowers and songs.

'Come, child, come,' called his parents, as he lagged behind, arrested by the toys in the shops that lined the way.

He hurried towards his parents, his feet obedient to their call, his eyes still lingering on the receding toys. As he came to where they had stopped to wait for him, he could not suppress the desire of his heart, even though he well knew the old, cold stare of refusal in their eyes.

'I want that toy,' he pleaded.

His father looked at him red-eyed, in his familiar tyrant's way. His mother, melted by the free spirit of the day, was tender, and giving him her finger to hold, said, 'Look, child, what is before you.'

The faint disgust of the child's unfulfilled desire had hardly been quelled in the heavy, pouting sob of a breath, 'M-o-th-er', when the pleasure of what was before him filled his eager eye. They had left the dusty road on which they had walked so far. It wended its weary way circuitously to the north. They had come upon a footpath in a field.

It was a bowering mustard field, pale like melting gold as it swept across miles and miles of even land, a river of yellow liquid light, ebbing and falling with each fresh eddy of wild wind, and straying in places into broad rich tributary streams, yet running in a constant sunny sweep towards the distant mirage of an ocean of silver light. Where it ended, on one side stood a cluster of low mud-walled houses, thrown into relief by a dense crowd of yellow-robed men and women from whom arose a high-pitched sequence of whistling, creaking, squeaking, roaring, humming noises, sweeping across the groves to the blue-throated sky like the weird, strange sound of Shiva's mad laughter.

The child looked up at his father and mother, saturated with the shrill joy and wonder of this vast glory, and feeling that they, too, wore the evidence of this pure delight in their faces, he left the footpath and plunged headlong into the field, prancing like a young colt, his small feet timing with the fitful gusts of wind that came rich with the fragrance of more distant fields.

A group of dragonflies were bustling about on their gaudy purple wings, intercepting the flight of a lone black butterfly in search of sweetness from the flowers. The child followed them in the air with his gaze, till one of them would fold its wings and rest, and he would try to catch it. But it would go fluttering, flapping, up into the air, when he had almost caught it in his hands. One bold black bee, having evaded capture, sought to tempt him by whining round his ear and nearly settled on his lips, when his mother gave a cautionary call, 'Come, child, come. Come onto the footpath.'

He ran towards his parents gaily and walked abreast of them for a while, being, however, soon left behind, attracted by the little insects and worms along the footpath that were teeming out from their hiding places to enjoy the sunshine.

'Come, child, come,' his parents called from the shade of a grove where they had seated themselves on the edge of a well. He ran towards them.

An old banyan here outstretched its powerful arms onto the blossoming jack and jamun and neem and champak and scrisha and cast its shadows across beds of golden cassis and crimson gulmohur as an old grandmother spreads her skirts over her young ones. But the blushing blossoms freely offered their adoration to the sun, in spite of their protecting chaperone, by half covering themselves, and the sweet perfume of their pollen mingled with the soft, cool breeze that came and went in little puffs, only to be wafted aloft by a stronger breeze.

A shower of flower petals fell upon the child as he entered the grove and, forgetting his parents, he began to gather the raining petals in his hands. But lo! he heard the cooing of a dove and ran towards his parents, shouting, 'The dove! The dove!' The raining petals dropped from his forgotten hands. A curious look was on his parent's faces till a koel struck out a note of love and released their pent-up souls.

'Come, child, come!' they called to the child, who had now gone running in wild capers round the banyan tree, and gathering him up they took the narrow, winding footpath which led to the fair through the mustard fields.

As they neared the village, the child could see many other footpaths full of throngs, converging to the whirlpool of the fair, and felt at once repelled and fascinated by the confusion of the world he was entering.

A sweetmeat-seller hawked, 'Gulab-jamun, rasgulla, burfi, jalebi,' at the corner of the entrance, and a crowd pressed round his counter at the foot of an architecture of many-coloured sweets, decorated with leaves of silver and gold. The child stared open-eyed and his mouth watered for the burfi that was his favourite sweet. 'I want that burfi,' he slowly murmured. But he half knew as he begged that his plea would not be heeded because his parents would say he was greedy. So without waiting for an answer, he moved on.

A flower-seller hawked, 'A garland of gulmohur, a garland of gulmohur.' The child seemed irresistibly drawn by the implacable sweetness of the scents that came floating on the wings of the languid air. He went towards the basket where the flowers were heaped and half murmured, 'I want that garland.' But he well knew his parents would refuse to buy him those flowers because they would say they were dear. So without waiting for an answer, he moved on.

A man stood holding a pole with yellow, red, green and purple balloons flying from it. The child was now carried away by the rainbow glory of the silken colours and he was possessed by an overwhelming desire to have them all. But he well knew his parents would never buy him the balloons because they would say he was too old to play with such toys. So he walked on farther.

A juggler stood playing a flute to a snake which coiled itself in a basket, its head raised in a graceful bend like the neck of a swan, while the music stole into its invisible ears like the gentle rippling of a soft, slow waterfall. The child went towards the juggler. But knowing his parents had forbidden him to hear such coarse music as the jugglers played, he proceeded farther.

There was a roundabout in full swing. Men, women and children, carried away in a whirling motion, shrieked and cried with dizzy laughter. The child watched them intently going round and round, a pink blush of a smile on his face, his eyes rippling with the same movement, his lips parted in amazement, till he felt that he himself was being carried round. The ring seemed to go fiercely at first, then gradually it began to move less fast. Presently the child, rapt, finger in his mouth, saw it stop. This time, before his overpowering love for the anticipated sensation of movement had been chilled by the thought of his parents' eternal denial, he made a bold request, 'I want to go on the roundabout, please, Father, Mother.'

There was no reply. He turned to look at his parents. They were not there, ahead of him. He turned to look on either side. They were not there. He looked behind. There was no sign of them.

A full, deep cry rose within his dry throat and with a sudden jerk of his body he ran from where he stood, crying in red fear, 'Mother! Father!' Tears rolled down from his eyes, hot and fierce; his flushed face was convulsed with fear. Panic-stricken, he ran to one side first, then to the other, hither and thither, in all directions, knowing not where to go. 'Mother, Father!' he wailed with a moist, shrill breath now, his throat being wet with swallowing of spittle. His yellow turban came untied and his clothes, wet with perspiration, became muddy where the dust had mixed with the sweat of his body. His light frame seemed heavy as a mass of lead.

Having run to and fro in a rage of running for a while, he stood defeated, his cries suppressed into sobs. At little distances on the green grass, he could see, through his wet eyes, men and women talking. He tried to look intently among the patches of bright-yellow clothes, but there was no sign of his father and mother among these people, who seemed to laugh and talk just for the sake of laughing and talking.

He ran hotly again, this time to a shrine to which people seemed to be crowding. Every little inch of space there was congested with men but he ran through people's legs, his little sob lingering, 'Mother! Father!' Near the entrance to the temple, however, the crowd became very thick: men jostled each other, heavy men, with flashing, murderous eyes and hefty shoulders. The poor child struggled to thrust a way between their feet but, knocked to and fro by their brutal movements, he might have been trampled underfoot had he not shrieked at the loudest pitch of his voice, 'Fa—ther, Mother!' A man in the surging crowd heard his cry and, stooping with very great difficulty, lifted him up in his arms.

'How did you get here, child? Whose baby are you?' the man asked as he steered clear of the mass. The child wept more bitterly than ever now and only cried, 'I want my mother, I want my father!'

The man tried to soothe him by taking him to the roundabout. 'Will you have a lift on the horse?' he gently asked as he approached the ring. The child's throat tore into wild, deep, shrill sobs and he only shouted, 'I want my mother, I want my father!'

The man headed towards the place where the juggler still played on the flute to the dancing cobra. 'Listen to that nice music, child,' he pleaded. But the child shut his ears with his fingers and shouted his double-pitched strain, 'I want my mother, I want my father!'

The man took him near the balloons, thinking the bright colours would distract the child's attention and quieten him. 'Would you like a rainbow-coloured balloon?' he persuasively asked. The child turned his eyes from the flying balloons and just sobbed, 'I want my mother, I want my father.'

The man still importunate in his kindly desire to make the child happy, bore him to the gate where the flower-seller sat. 'Look! Can you smell those nice flowers, child? Would you like a garland to put round your neck?' The child turned his nose away from the basket and reiterated his sob, 'I want my mother, I want my father.'

Thinking to humour his disconsolate charge by a gift of sweets, the man took him to the counter of the sweet shop. 'What sweets would you like, child?' he asked. The child turned his face from the sweet shop and only sobbed, 'I want my mother, I want my father.'

The Barber's Trade Union

Among the makers of modern India, Chandu, the barber boy of our village, has a place which will be denied him unless I press for the recognition of his contribution to history. Chandu's peculiar claim to recognition rested, to tell the truth, on an exploit of which he did not know the full significance. But then, unlike most great men of India today, he had no very exaggerated notion of his own importance, though he shared with them a certain naive egotism which was sometimes disconcerting and sometimes rather charming.

I knew Chandu ever since the days when he wore a piece of rag in the middle of his naked, distended-bellied body, and when we wallowed together in the mire of the village lanes, playing at soldiering, shopkeeping, or clerking and other little games which we invented for the delectation of our two selves and of our mothers, who alone of all the elders condescended to notice us.

Chandu was my senior by about six months, and he always took the lead in all matters. And I willingly followed, because truly he was a genius at catching wasps, and at pressing the poison out of their tails, at tying their tiny legs to cotton thread and flying them, while I always got stung on the cheeks if I dared to go anywhere near the platform of the village well where these insects settled on the puddles to drink water.

When we grew up, he still seemed to me the embodiment of perfection, because he could make and fly paper kites of such intricate design and with such balance as I could never achieve.

To be sure, he was not so good at doing sums at school as I was, perhaps because his father apprenticed him early to the hereditary profession of the barber's caste and sent him out haircutting in the village, and he had no time for the home tasks which our schoolmaster gave us. But he was better than I at reciting poetry, any day, for not only did he remember by rote the verses in the textbook, but he could repeat the endless pages of prose in that book so that they seemed like poetry.

My mother resented the fact that Chandu won a scholarship at school while I had to pay fees to be taught. And she constantly dissuaded me from playing with him, saying that Chandu was a low-caste barber's son and that I ought to keep up the status of my caste and class. But whatever innate ideas I had inherited from my forefathers, I certainly hadn't inherited any sense of superiority. Indeed, I was always rather ashamed of the red caste mark which my mother put on my forehead every morning, and of the formalized pattern of the uchkin, the tight cotton trousers, the gold-worked shoes and the silk turban in which I dressed; and I longed for the right to wear all the spectacular conglomeration of clothes which Chandu wore—a pair of khaki shorts which the retired Subedar had given him, a frayed black velvet waistcoat, decorated all over with shell buttons, and a round felt cap which had once belonged to Lalla Hukam Chand, the lawyer of our village.

And I envied Chandu the freedom of movement which he enjoyed after his father died of plague. For then he would do the round of shaving and haircutting at the houses of the high-caste notables in the morning, bathe and dress, and then steal a ride to town, six miles away, on the footrest of the closed carriage in which Lalla Hukam Chand travelled to town.

But Chandu was kind to me. He knew that I was seldom taken to town, and that I had to trudge three weary miles to a secondary school in the big village of Joadiala with the fear of God in my heart, while he had been completely absolved from the ordeal of being flogged by cruel masters as he had left school after his father's death. So he always brought me some gift or other from the town—a paint brush, or gold ink, or white chalk, or a double-edged penknife to sharpen pencils with; and he would entertain me with long merry descriptions of the variety of things he saw in the bazaars of civilization.

He was particularly detailed in his description of the wonderful English-style clothes which he saw the sahibs and the lawyers, the chaprasis and the policemen wearing at the District Court, where he had to wait for the journey home at the back of Lalla Hukam Chand's phaeton. And, once or twice, he expressed to me a secret wish he had to steal some money from the pitcher where his mother kept the emoluments of his professional skill, to buy himself a rig-out like that of Kalan Khan, the dentist, who, he said, performed miracles in the town, fitting people with rows of teeth and even new eyes. He described to me the appearance of Kalan Khan, a young man with hair parted on one side, and dressed in a starched shirt, with an ivory collar and bow tie, a black coat and striped trousers, and a wonderful rubber overcoat and pumps. And he recounted to me the skill with which this magician unpacked an Angrezi leather handbag and flourished his shining steel instruments.

Then he asked my advice on the question of whether, as a barber educated to the fifth primary class, he would not look more dignified if he, too, wore a dress in the style of Dr Kalan Khan. 'For though I am not a highly educated doctor,' he said, 'I learnt how to treat pimples, boils and cuts on people's bodies from my father, who learnt them from his father before him.'

I agreed with his project and encouraged him with the enthusiasm I felt for everything that my hero thought or did.

One day I was thrilled to find Chandu at the door of my house in the morning. He was dressed up in a white turban, a white rubber coat (a little too big for him, but nevertheless very splendid), a pair of pumps in which I could see my face reflected in clear silhouette, and he had a leather bag in his hand. He was setting off on his round and had come to show me how grand he looked in his new rig-out.

'Marvellous!' I said. 'Marvellous!'

And he rushed off towards the house of the landlord, whom he shaved every morning, myself following admiringly behind.

There were not many people in the street at this time. So I alone witnessed the glory of Chandu, dressed up as a doctor, except, of course, that he himself seemed rather self-conscious as he strutted up the street, carefully avoiding the taint of cow-dung cakes which the village women stuck to the walls, and the dirty water which flowed through the drains. But as we entered the home of the landlord, we met Devi, the landlord's little son, who clapped his hands with joy and shouted to announce the arrival of Chandu, the barber, in a beautiful heroic dress like that of the Padre sahib of the Mission School.

'Ram! Ram! Ram!' said Bijay Chand, the burly landlord, touching the sacred thread which hung over his ear since he had just been to the lavatory. 'The son of a pig! He is bringing a bag made of cowhide into our house and a coat of the marrow of, I don't know, some other animal, and those evil black Angrezi shoes. Get out! Get out! You son of a devil! You will defile my religion. I suppose you have no fear of anyone now that your father is dead!'

'But I am wearing the clothes of a doctor, Jagirdar sahib,' said Chandu.

'Go away, you swine, go away and wear clothes befitting your low status as a barber, and don't let me see you practising any of your new-fangled notions, or else I will have you flogged!'

'But Rai Bijay Chand sahib!' Chandu appealed.

'Get away! Get away! You useless one!' the landlord shouted. 'Don't come any nearer, or we will have to treat the whole house with the sacred cow-dung to purify it.'

Chandu returned. His face was flushed. He was completely taken aback. He did not look at me because of the shame he felt at being insulted before me, whose hero he knew he was. And he rushed towards the shop of Thanu Ram, the sahukar of the village, who kept a grocer's store at the corner of the lane.

Devi, the landlord's son, had begun to cry at his father's harsh words, and I stopped to quieten him. When I got to the head of the lane, I saw the sahukar with one end of the scale in which he had been weighing grain lifted in one hand, abusing Chandu in the foulest way. 'You little swine, you go disguising yourself as a clown when you ought to be bearing your responsibilities and looking after your old mother. You go wearing the defiled clothes of the hospital folk! Go, and come back in your own clothes! Then I shall let you cut my hair!' And as he said so he felt for the ritual tuft knot on top of his head.

Chandu looked very crestfallen, and ran in a wild rage past me, as if I had been responsible for these mishaps. And I nearly cried to think that he hated me now just because I belonged to a superior caste.

'Go to Pandit Parmanand!' I shouted after him. 'And tell him that these garments you are wearing are not unclean.'

'Ho, so you are in league with him,' said Pandit Parmanand, emerging from the landlord's home, where he had been apparently summoned to discuss this unholy emergency. 'You boys have been spoiled by the school education which you have got. It may be all right for you to wear those things because you are going to be a learned man, but what right has that low-caste boy to such apparel? He has got to touch our beards, our heads and our hands. He is defiled enough by God. Why does he want to become more defiled? You are a high-caste boy. And he is a low-caste devil! He is a rogue!'

Chandu had heard this. He did not look back and ran in a flurry, as if he were set on some purpose which occupied him more than the abuse which had been the cause of his flight.

My mother called to me and said it was time for me to eat and go to school or I should be late. And she could not resist the temptation to lecture me again about my association with the barber boy.

But I was very disturbed about Chandu's fate all day, and, on my way back from school, I called in at the hovel where he lived with his mother.

His mother was well known for a cantankerous old woman, because she, a low-caste woman, dared to see the upper-caste people as they never dared to see themselves. She was always very kind to me, though she spoke to me too in a bantering manner, which she had acquired through the suffering and humiliations of sixty-odd years. Turning to me she said, 'Well, you have come, have you, to look for your friend. If your mother knew that you were here she would scratch my eyes out for casting my evil eye on your sweet face. And you, are you as innocent as you look or are you a sneaking little hypocrite like the rest of your lot?'

'Where is Chandu, then, mother?' I said.

'I don't know, son,' she said, now in a sincere simple manner. 'He went uptown way and says he earned some money shaving people on the roadside. I don't know what he is up to. I don't think he ought to annoy the clients his father served. He is a child and gets funny notions into his head and they ought not to be angry with him. He is only a boy. You want to see him and go out playing, I suppose. Very well, I will tell him when he comes. He has just gone up the road, I think!'

'All right, mother,' I said and went home.

Chandu whistled for me that afternoon in the usual code whistle which we had arranged to evade the reproaches of interfering elders that our association often provoked.

'Come for a walk to the bazaar,' he said. 'I want to talk to you.' And hardly had I joined him when he began, 'Do you know, I earned a rupee shaving and haircutting near the court this morning. If I hadn't had to come back on the back bar of Hukam Chand's carriage early in the afternoon, I should have earned more. But I am going to teach these orthodox idiots a lesson. I am going on strike. I shall not go to their houses to attend to them. I am going to buy a Japanese bicycle from the gambling son of Lalla Hukam Chand for five rupees, and I shall learn to ride it and I will go to town on it every day. Won't I look grand, riding on a bicycle, with my overcoat, my black leather shoes, and a white turban on my head, specially as there is a peg in front of the two-wheeled carriage for hanging my tool-bag?'

'Yes,' I agreed, greatly thrilled, not because I imagined the glory of Chandu seated on a bicycle, but because I felt myself nearer the goal of my own ambition. I felt that if Chandu acquired a bicycle, he would at least let me ride to town on the elongated bolt at the back wheel or on the front bar, if he didn't let me learn to ride myself and lend me the machine every now and then.

Chandu negotiated the deal about the bicycle with an assurance that seemed to me a revelation of his capacity for business such as I had never suspected in him, from the reckless way he spent his money. And then he said to me in a confidential voice, 'You wait for another day or two. I shall show you something which will make you laugh as you have never laughed before.'

'Tell me now,' I insisted, with an impatience sharpened by the rhythm of the excitement with which the spirit of his adventure filled my being.

'No, you wait,' he said. 'I can only give you a hint at the moment. It is a secret that only a barber can know. Now let me get on with the job of learning to handle this machine. You hold it while I get on it, and I think it will be all right.'

'But,' I said, 'this is not the way to learn to ride a bicycle. My father learned to ride from the peg at the back, and my brother learnt to ride by first trying to balance on the pedal.'

'Your father is a top-heavy baboon!' said Chandu. 'And your brother is a long-legged spider. I,' he continued, 'was born, my mother tells me, upside down.'

'All right,' I said. And I held the bicycle for him. But while my gaze concentrated with admiration on the brilliant sheen of the polished bars, I lost my grip and Chandu fell on the other side with a thud, along with the machine.

There were peals of laughter from the shop of the sahukar, where several peasants congregated round the figure of the landlord. And then the sahukar could be heard shouting, 'Serves you right, you rascally son of the iron age! Break your bones and die, you upstart! You won't come to your senses otherwise!'

Chandu hung his head with shame, and muttered an oath at me, 'You fool, you are no good!' though I had thought that he would grip me by the neck and give me a good thrashing for being the cause of his discomfiture. Then he looked at me, smiled embarrassedly, and said, 'We will see who has the last laugh, I or they.'

'I will hold the machine tightly this time,' I said earnestly, and I picked it up from where it lay.

'Yes, break your bones, you swine,' came the landlord's call.

'Don't you care!' Chandu said to me. 'I will show them.' And he mounted the bicycle as I exerted all my strength to hold it tight. Then he said, 'Let go!'

I released my grip.

He had pressed the pedal with a downward pressure of his right foot, hard, and, as the wheels revolved, he swayed dangerously to one side. But he had pushed the other pedal now. The machine balanced, inclining to the right a little, so that I saw Chandu lift his rump from the saddle in the most frightening manner. He hung precariously for a moment. His handles wobbled dangerously. He was tottering. At this juncture, a mixed noise of laughter and sarcasm arose from the congregation at the shop and I thought that Chandu would come to grief with this confusion, if not on account of his utter incapacity. By a curious miracle, however, Chandu's feet had got into the right rhythm for pedalling and his handle had adjusted itself to his stiff hands, and he rode off with me running behind him, bursting myself with enthusiastic 'shabashes'.

A half a mile run and he repeated the trick.

Though I was very eager to share the joy of his newly acquired skill, I didn't see Chandu the next day, as I was being taken to see my aunts in Verka, straight from school.

But on the third day he called for me and said that he would show me the joke he had talked of the other day. I followed quickly, asking the while, 'Tell me, what is it all about?'

'Look,' he said, hiding behind the oven of the village potter. 'Do you see the congregation of men in the sahukar's shop? Try and see who's there.'

I explored the various faces and, for a moment, I was quite baffled.

'Only the peasants sitting round waiting for the landlord,' I said.

'Look again, idiot,' he said, 'and see. The landlord is there, his long-jawed face dirtied by the white scum of his unshaved beard.'

'Ha! Ha!' I shouted hilariously, struck by the contradiction of the big thick moustache (which I knew the landlord dyed) with the prickly white bush on his jowls. 'Ha! Ha!' I roared. 'A sick lion! He looks seedy!'

'Sh!' warned Chandu. 'Don't create ruckus! But look at the sahukar. He looks like a leper with the brown tinge of tobacco on his walrus moustache which I once used to trim. Now you run past the shop and call "Beavers, beavers!" They can't say anything to *you*!'

I was too impetuous a disciple of the impish Chandu to wait to deliberate.

'Beavers! Beavers! Beavers!' I shouted as I ran past the shop to the edge of the platform by the banyan tree.

The peasants who were gathered round the shop burst out laughing, as they had apparently been itching to, for they had noticed the strong growths on the elders' faces, though they had not dared to say anything.

'Catch him, catch him, the little rogue!' shouted the sahukar. 'He is in league with that barber boy, Chandu!'

But, of course, I had climbed up the banyan tree, from which I jumped on to the wall of the temple and shouted my slogan at the priest.

The rumour about the barber boy's strike spread, and jokes about the unkempt beards of the elders of the village became current in every home. Even those who were of high castes, even the members of the families of the elders, began to giggle with laughter at the shabby appearance of the great ones and made rude remarks about their persons. And it was said that the landlord's wife threatened to run away with somebody, because, being younger than her husband by twenty years, she had borne with him as long as he kept himself in trim, but was now disgusted with him beyond the limits of reconciliation.

Chandu did good business in town during these days and managed to save money, even though he bought new clothes and new tools for himself and gave me various presents.

The village elders threatened to have him sent to prison for his offences, and ordered his mother to force him to obey before they committed him to the police for a breach of the peace.

But Chandu's mother had, for the first time in her life, touched the edge of prosperity, and she told them all what she thought of them in a language even plainer than that in which she had always addressed them.

Then they thought of getting the barber of Verka to come and attend them, and offered him an anna instead of the two pice they had usually paid to Chandu.

Chandu, however, had conceived a new notion this time, newer than those he had ever thought of before. Having seen the shop of Nringan Das, the barber of the town, he had applied his brain to the scheme of opening a shop on the wayside at the head of the bazaar, in partnership with his cousin, the barber of Verka, and with Dhunoo and the other barbers within a range of seven miles from his village. He proposed his new idea to his cousin and Dhunoo and all the other barbers at a special meeting of his craft, and, by that gift of the gab which he had, besides his other qualities of the head and the heart, he convinced them all that it was time that the elders of the village came to them to be shaved rather than that they should dance attendance upon their lords and masters.

'Rajkot District Barber Brothers' Hairdressing and Shaving Saloon' has been followed by many other active trade unions of working men in our parts.

Duty

The midday sun blasts everything in the Indian summer: it scorches the earth till its upper layers crack into a million fissures; it sets fire to the water till the lakes and pools and swamps bubble, evaporate and dry up; it shrivels up the lives of birds, beasts and flowers; it burns into one like red pepper and leaves one gasping for breath with a bulging tongue till one spends one's time looking for some shady spot for even the most precarious shelter.

Mangal Singh, the policeman who had been posted on duty at the point where the branch road from the village of Vadala enters the Mall Road of Chetpur, had taken shelter under the sparse foliage of a kikar tree beyond the layers of white dust, after having stood in the sun for five and a half hours since dawn. In a little while, sepoy Rahmat-Ullah would come and relieve him, and he felt that he could cool down a little and prepare to go to the barracks.

The sun was penetrating even the leaves of the wayside trees, and there was not much comfort in the humid airless atmosphere, but after the cracking heat of the open, Mangal felt that this comparative shade was a blessing.

He was not, of course, like the delicate Lallas, rich Hindu merchants, who rode out into the gardens early in the morning and withdrew after 'eating' the fresh air at sunrise and never appeared till sunset, sitting in the laps of their wives drinking milk-water or lying sprawled about on the front boards of their shops under the cool air of electric fans . . . No, he didn't say as they would, 'I go for a pice worth of salt, bring me a palanquin.' Nor could he 'quench his thirst by drinking dew'. No, he was proud that he came from strong peasant stock and was a hardy policeman who could rough it: indeed, this police service was not active enough for him and he felt it a pity that he had not become a real sepoy, for there was more pay in the paltans and there were better uniforms, also free mufti and free rations. So he had heard after he had put the mark of his thumb down and joined the police force—but once done cannot be undone. And it was the blessing of the Gurus, as there was little chance of earning any extra money in the military; while, apart from the fifteen rupees pay, there were other small sums so long as confectioners continued to mix milk with water and so long as there was a murder or two in the prostitutes' bazaar, and so long as there were respectable Lallas who would pay rather than have their names mentioned . . . Why, even here on point-duty in the waste land—'your own is your own and another's is also yours.' For if the peasants offered tokens of grain and butter and sugar to the Munshi at the customs house, then why not to the police? That skinny little Babu at the octroi post had not the strong arm of the sepoy to protect them when they were being looted by the thugs in the market . . . He knew. After wisdom the club. If only he had been able to pay a nazarana to the Tehsildar, he would never have lost his land to Seth Jhinda Ram . . . But God's work was well done, man's badly. And, truly, if he had not pressed the limbs of the landlord, he would never have got the recommendation to join the police. And you learnt a great deal in the service of the Sarkar. And there was nothing better than Service: no worry, and there was so much izzat in it that these very cowardly city folk who laughed at you if you were a peasant, joined their hands in obeisance to you if you wielded a truncheon. And the rustics who had no notion of discipline or duty could be made to obey authority with the might of the stave, and if they didn't obey that, the fear of the handcuff—even a daring robber like Barkat Ali could not escape because one could blow the whistle and call the entire police force out. And the Sarkar is truly powerful. Like Alamgir, it leaves no fire in the hearth, nor water in the jar, to bring a man to justice . . .

He glanced at his dust-covered feet in the regulation shoes of rough cowhide, even as he congratulated himself on his lucky position as a member of the much-feared police service and wished he had really been in the army, for there the sepoys had boots given them. His puttees too were old and faded and there was something loose about the khaki uniform with the black belt. The uniform of the army was so tight-fitting. Perhaps the whistle-chain and the truncheon improved this and the red-and-blue turban was nice, but—he lifted his hand to caress the folds of his headdress and to adjust it, as it was heavy and got soaked with the sweat that flowed from his fuming scalp burdened by long hair on the lower edges . . .

The sun poured down a flood of fire on the earth, and it seemed as if the desolate fields covered with dense brown thickets and stalks of grass and cacti were crackling like cinders and would soon be reduced to ashes. A partridge hummed in its nest somewhere and a dove cooed from the tree overhead, giving that depth to the shade which fills the air with long, endless silences and with the desolate peace of loneliness.

Mangal Singh drifted a few steps from where he was standing and halted on a spot where the shade was thicker than it was anywhere else under the kikar trees. And, blowing a hot breath, he cupped his palms over the knob of his stave and leaned his chin on the knuckles of his joined hands and stood contemplating the scene with half-closed eyes like a dog who rests his muzzle on his front paws and lies in wait for his prey.

Layers of white-sheeted mist floated past his eyes in the sun-soaked fields, the anguish of a thousand heat-singed bushes, while the parched leaves of the hanging boughs of the wayside trees rustled at the touch of a scorching breeze.

One breath, a thousand hopes, they say, and there never comes a day without evening—but it would be very difficult to walk down to the barracks through this terrible heat. And he wished his duty was not up, that someone could fetch his food for him and that he could borrow a charpai from the octroi and go to sleep in the grove of neem trees by the garden of Rais Jagjiwan Das, or sit and talk to the grass-cutter's wife who had breasts like turnips. Only Rahmat-Ullah had an eye on her too, and he was sure to be here, as he preferred the desolate afternoon, thinking that he might get a chance when no one was about.

'I will have to walk back to the lines,' he muttered to himself and yawned. He felt heavy and tired at the prospect and his legs seemed to weaken from the knowledge of the unending trudge of three miles. He shook his head and tried to be alert, but the invisible presence of some overwhelming force seemed to be descending on him and his heavy-lidded eyes were closing against his will. He took a deep breath and made another effort to open his eyes wide through the drowsy stupor of the shade that weighed down from the trees. For a moment his body steadied and his eyes half opened. But how hateful was the glare, and how cruel, how meaningless, was life outside . . . And what peace, what quiet below the trees, beneath the eyes . . .

If a god should be standing here he could not help closing his eyes for a minute, he felt; and sleep came creeping into his bones with a whiff of breeze that was like a soft beauty retreating coyly before the thousand glares of the torrid sun which burnt so passionately above the silent fields . . . The heat seemed to be melting the fat in his head and to be blinding his eyes, and he let himself be seduced by the placid stillness into a trance of half-sleep . . .

Through sleepy eyes he was conscious of the whispering elements as he dozed, and his body still stood more or less erect, though his head was bent on the knuckles of his hand above the stave, and the comers of his mouth dribbled slightly . . .

'Shoop . . . shoop . . . shoop . . .' a snake seemed to lash his face at the same time as he saw the soothing vision of a dim city through the stealthy corners of whose lanes he was passing suavely into a house was effaced . . .

'Shoop . . . shoop . . .'

He came to suddenly and saw Thanedar Abdul Kerim standing before him, his young face red with anger under the affected Afghan turban, his tall lanky form tight-stretched, a cane in his hand, and his bicycle leaning against his legs . . .

'Wake up! Wake up, you ox of a Sikh! Is it because it is past twelve that your senses have left you?'

Mangal reeled, then steadied himself, his hands climbing automatically to his turban which had been shaken by the Inspector's onslaught.

'Shoop . . . shoop,' the cane struck his side again and stung his skin like a hundred scorpions. And a welter of abuse fell upon his ears, 'Bahin-chod, the DSP might have passed, and you are supposed to be on *duty*. Wake up and come to your senses, madar-chod!'

Quite involuntarily, Mangal's right hand left the turban and shot up to his forehead in a salute, and his thick, trembling lips phewed some hot stale breath, 'Huzoor, mai–bap.'

'You eat the bread of illegality,' the Thanedar shouted. 'I will be reprimanded and my promotion stopped, you swine!'

And he lifted his cane to strike Mangal again, but the sepoy was shaking with fright so that his stave dropped from his hand.

Mangal bent and picked up his lathi.

'Go and be on your point-duty!' ordered the Thanedar sternly and, putting his foot on the pedal, rode shakily away on his bicycle.

Mangal walked out of the shade, his shins and thighs still trembling and his heart thumping in spite of himself, though he was less afraid than conscience-stricken for neglecting his duty.

The heat of the sun made the skin of his face smart with a sharp pain where the perspiration flowed profusely down his neck. He rubbed his hand across it and felt the sweat tingle like a raw wound.

He shook himself and his head twitched, and he looked about in order to see if anyone had seen him being beaten. He wanted to bear the pain like a man. But his eyes, startled by the suddenness with which they had opened, were full of a boiling liquid that melted into fumes as he raised his head.

His throat was parched dry and he coughed with an effort so that his big brown face above the shaggy beard reddened. Then he paused to spit on the road and felt his legs trembling and shaking more than ever. He twisted his face in the endeavour to control his limbs and lunged forward . . .

'Ohe, may you die, ohe asses, ohe, may you die,' came a voice from behind him.

As he turned around, he saw a herd of donkeys come stampeding up the road in a wild rush, which became wilder as their driver trotted fast behind them in an attempt to keep them from entering the Mall Road at that pace.

For a moment, the cloud of dust the herd had raised on the sides of the deeply rutted Vadala Road obscured Mangal's view of the man, but then suddenly he could hear him shouting, 'Ohe, may you die, asses!'

Mangal ran with his stave upraised, in a wild scurry towards the driver of the stampeding donkeys, scattering them helter-skelter till some of them cantered the more quickly into the Mall and the others turned back and came to a standstill. He caught the driver up before the man had escaped into a ditch by the banana field. And, grinding a half-expressed curse between his teeth, he struck him with his stave hard, hard, harder, so that the blows fell edgewise on a donkey's neck, on the driver's arms, on a donkey's back, on a donkey's head, on the man's legs . . .

'Oh, forgive, Sarkar, it is not my fault,' the man shouted in an angry, indignant voice while he rubbed his limbs and spread his hands out to ward off more blows.

'You, son of a dog,' hissed Mangal as he struck again and again, harder and harder, as if he had gone mad, till his stave seemed to ring as a bamboo stick does when it is splitting into shreds.

The Liar

Labhu, the old shikari of my village, was a born liar. Therefore he had won the reputation of being the best storyteller in our parts. And though a sweeper of low caste, he was honoured by all and sundry. He was tolerated even to the extent of being given a seat at the foot of the banyan tree. And my mother did not insist too harshly on the necessity of my taking a bath to purify myself every time I had been seen listening to one of his uncanny tales with the other village boys.

Labhu was a thin, little man, with the glint of a lance and the glide of an arrow. His wiry, weather-beaten frame must have had immense reserves of energy, to judge by the way he could chase stags up the steep crags of the hills behind our village and run abreast of the bay mare of Subedar Deep Singh to whose household he was attached as a shikari, except when some English official, a rich white merchant, or a guest of the subedar, engaged him for a season. It was perhaps this wonderful physical agility of his that had persuaded him to adopt the profession of a shikari. Labhu had also a sensitive, dark face, of which the lower lip trembled as it pronounced the first accents of a poignant verse or the last words of a gruesome hunting story. And it was the strange spell that his tragic verses and weird stories cast on me that made me his devoted follower through childhood. He taught me to run with the hare and hunt with the hounds; he taught me the way to track all the wild animals; and he taught me how to concoct a cock-and-bull story to tell my father if I had to make an excuse for not being at home during the reign of the hot sun.

His teaching was, of course, by example, as I was rather a critical pupil.

'Labhu,' I would say, 'I am sure it is impossible to track any prey when you are half up the side of a hillock.'

'Acha,' he would say, 'I will show you. Stand still and listen.'

I did so and we both heard a pebble drop. Up he darted on the stony ridge in the direction whence the sound had come, jumping from crag to crag, securing a precarious foothold on a small stone here and a sure one on a boulder there, till he was tearing through a flock of sheep, towards a little gully where a ram had taken shelter in a cave, secure in the belief that it would escape its pursuer.

'All right,' I would say. 'You may have been able to track this ram, but I don't believe that yarn of yours about the devil-ram you saw when you were hunting with the subedar.'

'I swear by God Almighty,' he said, 'it is true. The subedar will tell you that he saw this terrible apparition with me. It was a beast about the size of an elephant, with eyes as big as hen's eggs and a beard as long as that of Maulvi Shah Din, the priest of the mosque, only not henna-dyed and red, but blue-black; it had huge ears as big as an elephant's, which did not flap, however, but pricked up like the ears of the subedar's horse; it had a nose like that of the wife of the Missionary sahib, and it had square jaws which showed teeth almost as big as the chunks of marble which lie outside the temple, as it laughed at the subedar. It appeared unexpectedly near the peak of Devi Parbat. The subedar and I had ascended about twelve thousand feet up the mountain in search of game, when suddenly, out of the spirit world that always waits about us in the living air, there was the clattering of stones and boulders, the whistling of sharp winds, the gurgling of thunder and a huge crack on the side of the mountain. Then an enormous figure seemed to rise. From a distance it seemed to both of us like a dark patch, and we thought it was an oorial and began to stalk towards it. What was our surprise, however, when, as soon as we saw it stand there, facing us with its glistening, white eyes as big as a hen's eggs, it sneezed and ripped the mountainside with a kick of its forefeet and disappeared. The mountain shook and the subedar trembled, while I stood bravely where I was and laughed till I wept with joy at my good luck in having seen so marvellous a manifestation of the devil-god of the tribe of rams. I tell you, son, please God I shall show him to you one of these days.'

'Labhu, you don't mean to say so!' I said, half incredulous, though I was fascinated by the chimera.

'Of course I mean to say so, silly boy,' said Labhu. 'This is nothing compared to the other vision that was vouchsafed to me, praise be to God, when I was on the journey to Ladakh, hunting with Jolly John Sahib.' And he began to relate a fantastic story of a colossal snake, which was so improbable that even I did not believe it.

'Oh, you are a fool, Labhu,' I said. 'And you are a liar. Everybody says so. And I don't believe you at all. My mother says I am silly to believe your tales.'

'All right, then, if you don't believe my stories why do you come here to listen to them?' he said, with wounded pride. 'Go, I shall never teach you anything more, and I shall certainly not let you accompany me to the hunts.'

'All right,' I said, chagrined and stubborn. 'I don't want to speak to you either.'

And I ran home bursting with indignation at having forced a quarrel upon Labhu, when really he only told me his stories for my amusement.

Labhu went away for a while on a hunting tour with the subedar. He didn't come back to the village when this tour finished, because Subedar Deep Singh's eldest son, Kuldeep Singh, who was a lieutenant in the army, took him for a trip across the Himalayas to Nepal.

During this time, though I regretted Labhu's absence, I lent my ear readily to the malicious misrepresentation of his character that the subedar and his employers, and occasionally also my father, indulged in; because, though superior to Labhu by caste, they were not such good shots as he was.

'He can only wait by a forest pool or a safe footpath to shoot at some unfortunate beast, this Labhu!' said the subedar. 'And often he shoots in the dark with that inefficient powder-gun of his. He is no good except for tracking.'

'Yes,' said my father, 'he is a vain boaster and a liar. The only beast he dared to shoot at while he was with me was a hare, and even that he hit in the leg.'

I waited eagerly for Labhu's return to confirm from his very mouth these stories of his incompetence, because, though incredulous of this scandal, I had been driven to a frenzy of chagrin by his insulting dismissal of me. I thought I would ask him point-blank whether he was really as bad a hunter as the subedar and my father made him out to be.

When Labhu came back, however, he limped about and seemed ill. I was very sad to see him broken and dispirited. And I forgot all the scandal I had heard about him in my bafflement at the sudden change that had come into his character, for he was now no longer the garrulous man who sat telling stories to old men and young boys, but a strangely reticent creature who lay in a stupor all day, moaning and murmuring to himself in a prolonged delirium, except that he occasionally hobbled out with a huge staff in his hand in the evenings.

I was afraid to go near him, because he always wore a forbidding, angry look. But the villagers didn't seem to think there was anything the matter with Labhu, as I heard them say, 'Now that we have no patience with him and his stories, he spends most of his time telling them to himself, the fool!'

I owed a loyalty to Labhu, for I had discovered a kinship in my make-up for all those extravagances for which the shikari was so well known.

So I went up to him one day, as he lay on a broken string bed near his mud hut, under the precarious shelter which a young pipal gave him.

'You have returned then, Master Labhu,' I said.

'Yes,' he said, 'I have been back some time, son. I looked for you, but you did not seem to be about. But you know, the man who is slain cannot walk even to his own house. This leg of mine pains me and I can't get about as I used to.'

'What happened to your leg, then?' I asked, realizing that he had forgotten all about our past quarrels and was as kind and communicative to me as before. 'Did you fall down a cliff or something?'

'No,' he said in a tired voice. And he kept quiet for a long while.

'What happened, then?' I persisted.

'You know, son,' Labhu began, at first pale and hesitant, then smiling and lifting his eyebrows in the familiar manner of the old days, 'I went away on a hunting tour in the pay of the subedar's eldest son, Kuldeep Singh, and some of his friends. Well, we went to Nepal through the Kulu valley. They had no experience of hunting in this or in any other part of the world, and I led them across such trails as I knew and such as the local shikaris told me about. That boy, Kuldeep, I don't know what he does in the army, but he can't shoot at any range, and the sahibs with him were clumsy, purblind white men. I would point to a beast with my stick, and, though they could see the hide before their eyes, they bungled with their guns or were too noisy on their feet, and away crashed the bull which we had been tracking. I would grunt, shrug my shoulders and did not mind, because they were like children. They had finished hundreds of cartridges and had not shot anything, and daily begged me to help them to secure some game.

'At first I told them that game doesn't taste sweet unless it is shot by oneself. But at length I took pity on them and thought that I would secure them a good mixed bag. I shot twelve tigers with my gun and fifteen panthers in the course of seven days, and many stags.

'On the eighth day we saw a monster which had the body of a bear, the head of a reindeer, the feet of a goat, the tail of a wild bull and a glistening, fibrous tissue all round it like the white silken veil which the Rani of Boondi wore when she came to visit Subedar Deep Singh's wife. Kuldeep Singh and the sahibs were very frightened of this apparition and said it was the devil himself who had the shape of an earthly being and who would soon breathe a breath which would mix with the still air of the night and poison life.

'They were all for killing it outright, while I was sure that it was only a princess of the royal house of Nepal who had been transformed by some magician into this fantastic shape and size. And I wanted to catch it alive and bring it home to be my bride.'

Labhu went on to relate how beautiful she was and how he resolved to restore her to her normal self by reading magical incantations.

'I told her I loved her,' he continued, 'and she smiled shyly. But some fool, I think it was the subedar's son, fired a volley of shots, which frightened her so that she ran, became one with the air and began to ascend the snowy peaks of Kailash Parbat.

'I was bent on rescuing my beloved, and I leapt from one mountain to another, calling after her to stop. But that idiot Kuldeep and the sahibs kept on shooting and roused the magician who kept guard over her. And this evil sage threw a huge mountain of snow at me to kill me.

'I just blew a hot breath and the mountain of snow cracked into a million pieces and hung about the sky like glittering stars.

'Then the magician struck the earth with his feet and opened up a grave to bury me alive. I leapt right across the fissure and found myself on a peak in the land of the lama who never dies.

'By now, of course, the magician had hidden the beauty away in some cave. So I gave up the chase, as there was the doom of death about this beauty, anyhow, and I made one leap across the Himalayas for home . . .'

'And as you landed this side of the mountains you sprained your foot,' I said.

Labhu lifted his eyebrows funnily in the manner of the old days and, laughing, said, 'Have I told you this story before, then?'

The Maharaja and the Tortoise

Of all the ancient (and, of course, noble) princely houses which have succeeded in preserving, by natural and artificial means, the continuity of their bloodstream through the ages, the line of the Maharajas of Udhampur, of the Suraj-Bansi clan who claim their descent from the Sun, by way of the god-king Ram, is the most ancient and most noble.

They are proud and warlike chieftains whose chivalry is a by-word in Indian homes, whose jewels and diamonds and rubies and sapphires and elephants are coveted by all the shopgirls of Europe, and whose splendid contributions in men, money and materials to the British Raj, in bringing law and order to India, have been recognized by the Sarkar through treaties which appoint them the guardians of millions of the poor, and by the grant to them of various titles, certificates and scrolls.

Besides being confirmed a 'Descendant of the Sun' by special decree of the Government of India, on the death of his revered father Maharaja Gulab Singh and on his accession to the ancestral throne, His Highness Maharajadhiraj Sir Ganga Singh Bahadur was made Knight Commander of the Star of India (2nd class) for his services as an orderly to His Majesty the King-Emperor at the Coronation Durbar at Delhi. And he was awarded a salute of twenty-one guns for supplying a whole brigade of sappers and miners and for his valiant services in the field and at home during the War. The Hindu University of Hathras had conferred on him the honorary degree of Doctor of Laws for contributing lavishly to its funds and several women's clubs in America, and the Honourable Society of Haberdashers of the United Kingdom had elected him an honorary member. Besides these, a long list of chosen letters of the Latin, Arabic and Sanskrit alphabets had accrued to his name during the years.

Be it said to the credit of His Highness that though he was gracious enough to accept all these honours, and had indeed in his younger days been eager enough to seek them, the superabundance of these titles, mostly couched in Angrezi speech which he did not understand, seemed to him irrelevant in his mature years, except as the necessary adjuncts of a modern existence, like the patent-leather shoes, and the eighteen-carat gold watch studded with diamonds, which he wore on special occasions with the ceremonial robes of the ancient and princely house of Udhampur.

For, in spite of his loyalty and devotion to the British Crown and his consequent assumption of the privileges that this devotion and loyalty brought in their train, His Highness had never really accepted the suzerainty of the dirty, beef-eating race of which even the kings were used to wiping their bottoms with paper. He was a strict Hindu and, being true to the great traditions of his house and conscious that its eminence among the princely houses was founded more on the spiritual than the temporal power associated with his ancestors, he valued only one title, 'Descendant of the Sun', and did not care for the other decorations.

In fact, as he grew in age, he had been inclined to care less and less for the things of this world and more and more for the things of the spirit. But, since the habits which he had cultivated in his hot-headed youth, and the responsibilities of his position as the head of his State did not altogether conduce to renunciation, he had compromised and accepted the appurtenances of a modern existence at the same time as he sought to deepen his faith in the invisible, ethereal God and to cast off the false cloak of the flesh.

Now, as everyone knows, even the greatest saints and prophets of this world have found it difficult to achieve the ideal of complete detachment or non-attachment. The Lord Buddha who preached the cessation of all desire in order to rid the world of suffering died of meat-poisoning. And Jesus wept in vain. And Lao Tze suffered from pangs of bad conscience about his love of the world, and the gout.

It is not to be wondered at, therefore, if His Highness Maharajadhiraj

Sir Ganga Singh Bahadur failed in the pursuit of God. For this evil iron age imposes certain limits even on the most heroic sons of India! Hedged in between a diabolical Sarkar, whose real feelings about him were difficult to discover in spite of his intimacy with the political resident, Sir Francis Wimperley, and a people who were always clamouring for something or other, His Highness was in a doubly difficult position in realizing the great spiritual ideals of his inheritance.

The catastrophe which led to his disillusionment is one of the most important miracles of religious history in the world and has become a legend to all true followers of the faith, besides being the greatest spiritual crisis in the annals of Rajasthan since the johur, the last sacrifice by the Rajputs when they were besieged in the hill fort of Chitore by the lusty slave-king of Delhi, Ala-ud-din, and since the performance of suttee by Queen Padmani, who burned herself with her female companions rather than yield to the conqueror.

It so happened that as Maharajadhiraj Sir Ganga Singh reached the age of forty and felt he was getting old, he sought the advice of Pandit Ram Prashad, who was both the high priest and the prime minister of Udhampur, to prepare an easy passage for his journey to the next world.

Pandit Ram Prashad, a clever little lawyer who had been able to maintain his position in the State for seven years—a longer term of office than had been enjoyed by any other vizier, because he was superior in cunning to all the other courtiers—advised His Highness that, according to the holy books, on the appearance of every full moon, he should donate his weight in gold to the priests, entertain seven hundred of them to a feast in the palace and take to prayer, mentioning the name of God three hundred and seventy-five times on the rosary after offering oblations every morning to his ancestor, the Sun, seated in the lotus seat by the edge of the Ganges. If this ritual was not followed, said the pandit, His Highness was in grave danger because, the access to heaven apart, he would have prolonged illnesses, as the planets Saturn and Venus were daily clashing in the scroll of his horoscope.

As the palace of the Maharaja of Udhampur was situated on the edge of the desert of Rajputana, and the River Ganges flowed about a hundred and fifty miles away up north, His Highness was hard put to it to understand how he could offer oblations to the Sun sitting by the Ganges. But Pandit Ram Prashad had a more agile mind than His Highness, or, for that matter, anyone else in Udhampur. He immediately called Sardar Bahadur Singh, a contractor who paid the best commissions, and arranged the construction of a tank which was to be filled from the River Ganges by means of a pipeline all the way from Hardwar, where the holy river first enters the plains from the hills. The cost was to be a meagre hundred and eighty lakhs. And he presented this plan to His Highness.

Needless to say, money was no consideration to His Highness Maharajadhiraj Sir Ganga Singh Bahadur, as everyone knew that he had given a hundred lakhs to the Sarkar during the war and had spent forty lakhs on a fleet of Packards which broke their axles on the rutted, unpaved tracks of Udhampur and lay rusting in the stables. So that when Pandit Ram Prashad laid the scheme before His Highness, he nodded assent even as his bleary eyes, yellowed by the smoke of opium, closed in a half-sleep and he sank deeper into the cow-tailed cushions, the carved silver handle of the long tube of his hubble-bubble dropping from his hand.

There is a sacred belief in India in a system of government called the Ram Raj. According to this, the monarch is regarded as the father–mother of a happy family, which not only includes the male and female members of the royal household but even the dirty, ragged, lice-ridden common people of the kingdom. Since it was said in Udhampur that all the Rajputs from the Maharajadhiraj downwards were cousins who once belonged to the same clan, caste and race, the belief in Ram Raj in this State was most intense. But though the kinship on which this belief was founded was not too obvious during those resplendent feasts which were held in honour of visiting officials at the palace, it appeared on other occasions, especially at times of national emergency when the people were asked to give up their own occupations and help to increase the prestige of their spiritual and temporal head by dedicating themselves to some duty in the service of the State.

When the plan of building a tank by the palace and connecting it by a pipeline to the Ganges was conceived in order to enable His Highness to offer oblations and prayers to his ancestor the Sun, all the manhood, as well as the womanhood and even the childhood, of Udhampur were conscripted to help in the building and earn the blessings that would indirectly accrue to them through the Maharaja's realization of easy access to heaven.

Though there were some in Udhampur who thought the scheme fantastic, others believed that the Maharaja, who had once spoiled his religion by crossing the black waters and shaking hands with people who ate cow's flesh, and by whoring and drinking, was now returning in his old age to the right path. And they accepted a mere pittance from the contractor and willingly worked day and night, sweating and straining, with the thousand names of God on their thirsty lips and the roots of wild plants in their bellies, to complete the work.

It did not take many months before the long line from Hardwar to Udhampur was laid and a beautiful square tank built, connecting the palace by means of three steps with the holy water.

With that large-heartedness which was characteristic of His Highness's family, capable of the uttermost hatred for the enemy and the tenderest solicitude for those who had won favour, the Maharaja had all those who had pooh-poohed the plan of constructing the tank flogged and banished, and all those who had helped in preparing the conditions through which he was to perform the prescribed ceremonies feasted. And there was some weeping in Udhampur, but also much rejoicing; and, as always happens on such occasions, the shouting and the laughter drowned the tears.

For a few days after these celebrations, His Highness could not start practising the prescribed ritual of offering prayers and oblations to the father Sun, from whom he was descended, because it seemed difficult, after the feasts which were held on the auspicious occasion of opening the tank, to settle down to the serious business of praying every morning, especially as His Highness had never been an early riser, and also because he was not feeling too well after the effect on his liver of rich food during the banquets.

When a number of digestive powders had restored his liver somewhat, the Maharaja developed gout in his left foot, and that made it difficult for him to stir from the velvet cow-tailed cushions on which he reclined, swathed in bandages and Kashmir shawls.

This enforced delay in search of the kingdom of heaven fortunately gave His Highness time for some heart-searching as a preliminary to the prayers which he was soon going to undertake.

He asked himself whether the favourite young Rani, who had come in the palanquin sent by a prince of Nepal on the inception of the project for building the tank, was not right when she insisted that he should have his proud beard, which spread in two different directions at the chin, shaved off. Did it really make him look old? And was it a fact that the Angrezi log considered a man young at sixty? If what General Bhola Singh, the commander-in-chief of his army, had told him was true, that by taking a paste made of the powdered flesh of a male bear's organs one could rejuvenate oneself and even become the father of a child, then he had only to set his hunters searching for game and not despair or feel old at forty . . . Why impose on himself the duty of offering oblations and saying prayers, anyhow, when one could easily get the priests to repeat the holy verses for a little money, or even get them to say that the feasting of a thousand priests or the bestowal of gifts to a shrine could ensure one's salvation? He had never learnt any sacred verses and formulas and, after all, what was he to say to the Sun if, indeed, he did go down to the tank at dawn and throw water skywards? The longer he reclined on the cushions and the more his gout pained him, the more such doubts and misgivings assailed him. And he twisted his beard between the forefinger and thumb of his left hand as he rested his head on his right. But a good mixture of opium and tobacco in the chillum of his hubble-bubble dispelled every thought and he succeeded in postponing the awkward decision for days on end.

But, for some curious reason, Pandit Ram Prashad kept on plaguing the Maharaja with inquiries about when His Highness was going to begin saying the prescribed prayers. Besides the clashing of the planets Saturn and Venus in His Highness's horoscope, said the prime minister, the construction of the tank and the pipeline from Hardwar had almost emptied the State treasury. The only way of collecting new taxes from the peasantry was by sedulously persuading them to believe that His Highness's prayers would bring merit to the whole kingdom, as the prayers of no other person could. The fellow was so persistent that he nearly bit off the Maharaja's ears by his constant bullying and nagging. And he absolutely refused to point any other way of securing the advantages of heaven, although previously he had prescribed the feasting of seven hundred priests in every emergency as a way of getting out of the more arduous sacrifices.

The Maharaja's pretences about his indisposition, his ignorance of the sacred verses, etcetera, were met by the argument that by attaining purity of heart he would attain good health. And since His Highness could not confess that the real reason for his lack of pious zeal was that he wanted to have one last fling before he regarded himself as an old spent man, fit only for the mumbling of prayers, he found himself in a corner.

One day, indeed, he burst into a regal rage and declared that it was not necessary for him, the Descendant of the Sun, to pray in order to be taken into favour by his ancestors, and that no dog of a Brahmin could force him to renounce life at the age of forty.

But Pandit Ram Prashad respectfully assured him that if, after spending all the revenue of his State, he did not devote himself entirely to religion, and if he, the prime minister, was not given a free hand to rule the State in the best interests of the praja, he would have to declare the treasury bankrupt and beg the British Sarkar to force His Highness to abdicate and appoint a court of wards.

The Maharaja had no option but to submit to this threat. However, he sought a few days' grace from the prime minister on the plea that he wanted to learn the words of the *Gayatri*, the hymn to the Sun, before he started to pray, but really in an attempt to evade the ordeal should something happen in the meantime to make that possible.

Pandit Ram Prashad appointed a priest to come and help His Highness to memorize the *Gayatri* mantra. And His Highness had perforce to listen to the recitation hundreds of times. Long before he had learnt the whole thing by heart he pretended that he knew it, as it was the only way he could keep the prime minister's abominable nominee away from the palace.

At length, the day was appointed when the Maharaja was to begin worship on the edge of the tank and to bring merit to himself and his subjects.

With the beating of drums, the blowing of conches, the striking of cymbals and gongs and the tolling of bells, His Highness rose at dawn from the side of his favourite consort and, with his feet swathed in bandages, for he still suffered from gout, he limped down the three steps which led from the balcony of his Diwan to the edge of the tank, where Pandit Ram Prashad and the other courtiers, priests and people had preceded him.

The eastern sky was colouring with a rosy flush as the refulgent visage of the Sun, the ancestor of Maharajadhiraj Sir Ganga Singh Bahadur, showed up over the rim of the hills beyond the desert.

The whole congregation dipped themselves for a ceremonial bath in the sacred water. Pandit Ram Prashad, in his capacity of high priest of the kingdom, then led the prayers.

The prime minister and the other priests would lift the holy water from the third step of the tank in their upturned palms and, showing it to the Sun, pour it before them to the accompaniment of the *Gayatri* mantra.

The Maharaja followed them rather dreamily, as his eyes did not seem to have quenched their sleep during the night.

After the recitation of mantras was over, the congregation sat down in the lotus seat on the lowest step of the tank to repeat parts of the *Bhagvad Gita* and to contemplate the vision of God in their souls with closed eyes, as is prescribed by the rules of Hindu ritualistic worship.

His Highness was afraid that if he closed his eyes tight to contemplate God he might fall asleep and tumble into the water. So he had to be vigilant if only to keep himself balanced in his seat. As he kept opening his eyes and shutting them, he saw what appeared to be a piece of round green moss floating among the flower petals and the rice which had been copiously sprinkled by the congregation during the singing of the hymns.

The continual hum of the prayers recited by the priests became monotonous, and His Highness, catching himself half asleep, deliberately opened his eyes and scanned the landscape. Millions of his devout subjects who had helped to construct the pond were gathered all round, apparently happy to be sharing in this communion which he had graced by his presence.

Feeling that he might be observed, he bent his head. The curious piece of moss had now floated near his bandaged feet, as if drawn by the dirty-looking green potion showing through the bandages which the barber of the palace had wrapped round his feet. His Highness could not move his hands to throw away the scum as he held them in the prescribed posture like the opening petals of the lotus flower, on his knees. And yet he did not want the scum to stick to his gouty feet. He dared not move his body at all, lest Pandit Ram Prashad should rebuke him for inattention afterwards. And yet he felt he must do something about it. In his panic, he thought he could stir the scum away with a slight movement of his feet without attracting the attention of any member of the congregation or the priests . . .

With one brisk little movement he stirred his left foot in the water and closed his eyes, sure that if he did not see himself do this no one else would.

But there was a sharp shooting pain near the big toe of his foot and he lifted his eyes with a dazed look of horror in them.

A little piece of pale-brown flesh floated before him and a stream of blood was spurting from the bandages between his toes like a miniature fountain.

'A tortoise! A tortoise!' the priests shouted, and drew back with upraised hands and scurrying legs.

'The tortoise has bitten off the Maharaja's toe!' a courtier shouted, lifting the piece of flesh from where it was sinking behind the disappearing tortoise.

'Murder! Murder!' shouted another courtier.

'Blood!' shouted a third.

'Keep quiet! Keep quiet!' shrieked His Highness, as he felt half afraid that the prime minister would rebuke him for ruining the ceremony by this unseemly behaviour and the millions of his subjects might regard this inauspicious accident as the harbinger of more trouble to come.

But the frightened priests and the cowardly courtiers fled up the palace steps. And cries of Ram! Ram! Hari! Hari! arose from the throngs of people on the other sides of the tank. For everyone now believed from the pandemonium at the three steps that some evil had befallen the Maharaja.

With a resurgence of princely pride, His Highness stood where he was and, though his face twitched and he went pale all over, he waved his arms in the gesture which signifies the casting of a blessing, in order to assure the people that he could maintain his composure even when his courtiers flew in a panic.

At this instant, his own astonishment at his calm filled him with a greater degree of princely pride and he confronted Pandit Ram Prashad, the prime minister, who stood on the first step casting the shadow of his presence on the Maharaja, with an accusing stare in his eyes.

'Catch that swine! Catch that robber who has run away with my big toe!' the Maharaja shouted. 'Don't stand there looking at me! It is your infernal advice which has led to this . . . I shall break your head if you cannot catch the culprit and bring it to justice!'

And, shaking his hands at the prime minister, glaring at the retreating figures, shouting, cursing, moaning and whimpering, he limped up the three steps, fainted, and fell face downwards on the marble floor.

The women of the zenana came weeping up to the balcony and there was mourning in the palace as well as in the capital, as if the

Maharaja were dead or dying.

But with a dauntlessness deriving from the Himalayan blood in her veins, the favourite Rani took His Highness in hand: she issued a proclamation to the people under her own name, giving a full account of the accident, and assuring the populace that the Maharaja was well on the way to recovery and would soon see that the perpetrators of the attempt on his life were brought to justice.

The prime minister now realized that his attempt to wrest control of His Highness's earthly kingdom by pointing out to him the advantages of the kingdom of heaven had failed. And recalling how even in the moment of his direst pain, when he had been bitten by the tortoise, the Maharaja had kept calm while he and the other courtiers had fled to safety up the steps, he now felt afraid of the weak, opium-eating monarch whom he had thought as wax in his hand to twist as he liked. He did not know what kind of retribution the Rajput in His Highness would demand from him if he didn't produce the culprit tortoise. And yet what could you do to a reptile to revenge yourself? Have it killed? But there would surely be no satisfaction in that, as most of the water creatures had cold blood anyhow. Apart from the Maharaja's words before he fainted, however, the favourite queen's behaviour was menacing.

He forthwith ordered the fishermen of Udhampur to lay their nets and catch the tortoise which had bitten off the big toe of His Highness's right foot, and he offered the prize of a rupee to the man who would produce the reptile dead or five rupees to the man who would produce it alive.

It was not long that this prize remained unearned. For during the very next hour fishermen brought several tortoises, dead and alive, in baskets to the prime minister, who was hard put to it to discover which was the tortoise that had bitten off the toe of His Highness's right foot. And, for a moment, he was perplexed. But with that genius for inventing stratagems which is the secret of diplomacy, he had all the tortoises but one thrown back into the tank, and then he went to His Highness's presence, bowed obsequiously, and said, 'Your

Highness's orders have been carried out. The tortoise has been caught. Would Your Highness give the necessary command?'

Maharajadhiraj Sir Ganga Singh Bahadur's princely pride, fanned by his favourite consort's care, had crystallized into a stubborn sense of hurt dignity. His Highness shouted to the prime minister, 'Bring this beti-chod tortoise before the court and let it be tried before me and let a just punishment be meted out to it and all the other culprits! . . .'

It seemed a ridiculous thing for the Maharaja to want to try a tortoise in his court. But the prime minister was used to the strange and absurd whims of His Highness. He kept cool and had the tortoise brought into the court.

On seeing the reptile waving its head in the basket, His Highness ground his teeth in fury and, foaming at the mouth, exclaimed, 'Bring it up here so that I may trample upon it with the foot which it has disabled!'

'Sire,' the prime minister advised, 'it has sharp, knife-like teeth, and may bite off the whole of your royal foot.'

This restrained His Highness from taking the law into his own hands immediately. But he pompously proclaimed, 'We, Sir Ganga Singh Bahadur, Maharajadhiraj of Udhampur, scion of the Suraj-Bansi clan, constitute ourselves as the supreme judge of this court as well as plaintiff and prosecutor in this case. Let whosoever dares to come to the defence of this infamous tortoise who bit our toe speak in its defence. But be assured that if the guilt be proved against the said tortoise, then both the reptiles—the said tortoise and its counsel— shall be beheaded instantaneously in our presence.'

The redness in His Highness's eyes, as well as the cracked fury of his stentorian utterance, was obviously an attempt to imitate the violent and grandiloquent manner of public prosecutors in the fascist states which he had visited during his last European tour. The prime minister came forward and said, 'I shall defend the culprit.'

There were whispers of pity, remorse and joy in the hall, as the noblemen, the courtiers and the servants were sure that the bleeding, bandaged toe of His Highness was the surest proof of the guilt of the tortoise, and would, in being proved, involve difficulties for the prime minister since he had the temerity to defend the reptile.

'Acha then, proceed, you, dog of a Brahmin,' the Maharaja roared, confirming the worst fears of the audience, his anger taking force from the pain in his foot.

'You are my father–mother,' said the wily Ram Prashad without being ruffled by the Maharaja's abuse, 'as you are father–mother of the people of this land. But I have been responsible for encouraging Your Highness to have this tank constructed, and I have a plea to make.'

'Make it then!' said the Maharaja.

'Sire!' began the prime minister, adopting the familiar and time-worn method of flattery. 'Your Highness is a scion of the Sun and, therefore, the greatest and the mightiest prince in the land. Your counsel is heard in far lands and your fame has spread into the farthest corners of the world, even in the lands of perpetual ice and snow where you have travelled. But Your Highness may be pleased to know that, according to the holy books, it is a sin to kill a Brahmin, and punishable by the consignment of the killer to twenty cold hells. Therefore I am free from attack from the highest as well as the lowest of the land.'

Having secured immunity for himself with the aid of Manu's four-thousand-year-old code, which is recognized in part by the Government of India and of course as a whole in the native states, he proceeded to apply his peculiar religious-forensic knowledge to the defence of the tortoise.

'As for this reptile, the sages of old prophesied that the God Vishnu would be born in the iron age in the form of a tortoise and would be transported through an underground passage to a tank specially built for it by a Descendant of the Sun. And that, by the sacrifice of a toe of the said Descendant, the world would get the first sign that the God Vishnu, the Antecedent of the Sun, had come to live in the old land of Rajasthan again. After that event, the old ideal of Ram Raj, of a perfect kingdom, would be realized in the State . . .'

And he further stated that if His Highness would recognize this sign, and forgive those whom he considered his enemies, he would have the gift of a son and heir born to him by his youngest queen and get a safe passage to heaven into the bargain. Otherwise, he said, a lifelong curse would descend upon the Maharaja: he would be made to abdicate and the Suraj-Bansi clan would die out for ever.

'Incarnation of Vishnu!' mocked a courtier who had ambitions to the post of prime minister and therefore hated Pandit Ram Prashad and saw through his machinations. 'Incarnation of the devil! That tortoise has disabled His Highness for life and it is made out to be the vehicle of God!'

His Highness's vanity was flattered by the prime minister's explanation. But, driven almost crazy by the pain of his injured foot, he sweated and blew hot whiffs of breath as he rolled about in a frenzy of indecision on the cushions on which he leaned.

'I have fulfilled my mission in warning you of the portents,' said Ram Prashad to make up His Highness's mind for him.

'What proof is there,' said the courtier who was the rival of the prime minister, 'that this is the tortoise which is, of all the tortoises in the tank, the incarnation of Vishnu?'

'What proof is there,' parried the prime minister, 'that this is the tortoise which bit off the toe of His Highness's right foot?'

The Maharaja seemed to be overcome by the prime minister's logic.

'To be sure, Pandit Ram Prashad seems right,' he said, scratching his beard. 'For the portents, as he described them, tally with the legend that God appears to every scion of the Suraj-Bansi clan.'

'But, Sire!' said the enemy of the prime minister. 'What proof is there that the miracle would happen in this manner? Where are the holy books which lay it down?'

'Pandit Ram Prashad is a holy Brahmin apart from being a vizier,' said one of the partisans of the prime minister.

And there was a way of words, an exchange of fiery glances, and tempers threatened to rise, and were controlled only by the state of His Highness's health.

'What judgment should I pass in the circumstances, Panditji?' asked

His Highness reverently of the prime minister.

'I would suggest that you order this tortoise to be taken back to the River Ganges whence it came,' said the prime minister, 'so that if, as I say, it is the incarnation of the God Vishnu, it will come back and manifest itself again.'

That course of action appealed to His Highness's way of thinking. If it was really God Vishnu, it would come back and do something to reveal itself, though he would not like it to do so in quite the same way as the last time; and if it was only a tortoise, this would be the best way of getting rid of the nuisance and yet to save face after all the brave words he had used and been unable to act upon. His Highness therefore delivered judgment accordingly.

In the law reports of Udhampur state, published by His Highness's Government, in emulation of the practice of England, where justice is mainly custom and precedent, the sentence reads as follows:

'We, Sir Ganga Singh Bahadur, Maharajadhiraj of Udhampur, scion of the Suraj-Bansi clan, Knight Commander of the Star of India (2nd class), etc., order that the tortoise in the palace tank, which is suspected of being either an arch-criminal or the incarnation of the God Vishnu, be exiled to the River Ganges for a year, so that it can prove its authenticity by a miracle of divine will,' etc.

During that year, a tortoise bit off the five fingers of a washerman who was cleaning clothes by the tank, and a son of God was born to the favourite Rani.

At the instance of the prime minister, His Highness the Maharaja declared a public holiday to celebrate the latter event. And everyone believed that the God Vishnu had become incarnate in the old Maharaja and that Ram Raj had come to Udhampur, that it had become a perfect State.

A Rumour

'How far be the town of Bariwal from here, brother?' Dhandu asked a man who sat by a small sweet-stall on the roadside. And while the stall-keeper lifted his dreamy head from where it lay in his interlocked arms, Dhandu mopped the sweat off his black, burnt forehead with the five stubby fingers of his right hand, phewed a hot breath from under his white drooping mustachios, and scratched the bristles of a day's growth of white beard.

'Only a mile,' the stall-keeper murmured.

It seemed to be a mile from everywhere, and, during the three days he had been walking, the miles had seemed to be endless.

'I be from the village of Deogarh,' Dhandu volunteered the information to the sleepy stall-keeper, apologetically, 'a carpenter by trade . . . And I be going to the mill at Bariwal, brother.'

The stall-keeper skimmed the sugar-coated gram, which lay covered with a swarm of flies on the huge iron plate by his side, with his hand, and then looked at Dhandu. But old Dhandu still had some of the gram which his wife had roasted for him to take on his journey, in the bundle on his back, and he did not feel justified in making any extravagant purchases until he had got the job in the mill. He sheepishly withdrew his eyes from the stall and began to walk away.

The winding road was already glowing red-hot under the sun and the small stones and splinters on its frayed edges got into the cracks of his bare heels. He felt guilty that he hadn't hurried to his destination before the sun soared too high. But the dawn had been so cool, and his old, weary limbs couldn't shake off the sleep. And then he had stayed to rub his forehead at the temple, as this was the morning on which he had to buy work, and he needed the blessings of the Gods . . . 'Ram, Ram, Ram,' he muttered the name of God, lest Divine Grace be withdrawn from him for grudging the time he had spent in prayer, and he moved along the dusty fringe of the road with considerable alacrity. As he walked, he looked away into the wheat fields in the shallow valley by the roadside. What fields! Small, weak, spindling stems, one hand high, with hardly any ears of corn!

For a moment, the scorching rays of the sun, slanting on the road, blinded him, and he could see only some vultures perched on the hillside by the carcass of an ass, their twisted beaks shining like bright silver in the glare . . . But, there before him, down the road, was the town: tall brick-built houses and small brick-built houses, and squat, flat-roofed mud huts and uneven thatched cottages, and onion-domed mosques and conic temples like the mountain peaks, and a higher tower that fumed at the sky . . .

Dhandu hurried, almost as if his feet were being impelled by an increased eagerness to reach the town and devour everything that was in it.

Suddenly there was the clanging of vehicles on his right, the raucous loud bellowing of horns, more noisy than the sound of snaky bugles which the ascetics blew at the shrine of Durga Devi at the festival of Kali in Bilaspur, the shouting and yelling of men behind him, accompanied by the tinkling of bells and the ratlling of cane sticks on the wheels of carriages.

Dhandu blinked his eyes and saw that he had walked right into the crossroads and was, with an obstinate calf which stood munching at a bundle of greens it had pilfered from a vegetable stall, the cause of all the pandemonium.

Smiling and impervious to the abuse, the ridicule and the laughter of the drivers, the tonga-wallahs and the pedestrians, he lifted his legs with a love of life which surprised even he who had often forsaken himself to the tender mercies of Bhagwan, who had, indeed, wished, during the latest disgrace of his life, to die. And he got on to the side of a jostling crowd of tall villagers dressed in long homespun tunics and tehmets, and small townsmen, dressed in muslins, who chewed betel leaves galore, and babus who wore kot-patloons, and boat-like caps on their heads.

For a moment he stood bewitched, looking at an enormous red charabanc. He wished he had learned to mend these 'motus' instead of sticking to carpentry all his life. But they were made in Vilayat, it was said; and perhaps you had to go across the seas to learn to repair them . . . 'Better that I should get this job and arrange to call Sukhdevi. Bisheshwar, the weaver, said there were plenty of jobs for skilled workmen in the mill, and the pay was as much as a babu earned . . . But where is the mill? I must ask the way . . .'

As he furtively raised and lowered his dim eyes, he felt that everyone was intent on his own errand. He looked around to make sure again. No one was interested in him—except the pan-biri wallah who was beckoning him . . . Or was he just sprinkling water on the betel leaves spread under the wet rag? He contemplated the parting of the stall-keeper's well-oiled hair and the large freckled looking-glass, which occupied half his shop, beneath the bright picture of Krishan ji Maharaj, dancing on the crest of a cobra, studded with stars. 'Shall I go in and ask, for an hour's shame brings a day's rest . . .'

'Where be the mill, brother? Bariwal woollen mill?' he asked in a whisper, rushing up with alacrity and joining hands and twisting his lips under the thick mustachios with an abject humility.

'Keep aside, keep aside, it is early in the morning!' shouted the pan-biri wallah.

'I be from the village of Deogarh . . .'

'Pass on, pass on, it is early in the morning and I can't give you a pice. I have hardly yet made my bonnee and you beggars—'

'I am not a beggar—'

'Oh, go, don't make a row early in the morning, Baba, I have told you once and for all, go!'

'Where be the mill, brother?' Dhandu pleaded. 'I be from the village of Deogarh and I heard a rumour—'

'Oh, you want to go to the mill; you have heard a rumour that there is a job waiting for you there?' said the pan-biri wallah in an even voice which only half betrayed his cynicism. 'Go along by the fruit market there, see? The big gate in the high wall, studded with gems . . .'

Dhandu murmured gratitude with joined hands and plunged into the road, elated by the cheery manner of the pan-biri wallah.

'His end has come, darting into the road like that!' said the pan-biri wallah to the owner of a neighbouring cookshop.

But the road was clear at that instant except for a group of peasants who stood listening to the voice from a box outside a shop, by the opening of the fruit market. Dhandu entered a square, past the puddle of buffalo urine in the passage. Some sweating coolies were unloading baskets of mangoes in the shops. He had eaten plenty of mangoes at home but never had the fruit smelt so sweet to Dhandu's senses as in this market. Oh, the varieties of them! In the hills the mangoes were so small because the same old trees had to bear fruit year after year and no new cuttings were planted. He would have loved to have tasted one of these which looked like Sukhdevi's breasts before she had had her son . . . But if the mill was so near the fruit market he would be coming here every day. The pan-biri wallah seemed to have heard of the rumour. 'May God bless his auspicious words,' he muttered to himself and pushed ahead till he came to the corner of the fruit market where he thought was the opening leading to the mill. He could see the tall chimney of the factory beyond the stalls, but he could not see an opening.

He decided that he would ask someone the way again.

Little groups of men crouched, sat and slept on the straw in the shadow of the carts. One coolie near him was looking for lice in the seams of his tunic, which he had spread out on his knees while his bare body streamed with sweat; another was pulling lustily at a coconut-basined hookah; a third looked greedily towards some cart-drivers who were beating cream cakes for a cool drink in an earthen pitcher; and a fourth groaned uncannily as he slept . . .

'Where be the way to the mill, brother?' Dhandu asked.

No one answered and all the men remained intent on their preoccupations, since the question had merely been whispered to the different strata of smell in the overloaded air of the market, rather than to any person.

'I be from the village of Deogarh, brother, and I heard a rumour that there is a job for skilled workmen hereabouts. You be hill-men, too, brothers?'

The coolie who was smoking suddenly laughed a laugh which spluttered into a cough as it got caught in the smoke which he inhaled. And the other men looked up at Dhandu as much as to ask, 'Are you mad?'

'Don't laugh at one who is old enough to be your father,' said the man who was looking for lice, to his companion.

'The old fool! Fancy coming here where the coolies of the whole world have descended and crowded each other out!' said the man who was smoking.

'Go, go, Baba, there is your way,' the third man said wearily. 'Don't mind these bastards. You should have gone by the main road, but there is a short cut through that lane.'

'Acha, son,' Dhandu said. 'Will the jackal's cry kill the buffalo or the abuse of an angry man damage my soul?' And he proceeded.

There, he could see the tall chimney of the mill talking to the sky behind the irregular houses by the godowns. But where was the lane?

He walked through the market which swarmed with men and beasts of burden and carts and sacks and buzzing flies and wasps, till he could see the narrow opening of an alleyway with a folding iron door which was ajar.

'It is no shame to eat one's own bread or to earn it,' he said to assure himself before approaching the great doors of the factory. The spiked grandeur of the iron gateway towered above him and he felt small and irrelevant before the fine cock of a Pathan who stood dressed in a green drill uniform with a gun in his hand and a belt of cartridges round his chest.

He hesitated a little and scratched his beard to screw up courage. There was no one about, and the sentry had seen him. So he advanced, his head bent and his feet hitting against each other. His son had told him that it was the natural custom among the Pathans to salaam and not to join hands. He gingerly put his hands to his head and said,

'Salaam, Khan, I heard a rumour that there is a job for a skilled workman in the mill. I be from the village of Deogarh, a carpenter by caste.'

'Who told you the rumour?' said the Pathan, standing rigidly where he was, without the flicker of an eyelid.

'Bisheshwar Singh, a man from my village who worked here said so, Hajoor.'

'Ah, Basheshwar Singh! You are the friend of Basheshwar Singh?' said the Pathan, without changing his tone.

Dhandu's hopes, which had been slightly chilled by the laughter of the coolie in the fruit market, arose to see that the sentry knew Bisheshwar Singh. 'Han,' he continued, 'Bisheshwar Singh said that there is good money for a skilled worker in this mill.'

'Ah, Basheshwar Singh said so, eh? Basheshwar!' the Pathan iterated, grinding his words first softly, then hard, after which he smiled a good-humoured smile. 'Basheshwar Singh, the son of a dog! Basheshwar Singh! The seed of a donkey! . . .'

'You remember him then, Khan?' Dhandu asked, thinking that the Pathan was abusing Bisheshwar affectionately, as is the custom among intimate friends in Hindustan.

'Who doesn't know Basheshwar Singh?' the Pathan said, curling his lips like a viper. 'He was the ringleader of the strike in this mill and I would have murdered him like this.' He raised the forefinger of his right hand to his neck and then made the noise which the knife makes in butchering the neck of a goat. 'I would have murdered him if Dastur sahib had not prevented me. The illegally begotten Basheshwar! Rape of his mother! Where is he? I have to settle a feud with him! Where has he retreated—back to his mother? Rape of his sister! He and his associates beat me, beat me in the strike. And they stopped the mazdoors from paying me the interest as well as the principal. Dastur sahib, the coward, suspended him before I came out of hospital, otherwise Basheshwar and his life would have parted company. But he does not know that a Pathan never forgets . . .' And he rubbed the five fingers of his right hand over his face and took the ceremonious vow of vengeance.

'What does a strike mean, Khan?' Dhandu asked, to allay the Pathan's wrath before asking him for the job, for he still harboured a naive faith.

'Oh, do you joke with me?' the Pathan shouted. 'What means a strike? Has that illegally begotten sent you here to start trouble again? I shall shoot him if I see him—Labour Commissioner or no Labour Commissioner! And if you value your life, go your way!'

'But, Khan, I don't know Bisheshwar,' Dhandu said, with joined hands. 'I only heard the rumour in the village and I had lost my home and implements through the working of fate, so I came here, a three days' journey from my village, Deogarh; and I be a carpenter by trade . . .'

'You heard a rumour, eh, a rumour?' said the Pathan, craning his neck forward. 'The son of a donkey, a rumour!' And he laughed a crackling crow's laugh. 'A rumour! The sinews of an owl! A rumour!'

'Khan . . . is it not? . . .'

'Go, son of Khan, how can it be true!' the Pathan said, with a gurgle in his throat. 'Dastur sahib has sacked a number of mazdoors because the mill will soon go on short work.'

'But, Khan,' Dhandu persisted.

'Go, go, there are no jobs,' shouted the sentry, with a resurgence of anger. 'Go, son of Basheshwar, the gandu. Go, or I shall hand you over to the police! Go!' And he shook the double-barrelled gun and stamped his feet.

The violence of the Pathan's manner lifted the scales from Dhandu's dim, hopeful eyes and he saw that there was no getting past this sentry into the factory, as there was no passing through the hard wood of its gate or across its high walls with the broken glass studded on its cemented edges. For a moment he stood thinking that he could join his hands to the sentry. But the Pathan stood pulling himself to his full height, hard as a rock. Dhandu couldn't even lift his eyes to see. The thing before him, the wood of the door, the spikes on its crest, the pillars which supported the doors, even the shadow of the gateway seemed to weigh down on his brain. He hung his head, not daring to look up to the pendent strength of the gigantic objects about him.

'Go!' the sentry shouted again and stamped his feet.

Dhandu jumped and then began to walk away like a dog with his tail between legs, looking furtively back to see if the Pathan was following him.

His throat was parched; his legs trembled and seemed to sink beneath him; his whole frame, hardened by the toil of years, seemed to have grown suddenly numb . . .

He looked emptily before him as if he were walking through a void, completely unconscious of the sweat trickling through the rivulets of the furrows on his head, across his eyes, across his bearded cheeks, across his nose to the lips, the chin and the neck. Fascinated by the fear of the Pathan, he wanted to glance back again towards the gate of the factory, but his courage failed him.

'A rumour! A rumour! Only a rumour!' The thought tolled at the back of his brain like the echo of some distant thunder.

And he walked along dazed.

'So there were no jobs,' he muttered to himself as he stood still some distance from the scene of his humiliation. 'What was a strike, and what had Bisheshwar Singh done?' he asked himself, turning back to see if he was out of the danger zone. But there was no answer to these questions in his brain. As he cast another glance backwards he still felt dangerously near the factory gate. To get farther away from the hateful, unapproachable factory, however, and feeling that it would be easier if he kept on the move, he resumed his way.

He felt as if he were journeying at an ant's pace through a sandy desert, breathless and choked with the heat; his life seemed a heavier burden than he had ever carried . . . He had felt like this once or twice when he had the ague as a child, helpless and weighed down as if he could sink wherever he dropped if he let himself go, released the hold on himself. But then he had recovered from these illnesses and floated like a leaf in the hills, and he had gone adventuring into the fields without shirking work. Now, however . . .

'Ohe, get out of the way, ohe, get out of the way!' a cart-driver shouted, while he strained at the buffalo to stop the cart.

Dhandu became aware that he had stopped still without knowing that he had stopped.

He edged out of the way and tried to summon some thought which could illumine the darkness in his eyes. But no thoughts came into his head, only the feeling that he was just drifting along, knowing not where to go in this strange city, far away from his village, alone, without any friends or relations.

Honk! Honk! The horn of a lorry barked as it came from a sidestreet.

'Ohe, get aside, hurry, hurry, ohe, ohe, ohe . . .' the policeman on point-duty called.

'A rumour! So it was only a rumour, a rumour!' Dhandu continued to murmur self-pityingly in the empty shell of his brain, heedless of the calls. 'And Bisheshwar said every mazdoor gets thirty rupees . . . and Angrezi houses to live in, and meat to eat instead of lentils and rice—and there was really no . . .'

Honk! Honk!

'A rumour. . . .'

But the lorry from behind, in trying to avoid a headlong crash with the bullock-cart, had skirted round the road and knocked him down.

Instinctively he rolled, five, six times, the deafening roar of the engine, the shouts, the horns urging him on. But the inexorable wheels of the lorry, unchecked by the brakes, ran over him, crushing his ribs.

He put his hands to his heart and opened his mouth to shriek, but no sound came, though his heart was beating loudly. There was a sudden panic in his hot flesh.

What had happened?—Was he dead?'

His arms fell on his sides, the toes of his feet were severed clean from their joints and the entrails showed over the mess, torn from his insides. He strained his will in a brave effort to rise again, but he couldn't.

He waited patiently without a cry, as though if he remained cool and fearless, death would be warded off. But in the dusty heat of the forenoon his blood flowed and, before the people could drag him out from under the lorry, he was dead.

A rumour reached Deogarh some months later that Dhandu, the old carpenter of the village, had become a resident of the celestial heavens.

A Pair of Mustachios

There are various kinds of mustachios worn in my country, to mark the boundaries between the various classes of people. Outsiders may think it stupid to lay down, or rather to raise, lines of demarcation of this kind, but we are notorious in the whole world for sticking to our queer old conventions, prides and prejudices, even as the Chinese or the Americans, or, for that matter, the English . . . And, at any rate, some people may think it easier and more convenient to wear permanent boundary-lines like mustachios, which only need a smear of grease to keep them bright and shiny, rather than to wear frock coats, striped trousers and top hats, which constantly need to be laundered and dry-cleaned, and the maintenance of which is already leading to the bankruptcy of the European ruling classes. With them, clothes make the man, but to us, mustachios make the man. So we prefer the various styles of mustachios to mark the differences between the classes . . .

And very unique and poetical symbols they are too. For instance, there is the famous lion mustache, the fearsome upstanding symbol of that great order of resplendent rajas, maharajas, nabobs and English army generals who are so well known for their devotion to the King-Emperor. Then there is the tiger mustache, the uncanny, several-pointed mustache worn by the unbending, unchanging survivals from the ranks of the feudal gentry who have nothing left but the pride in their greatness and a few mementoes of past glory, scrolls of honour, granted by the former emperors, a few gold trinkets, heirlooms, and bits of land. Next there is the goat mustache—a rather unsure brand, worn by the nouveau riche, the new commercial bourgeoisie, and the shopkeeper class who somehow don't belong—an indifferent, thin little line of a mustache, worn so that its tips can be turned up or down as the occasion demands a show of power to some coolie or humility to a prosperous client. There is the Charlie Chaplin mustache worn by the lower middle class, by clerks and professional men, a kind of half-and-half affair, deliberately designed as a compromise between the traditional full mustache and the clean-shaven Curzon cut of the sahibs and the barristers, because the babus are not sure whether the sahibs like them to keep mustachios at all. There is the sheep mustache of the coolies and the lower orders, the mouse mustache of the peasants, and so on.

In fact, there are endless styles of mustachios, all appropriate to the wearers and indicative of the various orders, as rigorously adhered to as if they had all been patented by the Government of India or had been sanctioned by special appointment with His Majesty the King or Her Majesty the Queen. And any poaching on the style of one class by members of another is resented, and the rising ratio of murders in my country is interpreted by certain authorities as being indicative of the increasing jealousy with which each class is guarding its rights and privileges in regard to the mark of the mustachio.

Of course, the analysis of the expert is rather too abstract, and not all the murders can be traced to this cause, but certainly it is true that the preferences of the people with regard to their mustachios are causing a lot of trouble in our parts.

For instance, there was a rumpus in my own village the other day about a pair of mustachios.

It so happened that Seth Ramanand, the grocer and moneylender, who had been doing well out of the recent fall in the price of wheat by buying up whole crops cheap from the hard-pressed peasants and then selling grain at higher prices, took it into his head to twist the goat mustache, integral to his order and position in society, at the tips, so that it looked nearly like a tiger mustache.

Nobody seemed to mind very much, because most of the mouse-mustached peasants in our village are beholden to the bania, either because they owe him interest on a loan, or an instalment on a mortgage of jewellery or land. Besides, the seth had been careful enough to twist his mustache so that it seemed nearly, though not quite, like a tiger mustache.

But there lives in the vicinity of our village, in an old, dilapidated Moghul style house, a Mussulman named Khan Azam Khan, who claims descent from an ancient Afghan family whose heads were noblemen and councillors in the Court of the Great Moghuls. Khan Azam Khan, a tall, middle-aged man, is a handsome and dignified person, and he wears a tiger mustache and remains adorned with the faded remnants of a gold-brocaded waistcoat, though he hasn't even a patch of land left.

Some people, notably the landlord of our village and the moneylender, maliciously say that he is an impostor, and that all his talk about his blue blood is merely the bluff of a rascal. Others, like the priest of the temple, concede that his ancestors were certainly attached to the Court of the Great Moghuls, but as sweepers. The landlord, the moneylender and the priest are manifestly jealous of anyone's long ancestry, however, because they have all risen from nothing, and it is obvious from the stately ruins around Khan Azam Khan what grace was once his and his forefathers. Only Khan Azam Khan's pride is greatly in excess of his present possessions, and he is inordinately jealous of his old privileges and rather foolish and headstrong in safeguarding every sacred brick of his tottering house against vandalism.

Khan Azam Khan happened to go to the moneylender's shop to pawn his wife's gold nose ring one morning and he noticed the upturning tendency of the hair on Ramanand's upper lip which made the bania's goat mustache look almost like his own tiger mustache.

'Since when have the lentil-eating shopkeepers become noblemen?' he asked surlily, even before he had shown the nose ring to the bania.

'I don't know what you mean, Khan,' Ramanand answered.

'You know what I mean, seed of a donkey!' said the Khan. 'Look at the way you have turned the tips of your mustache upwards. It almost looks like my tiger mustache. Turn the tips down to the style proper to the goat that you are! Fancy the airs of the banias nowadays!'

'Oh, Khan, don't get so excited,' said the moneylender, who was nothing if he was not amenable, having built up his business on the maxim that the customer is always right.

'I tell you, turn the tip of your mustache down if you value your life!' raged Khan Azam Khan.

'If that is all the trouble, here you are,' said Ramanand, brushing one end of his mustache with his oily hand so that it dropped like a dead fly. 'Come, show me the trinkets. How much do you want for them?'

Now that Khan Azam Khan's pride was appeased, he was like soft wax in the merchant's sure hand. His need, and the need of his family for food, was great, and he humbly accepted the value which the bania put on his wife's nose ring.

But as he was departing after negotiating his business, he noticed that though one end of the bania's mustache had come down at his behest, the other end was still up.

'A strange trick you have played on me, you swine,' the Khan said.

'I have paid you the best value for your trinket, Khan, that any moneylender will pay in these parts,' the bania said, 'especially in these days when the Sarkars of the whole world are threatening to go off the gold standard.'

'It has nothing to do with the trinket,' said Azam Khan, 'but one end of your mustache is still up like my tiger mustache, though you have brought down the other to your proper goat's style. Bring that other end down also, so that there is no apeing by your mustache of mine.'

'Now, Khan,' said the bania, 'I humbled myself because you are doing business with me. You can't expect me to become a mere worm just because you have pawned a trinket with me. If you were pledging some more expensive jewellery, I might consider obliging you a little more. Anyhow, my humble milk-skimmer doesn't look a bit like your valiant tiger mustache.'

'Bring that tip down!' Khan Azam Khan roared, for the more he had looked at the bania's mustache the more the still-upturned tip seemed to him like an effort at an imitation of his own.

'Now, be sensible, Khan,' the moneylender said, waving his hand with an imperturbable calm.

'I tell you, turn that tip down or I shall wring your neck,' said the Khan.

'All right, the next time you come to do business with me I shall bring that tip down,' answered the moneylender cunningly.

'That is fair,' said Chaudhri Chottu Ram, the landlord of the village, who was sitting under the tree opposite.

'To be sure! To be sure!' some peasants chimed in sheepishly. Khan Azam Khan managed to control his murderous impulses and walked away. But he could not quell his pride, the pride of the generations of his ancestors who had worn the tiger mustache as a mark of their high position. To see the symbol of his honour imitated by a bania—that was too much for him. He went home and fetched a necklace which had come down to his family through seven generations and, placing it before the bania, said, 'Now will you bring that tip of your mustache down?'

'By all means, Khan,' said the bania. 'But let us see about this necklace. How much do you want for it?'

'Any price will do, so long as you bring the tip of your mustache down,' answered Azam Khan.

After they had settled the business, the moneylender said, 'Now, Khan, I shall carry out your will.' And he ceremoniously brushed the upturned tip of his mustache down.

As Azam Khan was walking away, however, he noticed that the other tip of the bania's mustache had now gone up and stood dubiously like the upturned end of his own exalted tiger mustache. He turned on his feet and shouted, 'I shall kill you if you don't brush that mustache into the shape appropriate to your position as a lentil-eating bania!'

'Now, now, Khan, come to your senses. You know it is only the illusion of a tiger's mustache and nowhere like your brave and wonderful adornment,' said the greasy moneylender.

'I tell you I won't have you insulting the insignia of my order!' shouted Azam Khan. 'You bring that tip down!'

'I wouldn't do it, Khan, even if you pawned all the jewellery you possess to me,' said the moneylender.

'I would rather I lost all my remaining worldly possessions, my pots and pans, my clothes, even my house, than see the tip of your mustache turned up like that!' spluttered Azam Khan.

'Acha, if you care so little for all your goods and chattels, sell them to me and then I shall turn that tip of my mustache down,' said the moneylender. 'And, what is more, I shall keep it flat. Now, is that a bargain?'

'That seems fair enough,' said the landlord from under the trees where he was preparing for a siesta.

'But what proof have I that you will keep your word?' said Azam Khan. 'You oily lentil-eaters never keep your promises.'

'We shall draw up a deed, here and now,' said the moneylender. 'And we shall have it signed by the five elders of the village who are seated under that tree. What more do you want?'

'Now, there is no catch in that,' put in the landlord. 'I and four other elders will come to court as witnesses on your behalf if the bania doesn't keep his mustache to the goat style ever afterwards.'

'I shall excommunicate him from religion if he doesn't keep his word,' added the priest, who had arrived on the scene on hearing the hubbub.

'Acha,' agreed Azam Khan.

And he forthwith had a deed prepared by the petition writer of the village, who sat smoking his hubble-bubble under the tree. And this document, transferring all his household goods and chattels, was signed in the presence of the five elders of the village and sealed. And the moneylender forthwith brought both tips of his mustache down and kept them glued in the goat style appropriate to his order.

Only, as soon as Khan Azam Khan's back was turned, he muttered to the peasants seated nearby, 'My father was a sultan.'

And they laughed to see the Khan give a special twist to his mustache, as he walked away, maintaining the valiant uprightness of the symbol of his ancient and noble family, though he had become a pauper.

The Cobbler and the Machine

Apart from the innocence of old age and youth, Saudagar, the cobbler of my village, and I shared in common a passion for the machine.

Saudagar, of course, was interested in only one machine, the small sewing machine which the village tailor wielded very ostentatiously on the footboard of his cavernous shop before the gaping rustics, who had often travelled fifty miles from their homes in the hills to see it— a grimy, black hand-machine in a casket, decorated with a tracery of leaves in yellow paint, that nibbled at the yards of cloth, like a slimy rat, at terrific speed. But I liked all kinds of machines which I saw in the town where I went to school every morning: the great big railway engine, whose phuff-phuff I had learned to imitate when we played at trains at the recess hour; the phonograph from which I hoped to hear my own voice one day; the motor car in which my father was given a lift by Lalla Sain Das when there was an election; the pushbike on which our second master came to school from his bungalow; the intricate mass of wheels and pistons which lay hiccuping in the powerhouse at the junction of the two canals; and the roaring monsters of iron and steel that converted the cotton and wool of our village into cloth at the Dhariwal mills. And even of sewing machines I had seen at least two varieties other than the one that Saudagar knew, and yet a third—a pedal-machine, adjusted to a chair with a leather belt across it, to which I used to see Baha-ud-din, the tailor in the Main Bazaar in the town, glued all day, and a similar upright contraption on which one of the employees in the Bhalla shoe shop sat sewing boots.

'Uncle Saudagar,' I said to the cobbler one day as I sat idly at the door of his dark straw hut while he stared across the street at Bhagirath, the tailor, revolving the handle of his sewing machine with amazing alacrity. 'Do you know you waste so much of your time sewing pieces of leather to the soles of people's shoes and then they complain that you don't sew them well and that the water gets into them? Why, you could have a machine like Bhagirath's, even superior, with a seat attached to it like the chairs the sahibs sit on. I have seen a man in the Bhalla shoe shop sewing boots on one.'

'Is there a machine like that, son?' said Saudagar incredulously, and yet vaguely convinced, as he had been for months since the tailor bought his casket machine, that there must be a contrivance for sewing leather as there was one for sewing cloth.

'Yes, Uncle,' I said enthusiastically, for to me all machines were still toys and playthings, rather than 'chariots which men could ride'. 'There are wonderful machines in the town if only you will go and see, but you never stir out of this hovel. Didn't you go to see the great exhibition at Lahore? My father tells me there was a great big boot there, all sewn by machine, in which people could play hide-and-seek.' I had seen the wonders of science in the school laboratory and the marvels in the streets of the town and wished rather too eagerly that they could come to my village, so convinced was I of the superiority of modernity over the old ways of the countryside.

'Well, son,' said the old man kindly, 'I have heard that there is a machine which can do the work of my hand, but I have never seen it. Ever since I saw the ready-made saddles, reins and collars in the stables of Thakur Mahan Chand, I knew they were made by a defter hand than that of man. And when the son of the landlord sent me the black leather boots which he bought in town to mend, I knew that they couldn't have been sewn by any human being. And truly, I have been looking at Bhagirath's sewing machine and wondering if there is a similar contraption for sewing shoes. But I am old and have not been to town these ten years. So I have not seen what this machine looks like. One day I must make a trip to see it. But, of course, I am too poor ever to be able to buy it. And perhaps God would curse my fingers and those of my pupils, and make them incapable of sewing at all, if I began to use this machine.'

'But, Uncle Saudagar,' I said, 'I tell you you will like this machine if you see it. And you will look like a sahib sitting on the chair which is adjusted to it. You will only need a basket-hat to complete your life and you will begin to eat and drink on a raised platform automatically. I wish my mother would let me convert that broken pitcher we have into a chair and I could use the manger of the cows for a table always.'

'I am an outcast, son,' Saudagar said. 'How can I presume to eat like the sahibs or be like them. And won't people laugh at me if they see me seated in a chair, sewing shoes?'

'But these people are fools, Uncle,' I said. 'They regard the sahibs as outcasts, too, even though the sahibs are clean. And these rustics have no idea of modern times. They are old fogies with junglee habits. They are oxen. They have no idea of the new life.'

'Yes, son, perhaps you are right,' said the old cobbler. 'God has created iron in the mountains. I suppose He meant us to make machines with it.'

'I have got a beautiful bolt I found in the playground, Uncle,' I said. I will show it to you, if you like.'

'I would like to see it, son,' said Saudagar indulgently. 'Now run along and go home. Your father might come this way and abuse you for wasting your time sitting in an outcast's shop. Run along and play with your fellows.'

'I will also bring you a picture of the sewing machine, if you like, Uncle,' I said, making an overture of friendship so as to win more easily the privilege of fidgeting around the cobbler's shop, for ordinarily he discouraged children from flocking around the door of his hovel and robbing his dim eyes of the little natural light that trickled through the aperture of the door.

'All right,' he said. 'All right, son. You must show me a picture if you can, though I don't know what use it is to show a man the likeness of a bunch of grapes when he will never be able to eat the fruit.'

But the spark that had failed to kindle a devouring flame in the heart of old Saudagar lit my flesh with the warmth of a new delight, for the echo of the old cobbler of my village handling a new machine reverberated in my brain like the voice of a wish that had become father to the thought. I ran towards home as if I were possessed by more than a love of the new toy that would be Saudagar's machine. I had a feeling that there might come to be in my village the atmosphere of a splendid, gorgeous wonder-house, in which great big iron frames, with a thousand screws and knobs assembled through the ingenuity of a man like my science master, created the power to achieve miracles.

I persuaded my class-fellows when we were coming home from school the next day to climb a high wall near the railway station and pull off a poster which showed an Englishwoman, with a bun on the top of her head, wielding a Singer sewing machine embossed on a steel plate in the shape of the letter S. And I brought it to Saudagar.

'This, Uncle,' I said, 'is the kind of machine which I told you you should have. Only this is for sewing cloth. But the one for sewing leather, which the man in the Bhalla shoe shop plies, is like it in appearance, except that it has a thicker needle.'

The old cobbler looked at the picture in wide-eyed wonder. I could see from the loving way in which he passed his hand over the surface of the steel that his imagination had caught fire from the picture of the sewing machine, bigger than Bhagirath's, which seemed to make him firmly believe in the existence of a similar machine for sewing leather, though he hadn't seen it.

And so charmed was he by the novelty of the instrument of which I had shown him the picture, that he asked us to bring the steel plate which we had stolen into his shop and leave it there for a decoration. And he gave us a pice each as compensation for our trouble.

It seemed to me that he had not kept the advertisement for the Singer sewing machine merely for decorative purposes, but because he wanted to see the likeness of the object which he had set his heart on buying one day. And my feeling was confirmed by the fact that whenever I went to his hovel now he would always say something about the shape of the needle in the picture not being quite clear, and of his inability to understand how one could get into the habit of pressing the pedal with the feet while one was sewing something on top.

'And the stool seems too small,' he said. 'It may be all right for the "lendis" to sit on, but how will such a crude old bottom as mine balance on it?'

'Don't you care,' I said, with an emphasis that gained weight from the earnestness and zeal I felt at the prospect of seeing the cobbler of my village achieve the dexterity of the man in the Bhalla shoe shop. 'A little practise and you will learn to wield it better than anyone else, and as for your old posterior, why, I have seen the heavy-bottomed memsahib, who is the wife of the city engineer, balanced on a stool like that in the veranda of her bungalow, as if she were seated on a comfortable horse.'

A look of wonder lit his dim eyes and, glancing at me with the tenderness of humility, he traced the curves of the steel plate on the picture of the machine printed in black-and-white against the green. And then he would close his eyes and, smiling, shake his head as if he were surcharged with the ecstasy of a knowledge in the hollows of his brain where phantasmagoric visions of himself at work on the new machine swirled in a mad delirium, the edges of enchanting top-boots, splendid, well-polished shoes, and strong-soled country shoes creating and destroying each other in an irrelevant disorder.

'But anyhow, the trouble is, son, where am I to get the money to buy the machine?' the old man would then say with a sigh, and continue, 'I don't know how I shall get it, and where it is to be got even if I had the money, which I shall never have.'

The grim sagacity of his practical argument defeated my intelligence, for I had no idea how many rupees the machine cost and where Saudagar was to get the money, but, of course, the address of the Singer Sewing Machine Company, England, was printed at the bottom of the picture, and I speculated that if that company manufactured sewing machines for cloth, surely they made those for sewing leather, and I said, 'It is made in Vilayat, and can be had from there, or perhaps through a commission agent in Lahore or Bombay, if not in our district.'

'Vilayat is very far away,' Saudagar said, 'and I shall never cross the seven seas even when I go to Heaven, because I have not done enough good deeds to earn the privilege of being able to travel in my next life. As for Lahore and Bombay, if anyone is going there from our parts we will make inquiries.'

But for days and weeks and months no one from our parts was going to Lahore, Delhi or Bombay, and I hugged the desperate enthusiasm for Saudagar's sewing machine in my heart till the cool waters of a placid existence had washed off the bright edges of my dreams. I went to see the cobbler as usual in the afternoons, but the topic of the machine was seldom mentioned, and instead the old man bent over the shoes he was mending, brushed his beard, and, with a mischievous light in his eyes, told me a story about some ogre or wild animal, or the witchery of an old maiden who died without ever being married.

One day, however, when I was waiting at the usual hour for my friends to emerge from their homes to play in a maidan near Saudagar's house, he called me and, with a weird chuckle that rose above the curve of his usual silence into a jerky shriek like the convulsive laugh of a madman, he said, 'Come here, son, and guess what has happened.'

'What is it?' I asked, at first completely taken aback, but then warming to the happy glare in his eyes with a sensation that the cause of Saudagar's sudden happiness was somehow connected with our project about the machine.

'You know, son, that Lalla Sain Das, the notary and cotton dealer, has gone to Vilayat on business. Well, he asked me to make him some gold-worked shoes to give as presents to his clients beyond the seas. When he came to collect them, he asked me politely whether he could do something for me while he was away. And I asked him to fetch a machine for sewing leather. He was very kind and said he would bring the machine most willingly. And what is more, that since he knew I was a poor man who couldn't pay him for the thing at once, he would buy the machine at his own expense and let me use it and pay for it by and by exactly as if it were a loan with a small interest attached to it. Now I have had this letter from the rail office and the Munshi read it and he says that it is the voucher for the sewing machine which Lalla Sain Das has sent from Vilayat and which is lying in the railway godown. So, please God, I shall have the machine after all. I am going to distribute sugar-plums among the brotherhood to celebrate the auspicious occasion when the machine comes, and I will make you a pair of Angrezi boots, since it was really you who told me about it.'

I clapped my hands with joy, took some breaths quickly, and stimulated my being with shouts of 'Marvellous! Marvellous!' And, either because I easily whipped myself into a kind of elemental buoyancy, or because it was the natural colour of my temperament, I danced in my mind to the cadences of a rhythm I could feel in the working of the machine, in its contours, in its dainty, intricate contrivances, its highly ingenious purpose, in the miracle it was to me, an architecture embodying mysteries which not only represented the exact formulas of science and mathematics, but was the magnificent toy, the plaything. And, of course, Saudagar's offer of a pair of Angrezi boots, such as I had been persuading my father to buy me for years, made me hysterically happy, for I felt that I could rise in the estimation of all my fellows by possessing footwear which was worn only by the sahibs and the rich folk.

'When will you actually get the machine, Uncle?' I asked eagerly.

'I shall go and get it tomorrow, son,' he said. 'It is after eleven years that I am going to town.'

'If you are in town, then, go and get the advice of the cobbler in the Bhalla shoe shop as to how to work it.'

'That is a good idea,' Saudagar said. 'Yes, I will do that. And since you have been so good to me, child, I shall take your measurements now and start sewing your shoes first on the machine.'

I would have stayed and talked about the possibilities of the new wonder to Saudagar if my friends had not been calling incessantly, but that afternoon I was too preoccupied by my ardour to put my heart into playing kabaddi, and I couldn't sleep in the night for the sheer excitement of sharing the glory of having inspired the old cobbler. In the morning I ran along to school, bound up in the curves of a rich stillness, the radiant exultation of a child whose fantastic dreams have, for the first time, achieved the guise of visible truths. And all day I was full of mischief—the tingling shadow of an ingrown largeness in my being played havoc with every mundane fact, the vastness of the creator laughed at people, and the depths of a realized truth mocked at impossibilities.

Off I went to Saudagar's shop immediately after I returned from school and, true as the very colour of my dream, even truer because harder, the sewing machine was before me, with the old cobbler seated on the stool adjusted to it, sewing a piece of leather, with beads of perspiration on his forehead, as his two pupils and a number of other people of low and high castes crowded into the hovel to see the wizardry.

'Come, son,' Saudagar said, lifting his eyes and breathing a mouthful of stale breath. 'This is the upper part of the boots I am going to sew for you, since you must have the first fruits of my acquisition.'

I smiled awkwardly and then felt a sudden urge to touch the wonderful new thing which was exactly like the sewing machine of which I had brought Saudagar the picture, except that it had no casket to enclose the upper part, but an anvil into which the needle darted like a shaft, probing the leather in between with the cotton in its eye. But I curbed my childish desire as, just then, Saudagar brushed aside the crowd which was also clamouring to touch it, and I only asked, 'When will my shoes be ready, Uncle?'

'You shall have them by and by,' Saudagar said. 'I will sew them at any odd times I get, because all the rest of my time must be devoted to turning out enough work to pay off the debt I owe on the machine to Lalla Sain Das, who is coming back tomorrow.'

My visits to the cobbler's shop became more frequent since I could always excuse myself to my parents by saying that I was going to the outcast's quarter to see how the boots that Saudagar had promised to make me were coming along. And as my old Indian shoes made of crude hide were wearing out and my parents would have had to buy me a new pair if Saudagar had not offered me the gift, I was allowed to go and waste as much time as I liked.

Saudagar had added a pattern of stitches to the shoes he intended for me during the first few days, but then he had hung them up as a sample on the door of his hut, and was mainly busy turning out Indian shoes by the dozen to defray the interest that accrued at the rate of fifteen per cent on the sum of one thousand rupees, which Lalla Sain Das had declared to be the cost of the machine plus freightage and taxes. Every time I went, the old man would pick up the sample and contemplate it with an air of absorption and say, 'Well, son, I believe I shall begin to sew the lining to them next week, and then I must send Majitha to get some leather for the soles and heels. Or would you like rubber soles instead?'

'No, I want leather soles and rubber heels, Uncle,' I said, swinging from the first disappointment of seeing the shoes no further advanced to a sudden excitement.

'You can't have both, son,' Saudagar would say kindly.

'I want to set the fashion,' I replied.

'But, son, let me make you an ordinary pair first,' said the old man, 'and then later—'

'When will they be ready?' I would ask impatiently.

'Tomorrow, by the grace of God, tomorrow I shall do something to them . . .'

But tomorrow and tomorrow and tomorrow came and went, and as my old Indian shoes were completely worn out and discarded, I trudged barefoot to and from school, and cursed both my parents for not buying me a new pair of Angrezi shoes and Saudagar for not completing the pair he had promised me.

I couldn't realize that my parents were poor and could not afford to buy me a new pair of English boots, and I was too obstinate to accept a cheap pair of Indian shoes. But Saudagar's work was pledged to Lalla Sain Das for the money the cobbler had borrowed to buy the machine, and I was disgusted.

'Let me buy you a good pair of shoes like your old ones,' my mother said.

'No,' I replied stubbornly. 'I want English shoes and you needn't bother because Saudagar is making them for me.'

'"Never trust a washerman's promise, nor a goldsmith's nor a cobbler's,"' she quoted the proverb.

But mine was the faith that would have moved mountains but for the fact that an act of God intervened. Saudagar, the old cobbler, fell ill and was unable to work for days, and when he got up from his illness he had to clear arrears of debt and work so hard on his ordinary job that he had no time left even to think of the shoes he had so lovingly cut and on which he had sewn the first stitches. And considering that he had not been able to pay up even the arrears of interest on the cost of the machine, there was little prospect of his ever completing the job for me.

I looked at the old man bending over the machine and working patiently as sweat poured from his face on to his neck and then on to the earth, and I felt constrained not to trouble him with my demands. And the mixture of resentment and pity I felt for the old man became transformed into a feeling of hate for the machine, for, as it stood hard, hard and unbending, it seemed to have become a barrier between Saudagar and me and the thing which had emphasized his self-interest so that he never seemed to put a stitch on anyone's shoes without insisting on being paid for it. And as he sat tied to the chariot wheels of doom, he also began to be more and more reticent, as if he were turning in upon himself to drink his own blood in the silent places of his heart, and the illumination of his natural manner disappeared behind a pale, shadowy face that was always dirty and grimy with a layer of scum on the sweat-covered beard. And still the sample shoes of English design meant for me stood unfinished, while he and his assistants worked furiously to produce enough to pay off the debt on the machine.

I shook the roots of hope from their foundation in my heart and rarely visited Saudagar's shop, thinking he would call me one day when the remorse of his unfulfilled promise had prompted him to finish making my boots.

But that day never came, for, worn out by the fatigue of producing many more shoes than he had ever sewn to pay off his debt, drained of his life-blood by the sweat that was always pouring off his body, he fell stone dead one evening as he recited the devotional verses:

'The days of your life are ending
And you have not made your accounts with God.'

In the amorphous desert of my familiar thoughts I felt the pain of a silent guilt, as I knew that I had, to some extent, been the cause of his death. If only I had known then that it was not enough for Saudagar and his pupils to love the machine and work it, but to own it, I could have defied the verdict of the village which said that Saudagar was killed by the devil disguised in the image of the sewing machine.

A Confession

I don't know why he had to say it to me. But, after listening to the address of Srijut Bishambar Dayal Bhargava on the achievements of the national renaissance during the last few years, I had to go home with Latif and, on seeing him ostentatiously lift the cloth from the sumptuous supper which his wife had left on the table, I had casually let fall the remark, 'I wonder how many coolies have been vouchsafed the advantages of a fifth meal like this, through the Struggle, or for the matter of that, of a meal at all.'

'You are a cynic,' Latif said, and in a characteristic lawyer's manner sought to defend the lovely food against my aspersions. 'You would not wish to deprive those of us who have the good things of the world of their enjoyment of them when you yourself are really trying to afford the poor the advantages they don't possess. You will produce utter chaos in this world if you do that, and law, authority and religion will all go by the board. As you know, there have always been inequalities in this world; the sheep always want to be led, and they want God as much as bread. So it was in the past, so it is in the present, so it will be in the future.'

'I am probably a prig,' I said. 'I have an awful conscience because I feel that the humiliation of the poor is also my humiliation.'

For a while there was a tension in the atmosphere and we went on eating quietly. It was a delicious meal—rissoles, with pickles of various kinds and dry chapattis to eat, and some French white wine to drink. I was enjoying it immensely and yet trying to restrain myself from betraying this either by word or sign, as I didn't want to show that this was a special occasion, and that never since my return from Europe had I tasted French wine.

'I want to say something to you,' Latif began suddenly, dropping his knife and fork. And as I looked up at him, his face was flushed with a certain agitation and his eyes bent down.

'Go ahead,' I said. 'What is it?' And, perhaps because I pronounced those words rather indifferently, Latif hesitated for a moment, looked at me furtively, as if to make sure that I wouldn't laugh at him, and then, leaving his food, burst out quickly, earnestly, in English, as if he wanted to get it over in a mouthful:

'I want to confess something to you. It is sincere. I didn't realize it till now. Honestly! You know I have been a Municipal Commissioner for some years, and this and my practice leave me very little time even to say prayers . . . I am lucky to have met such an esteemed person as you. In fact, I wrote to my brother in Delhi and told him that you were gracing our house with a visit. So you will realize that it wasn't my fault altogether . . .'

He paused for a moment. I didn't know what all this rigmarole was about. I was slightly embarrassed by his kindly references to me. But what was he getting at? I made a vague guess or two as to what he was going to say, but before my speculations had taken any shape he resumed his narrative, with the same terrific hurry to get it over with which he had begun.

'I was going up to argue the Habib-ud-Din murder case, the appeal for which was to come up before Mr Justice Thakur Das at eleven-thirty this morning, and having missed the Frontier Mail at eight because that bahin-chod sala coachman of mine didn't wake me, I reached Lahore by an ordinary train at eleven . . .'

Something seemed to get stuck in his throat at this and he coughed noisily and, leaning over his chair, spat into the veranda decorated by palms and evergreens. Then, twisting the muscles of his face with anger at the interruption, he began hoarsely:

'I must see the Hakim about this bahin-chod cough . . . but I am always so busy, honestly! . . . You know what a big station Lahore is. The train came into the platform number twelve after its usual slow crawl; it becomes slow like an ant from Mughalpura cantonment to Lahore junction. And there was such a crowd of those uncouth, cumbersome peasants and third-class passengers, struggling to rush up the bridges, knocking your sides about with their staves and their bundles and their bedsteads, you know. I shouted for a coolie to come and bear my suitcase and take me by some less crowded way to the exit near the first, second or inter-class booking-office in the hall where I could get a tonga.

'The man, a dingy little poorbia with a shrivelled face, looked cunning. I didn't like him from the beginning, as he kept very dumb, but he must have been clever, for though he pretended to be a fool, he made a mysterious sign for me to follow . . .'

Saying this, Latif shook his head and lifted the lid of his left eye, as if to emphasize his estimate of the man's suspicious character, smiled while he paused to create a deliberate suspense, and went on:

'Obviously he had made a practice of smuggling gentlemen who travel "without" out of the station, because he took me through the kitchen of the first-class restaurant, through an assistant stationmaster's office on platform number twelve, across the rails by the steaming engine of the Karachi Express, through a soldiers' canteen, and then by a short cut over an empty bridge on to platform number one. He must have been a rogue, as he looked surprised when I took out my ticket to hand over to the ticket-collector at the gate. I am convinced that this coolie imagined me to be "without" as he was almost walking through the doors of the goods godown of his own accord when I called him and directed him towards the proper exit. I am sure he had made a habit of smuggling people for a little bakhsheesh. Honestly! There could be no doubt about that, but . . .'

At this Latif saw that my glance was averted from him, and he paused, perhaps because he felt apprehensive that he was not carrying me along with him.

'And then?' I said, affecting an indifferent manner.

'I hailed a tonga when I got outside, but the tonga-wallah was insolent and, seeing that I wanted only a single seat, beckoned a family of five who were waiting for a conveyance. On seeing this, my coolie ran and fetched another tonga for me without my asking him, a thing which made me very angry because I knew that he would want an extra tip for doing that. These railway coolies are pukka badmashes. He put my briefcase into the tonga and, without salaaming or anything, hurriedly stretched his hand out and said, "Huzoor."

'"Acha, be patient, I am not running away," I told him, as the man's abruptness irritated me. I felt that if it weren't for his knowledge of the intricate ways of the station I could easily have borne my briefcase, and I felt that he hadn't earned his wages . . . As you will admit, a small case isn't heavy . . . and I couldn't help hating the man for his insolence as he stood. Baba, whatever you may say, these people have raised their heads to the skies and, because they have no breeding, they are absolutely insulting. This man had a sullen expression on his face, and preened himself, though he was an ugly poorbia, because he had twisted his white mustachios, discoloured an orange-red by tobacco on the ends, upright, and had had a perfectly clean shave even though his jaws were ugly and hollow . . .'

I was going to interrupt Latif by saying that the fact that the man had had a shave and had put out his hand without undue ceremony didn't necessarily mean that he was insolent, but I had hardly opened my mouth when he lifted his hand and raced on eagerly.

'I did not mind, really. I put my hand into the pocket of my patloon for the small change I had. I could feel a rupee and four anna bits. I took the two nickel anna pieces out of my pocket and gave them to him with a smile, admonishing him jokingly, "You must give up your illegal traffic in smuggling people without tickets across the station." But the damn sala said curtly, "Huzoor, the rate of bearing a case is four annas."

'"You are barking an untruth," I said, as his insolence made me very angry indeed. You will admit that the provocation he was offering me was great, particularly as I was in a hurry and he knew he was delaying me. I admit that I was wrong in losing my temper and talking to him impatiently, but I assure you I tried to be as reasonable as I could, and I said to him in a gentlemanly way: "*Bhai*, accept what you have been given and don't make a row." But he caught hold of me, not in supplication, mind you, but to prevent me from going. So you see that I was justified in thinking he was a rogue. "Accept what you have been given," I said, "or I shall hand you over to the police for carrying on that illegal traffic in conveying people without tickets across the station."

'"Huzoor, Huzoor, give me my dues," he insisted, bending and joining his hands. Perhaps I was harsh on him, but I didn't believe him when he said, "I don't want anything more than my wages," particularly as he began to insult me openly, saying, "Most people give me a tip, but you look like a kanjus sahib, so I shall be content if you give me my wages only."

'I was enraged at his calling me a miser sahib, as anyone might be on being spoken to like that by a mere labourer. But I was getting late for the court, and, controlling my anger, I began to board the tonga, feeling that if I had had more time perhaps I would have bargained with him and paid him a little more, as, sincerely, I didn't want to deprive him of his just dues. But he held me back by the lapels of my coat and whined, "Huzoor, Huzoor!"

'I was so annoyed by the touch of the sala's dirty hands preventing me from getting on the carriage . . . You see he was being impudent and impertinent, and I might have fallen, the way he pulled me, as I had one foot on the footrest. Then I lost my temper. I descended, and, turning round, gave him a kick so that he fell back weeping. I am sorry I did that, but, sincerely, what else could anyone have done?'

Latif paused as if he had finished his narrative, and he looked at me at once guiltily and as if he wanted to enlist my sympathy for his righteousness and honesty. My face was set without a flicker and yet he must have seen that I considered him blameworthy. He lowered his voice and sought to unburden himself more humbly.

'Some people gathered round to see what was up, and I saw a policeman approaching. It seemed to me a disgrace that I, a respectable citizen, a municipal commissioner and a vakil, should get involved in an unpleasant scene like that, particularly as I don't like being in a crowd. I get an awful feeling of claustrophobia when I am surrounded—it makes me feel very nervy. So, for a moment, I thought of putting my hand in my pocket and flinging another two annas at him, to have done with it all. But frankly, I was keeping two annas to pay the tonga-wallah, and I wanted to economize, because when you live to a certain standard, you see, you have all kinds of expenses to meet, particularly if you have a large family to keep. And I didn't want to change a rupee. And then something very awkward happened: a voice called, "What is the matter, Latif?" and I recognized the face of Gulshan Rai, who is an advocate of the High Court, Lahore, and a friend of mine since college days.

'"Huzoor, I bore the sahib's case from platform number twelve to the hall, and the rate is four annas, while the sahib has only given me two annas," the coolie blurted out before I could say a word.

'I felt utterly humiliated in the eyes of Gulshan Rai and my anger knew no bounds, but I couldn't do anything. Although I would have felt very sorry before you, as it is below my dignity to have been involved in that row, I could have kicked that badmash. I only said to Gulshan, "This man is a fraud." And, sincerely, whatever may have happened, I still believe that he was what I say he was. I told everyone, "I think this man helps people without tickets to get out of the station, and I won't pay him a pice more."

'"Oh, come," said Gulshan, "pay him two annas more."

'At that I thought of saving my face before Gulshan, as I knew the story would spread in the Bar room and my prestige might be damaged, and I pretended to look in my pockets for change and got out a rupee. I don't often do that. Sincerely. Please believe me. In fact, people will tell you that I am very generous, as I certainly have given more garden parties in this municipality than any other respectable citizen. I don't know what you will think of me. But I did that. And perhaps I am to blame. I don't know what possessed me but I did that.'

His face reddened and he looked very excited, his words now hurtling one over the other.

'"I have got two annas," Gulshan said. "Don't change the rupee." And he threw the two annas at the coolie, saying, "Now run away, my friend, and don't make any fuss. The sahib is in a hurry."

'I wish I had done to the man what Gulshan did at the very start, and there wouldn't have been any unpleasantness, but I was boiling with fury. "Go now and get out of my sight, otherwise I shall hand you over to the police," I said.

'Gulshan was also going to the court and he shared the tonga with me, and, though I insisted on paying the fare, he said I had no change and he paid at the end of the journey.'

After saying this, Latif laughed, a half-embarrassed, half-real chuckle. Then he became silent and sat with his head bent down shamefacedly, glancing at me from the pupils of his eyes and opening his lips as if to ask me something, to ask my opinion, my verdict on this affair. And I felt that he expected me to be kind to him and yet admonish him exactly as he had himself done while narrating the incident, now being kind to himself and justifying his behaviour, now admitting his guilt. But there was a pause as I was too embarrassed to say anything. At length, with an effort that made his words tremble, he broke the silence and burst out almost hysterically, 'I couldn't argue my case in court. My words seemed to get stuck in my throat like jagged-edged knives, and my mind kept forgetting the points. I was so confused . . .

'And now, I don't know, but I can see that coolie arise from behind my head before my eyes, his blood-streaked eyes, bending over his joined hands, crying and whining and protesting like a black wasp into my ear, whining . . .

'And at times today I have felt he was following me about. Ugly monolith of a man. Threatening me. With his outstretched, demoniac claws. Threatening me. Threatening me. Just threatening me. A dirty, uncouth creature! Threatening me . . .'

A Promoter of Quarrels

'It is a furlong if you stand, two miles if you sit, and six if you eat,' said Basanto.

'The angry man listens to no one,' said Hiro.

And they crouched impatiently a few yards away from the shop of Seth Nanak Chand, confectioner, with their pitchers of milk before them as they assembled the colourful rags of their clothes round them in the early wintry cold of the hills. They were cowherd women who had travelled through the dawn uphill from the village in the valley by which they lived in a nomadic colony under the trees.

'Yes, this one has eaten the deaf man's sugar,' Basanto said, with a disgust which gathered the wrinkles of her forty years into an ugly knot on her face.

'He has got plenty of sugar, Aunt,' said Hiro, looking greedily at the sugar-plums, jalebis, the cream cakes and crude sugar candy which lay tier above tier on Nanak Chand's counter, open to the attacks of the lean and hungry flies.

'What food to the hungry? What pillow to the sleepy?' Basanto said. 'Child, it is not in our luck to eat such delicacies. The other day when I asked Nanak for a bit of sugar candy for your cousin, he said, "It is a rupee a seer; how many annas-worth do you want?" And, of course, I took my own face and went away, for what is there to stop the mouth from eating a rupee-worth once you begin to buy? I had wanted a little gift to sweeten the mouth of my boy . . .'

'I have forgotten how to eat sweetmeats,' said Hiro. 'It is such a long time since I tasted a sugar-plum.'

'I will buy some today. I have brought some extra milk to pay for the sweets.'

'Come, come and show me the milk, Basanto. Hiro, come, come, hurry up,' said Nanak. 'The sahibs will be waiting for their tea: you don't know that the goras have their breakfast in bed.'

'Come, Aunt,' said Hiro eagerly, and lifted the pitcher onto her head with her young arms.

'Give me a hand, ni, before you rush away,' said Basanto. 'I know you are in a hurry to eat the rice cakes, but help an old woman. And, anyhow, I am first; you weren't born before I began to sell milk to Nanak.'

'Come, come, don't fight,' shouted Nanak, the gold rings in the lobes of his ears shaking with the force he put into his words.

Hiro lowered the pitcher from her head to the earth and helped Basanto with her vessel. Then she took the opportunity to untie a knot of her apron in which she had been saving coppers and, emptying them into her hand to buy some sweets, lifted her pitcher and took it nearer to Nanak Chand's counter.

'I want my account settled, Sethji,' said Basanto, as she lowered her pitcher of milk. 'We are moving down to the plains with our cattle as the winter has come; we were drenched in the rain last night as the trees are not much protection; and we have to pay the grazing tax to the Sarkar before we can leave, or they will take our clothes off.'

'You should have a house built,' said Nanak.

'We are not rich seths like you,' Basanto said.

'Good work, good pay,' said Nanak.

'Good pay, good work,' put in Hiro.

'You, you are worth a lakh of rupees,' said Nanak. 'You can get the pay without the work.'

'Why, I haven't even been able to get the gift of a sugar-plum all this time,' said Hiro, and she threw her apron over her head modestly.

'You can fill a glutton's stomach, but you can't fill her eyes,' said Basanto, who was jealous of the seth's attention to Hiro. 'Are you eating rice cakes or bargaining? Here, take the milk. Where is your servant today?'

'Ohe, where are you? Ohe, Munshi Singha,' called Nanak, scratching himself between the loins.

'Ayaji,' a pale young Sikh boy answered, with his head bent and his chin thrust back in abject humility. 'The cauldron is cleaned and ready.'

'Come and take their pitchers and pour them into the cauldron—there, where the cauldron is; don't be fetching the huge thing here,' said Nanak.

And as Munshi came, showing his ribs and knees through his torn long tunic and pyjamas, Nanak heaved his bottom-heavy body from the greasy cushion on which it rested and went into the black cavern of the shop, saying, 'I will get the leavings of yesterday's boiled milk for you two cowherd women.'

'Why, aren't there any dogs in this bazaar to throw them to?' said Basanto. 'You have never given anything worthwhile away.'

'Ohe, Munshi, keep Hiro's milk separate to take to the sahibs and pour Basanto's into the pan,' said Nanak as he retreated.

'Attend to my pitcher first, vay kaka,' said Basanto to Munshi. 'I have to get back to my children. Look at the sun soaring. Have you ever seen a day going? The cattle must be waiting to go out. And I have to collect the money from your master . . .'

'What difference do halt and march make to a beggar?' said Hiro, with dumb humility. 'Take my aunt's milk first, Munshi.'

'Wait till you grow up, my girl,' said Basanto. 'You will have to work and rear children on nothing. Now you eat the bread of illegality from your parents and they eat the bread of illegality by getting you, with your youth, to run errands for them shamelessly. I wouldn't let my daughter sit about in the bazaar, open to everyone's gaze, talking and joking and laughing with all these lewd shopkeepers, who put the price of your body at a lakh. A young girl like that, fancy, sisters. I don't know what the world is coming to! In my time . . .'

While Munshi was carrying Basanto's pitcher of milk into the shop, Hiro heard a loud splash of—what was it?—water! And then she saw Seth Nanak Chand emerging with the leavings of yesterday's boiled milk in an open brass pot.

'Ohe, bring the cauldron out after you have poured the milk and bring the thermometer,' shouted Nanak Chand to the servant. 'You can't see anything in the dark there.'

'Give me an anna-worth of sugar candy,' said Hiro, showing the four pice in her hand to Nanak.

'Throw the pice,' said Nanak, with the scrupulosity of the Hindu. And he weighed the sweets in the scales and poured them into a piece of wastepaper and threw the parcel at the virgin 'worth a lakh of rupees'.

Munshi brought the cauldron, straining every muscle of his body to keep the unwieldy thing from upsetting. His pale face flushed as he succeeded in balancing it on the fireplace by Nanak's greasy cushioned counter.

'Where is the meter?' Nanak asked, fumbling for the instrument on the dust-covered greasy wall behind the door. And he ordered the panting Munshi, 'Come, now, pour the other pitcher into that tin, for the khansamah boy will be coming.'

At length he found the meter. He wiped it with an end of his dirty loincloth and dipped the instrument into the milk.

'So you have taken to deception, have you, Basanto?' he said.

'Why?' exclaimed Basanto.

'Why, is there anything wrong?' asked Hiro, tying the sweets in an end of her apron.

For a moment Nanak paused with deliberate theatricality and made his grim face grimmer. Then he said, 'There is water in this milk.' And screwing his face into a knot of anger, he turned to his servant, 'Bring the other milk here too, ohe, Munshi.'

The boy fetched the cauldron containing Hiro's milk and Nanak dipped the meter into it.

'There is something black in the pulse!' said Hiro, trying to connect the splash of water which she had heard on Nanak's retreat into the shop and the discovery of water in Basanto's milk.

'Acha, there is something black in the pulse, my fair one!' Basanto burst. 'There is something black in the pulse! Eh! Only the crow understands the crow's language! How dare you talk of me like that! May nothing remain of you! May your face be cursed by the black pox! How dare you say that I have brought diluted milk to the market! How—'

'Auntie, I am not saying anything against you. Why do you begin to abuse me? Look, he is judging my milk there, too . . .'

And she turned to Nanak. 'You daren't say that there is water in my milk, you dare not, seth, for I milked the cows myself.'

'I don't know how you do it,' said Basanto, before Nanak gave his verdict about Hiro's milk. 'I know how you can make the cows drink water before you milk them, if you don't put water into the pan! Taking the bread out of my children's mouths!'

'Yes,' said Nanak, 'this is very thin, and something has been done to the milk though the meter can't detect it . . .'

'No, sethji, it can't be!' protested Hiro. 'On the oath of God, on the oath of my father and mother, on the oath of those who are dearest to me, there is no water in my milk.'

'And there is in mine, you bitch!' shouted Basanto. 'Go like the dog! Come like the cat! Go, go, eater of your masters. May that father of yours die and leave your mother a widow! May you become an orphan! May you all die! I shall buy up Nanak's shop and distribute sweets when you all disappear from this world!'

'Ni, come to your senses, Auntie,' Hiro said. 'You silly old woman, why do you want to cut my throat? A single stick will neither burn, nor light, nor shine. You should rage against that promoter of quarrels, there! . . .'

'I will call the policia there and hand you over if you call me a promoter of quarrels,' said Nanak, working up into a bluff rage. 'You quarrel among yourselves, you low cowherd women, and put the blame on me. How dare you be so insolent?'

'You dare to call the policia,' said Hiro. 'I will spit on you. I know what you do when you go inside; Aunt Basanto doesn't.' Her rage stifled her speech. And she flushed an indignant red at the callous and deliberate roguery of the seth and the machinations with which he had built himself a protuberant belly and a palace in the city, for he himself had told her some of the tricks of the trade in a moment when he wanted to win her confidence, and her body, but the dumbness of generations of servitude prevented her from saying anything.

'Of course Aunt Basanto doesn't know anything, and you do, you upstart!' said Basanto. 'Do I need a mirror to wash my hands with? You whore! So you have been inside. And you can talk. But some talk and use their tongues while I use my hands.'

And she leapt at Hiro with her claws outstretched and, tearing the rag of apron from the girl's head, pulled her hair, and dug her nails into her neck, shouting the while, 'I will comb your matted hair with a firebrand, you bitch! You daughter of a pimp and a whore! I will pour the boiling water of my rage on your head! I will eat you alive!'

Munshi rushed between them and tried to separate them.

'Leave them to it, ohe boy, let the thieves kill each other!' Nanak said. 'Eat till you are full, fight till your skull is cracked.'

But the boy parted the two women, dragging Basanto away as she still shouted, 'I will eat her and all her relations! By the Pir, I shall eat her . . .'

'Whether you eat or not, the mouth of that wolf there is dreadful,' said one of the crowd, which had gathered round to see the tamasha, in a hoarse whisper to quieten her.

'He is only encouraging you to fight,' said Munshi, putting his hand on the corner of his mouth to deflect his voice. 'He put . . .'

But Nanak was within audible distance and was staring with his furtive eyes so that the boy could not tell her that it was his master who had put the water into the milk, and that her companion meant nothing more when she said she saw something black in the pulse but that she suspected he had done the trick when he went in.

'Acha, settle my account,' said Basanto, a glimmer of the truth dawning upon her through Munshi's whisper.

'Sweet and brakish are all one price,' said Nanak, 'and that means no price . . . I don't know when you have given me bad milk and when you have given me good milk. But I know that I have had to pay the policia good money in order to prevent him from taking me to the lock-up. Now they will catch the real culprits, because each of you has accused the other before my servant and all the people here . . .'

'Oh, Seth Nanak Chand, give her the money and end this row,' said a neighbouring shopkeeper in the crowd.

'Yes, yes, give them the money and let them go,' said another man.

'No, no, they are thieves,' said Nanak.

'Ohe, come, Seth Nanak Chand, let them go,' said a neighbouring grocer who still sat in his shop.

'Acha, now you bitches,' said Nanak. 'I think it charity on my part that I give you a rupee each for the milk which you have supplied me with this month, though I could have handed you over to the policia . . .' And he threw a silver coin to each of them out of his rusty iron cash box.

The women were dumb. They had exhausted themselves quarrelling and hadn't the breath to haggle.

'Go, go now, before I call the policia.'

'Go, go, the black crow will only yield black milk,' said a kindly neighbour.

'Go, go, the cash tenant needs no sponsor,' said another man.

They picked up the coins gingerly. Then Basanto said to Hiro, 'Come, child, he eats eight bowls of milk and sixteen sugar-plums, while we eat the dust and drink the blood of our livers . . .'

'Yes, Auntie, there will be no grief at his death, except among the crows,' Hiro answered.

And they 'took their own faces' and walked away.

Lullaby

'Sleep
Oh sleep,
My baby, sleep,
Oh, do not weep,
Sleep
Like a fairy . . .'

sang Phalini as she rocked her little one-year-old Suraj Mukhi in her lap, while she fed the machine with handfuls of jute.

Would he ever get to sleep?

'Sleep
Oh sleep,
My baby, sleep . . .'

His flesh was so warm. She could feel the heat of his little limbs on her thighs, a burning heat which was mixed with a sour smell. He must be ill. All day he had not shut his eyes, all day he had sobbed and cried.

The engine chuk-chuked; the leather belt khupp-khupped; the bolts jig-jigged; the plugs tik-tikked; the whole floor shook like the hard wooden seat of a railway train.

And she had to go on feeding the gaping mouth of the machine. 'Bap re bap, why is this bitch barking?' the sharp-tongued woman who sang folk songs, and could brook no one else singing, called to the other women.

'Sleep,
Oh sleep . . .'

Phalini felt her throat growing hoarse with the jute fluff she had been swallowing since she had let the fold of the apron rag, with which she ordinarily padded her mouth and nose in the factory, fall loose. The fluff seemed to be everywhere—on the walls, over the machine, on her face. She could feel it streaming down her nose, her cheeks, to the silver ring round her neck which was green with sweat. She cast her eyes over her nose and felt how ugly it was as it stood out from her hollow cheeks. That is why she had pawned her big silver nose ring which her mother-in-law had given her in the dowry, and refused to adorn her nostrils even though it was a bad omen to take off your jewellery.

'Ooon . . . ooon . . . ooon . . .' Suraj Mukhi cried. The sharp, feeble cry stirred the black night of Phalini's soul as the air stirs the water, but the child's voice was drowned in the dithyrambic hum of the preparing-shed in the factory.

'Sleep
Oh sleep,
My baby, sleep,
Oh, do not weep,
Sleep . . .'

she sang, bending over the child's head till she almost touched the feverish brow and kissed the close-fisted hands which Suraj Mukhi was rubbing on his eyes, even as he cried. And then she threw another handful of jute into the jaws of the monster.

Her own voice sounded to her like the whisper of a broken reed, completely out of tune today, as it had seldom been out of tune when she sang the work song:

'Roller
Roll
Spread jute
Open mouth,
Rise jute
Fall seeds,
Work into cloth.'

Her big troubled eyes roved away from the child to the gaping mouth of the machine, beyond the black, greasy bolts and knobs and pistons, above the fumes of the thick, sickly, tasteless air in the shed.

The engine chuk-chuked; the leather belt khupp-khupped; the bolts jig-jigged; the plugs tik-tikked; the whole floor shook like the hard wooden seat of a railway train.

She felt giddy.

She had felt like that five months before she had given birth to a child: an oily taste in the mouth with a bile under the tongue that seemed to go quivering into the swollen pitcher of her belly and bring the entrails up to her throat. But the quickening under her navel and the memory of her lover's face seemed to offset the nausea. She tried to think of him now, as he had looked when he first came down from the northern hills.

The wild, wispish boy with large brown eyes which had flashed when he had talked to her husband, Kirodhar, but which were so shy when he looked at her. Suraj Mukhi's eyes were like his. Also Suraj Mukhi's limbs smelt like his. But he would never know that he was the father of the child. Why, he was a child himself. He had come like lightning and gone like the thunder of the northern hills . . .

Where had he gone, she wondered. Had he only come to give her the pang of parting? Where had he gone? It was now summer again and he was here last summer. For days she had scanned the horizon of the sky above the city, towards the north in the direction where he had gone. But he didn't seem to be anywhere in the large breathless space. Only Suraj Mukhi lay in her arms. And the sun, after which she had named the child, stood high. And the tears rolled down her scalded face to her chin, across her cheeks, before she realized that she was weeping . . . Oh, where was he, the gay child, her lover, her baby, so simple, so stubborn, so strong?

'And I shall grow old and grief, not Kirodhar, shall be my Lord . . .'

'Ooon . . . ooon . . .' the child moaned.

The engine chuk-chuked; the leather belt khupp-khupped; the bolts jig-jigged; the plugs tik-tikked; the whole floor shook like the hard wooden seat of a railway train. And she had to go on feeding the mouth of the machine.

'Bap re bap, what is the matter with the brat? Can't you keep him quiet?' said the woman next to her.

Phalini saw him as she had seen him in a dream one day, standing by her side, smiling to her so that she had wanted to clasp him close to her breast. But when she had stretched her arms towards him, she had suddenly wakened and found herself groping in the dark towards Kirodhar, who had thought she wanted him and had taken her. He must be somewhere in the far-off hills, doing what? . . . Wandering perhaps, happy and free, while she was caged here with his child.

She bent down to look at the child. His eyes were open, his face was still, he cried no more. That was good, she could feed the machine with more jute.

'Sleep
Oh sleep,
My baby, sleep . . .'

she sang, and she smiled at him and rocked him again. Suraj Mukhi's eyes just stared at her; rigid and hard his little hand lay on the side.

She swayed on her haunches and left the jute.

The effigy lay still.

Dead.

She gave a long, piercing shriek which tore through the ceiling.

She slapped her cheeks and beat her palms on her breast, crying in a weird, hollow voice, 'Hai, hai.'

'Bap re bap, why is she crying, this bitch? What is the matter with her?' said the woman next to her.

'My child, my child, my child . . .' Phalini cried, crazed and agonized as she tore her hair.

The women crowded round her.

'What is the matter?' the forewoman called. 'Why are you bitches running amok?'

The engine chuk-chuked; the leather belt khupp-khupped; the bolts jig-jigged; the plugs tik-tikked; the whole floor shook like the hard wooden seat of a railway train . . .

The Terrorist

He casually presented the slip to the sallow-faced English Inspector of Police who stood at the entrance of the Legislative Assembly buildings in New Delhi. He was making an histrionic attempt to look perfectly unsuspicious and ordinary. He pretended to be lost in admiration of the colossal pillared and domed sepulchre of Sir Edwin Lutyens' architectural dreams without knowing anything about the laws of architecture. He thought that the pretence would work.

But there was an uncontrollable tremor on his lips.

Lest the Inspector of Police notice him pursing his lips tight and lest his bent head arouse suspicion, he brazenly stared straight at the policeman and deliberately waited in that position.

'ADMIT SARDAR BIR SINGH TO THE PUBLIC GALLERY OF THE INDIAN LEGISLATIVE ASSEMBLY' the ticket read in his mind's eye, and he recalled the childish handwriting in which the signature of Rai Bahadur Sir Gopal Chand was sprawled underneath.

Nobody could find fault with that card. He could not have got a more authoritative guarantor than the Deputy President of the Legislative Assembly. 'And I feel I look perfectly calm,' he said to reassure himself.

All this went through his mind in a flash.

'All right,' said Captain Beatty, alertly looking up to Singh with his hard blue eyes and noticing not the slight tremor on his lips nor the surreptitious manner in which he had lifted his chin, but the face without a blemish; a handsome, wheat-blonde face, with a forehead, shadowed by a khaki polo topee, inflamed by pink-white cheeks, which tapered from the edges of the sharp nose over a regular, expressive mouth down to the chin, whose determination was sadly flawed by the pit of a dimple. 'A Kashmiri pandit, presumably,' Beatty thought, 'a relative of Sir Gopal Chand or a rich university student.' And he dismissed him from his mind because, except that the boy was handsomer than most, he seemed to Beatty like all the other 'native' students who crowded into the public gallery of the Chamber to hear debates, dressed in Ranken & Co. suits and expensive polo topees; such as he himself could not afford on account of those infernal Whiteway Laidlaw bills for Dorothy's dresses which literally poured in by every mail from Bombay.

'I hope that Vasu Dev has got in without any difficulty,' Singh said to himself as he walked up the carpeted stairs and approached the gallery. And he looked past the roped gangway, over the heads of the people who had already taken their seats on his left and right. 'Vasu Dev, Vasu Dev . . . no . . . no . . . yes . . . there was Vasu Dev . . . looking . . . yes . . . yes, quite unconcerned . . . there, on the left in the front row. Shabash! Bravo!'

A light negative shock of electricity passed through his body as he felt for the bomb in the pocket of the overcoat hanging on his arm.

He felt faint.

There was the positive impact of the hand-grenade in the pocket. He recovered his balance.

He had forgotten to take off his hat, as is the European custom on entering the room. He immediately did so, a little flustered that he might have been noticed with it on all that time. In order to offset any critical gaze that might have noticed him, he walked on, looking straight on his right with a hard, impenetrable glint in his eyes, as if that were his usual manner of looking at the world.

There was no seat in the front row on the right, except at the extreme end.

'Stupid,' he muttered to himself, 'that is the fruit of being late. If my coat brushes against any of these fools who have come like dogs to hear the old, old debates again under the new reforms, the vessel will be broken. I had better pass through the empty seats at the top and get to the edge of the gallery that way.'

He retraced a step, turned right, and walked quickly but carefully past the folded seats. His feet felt marvellously active, his head was clear and light, though his face seemed covered with perspiration.

As he sat down ostentatiously, he was afraid of the bomb exploding on his thighs. He caressed his coat lovingly and, putting it down before him gently, drew his trousers to a comfortable fold above his knees. He had never been very keen on preserving a faultless crease.

To avoid the squinting gaze of the man next to him—a Muhammadan with a red fez, frock coat and baggy trousers—he looked into the distance on the left and wondered if he would be able to see Vasu Dev, and whether Vasu Dev would be able to see him, to time the actual throwing of the bombs by signs.

He could not discover Vasu Dev at first glance. He withdrew his eyes. He dared not look left too actively at once. 'Not yet,' he said to himself. 'I will settle down first and behave as an ordinary visitor.'

He simulated the manner of an eager young man who had come to the Assembly Chamber for the first time in his life, looking as if fascinated, at the fake classical frescoes which decorated the lunettes under the Gothic–Moghul–American arches of the vast dome of the Assembly building.

The tempera paintings, executed on a background of gold, described the Hindu seven stages of life: birth, childhood, student life, love, family life, work, renunciation. The decorative floral details surrounding the hieratic medallions did not please him. The unhappiness, the grief, the suffering of all those phases of life which he had seen in the country about him had given a sardonic twist to his thin lower lip, and his eyes looked on at things contemptuously lest his romantic heart illumine them to the beauty of the world, to the joy of life.

But in a large hemisphere before him on the wall under the dome, he saw the picture of the Buddha preaching to his disciples. The endless hours during which he had sat at the feet of the yogis and ascetics in the various religious shrines, when he had had to live in disguise after he looted the Calcutta Mail at Kakori and there was a price of a thousand rupees on his head, and after he had raided the Chittagong armoury, came to his mind. They had taught him the great doctrine of securing release from the trammels of existence exactly as did the Buddha. They had pointed a way beyond suffering, beyond the essential unavoidable abomination of suffering. They had described to him the beauty of death. And now he was going to realize that beauty. Only, they had said that one should wait for the culmination patiently. He differed from them there. Death in action, death for such a noble cause as fighting for the honour of the motherland—that was a glorious death. Even according to the enthusiastic Hindus who believed in being born again and again to bear the oppressive sorrows of life from birth to death, one achieved a greater rebirth by doing great deeds. And Guru Gobind and a hundred other saints of his own religion, Sikhism, had achieved martyrdom by fighting against foreign rule. 'Shanti, Shanti, Peace,' the holy men used to say, and truly the Buddha in that picture looked the very embodiment of peace; but, he wondered, had the Buddha known the glory of sacrifice in war? Those Communists were right when they talked of revolution, but why did they believe they would become immortal on earth when all religions have taught that immortality is to be achieved only in heaven? Theirs was the militant optimism of materialists and sensualists. They believed that suffering was not inevitable, that they could end it. But they would only conquer the whole world and lose their own souls. No. Death is the only way of securing release from the trammels of existence. All things end in death. 'If India had been free, I would liked to have waited for death in peace. As it is, I must die in battle. And the battle is going to rage now.'

His gaze fell on the red plush of the curtains on the tall doors of the Chamber with the hated symbol of the British crown embroidered on them in gold. 'Those curtains are the colour of blood, blood when it has dried,' he said, with a malice born of revenge, which seemed to find a morbid delight in the mysticism of blood, in the pure joy of violence, destruction and annihilation. 'I wonder if they were deliberately chosen to be of that colour by the government which has won India by the sword and wants to keep it by the sword, chosen by my enemies who believe in bloodshed as I do. Well, soon I shall dye this whole Chamber in the colour of blood. That will be a fit answer to the insolence of these British!'

He felt the blood rise in his veins and colour his face with the wild flush of pride at these thoughts, the flush of pride and power and glory.

He recalled that he had experienced this feeling always at the most critical times in the short history of his life when he was about to kill someone or commit a robbery. He had felt it, for instance, before he shot one of the most prominent police officials at Lahore, and when he had exhorted the crowd at Sholapur to avenge themselves on the British by an open insurrection. It was a beautiful feeling, subtle and warm, like the intoxication of wine. It made one confident and strong . . .

The thud of awkward feet shambling down into the empty rows of the gallery, the shifting and shuffling of those who were already seated and made room for the newcomers peevishly or with exaggerated courtesy, disturbed his thoughts and annoyed him.

'Fools!' he muttered. 'Fools!' And he tried to ignore them by looking around.

A row of scarlet-complexioned Englishmen in frock coats, white shirts and those handkerchief ties (with the pearl pins) which he had never been able to tie, were coming into the distinguished visitors' gallery, with their wives and daughters, looking superior in silver-fox furs. 'No Indians?' his heart asked. 'No Indians among them?' 'No Indians there,' his eyes brought back the answer. His soul rose in a fit of indignation at the insult he thought implicit in this. 'Why are there no Indians in the distinguished visitors' gallery?' he asked. 'Aren't there any Indians left who can defend their honour against such insults? They should make it a point to be there, even if only to keep up the prestige of India before these red-faced monkeys. Surely they are allowed to go in there.'

In the press gallery, beyond the distinguished visitors' gallery, however, he could see two Indians seated beside an Englishman. That was gratifying. 'Though, of course,' he said to himself, 'they must be representatives of the Associated Press of India, which is an English organization.'

A stream of politicians was entering the Chamber past the head chaprasi of the Assembly, whose flowing grey beard wagged over the golden braid of his long red coat every time he greeted a celebrity.

'Fools! Fools! They let themselves be hoodwinked into believing that they now control the destiny of their country,' he muttered. 'They are just like buffaloes and bullocks, the bloated idiots with bored faces!'

He hated them with a hatred of youth's fire against middle-aged indifference.

'Fools! Fools! Bigger fools, those Swarajists! Even they have been taken in by the British.' He fumed inside himself to see some of the sombrely clad members of the Swaraj Party shaking hands with Sir James Ferguson, the Home Secretary, with cordial smiles on their lips. 'Time servers!' he said. 'Opportunists! They only joined the Congress because they wanted to get into the Assembly and to get jobs for their relatives! Traitors!' His feverish eyes explored the faces of the dishonourable Members even against his will.

There . . . there was that black Madrasi lawyer and traitor, Law Member of the Government of India, Sir Krishnaswami Iyer, in his small child's turban, embroidered with gold, and a tight, ill-fitting navy-blue suit, looking more like a scavenging crow than ever with his long, polished nose.

And there, entering the door, was that rich Parsi traitor, Sir Dadiji Maneckji Bottlewala, in English morning dress and a pointed French beard—typical member of the community which fancies itself more English than the English.

And there was that illiterate, hawk-nosed, fanatical Muhammadan camel of the desert, son of the prophet, Captain Sir Nasarullah Khan, flaunting the tail-end of his turban and his military uniform.

'Traitors! Traitors!' he muttered in disgust. 'Traitors! I wish I could blow them up at once. But wait till they have arranged themselves! I will upset them!'

His eyes fell on the beautiful white face of Lalla Dwarka Prashad Sharar, the leader of the Congress Party, the folds of whose homespun tunic and loincloth fell gracefully on his body like those of the Roman statues in the Lahore Museum. He admired that man. He would have liked to have been like him. He would have liked to have been his son so that he could have inherited the mantle of that distinction which raised the Lalla to the eminence of a virtual symbol of India. He recalled the occasion when he had first heard the great man speak at the Calcutta Congress. What an orator! The periods of his speech still rang in his ears. The fire of his incitements had sent him raiding, looting, killing, to revenge the wrongs of India. A member of the official nominated party had come to speak to the Lalla. Singh withdrew his eyes in disgust at the fool who dared to brush up against his hero.

'I must get ready,' he said to himself.

Before feeling for the bomb in the pocket of his overcoat, however, he leaned over the balustrade before him.

The Chamber was now full, above him, below him, about him.

There was a noise of indistinct talk going on, almost like a blurred whisper, punctuated by chatter.

The atmosphere was congested and warm.

He took a deep breath as if he were suffocating. It seemed to make him shiver.

'It is cold,' he tried to assure himself. 'I must soon get active. Then I shall get warm. I had better try and get ready to signal to Vasu Dev.'

He looked towards the left gallery.

The visitors in the public gallery were craning over the red plush of the balustrade and obstructing his view. He could not see Vasu Dev.

He retreated into himself.

A curious emptiness had taken possession of him. It seemed as if he had ceased to exist. But his face was hot and swollen. His ears felt like red, transparent hot iron. His eyes seemed full of molten lava. He tried to pull himself together and to concentrate on the deed.

He had no capacity for abstract thought left, however. The deed that he was going to perform presented itself to him only as a fact in history, in his own chequered history. It was an incident in his life, the last, final incident in his spectacular career, the act which would crown all his efforts at revolt.

Below, everything seemed ready for the Speaker to come in. He waited anxiously to watch old Mr Jay Dass Hartal take the chair. 'One of the bravest Indian politicians!' he said in his mind. 'His position as the first Indian President of the Assembly, won after arduous debate, is a glorious victory for the motherland.' He recalled that the sage had blessed him at the Cawnpore Congress. 'I wonder if he knew that I believed in shedding blood,' he asked himself. 'Still, he was kind to me, even though he had the liberal's horror of taking life. It would be a pity if he were killed when I drop the bomb. But he is old anyway. And I will try to throw the grenade near the official benches.'

No more thoughts came into his head for a moment.

He stared blankly into the air.

Then his glance fell on his knees strongly planted before him, between which lay the overcoat, in the pocket of which was the bomb. His knees began to shake a little.

He diverted his eyes to scan the texture of his overcoat. It was a plain tweed and not stimulating to thought.

He felt as if his head were made of wood which had suddenly become impenetrable to the air.

He shook himself with a slight, hesitant movement of his body and felt as if he were trembling.

Feeling that people about him might become aware of what was going on inside him, he bent his head and looked into his mind's eye.

He felt as if he were shut off from the rest of the world in a dark chamber, alone, a speck of darkness.

But then he became conscious of the presences about him, above all, below him. It was comforting, though oppressive.

He wished he could throw the bomb and be done with it.

He suddenly caught Vasu Dev's eyes.

The unbearded young college boy looked wild and furtive, disturbed, yet somehow convincing enough. Yes, he could be depended upon. Had he not drunk water out of the same cup—the symbol of the bitter poison of death? Had he not vowed undying eternal brotherhood and devotion to him, his leader, the liberator of India?

Singh struck the palm of his right hand against his heart and, with his gesture and the movement of his eyelids upwards to heaven, tried to communicate that he loved him and that they were to trust in God above and do the right—throw the bombs soon.

It occurred to him in a flash that he had forgotten about the challenge he had intended to utter when he threw the bomb. 'The Challenge! The Challenge!' he said. 'The words which will spread throughout the length and breadth of India like wildfire, words as memorable as those of Proudhon and Mazzini: "I die for my motherland. I become a sacrifice for it. I have tried to avenge Bharat Mata against the devilry of the British!"' He exulted to think that tomorrow these words of his speech would form the headlines of all the newspapers in Hindustan. He had printed the words on leaflets, so that if all died in the Chamber, the printed matter would remain. He felt for the papers in the right breast-pocket of his jacket. They were safe . . .

The Speaker entered, his long, flowing beard giving a prophetic dignity to his English wig and gown made of homespun cotton material.

The House rose with a rustle.

The Speaker took his seat on the high, throne-like chair.

The members sat down, shuffling, hustling, bustling, talking, whispering.

For a moment all was still again.

Singh saw, or imagined he saw, the three English ministers at the head of the official benches smiling derisively at the ceremonious looks on the faces of the Indian members, as if they who had created democracy could afford to laugh at the mock heroics of these natives whom they were educating in the methods of debate.

He frowned with resentment at so subtle an insult and nearly pulled out the handkerchief from his cuff to wave to Vasu Dev, which was the signal for the bombs to be thrown simultaneously.

He tried to calm down, to control himself, to go about the business clearly, coolly, deliberately.

But he could not get over the insult implicit in the derisive smile of the English ministers. He felt hot with exasperation, fumed with rage. The memories of the insults which he had suffered at the hands of British seemed to come back to him.

His eyes dimmed with a vague emotion which he did not really feel. He tried to work himself into a towering rage. But his throat seemed parched. He did not know if he would be able to utter the words of his speech when the time came.

The Speaker struck the bell on the desk.

Singh started. His legs seemed to sink beneath him. His heart throbbed violently. His body was perspiring.

He hurriedly put his hand into the pocket of the overcoat and drew out the bomb wrapped in a silken handkerchief.

His heart drummed against his chest now. His temples palpitated. His brain felt dizzy. The words of the challenge seemed to slip through his mind.

He hastily drew the printed leaflets out of his pocket.

His hands were shaking.

He breathed a deep breath, opened his eyes wide, tightened his muscles and prepared to rise.

The Speaker rose.

Singh rose too.

Before the Speaker's eyes had lifted their lids, Singh had flourished the silken handkerchief like a juggler, swept a glance at the Chamber, and thrown the bomb into the air.

'Shoon shut!' The bomb fell at the feet of Sir Arthur Rank, the Finance Minister.

'Hai!' Singh heard a cry like Vasu Dev's.

He looked and saw that the boy had been arrested by those about him with the live bomb still in his hand.

'Ooof! Oh, Heavens! We are dead! Undone!' The cries rose from the Chamber and there was complete pandemonium, the cowardly members rushing from their seats and falling over each other, the braver men standing away from their seats.

'Cowards! I become a sacrifice for the mother . . .' Singh shouted.

The old President called the members to order. But his gaze had soared to the public gallery where two men were being held by several others.

Singh's eyes were blurred by the blood that had risen in them. Fire burned in his brain, the fire of strength. Fire swirled in his body as he struggled to wrest himself from the grasp of the policemen about him. He was blind with blood.

A sharp slap fell on his face.

His eyes opened and he faced Beatty.

Tinkle! Tinkle! The President rang the bell and called, 'Gentlemen! Gentlemen! The bomb did not explode! Please return!'

'Oh, what evil stars have robbed my instrument of its power!' roared Singh, writhing histrionically.

'Bahin-chod! Sur ka bacha! Hosh karo!' shouted Beatty, again striking Singh's face.

Singh turned his other cheek deliberately, histrionically simulating the appearance of Christ on the cross, and shouted, 'If they hit you on the right cheek, turn your left . . .'

The visitors in the public gallery who had fled when they heard the bomb drop now came crowding around to see the terrorist, with horror-struck eyes and pale faces. As Beatty and two English police sergeants goaded Singh up the stairs with the butt ends of their revolvers, he smiled at the visitors, an automatic smile with a willed patriotism behind it. But for all its patriotism it was a ridiculous smile, the smile of a man who puffed his cheeks when he meant to twist his lips, the smile of a youth who had been suddenly paralysed by fear.

'I sacrifice myself for . . .' he roared, but the roar ended in a hoarse whisper.

The policeman dug into his ribs and pushed him forward.

'I. . .' he struggled to say with all the force of his voice.

The word sounded hollow as it struck the dome of the Chamber.

A Kashmir Idyll

It was about ten years ago, during a brief visit to Kashmir, that the incident I am going to relate took place. But neither time nor space has blurred the deep impression it made on me then, and it has haunted me for many days, so that I must needs put it down.

There were originally four of us in the party, including myself, the three others being a tall, imposing Sikh gentleman, both tailor-made and God-made; a sensitive young poet, a Kashmiri whose family had emigrated to the plains and made good as Kashmiris always do when once they have left the land where, though nature is kind and generous, man has for centuries most foully and cruelly oppressed man; and a hill boy who cooked for us.

We had loaded our luggage on a tonga and walked the three hundred and seventy-five miles on the road from Jammu across the Himalayas in slow stages, by the beds of the silent Ravi and the surging Chenab. On the peak of the Banihal we had held conversation with the wind that comes from the Kashmir valley, bearing a load of loveliness and pain, the golden exhalation of the saffron and the white sighs of a people who toil unrewarded.

We had descended to the natural spring of Ver Nag from which a few drops of water trickle into a stream that becomes the River Jhelum at Islamabad, where it divides the whole valley into two halves and flows into Lake Wullar and then cuts its way through two hundred miles of mountains into the plains.

From Ver Nag, a village of dark and labyrinthine streets full of small mud huts, the multi-coloured flowers on whose roofs give no hint of the misery which dwells within, we had traversed the main valley by a dusty road bordered by cubist poplars and cypresses.

We had made our headquarters in a houseboat at Srinagar. Then, taking the advice of a tourist's guide book which the government of His Highness the Maharaja of Kashmir had designed specifically for the use of English visitors, though a few Indians also took advantage of it if they had a smattering of the wonderful, official language, we had decided to undertake short trips to the remote valleys and the unspoiled outlying ranges of the Himalayas within the borders of Kashmir.

We visited the Sonamarg valley where the scarlet eyes of the morning are blinded by the glare of the snow that lies perpetually on the mountain peaks, leading through the Zogila Pass to Chotta Tibet, and where the sleep of the night is continually disturbed by the growling of the angry Indus rushing through glaciers and across high rocks and boulders on its tortuous passage across the Punjab.

We pushed by a difficult track across a crumbling mountain to the cave of Amarnath, where the dripping of water from melting crystals form a snow image of the shape of a phallus, which the superstitious go to worship in thousands at a particular time of the year, believing it to be the penis of the Great God Shiva.

We went to Gulmarg, the valley of wild roses; to Lilanmarg, where the lilies of the field grow for miles and miles and miles, angelic and melancholy. We ascended to Aparwat, the high peak above Gulmarg, on top of which is a crystal-clear pool that echoes back the faintest whisper.

We saw Gandarbal and Hari Parbat, the Shalimar and the Nishat; we went everywhere, devouring the beauty of Kashmir's landscapes, trudging along its byways, loitering among its stars, squandering whole days and weeks in search of exquisite moments.

And then there was nothing left to do except to sail among the waterways of the valley, to seek new harbours for our houseboat in the Dal lake and in the shadows of the various gardens, wherever the caprice of our idle wills directed the heart-shaped oars of our boatmen.

A cousin of the poet of our company, a nobleman and courtier of His Highness the Maharaja, who had sought us out in an obscure corner of the Dal, and showered the blessings of fruit and meat and drink upon us with a generosity that betokened his eminence and his affluence, offered us the hospitality of an island he possessed nearby.

Though grateful for his kindness, we had been finding the gentleman's hospitality rather embarrassing, because it involved us in a friendship with the great man which we could not spontaneously accept. For His Grace was rather a silly young man with the manners of a lout and a high blood pressure in his too opulent flesh, so we excused ourselves by saying that we were intending soon to complete our tour of the valley by going in our kitchen-boat to the Wullar. But it was not so easy for us to escape from the tentacles that he spread around us by that slick and sure turn of phrase that had so obviously carried him to his high position at court. He suggested that if we didn't accept his hospitality he would like to accept our hospitality and accompany us to the Wullar 'in your kitchen-boat for a change, because,' he said, 'I am tired of this grand style in which I have to live, and would like to be one of you.'

We were so bounden to the Nawab Zaffar Ullah, as the worthy was called, for the many favours he had heaped on us that we naturally could not refuse him, even though he became more patronizing and added that not only would he like to come with us, but two of his most intimate friends would like to accompany us also, and that he would like to supply provisions and order extra boatmen for our service on the way.

We were in for it, and we accepted all his offers because it would have been more strenuous to find excuses than to let ourselves become completely ineffectual pawns in his high hands. And, accompanied by him and his friends (a surly little judge of the High Court of Kashmir, and a most superficial young trader in hides and skins), we started one evening.

The shades of night were falling and we floated through the heaven and the earth in a dream as yet slightly disturbed by the Nawab and his companions.

The river flowed, and our boat flowed with it, without much help from our boatman, his wife, his sister, or his little daughter.

But we had hardly retired to the silent places of our heart when dinner was announced.

The Nawab had brought a sumptuous meal prepared by his servants, all ready to be served—rice coloured and scented with saffron, curried fowls perfumed with musk, and there were goblets of champagne, bottled in 1889.

Having compromised us into accepting his delicious food, it was only natural that the Nawab should deem it fit to amuse us with the gift of his speech. He told a few dirty stories and then launched into a discourse of which the ribaldry was so highly spiced with a deliberate obscenity that whoever felt nauseated or not, I, at least, who have never been over-righteous, turned aside, thought of the pride of my emotions, made my words the stars and surrendered myself to the bosom of the night.

When we awoke at dawn, our boat had unbarred the floodgates and glided into a veritable ocean of light. For, as far as I could see, for miles and miles, the azure waters of the Wullar spread around us, fluttering a vast expanse of mercury within the borders of the fiery sun-scorched hills.

The Nawab sought to entertain us with a song. But his voice was cracked and only his two friends sat appreciatively acclaiming his genius, while we wandered off to different points of the boat, helping with the cooking, dressing or lazily contemplating the wizardry by which nature had written a poem of broken glass, crumbling earth and blue-red fire.

For, truly, the Wullar is a magnificent spectacle under the red sky at morning.

I gazed upon the placid plain of water spellbound, enchanted. I lent myself to the whispers of the rippling breeze that was awakening the sleepy lotuses: tempted by an unbearable desire to be one with it, I plunged headlong into its midst and bathed in it to my heart's desire. Then I sat, sedulously noticing the blandishments of the elements from the shadow of a canopy under which the Nawab and his friends played cut-throat bridge.

By ten o'clock we had crossed the lake to Bandipur, a dull, insignificant little village on the road to Gilgit, the last stronghold of British Indian power before the earth ventures out into the deserts of Central Asia, uncharted except by shepherds till the Soviets brought the steel plough of prosperity there.

The Nawab here ordered the tehsildar to bring him ten chickens, five dozen eggs and some fruit for our delectation. And he took us about to the dirty houses of the village to show us off, or rather to show himself off, to the poor inhabitants of the township.

Our boatman came running and said that we should hurry because he wanted to row us across the middle of the lake before noon, as a squall generally arose in the Wullar every day at noon and it was likely to upset the boat if the vessel hadn't already crossed the danger zone before midday.

The Nawab abused him in Kashmiri, a language in which curses seem more potent than prayers.

We pressed the boatman's point, and since His Grace could not swear at us, he said he would get a man on begar (forced labour) to help the boatman and his family to row across the lake more quickly, and he tarried.

The boatman came again after half an hour and found us all waiting impatiently for the Nawab's return from a visit to the lavatory: His Grace had suddenly thought it fit to have a haircut and a Turkish bath in a hamam, and he didn't care what happened to us. When he did emerge from his ablutions, and heard not only the insistent appeals of the boatman, but our urgent recommendations, he, as a mark of his favour, clemency, or whatever you may call it, forthwith stopped a young man of the village who was walking along the cobbled high street and ordered him to proceed to our boat and help to row it to Srinagar.

'But Srinagar is fifty miles away, sir,' said the young man, 'and my mother has died. I am on the way to attend to her funeral.'

'Swine, dare you refuse?' snarled the Nawab. 'You are a liar!'

'No, Nawab sahib,' said the man, joining his hands. 'You are like God in mercy and goodness. Please forgive me. I am footsore and weary after a twenty-mile march in the mountains where I went to fetch my uncle's donkey. And now my mother has died and I must see the mullah about securing a place for her burial.

'Run, run towards the boat,' bawled the Nawab, 'or I'll have you flogged by the thanedar. Do you not know that this is the kingdom of which I am a nobleman. And you can't refuse to begar.'

'But, Sarkar . . .' murmured the young Kashmiri, his lips trembling with the burden of a protest which could not deliver itself in the Nawab's face, which glistened not only with the aura of light that the barber's massage had produced but with the anger which the man's disobedience had called forth.

'Go to the boat, son of an ass!' shouted the Nawab and raised his hand.

At the mere suggestion of the Nawab's threat to strike, the young man began to cry a cry which seemed childish and ridiculous in so grown-up a person, particularly because there were no tears in his large, brown, wide-awake eyes. And he moaned, 'Oh, my mother! Oh, my mother!' mechanically, in a voice which seemed to express more the cowardice of the Kashmiri which has been bred by the oppression of one brutal conqueror after another, than his very own real hurt.

But the Nawab was too thick-skinned to see the hurt in the man's soul. He looked at the big eyes weeping without tears and heard the shrill crescendo of his cry, and began to laugh.

'Let us leave him, Nawab sahib,' we said. 'We will give the boatman a hand and row across the lake to safety if we hurry.'

'Wait, wait,' the Nawab said, as he caught hold of the man by his left ear and, laughing, dragged him towards the boat.

The begari, who had begun to cry at the mere suggestion of a threat, howled the heavens down at the actual impact of the Nawab's hand on his body, while the Nawab, who had only laughed derisively at first, now chuckled with a hoarse laughter which flushed his cheeks.

The man extricated his ear from the Nawab's grasp as we were about five yards from the boat, and, perhaps because he thought he had annoyed His Grace by so overt an act of disobedience, he knelt down at his feet and, still weeping and moaning, joined his hands and began to draw lines on the earth with his nose as a sort of penance for his sin.

At this the Nawab burst into redoubled laughter, so that his face, his body itself, seemed to swell to gigantic proportions and tower above us all.

'Look!' he said, flourishing his hands histrionically without interrupting his laughter.

But the situation which had been tense enough before had become very awkward now as the man grovelled in the dust and rolled about, weeping, wailing, whining and moaning and sobbing hysterically with the most abject humility.

'Don't you weep, don't you moan, fool!' said the Nawab, screwing his eyes which were full of the tears of laughter, and he turned to the boatman, saying, 'Lift the clown from there and put him on the boat.'

The boatman obeyed the commands of the Nawab, and His Grace having stepped up to the deck behind the begari, we solemnly boarded the vessel.

The begari had now presumably half decided to do the work, as, crying his hollow cry and moaning his weird moan, he spat on his hands and took up the oar.

The Nawab, who cast the shadow of his menacing presence on the man, was more amused than ever, and he laughed hysterically, writhing and rumbling so that his two friends caught him in their grasp and laid him to rest under the canopy. He sought to shake them off with the weight of his belly and with the wild flourishing of his hands and the reverberating groans of his speech which came from his round red cheeks, muffled with continuous laughter.

The boat began to move, and as the heart-shaped oars tore the water aside, the begari ceased to cry and grieve with the same suddenness with which he had begun.

'Look!' the Nawab bellowed, his hysterical laughing fit ending in a jerky cough which convulsed him as a spark of lightning shakes a cloud with thunder. 'Look!' he spluttered and pointed towards the begari.

But the balls of his eyes rolled suddenly; his face flushed ghastly red and livid; his throat, twisting like a hemp rope, gave vent to gasping, whistling noises, and his hand fell limp by his side.

We all rushed towards him.

One of his friends had put his hand on the Nawab's heart, another was stroking his back.

A soft gurgle reverberated from the Nawab's mouth. Then there was the echo of a groan and he fell dead. He had been choked by his fit of laughter.

The boat rolled on across the still waters of the Wullar the way it had come, and we sat in the terrible darkness of our minds, utterly silent, till the begari began to cry and moan again, 'Oh, my mother! Oh, my mother!'

Lottery

There are certain words which so nearly approximate to the basic emotions of the human heart that though they may belong to one language they easily become current in all the others. Lottery is one of those universal words, and its general acceptability is due largely to the bit of the gambler that there is in every human being, to the belief in luck, fate, or accident of chance, of most people in a universe where little is certain. That one person, from among the millions who buy a ticket or a voucher, should receive a sudden windfall from the money contributed by these millions—that is what most human beings desire in this world of grandiose palaces and empty barns.

There was nothing surprising, therefore, in the fact that Kanahiya, the illiterate hillman from Kangra, who was watchman of the Imperial Bank of India, used the word lottery with almost the same frequency as he smoked a cigarette or puffed at his coconut-basined hookah. In fact, this was only to be expected, because, having retired from the army with nothing more than the bluff of the exaggerated prestige of sepoyhood, and a pension of three rupees a month, and seeing large sums of money change hands on the counters, or lying in the vaults of the bank, where he had secured a job following demobilization after the last war, he was, in one way or another, constantly aware of money. Full of admiration for the rich cloth and grain merchants who came to deposit their cotton bags of rupees at the bank every day, saluting the sahibs who drove up in big limousines to negotiate deals, their pockets bulging with paper notes, he had independently evolved the prayer, 'Make me rich, make me rich quick, O God, make me rich,' which he hummed in certain secret moments.

The prayer was, of course, never answered, for, as everyone knows, money does not fall like manna from heaven; there is not even a cash system in the celestial sphere, only barter.

So after many vain attempts at getting rich quick, by repeating his prayer, Kanahiya suddenly remembered one day that in the holy books which the village priest used to recite every morning, there was something to the effect that only those who work or do something to realize the ideal they seek in prayer find their requests to God answered.

Now, he could not become rich quickly by doing very much in the way of business, because he had no capital. And he could not become rich by getting a more lucrative job, because jobs had been as scarce during the past years as phoenixes—which are supposed to elevate one to kingship if they ever pass over one's head. So, tied to his post, on his unmilitary sentry go at the gates of the bank, his double-barrelled gun in his hand, he had sought to find a way to do something to get rich quick.

At last he had ventured very timidly to ask a manager who was going home on leave how white men came to be so rich. The sahib, giving the watchman a little bakhsheesh, had laughed and casually said, 'Kismet,' mere luck. On being pressed further by the persistent Kanahiya about the secrets of white men's success, and how he could emulate the example of the Westerners, the Englishman had jocularly said, 'Try a lottery.'

At first Kanahiya had not been able to understand what the manager sahib meant. But then he had asked Babu Radha Krishan, head clerk of the bank. The Babu had explained to him that there was a lottery called the Calcutta Sweep, for which one bought a share in a ticket at the modest price of ten to twenty rupees, and this might bring one a lakh of rupees if the number of one's ticket coincided with the number of the horse in the race run in Vilayat.

Ever since then, the word 'lottery' had become a kind of monosyllabic prayer, a watchword, catchword, cliché, phrase, proverb or whatever you would like to call it, on Kanahiya's tongue. He mumbled it to himself in secret moments when no one was looking, specially at bedtime or in the early morning, and he would talk about it to his friends on the least little excuse.

'You know,' he would say to Badri, the coachman of Lalla Banarsi Das, who came on a buggy to the bank, 'there is a magical lottery run in Vilayat, by which, if you buy a ticket, or a share in a ticket, you can become a lakhpati overnight if you are lucky to have the horse of your number come first in a race.'

'Aye, to be sure,' said Badri dubiously, 'but if it was as easy to become lakhpatis by this lottery you speak about then our Lallas would sit at home with their wives rather than sweat in their shops in the cloth market.'

But as his friends were cynical, Kanahiya would talk about lottery to strangers, mostly because he was talking aloud to himself to confirm his own faith in this extraordinary way of making money. Like his friends, however, the strangers dismissed all his talk about the lottery as the vapourings of a gullible fool. And if he invoked the fact that the Manager sahib himself had told him to try a lottery, they said that the sahib had been merely pulling his leg. Babu Radha Krishan's confirmation of the sahib's suggestion, and the details about the Calcutta Sweep lottery which the clerk had given him, seemed to his hearers the complicated talk of a half-baked learned man who was a danger to learning as well as to life.

The dream to get rich quick goaded Kanahiya on, however, in spite of everyone, especially after he had consulted Babu Radha Krishan again and again about the exact details of the Calcutta Sweep lottery. And to clinch matters, Babu Radha Krishan offered his services as an intermediary to buy him a share in a ticket for twenty rupees.

Kanahiya had been saving up two rupees a month for years and had piled up two hundred or so rupees in the bank in this way. Further, he had himself turned banker to the poor washermen, sweepers and cobblers who lived in the stables of the gentry in Queen's Road, Amritsar, where he himself occupied a room in an outhouse of Babu Radha Krishan's bungalow. He had earned a fair bit of interest on the money he lent out, so that his total fortune was something like three hundred rupees. 'You can well afford to risk twenty rupees on this lottery,' Babu Radha Krishan said to him, 'rather than go on talking about it and asking questions all the time. I know you have lots of money buried somewhere under the earth in several pitchers.'

The miser in Kanahiya made him hesitate, but the gambler in him egged him on, so the Babu settled the matter for him by actually making him buy a share for ten rupees in a ticket for the Calcutta Sweep, in which he himself had bought a share.

During the period when the great race was to be run, somewhere in Vilayat, and the result of the stakes was to be declared, Kanahiya's obsession with lottery became a positive mania. He would pester Babu Radha Krishan for news of the result every day; he would stop all the big lallas to ask them if they knew anything about the Calcutta Sweep; and he even dared to go up to the new Manager sahib, the forbidding little Mister Strong with the bald head and the ginger eyebrows, and asked him about the race. As this sahib, who was not given to levity, said that the result would be out soon and that he himself had bought a ticket in the sweep, Kanahiya calmed down a little and waited with characteristic oriental patience. His faith in the myth of lottery became so solid, indeed, that when he talked about it now to his friends he did so casually, as though it were an institution as solid as the Imperial Bank of India, only varying from this established firm in that it brought a million-fold interest on one's investment rather than the interest of three per cent.

At last Babu Radha Krishan called on him at his hovel in the outhouse one day with a newspaper in his hand and said that the result of the lottery had been declared and published and that, unfortunately, neither he nor Kanahiya had won anything; but that a peasant, a mere yokel in America, had got the lakh of rupees for the first prize and that two English lords had won the second and third prizes.

The bottom seemed to fall out of Kanahiya's world. He seemed to go pale and almost collapsed with disappointment, so that Babu Radha Krishan had to fetch smelling salts to revive him. Fortunately for Kanahiya it was a Sunday and he did not have to go to work, and he slept the clock round after he had swallowed some medicine which the Babu gave him.

For a few days afterwards he kept to himself and tried to avoid everyone he knew, both at the bank and among the colony of menials in the stables and outhouses of Queen's Road. His only consolation was that he had not been talking about the lottery overmuch for the last few days, because he had been too worried and expectant about the result. And now he hoped that people had forgotten his pet interest and would not ask him what news he had of the lottery and whether he had become a lakhpati. As the strain of earning a living kept most of his own circle of friends busy, and none of them could read a paper, none of them asked him any awkward questions. Only the manager sahib jocularly remarked, 'A good salary for honest work is better than speculation, eh, Kanahiya. Specially for poor people like you and I!' Luckily no one else was listening when the sahib said this; and anyhow, if someone had been there, Kanahiya was assured that they wouldn't have known what the talk was about, since the manager had not mentioned the word lottery.

In fact, Kanahiya so hated this word now that he could not even bear to think of it. All he was concerned about was to somehow make good those ten rupees which he had gambled and to try to save a little more money by pulling in his expenses. He forthwith raised the rate of interest he charged on the loans he gave by an anna in the rupee and became the careful watchman he had been before the mania for this lottery had taken possession of him.

But though he made good his losses on the gamble during the next year and was fairly content, the dream of getting rich quick often assailed him at nights. He would see himself as the landlord of his village, strutting about like a peacock in his fields full of corn, or as a rich lalla, splendidly clad, promenading in the Kangra valley, eating mangoes and bathing in the river, before going home to a handsome bejewelled wife. He did not take much notice of these nightly aberrations of his soul, but he did feel afraid that never now would he be able to return to his village as a rich man and marry the daughter of Subedar Raghunath Singh, as he could have done if he had become a lakhpati.

Hardened, careful and cynical, he resisted all temptations, however, and tried the safe and sure path of success through saving pice rather than risking an anna to make a rupee. And he evolved a corresponding philosophy to help him to live this modest life: 'A Rajah is a Rajah,' he would say, 'a watchman is a watchman, and a washerman is a washerman. So men were born, each in his place. No one should look at another's buttered bread and cultivate envy or greed. All I want is a bed to lie on, food to eat and work to do to keep myself from thinking too much . . .'

'And a wife to sleep with,' put in Shankar the washerman.

'No, no, I have no use for women,' Kanahiya said. But when he went to bed that night he felt that there was some truth in what Shankar had said. 'No home is complete without a woman,' he said to himself. 'And, to confess the truth, I have always envied Shankar his wife, Sobha, almost as fair as the memsahib of Mr Strong, and with a bottom which winks at one with every step she takes.'

She was the kind of woman he wanted; in fact there was no other woman like her, and it was her he wanted, he said in his mind. But how was he to get her? Another man's wife? It seemed impossible! . . .

Only, as he contemplated the smiling, happy young form of Sobha in his mind, he realized how often he had looked at her with desire. And if, as the holy men said, to look at a woman with desire was tantamount to having had her, then he had already possessed Sobha in a kind of way. So that even if he eloped with her, there would be no question of sin in it; he would be only claiming a woman who was his by all the rights of love. And how could he run away with her? How could he get another job to survive? And what would people think? He was afraid. He must forget all about this and go to sleep.

Kanahiya tried hard to go to sleep that night, but the agitation which possessed him mounted higher and higher in his brain, while he tossed from side to side on his bed and cried, 'God, give me sleep!' After the wrestling of various colloquies in his mind, as he was going over the incidents in his life, he recalled the disillusioning business of the lottery. A sudden illumination possessed him: he would not himself risk any more gambles of that sort, but he would persuade Shankar to borrow ten rupees from him on the mortgage of his wife Sobha, and as the washerman was unlikely, as he himself had been, to become a lakhpati, he would keep Sobha; for Shankar was already heavily in debt to him and would never be able to pay off the mortgage with interest and get his wife back. That plan settled in his mind, Kanahiya slept the sleep of peace during the rest of the night.

When he woke up in the morning, he exposed the plot to the rays of the sun above his head, and, lo and behold, Surya could not outstare him or make him feel ashamed. He tested the plan under the cold shower of the copious water that flowed from the lion-mouthed pump by Gagar Mal's serai, and the design in his mind emerged crystal-clear and pure after the bath. He contemplated the world of men and women about him at the end of Queen's Road and no one seemed to point the finger of accusation against him.

On the way to the bank, therefore, he called on Shankar and said, 'Why, ohe Shankar, what about paying me some of the money you owe me. The interest alone has piled up to ten rupees.'

Shankar stood silently by the donkey on whom he was loading bundles of clothes to go and wash at the ghat; he did not know what to say. To be sure, he had borrowed twenty rupees almost five years ago to celebrate the wedding of his younger brother, but he had not been able to save a pice in these hard times to pay back the capital or the interest on it. What could he say? At last he spoke, 'Acha, bhai, it is early morning and I am going to the ghat, while Sobha is baking bread to take with us. I shall give you an answer tonight and see if I can find a little ornament to sell or pawn to pay off the interest.'

'This is no talk,' said Kanahiya, putting the heat on. 'I want some of that money.'

'But, brother, it is early morning, and we have hardly awakened yet.'

'Son of the donkey, you are making excuses!' shouted Kanahiya. 'I am a watchman, once a sepoy, and I know how to wake you up properly.' And he flourished his musket at the washerman.

'That would only put me to sleep,' Shankar laughed.

'Oh, illegally begotten, I mean business,' Kanahiya threatened.

'Acha then, let us discuss business,' said Shankar, holding the donkey's ear in one hand and offering Kanahiya a seat on the string bed with the other.

'Unless you pay me the whole of the money which you owe me, by tonight, I will take you to court,' said Kanahiya peremptorily.

'He drinks most of his wages away,' said Sobha from the kitchen. 'Now this will teach him a lesson. He should have saved. He didn't even buy me a skirt.'

'Shut up, prostitute!' Shankar said. 'Don't you interfere in men's business.'

'She is right,' said Kanahiya.

'Yes, watchman Kanahiya sahib, he fights with me when he gets drunk, and even beats me,' Sobha said.

The washerman sank into the string bed and sat silent and defeated.

'Answer me!' Kanahiya bawled.

'What can I say?' said Shankar, after a long pause.

'Well, then, I can suggest a solution to you. I will give you ten more rupees—'

'Oh, generous watchman sahib, he will only drink it,' said Sobha.

'No, he won't do that,' said Kanahiya masterfully. 'I will give him ten more rupees if he mortgages you, Sobha, to me. With ten rupees he can buy a share in a ticket for the lottery and, if he is lucky, he may become a lakhpati and claim you back, as well as pay his dues to me. If not, he forfeits you . . . Those are my final terms.'

'But, Maharaj!' cried Sobha.

'Oh, Kanahiya seth! You never won that lottery, so what chance have I?' said Shankar, his hands joined in supplication.

'I tell you, those are my final terms,' said Kanahiya. 'Think them over during the day; in the evening I must have a settlement. Try your luck; you may be luckier than I.'

And, saying this, he stalked away towards the bank.

All day Kanahiya was in a flutter as he contemplated the rounded contours of Sobha's body in his mind, as he thought of her firm breasts and her fair face. She had sided with him clearly, he felt, in the quarrel with Shankar, that she seemed more than willing to be mortgaged to him in spite of her last show of protest. Besides, he could give her a cake of Pears soap and some electroplated trinkets and win her love. That word lottery, he gratefully thought. Surely there is a magic in it. Only he hoped that Shankar would not be able to raise the money to pay him off during the day. Anyhow, he had some documents prepared by the munshi of the bank to secure his plans to get Sobha.

After the bank closed, he hurried to the washerman's house and, flourishing the musket of his gun in his right hand, demanded, in a hissing whisper, 'Why, ohe Shankar, what have you decided?'

The washerman stood silently ironing clothes in the dark room which was both laundry and home to him and Sobha.

'Speak!' blared forth Kanahiya.

Shankar stopped ironing, but could not even lift his head to face the moneylender.

'Don't you see that I have made you a fair offer? You may be lucky and the ten rupees lottery share I have bought you may rid you of all financial difficulties.'

But in the boundless misery of Shankar's heart there was no room even for a particle of faith or even a ray of hope. He just sank down on his knees and, with tears in his eyes, begged Kanahiya for a little more grace.

'The seed of a donkey!' Kanahiya roared in a stentorian voice. 'Be a man and take the chance I am offering you!'

'You, asking him to be a man,' Sobha put in. 'You, a sneaking worm who has designed this plot to ensnare me. Go, you are less than a worm, you are a puffed-up ox from the hills with your notions of lottery. Have you become a lakhpati that you demand me from the man to whom I am married?'

'Sobha!' exclaimed the amazed Kanahiya, the pallor of chagrin on his face. 'But I thought you said you had no use for this drunkard anyhow!'

'Get out of here!' the washerwoman said regally.

'You bitch of all the dogs in the washerwoman's brotherhood!' shouted Kanahiya, lifting his double-barrelled gun. 'Silent, or I will murder you!' And for a moment he simulated the manner of the dacoits in the films made by Malabar Talkies. Turning theatrically to Shankar, he said, 'Here is the ten-rupee share in that lottery ticket I have bought you . . . And you, Sobha, come, I will make a woman of you!' And he went towards her.

'I will make you into a man if you don't look out and dare to touch me!' Sobha said.

'Come, don't be difficult,' said Kanahiya, wakening to her in the crisis which meant love or despair for him.

Sobha slapped him on the face with a sharp, clear stroke, while Shankar trembled.

The hillman's blood rose to boiling point at the insult and he lifted Sobha clear from the waist and carried her out, leaving the wailing Shankar behind. The outhouse in which the washerman lived was hidden from public view and no one heard the shrieks of Sobha nor the moans of her husband.

Locking her up in his own room, without bread or water, Kanahiya sat down on a charpai outside, smoking the hubble-bubble even as he trembled to think of the future. He was afraid that Shankar might call the police, or that the neighbours might tell on him and that the whole of his high-handed behaviour might cost him dearly in the end. But he had taken the precaution of forging a paper, transfixing the thumb-mark signature of Shankar from a previous deed to a new deal in which the washerman had promised to hand over his wife as a mortgage for arrears of debt and a ten-rupee share of the lottery. Sobha had been too outspoken to everyone in the neighbourhood to evoke any sympathy, and Shankar being weak, Kanahiya hoped for the best.

Sobha banged at the door and cried 'Dohai' for a long time, until, exhausted, she fell asleep.

Kanahiya went in and, placing some sweets by her, locked the room and slept outside.

When Sobha woke up at dawn and found that he had not touched her, but had instead left sweets by her bed, she, who had been a drudge in Shankar's house, weakened towards Kanahiya to some extent. And when he proposed that he would give up his job and elope to the hills with her she did not protest too loudly.

Before anyone was up in the outhouses, and while Shankar had gone to the cantonment to fetch his uncle, who was employed in a regiment and could get a colonel's letter to enforce his demand for the return of his wife from a mere civilian, Kanahiya bundled Sobha into a yekka with a few belongings and caught the dawn train from Amritsar Junction to Pathankot.

Having plied Sobha with all the gifts that he could buy at Pathankot, Kanahiya headed for a village where he knew a friendly sepoy, and there he remained in hiding for a month or two. Sobha yielded to him after a few more sanguinary battles, for cream cakes would soften any poor woman's heart, and hot milk with jalebis accelerates the process of conquest. Kanahiya had had a letter of resignation written by a munshi at Pathankot, and rested and enjoyed himself to his heart's content.

Then, sober, careful man that he was, he thought of ending his holiday and putting his affairs in order. He had about three hundred rupees in cash and a hundred and fifty owing to him from various clients in Amritsar, apart from the money Shankar owed him, of which he had generously thought of making a free gift to the husband in token of his mistress. With five hundred rupees, he was told he could buy a new house and a plot of land sufficient to grow two crops a year. But how was he to get his money back from the clients: he would have to go back to Amritsar once again.

He pondered long over the pros and cons of so hazardous a venture. At last, his gun in hand, and his gambler's instinct emergent again, he decided to risk it.

So off he took Sobha to Pathankot by yekka, decked in the best hillwoman's finery, and boarded the night train to Amritsar.

Arriving late next morning, he took a tonga and headed straight for Queen's Road. But the tonga-driver found it difficult to negotiate his vehicle into the path which led to the outhouses of the washermen and sweepers, for a vast concourse of menials was gathered together there, drinking and laughing and singing, dressed in the gayest clothes.

Was it the Holi festival when the washermen were prone to get very excited, or was someone being married, he wondered.

At last he asked the tonga-driver to ask someone what all the jollity was about.

'Why, don't you know?' said the tonga-driver. 'The whole town knows that the washerman, Shankar, has won the share of ten thousand rupees in the lottery. His ticket came third. I thought you were his guests coming here for the celebrations.'

Kanahiya's face fell. He clutched at his heart and nearly fainted.

'Stop!' he ordered the tonga-driver. 'Wait a while.'

And then he turned towards Sobha.

'You can wait or do what you like,' she said, jumping off the tonga. 'I am going back home.'

And before Kanahiya knew where he was, she was running towards the outhouse which was her home. The bird had flown out of his grasp, and, what was more, he could not now, since Shankar had become a rich and influential man, stay in the neighbourhood lest the washerman put the law on him.

'It's all a lottery—life,' said the tonga-driver sympathetically. 'Do you want to get down or do you want to go back? She has gone. If I were you, I should cut my losses and depart in peace.'

The tonga-driver had echoed his inmost thoughts. He had played high stakes and lost; he had played low stakes and the consequences were the same. Life was, indeed, a lottery nowadays. He sighed and said, 'Brother, I'll go back to the station and catch the twelve o'clock train.'

The beat of the dholki in the outhouse of Shankar and Sobha fell like the strokes of final doom on his heart and he held his head in his hands.

'Come on, be a man,' said the tonga-driver as he looked around after lashing his horse into a canter . . .

Mahadev and Parvati

Where the milk-white Ganges meets the dusky Jamuna are a few islets and sandy beaches on which the Kumbh Fair is held every twelve years. It is one of the most spectacular and enormous congregations in India, attracting to it the devout and the undevout from every corner of the land, full of the loftiest aspirations, fears and hopes, hungry for the food of the gods, thirsty for the waters of immortality. Preparations for the fair go on months ahead. The sadhus and ascetics have narsinghas of copper made to blow their greetings across the Himalayas to Lord Shiva from whose mouth the River Ganges is supposed to flow. The Brahmin priests rub up the mnemonic verses from the ancient holy books and evolve a more mysterious and magical ritual than that of previous years, for worship with them is like jugglery, the better the trick the bigger the price earned on it. And the people put by more and more money from their earnings to offer it to the holy men and the priests in order to secure easy passports to heaven.

Though the city of Prayag, where the confluence of the Ganges and Jamuna takes place, is a far cry from Colombo in Ceylon, in the mind of Parvati, the wife of the engineer Mahadev, it had assumed a significance more subtle than that which she could associate with the nearer shrine of Rameshwaram on the Cape Comorin, or even with the historic temple of Madurai near Madras. She had found her grasp on the fear of her husband slipping for some time, and she thought that a pilgrimage to Prayag, where the breath of the male Shiva weds the fiery dark Kali, might in some way cast a spell on him. Mahadev himself would rather have gone to the temple of Konark at Jagannath Puri, for a change of air and to see some of those famous erotic sculptures which are supposed to stir even the most jaded appetites to new fiercenesses of sexual fury. But the power of an Indian woman's persuasive tongue is only second to that of an American.

So off they went to a suburban railway station by Colombo and boarded a train for the north. Originally Tamils from Coconada, they sighed with nostalgia at the first glimpse of India from the small ship which crosses the short channel from Ceylon to the mainland.

And Mahadev would still much rather have gone to Ooty to drink a little beer in the cafés of the hill station and, if possible, to pick up some Englishwoman like those with whom he had had great success as a student in London. Instead, however, he had to stick to the route planned by Parvati, which led along the straight and narrow tracks of the Madras railway. They had two trunks in a second-class carriage all to themselves till Nagpur, but after that the throng of pilgrims began to increase and they had to squeeze into a corner, sit sweating, soot-covered and heavy-lidded with sleep. By the time they were a few hours' journey from Prayag, there was no room in the carriage to throw a til seed. What will not men and women endure to hang on to each other!

At last they reached Allahabad Junction on a torrid morning. Mahadev suggested that, in view of the congestion, it was best to stay at the Parsi hotel in the civil lines, and to motor over to Prayag a few miles away. Parvati conceded this as she had been pushed about enough by others more grasping after each other, and heaven, than her.

It was with great difficulty that they secured accommodation in Messrs Dinshaw's English-style guest house, for other professional men, too, from all parts of India seemed to have been led by their devoted wives, or the pull of their inherited faith, to the Kumbh Fair. And the atmosphere of the ramshackle hotel, with its tawdry Victorian furniture and pictures of Edward VII, seemed to the mind of the engineer Mahadev, from the slightly more advanced Ceylon, to be alien and inhospitable.

Parvati, who had been born in the house of a rich Tamil merchant in Malaya, and been married to Mahadev because he had found the dowry of two lakhs of rupees accompanying her a sufficient compensation for her lack of physical charm, was more compromising and docile. For she felt she was nearing the moment when she would realize that union with her husband through the influence of the vision of the two rivers meeting, which she had built up like a myth in her mind.

Mahadev was feeling sleepy, but he had to look for a taxi if they were ever to get to Prayag to have a dip in the waters of the Sangam before the sun rose too high; and, of course, taxis were non-existent on this auspicious day, having been requisitioned by the grandees and princes, who can always buy their way to heaven. The couple stood on the roadside and waited for a yekka. But these were chock-full of people from the civil lines on the way to Prayag, and the pilgrims from Ceylon waited in vain. At length someone advised them to trudge it by a short cut. They took the advice and set off.

The rising heat of the morning, the dust of the road and the worry of it, all made Mahadev miserable as, like a good Hindu husband, he walked four yards ahead of Parvati, a polo topee on his head, a white linen suit covering his sweating, heavy-limbed body, his feet thumping at an angle of forty-five degrees.

Their steady patience was, however, soon rewarded, because a yekka-driver picked them up onto his overloaded carriage, even though it was for the exorbitant sum of five rupees a fare for less than five miles.

Soon they were in sight of the River Ganges. And, already, feeling the impact of the cool breeze which rises from its snow-fed waters, Parvati felt her soul bursting with hope like a lotus. Even Mahadev was excited by the sight of the congregation on the riverbanks, scattered like shining white blossoms among the groves.

Every instant the din of the fair grew louder. And before long they had alighted and were part of the throng. Mahadev did not know if it was the contagion of togetherness which inspired him, but he dragged Parvati forward with great gusto through the crowd, shouting encouragement to her so as to be heard above the babble of men and women praying, talking, above the persistent calls of the hawkers, the obstreperous wailing of the beggars, the ear-splitting whistles of the toy-sellers.

As they penetrated farther, however, the thrill of community seemed to become suffocating, and Mahadev felt as if he would never get out of the clutches of the swarms of beggars—the blind, the deaf, the dumb, the leprous cripples minus an arm or a leg—all clutching for money and droning like wasps.

'Come this way to the river, sahib,' said a white-robed man, the imprint of sandalwood paste on his forehead clearly showing that he was a priest.

Mahadev felt relieved. And soon he and his wife were out of the claustrophobic atmosphere, seated on a platform by their rescuer, who seemed to be the partner of a hefty Brahmin who presided over the ritual of the dip in the confluence of Ganges and Jamuna.

Mahadev, who had travelled a lot and had endless experience of European guides, might have guessed that a tout is a tout, on the banks of the Ganges as well as on the quay at Marseilles, but for the fact that hardly had he and his wife sat down than the head priest took them completely in his charge and began to weave a fantastic web of mumbo-jumbo verses around the couple's heads, breaking the sacred word into their ears, touching their noses, their chins, and sprinkling the ash of dhup on their bodies.

The couple did not speak Hindustani and the priests did not know Tamil or English, except for the tout who spoke a few words of broken Angrezi, but the language of gesture always becomes very potent in such circumstances.

After a lot of spell-binding, the tout tied the end of the loincloth Mahadev had assumed with the dhoti of Parvati, having, it seemed, understood the peculiar reason for the couple's pilgrimage. And he led them to the river.

Amid the chants of the holy men, devout worshippers of the Sun, and the hissing prayers of the other men and women themselves, Mahadev and Parvati soaked themselves thoroughly in the water on the spot where the Ganges and Jamuna become one, and dripping, emerged, the ends of their wet clothes still tied together.

The tout led them back to the platform, where the high priest greeted them with more hymns and verses, even as he scattered rice over their heads and made them smell the smoke of sandalwood.

Mahadev and Parvati were by now on the way to being hypnotized into the feeling of togetherness, which they had come here to realize. And, beaming with warm smiles, they stood with joined hands before the agent of God, waiting for the union of their two minds which they felt sure was approaching steadily as the ceremony became more and more intricate. Parvati was praying in Tamil that as Ganges is united with Jamuna, her lord and master would remain united with her and that they would return here together in twenty years.

Suddenly, however, the high priest made a sign as if he was testing a silver rupee on the thumb and forefinger of his right hand.

Through his bleary, half-asleep eyes, Mahadev saw it, but did not take any notice.

The high priest repeated the sign and lifted the ten fingers of his hands and said, 'Huzoor!'

Mahadev was used to being addressed as Huzoor and stood with his head upright like a lord of the earth.

At this the tout ducked his head forward before Mahadev's gaze and said, in broken English, 'Rupee one thousand!' And thrusting his palm forward, said, 'Give.'

Mahadev opened his eyes wide with astonishment and incomprehension.

'One thousand, charge for ceremony! Understand? Give now!'

The tout's words were like hammer blows.

Mahadev swept his wife's face with a sharp glance and then, blinking his eyes, he waved his head, saying, 'No.'

'Put money here,' the tout said, rapping his knuckles on the platform.

Parvati nudged her husband to goad him to render forth unto God the price of His acceptance of her prayer, though she had no idea how much God was demanding.

In order not to give her the impression that he was being mingy or mean over the offerings, Mahadev joined his hands meekly to both the priest's and said, 'Fifty rupees.'

'How much does he say?' the old priest asked the tout.

The tout told him in Hindustani. Whereupon the high priest poured out a flood of Sanskrit imprecations asking the Gods to come and witness the impudence of the couple. And the tout shouted at Mahadev in a mixture of English, Hindustani and Punjabi, a great deal about how these dirty, beef-eating southerners come and want to expiate their sins by offering a few pices to the servants of God . . .

'One hundred rupees!' Mahadev offered generously to avoid the fuss.

The tout caught hold of the knot on the dhotis of the couple and began to sever it.

Parvati turned and saw the symbol of her togetherness with her husband in danger of being destroyed. She began to weep, and caught hold of Mahadev's arm with tender, supplicating hands.

Mahadev patted her on the head even as he addressed the tout in English and appealed to him to be a gentleman.

'Give a thousand rupees at once! Or I will break your head!' the tout answered. And he flashed his red eyeballs menacingly at the engineer.

The high priest added his quota of bullying and remonstrance.

A crowd began to gather together, muttering all kinds of malicious and unfriendly sentiments about southerners.

Mahadev felt the same claustrophobia now as he had experienced on his arrival at the fair. With a pitiful sob he put his head on his joined hands and knelt before the high priest, begging to be excused and offering two hundred rupees.

The high priest dismissed his abject apology with the most perfunctory of godly gestures.

And the tout, feeling that he had broken the pilgrim's will, struck Mahadev on the head, saying, 'Get up. You won't escape this way. A thousand rupees and no less!'

'Oh, don't be so cruel,' said a kindly pilgrim, coming to Mahadev's help. 'He is a stranger in these parts.'

'Go, go your way, and leave our votary,' the tout answered.

Weeping huge tears which fell on his chubby cheeks, Mahadev pulled Parvati near him and then explored for his wallet in the pocket of the shirt he had left behind before going to dip in the Sangam. It was not there. He looked furiously in the other pocket. No, he recalled he had put it in the pocket he had searched first. Panic-stricken, he took up his trousers and dug his hands into its two pockets. There was no sign of the wallet. The pallor of death spread on his face and he turned towards the high priest and the tout, now angrily, accusingly.

'A thousand rupees!' the tout said.

'You have stolen my money!' Mahadev shouted. 'Give me my wallet or I will call the police!'

'The thief threatening the sheriff!' the tout said to the crowd and raised his hand to strike Mahadev.

Parvati was weeping hysterically now. The ceremony of her innocent desire had been drowned in this vulgar brawl.

Mahadev looked at the two priests helplessly and, with a sudden loathing that would not transgress the code of good manners he had learnt, he surveyed the crowd for the figure of a policeman. There seemed none within reach.

'If you want to spare yourself more trouble at their hands, sir, please go away,' a well-spoken pilgrim suggested.

Mahadev picked up his clothes and, putting his arm round Parvati, moved away. He had never felt so near her before . . .

The Thief

The 'hoom' of the summer months in India is inexplicable, except in terms of an airlessness which seems to dissolve everything about one slowly and surely into a vague nothingness. Perhaps only a graph could illustrate it, because it is as much a sound effect as sense data, and sound can be drawn. Or, maybe, one could dispose certain daubs of paint in such a way as to break the exact symbolism of the Wheel of Life in a Tibetan scroll, and show all the concrete objects falling away, crumbling like the edges of the earth on judgment day, the stars breaking, the comets shaking, the seas full of fire and the sun alone standing there on high, a magnificent orb of brightness; a cruel, blood-sucking demon, scorching all sentient things as in some prehistoric war of the elements.

Ganesh always felt the listlessness of half death when he got up in the mornings, the heavy lids on his eyes literally ached as they opened, and no amount of stretching would stir the cells of his body into a sense of more than the doubt that he existed. So he generally crawled out of bed and proceeded towards the small balcony on the first floor of his ancestral mansion, there to inhale deep breaths of any air that was going. But there was seldom even a movement of a leaf or a dust speck such as could be called a breeze. Only the 'hoom' mixed here with certain asafoetid smells which rose from the open drains of damp lanes, the smoke of centuries and the rubbish of days that ran like a sore out of the huge bin on the corner of Gupta Road (named after his family) and King George's Road (named after George V, 'the Sailor King', who stood enshrined in marble fifty yards away in his coronation robes).

Although the 'hoom' persisted and there was no fresh air to breathe, there was a good reason why Ganesh Prashad repaired to the balcony with such unfailing regularity. For, since the scarcity in the South, the town's population had swelled with beggars, and among them was a woman with a child who had taken shelter on the marble steps at the foot of old King George's statue.

The slippery pads of her buttocks swayed before his gaze in zig-zags, as she walked away from the rubbish bin to the steps of the statue, after collecting a crust or a raw vegetable peel to chew. And as she drifted about like this, Ganesh felt a yearning in his blood, and his breath came and went quickly, until he was nearly choked in the utter hush of the mornings with the heat produced by the maddening waves of desire. His aching eyelids ached more sharply in the blinding glare and yet he could not keep his eyes from groping across the blaze, among the group of people who clustered around the steps of the statue or the rubbish bin, for the form with the swaying hips.

The fascination had been overwhelming from the start, for the first impression of the triangle formed by her thighs had made his sensations swirl in a giddy wave. But the memory of this impact had been sucked in by the sagging nerves of his sleep-doped body, and had gradually become a vague reaction with which other elements had mingled.

For instance, he had felt a distinct wave of nausea-cum-pity when he had seen her pick up a rotten banana peel from the rubbish bin and lick it. And he had wanted to run down and tell her that she would get cholera if she ate anything out of that bin. But he was afraid that if he went and singled her out for sympathy the other beggars might notice him and beat him up, for they still seemed to have enough strength left to guard the honour of their women-folk vigilantly. And as he could not do much about it he had just stood and stared at her, with the dull thud of an ache at the back of his head.

On another day, Ganesh had seen the beggar woman feeding her child on a bared breast. And that had aroused a feeling of unbearable tenderness in him, a tenderness, however, which gnawed at his vitals and aroused a lust of which the nether point was fixed somewhere in the memories of his own childhood.

And later, all these feelings had mixed with yet another—with a disgust he had suddenly felt on imagining her unwashed, dishevelled body in his arms, the putrid sore of her mouth touching his, the mouth which had eaten dirt and the filth of the rubbish bin, which had drunk the scum of the drains.

And yet, in spite of all the contradictory feelings, the first fascination of her swaying buttocks lasted, and the irresistible feeling which spread the confusion of a cloud over his senses, so that time and space ceased to exist and no consideration of duty or shame baulked his drunken gaze. And under the impulse of this distended desire, he would stand fixed to the balcony the whole morning though he be late for the office, until his elder brother, with whom he worked in the family firm of solicitors, began to notice the waywardness of his behaviour.

Once, he had tried to work up enough audacity to attract the woman's attention. But, being a timid respectable creature, he had to summon all the crazy impulses in his being to exercise the demons of destruction in him and beckon them to help him. The whole thing was a joke, he had sought to tell himself, the whole world was a joke and nothing was really stable. He himself, inheriting half the wealth of his dead father, was yet a slave to all the inhibitions and prohibitions of his elder brother and sister-in-law, living a confined, conventional life, contrary to everything he had learnt at college, and in full view of the disintegration, death and disease about him. And if it was all a joke, then this woman was a leer, an abject, worthless nothing, an ignorant, illiterate and dumb creature except that she possessed a pair of hips like boulders, the swaying of which excited him and from which he might get the pleasure of a moment, a mere particle of time in the long aeons of eternity where nothing counted or mattered. But, though the need for hypocrisy and circumlocution to build up an argument resulted in the coining of a number of euphemisms, he could not get away from the basic human feelings of pity and tenderness.

For, every day he was reminded of the incident in his youth when he had accused a beggar, who used to come up the lane on the right hand side of this house, of stealing a silk dhoti from his study on the ground floor, and had stood by while the servants beat up the beggar. In his younger days he had willed himself into the belief that he had actually seen the beggar rush out of his room with the dhoti, but since then he had felt less and less sure about it, and was, in fact, convinced that he had been guilty of snobbery with violence against an innocent man. And now, this hangover of an unkind act against one beggar had become an undertone beneath the lust for another, and the mingling of these made for a restlessness which was obvious in the increasingly frequent nervous twitch of his neck.

As he stood there one day, he felt he could not bear it. He could see the woman's breasts undraped, where her sari had slipped off as she crouched by the statue and washed the grit out of her child's eyes. And he felt the rustling of a strange song in his ears, the loam-song of dizzy desire mounting to the crescendo of a titanic choir. And the flow of a passionate warmth spread from his loins upwards to his eyes, making them more heavy-lidded and soporific than they had been when he had just awakened.

For long moments he tried to check his instinct to look deeper, to caress the amplitude of her haunches, an instinct which was driving him crazy. But he could feel her presence inflaming his body like a slow forest fire, which comes creeping up from the roots like smoke but becomes a wild red blaze suddenly in one crucial moment.

And as he was choked with desire, his neck twitched like that of a snake in the burning forest, and his vision was clouded altogether. Breathing heavily, hot, suffocated, he lifted his elbows from the wooden railings on which they rested and tried to steady himself.

The woman had now picked up her child and was feeding him at her right breast as she sat cross-legged on the ground. But the little one was whining, and shrieking, partly from the pain he had felt at having the thick crusts of grit removed from his eyes, but mainly because there was hardly any milk in his mother's breasts.

Ganesh's passion seemed to congeal as he heard the cries; he could feel an almost tangible loosening of his flesh, and though he was still soporific, he realized that he must go and bathe and dress.

But, even as he was withdrawing his gaze after a furtive stare at her haunches, he saw her hit the child with the palm of her hand and thrust the nipple of her left breast into his mouth. As Ganesh lingered to see what her second breast looked like, he heard the child yelling continuously. And, now, as though it were a revelation, the fact dawned upon him that there was no milk in the woman's breasts and that her child, who gnawed at her like a hungry rat, was shrieking with the need of his young life for sustenance.

He stood tense, as though he had had a vision, and his head was bent with a humility such as he had never known before, a craven, abject feeling of shame that a mother should have to hit her child in his presence because she had no milk in her breasts to give him, that she should have no milk because probably she had had no food herself. The joke, if it was a joke, the leer of her mouth, as well as the general ridiculousness of the world, was far too grim a joke to be merely laughed at. And, though she was unknown to him, an utter stranger, here today and dead tomorrow, she concerned him, if only because he had allied himself in his mind with desire for her . . .

As soon as the passion had become compassion in his body he had decided upon a course of action.

He turned around with a face knotted as though with revulsion against himself, and rushed downstairs towards the kitchen. It was just possible that by some miracle his sister-in-law might still be having her bath or lingering over her prayers. If so, he could get to the storeroom and get out a bag of grain and give it to the woman and her family on the steps of the statue.

When he got to the kitchen, he found that the course was, indeed, clear. There was only Biju, the servant boy, peeling vegetables there. But the storeroom was locked and the keys, ostensibly, hung at one end of his sister-in-law's sari.

'Where is bibiji?' he asked the servant impetuously.

'She is having a bath,' Biju said.

Ganesh swayed histrionically as though to yawn and stretch in order to bluff the boy. Then he drifted away up the stairs towards the bedroom occupied by his brother and sister-in-law. His brother would be away on his morning's constitutional in the garden, and, with luck, his sister-in-law had undressed in the bedroom and left her bunch of keys there.

With beating heart and anxious face, he sneaked into his brother's bedroom and looked around. He was lucky. The bunch of keys was on the dressing table. He took it.

But, before rushing down with it, as the wild cries of the beggar woman's child were terrorizing him to do, he sought to cover his manoeuvre and to give himself time. He went towards his room and called out, 'Will you be long in the bathroom, sister-in-law?' He knew that she would be longer out of sheer cussedness if only he showed any anxiety to make use of the bathroom.

'Yes, I am washing my hair,' came the answer.

Ganesh's face coloured with glee at the success of his ruse. The only thing that remained was to get the servant boy out of the way. So he called out from the inner balcony, 'Biju, go and get me a packet of razor blades from the shop. Here's a rupee coming down.'

The servant boy knew that he could always keep any change that was left over from a rupee when Ganesh sahib sent him shopping. He came eagerly enough into the compound and, picking up the money, ran.

Ganesh went down quickly and opened the lock of the storeroom door. He felt he heard a chorus of accusing voices and paused for a moment, but realized that it was only his heart pounding against his chest. And though he could not remember the shrill cries of the beggar woman's child any more, he remembered the way the little rat nibbled at his mother's breasts. For a moment he felt a fool going into the storeroom, a place he had seldom entered. But then he plunged into the dark.

His brother had hoarded quite a few bags of wheat and rice. So it was not difficult to spot them. Only, he didn't know whether it would be a bag of wheat or rice that he would be taking away. He did not pause to deliberate any more, however. He merely strained to get a grip on the nearest bag.

After rubbing his hands, which were moist with perspiration, on his pyjamas, he caught hold of the bag and lifted it coolie-wise on his back. Then he scrambled out and made for a small alley on the side of the house.

Hardly had he got to the middle of the passageway when he met Biju, who had come back after buying the razor blades.

'Let me carry it, babuji, let me carry it,' the boy said.

Ganesh was in a panic.

'Get away, get away,' he said.

But as the boy persisted, he thought that he might as well give the load to Biju, as, at any rate, he himself wouldn't look too dignified crossing the stretch between the opening of the gulley and the crowd of beggars by the statue.

'Where shall I take it?' Biju said.

'Give it to the beggars out there,' Ganesh said.

The servant boy looked askance but obeyed the orders.

Ganesh returned towards the storeroom to lock it up and restore the keys to his sister-in-law's dressing table.

'Where are my keys?' he heard a voice. But he thought that it was his own bad conscience shouting as it had done before.

'Who has taken the keys? Biju? Where are you? Have you taken my keys?'

Ganesh could not now mistake the source of the voice.

He drifted away from the storeroom door and ambling along as though he had come from a leisurely session in the lavatory below, he said, 'The storeroom is open. Your keys are lying here. Of course, the servant must have taken them . . .'

His heart beat like a tom-tom in hell now that he had lied. And he cursed himself for his lack of self-control.

The sister-in-law returned to her room, thinking that the servant had, indeed, taken the keys to get some condiments out of the storeroom.

Ganesh waited for Biju to come back, so that he could conspire with the servant boy to cover up what he had done.

'Don't tell bibiji about the bag of grain,' he said when the boy returned. 'And where are the blades?'

Biju showed him both the blades and the change on the palm of his hands.

'Keep the change,' Ganesh said. And he proceeded upstairs.

Like all people who try to be clever and hatch plots to carry out a design, he forgot to do one or two things which were essential to bluff his sister-in-law. For instance, he did not tell the servant boy the details of his plan about the bag of grain. Nor did he ask him to pretend that he, Biju, had taken the keys from the mistress's table to open the storeroom door and get some condiments out. And when his sister-in-law arrived downstairs and asked for the keys, the servant boy innocently said he knew nothing about them.

Of course, on sensing the real nature of the situation, he began to invent a lie to the effect that he had taken the keys from Ganeshji to fetch an empty bag out.

The lady of the house was nothing if not a shrewd, knowing housewife, instinctively aware of the subterfuges, lies and innuendos of all the members of the household. She caught the servant boy in the trap of prevarications that he had begun to make. And, when, on top of the incriminating evidence which Biju gave against himself, and Ganesh said he had seen him carry a bag of grain out of the house, the lady got her husband to beat the servant boy and throw him out, so that he could be free to join the beggars outside, whom he loved so dearly.

In spite of the many more lies he told, the servant boy was, however, throughout, as stubborn in refusing to tell upon Ganesh as this gentleman was in concealing the truth which might have cleared up the matter.

The imperturbable calm of Ganesh's behaviour after this incident was only broken when he saw the beggar woman again the next morning. His neck twitched more furiously, and his heavy-lidded eyes blinked, as if someone were digging pins into them, especially because he saw the servant boy, Biju, seated by her almost as though he had taken complete charge of her.

Professor Cheeta

Professor Cheeta heaved himself up from his seat on the top of the 77 bus immediately after it had left the Russell Hotel and, in the absence of the conductor upstairs, pressed the red knob of the bell with all his might.

The driver looked around with a scowl on his face, the passengers all stared hard, and the conductor, coming to the top of the stairs, mumbled some of the spiciest words in the unacknowledged but most telling and forceful vocabulary of proletarian speech.

The bus hesitated under the clock of Sir Isaac Pitman's Typewriting School, but did not stop until it had gone well past Peter's Bar by the Burlington Hotel, almost opposite Bloomsbury Place.

That is exactly where Professor Cheeta had meant it to stop.

'Come on now, oldie, your bus fare finished at Russell Square y'know!' the conductor shouted.

'Perhaps he does not understand,' a passenger said.

'Oh yes, he does! He comes this way every afternoon!' the conductor said.

'Thank you, thank you!' Professor Cheeta said sheepishly as he struggled down from the bus, breathing heavily. 'Thank you . . .'

'Come on then—I thank you!' the conductor said ironically, 'Come on . . .'

Seemingly undaunted, he stepped down from the deck of the bus hurriedly but carefully, deploring the fact that there was so little respect for old age in the world nowadays, and he began to walk down the pavement with mincing steps, followed by the humorous invective of the conductor.

Professor Cheeta was on his way to the British Museum Reading Room to research on the morphology of certain nouns and verbs in the Sanskrit, English and German languages, with a view to establish the cultural affinities of the Indo-Germanic peoples in particular, and the world in general, so as to promote world brotherhood, peace, tolerance and goodwill among men. He had started this particular enquiry about twenty-five years ago on the rebound against the fanatical nationalism of his earlier days and the terrorism with which he had toyed. But, as his research was nowhere near completion and as world tension grew, he was thinking of doing something more immediate, to write a short piece, a poem, to contribute his share to the solution of the difficulties of our troubled times. But almost every day he came into conflict with someone whose look or word implied 'black man' and his earlier terroristic impulses re-asserted themselves. He could not concentrate enough to put anything down and felt as though life were crumbling away around him. Now and then he walked the whole distance from his home in King's Cross Road in order to keep his thoughts together. But he was too old at sixty-four and couldn't keep it up. The life of poetry and reflection seemed to him more and more irreconcilable with the world of buses and trams.

Still, he rolled along at amazing speed on the short, squat legs which carried his top-heavy, stocky little frame, loaded with clothes. For, summer or winter, he wore two shirts, a thick waistcoat made of eiderdown, a rough suit, a large, frayed overcoat, a coloured muffler round his neck, another tied as a turban on his round head, which fell almost over his ears and covered his round coffee-coloured face.

He could not resist looking at the shop windows of Harding's bookshop in Great Russell Street, mumbling to himself names of the books displayed. Then, suddenly with a jerk, he tore himself away as if he were in a special hurry to get to the Reading Room and did not want to linger. For, ordinarily, he did not regard the Reading Room as a library, but more as a social club where he met all his old friends and cronies among the international fraternity of scholars, cranks, exiles and refugees who had also been researching here for years, monuments of industry and patience who emerged from their lonely attics and converged here towards the late afternoon.

'You are late today, Professor?' the tall, top-hatted beadle said by way of a greeting.

'Hello, Mr Jenks!' the professor returned the greeting.

''Ow are you? And the wife?'

Jenks's perennial inquiries about the wife had always embarrassed him, for, from the first, Peggy had patronized him by saying that she was marrying him, a coloured man, against the wishes of her family; and he had never got on with her. 'Rather seedy! Rather seedy, you know, Mr Jenks, my wife is rather seedy,' he said hypocritically and then sought to change the subject. 'The weather has not been too good . . . The sun! Oh, the sun of my country!'

'Too hot for me!' Jenks said, 'When I was in your country up in Chitral, I had malaria. Yes, too hot for me, your country!'

'And it is getting hotter—what with Gandhi!' interjected the dour policeman who stood by the gate.

But the professor was not really listening. The mention of the sun had excited a train of thought in his mind and he mumbled academically to himself, 'The sun has many names, Brahma, Vishnu, Krishna, Surya, Apollo, Ra, Isis, Phoebus, Thor . . .'

'And mumbo-jumbo,' said the porter with a laugh.

The professor did not take any notice of Jenks, but began suddenly, spontaneously like a child, to weave a rhapsodic chant about the sun, as children do when they are fascinated by a word.

'I am the son of the Sun
the true son of the Sun,
descended from the tribe of the worshippers of Surya,
baked in the fire of the Lord . . .'

'Breeds a lot of maggots, the Sun!' said Jenks.

But the professor did not heed him and walked away with a wave of the hand, singing snatches of little verses and soliloquizing in his rhapsodic manner.

'I am the circle above the zone of the equator
who stirred the seas
and shook the mountains,
who hurled the earth
into the mounting storm
of light . . .'

'He's off his head!' Jenks said to the policeman.

'Poet, and don't know it!' the policeman answered.

As Professor Cheeta walked along, talking to himself and chanting the words of certain half-forgotten poems, absent-minded and unconcerned with everyone else, he was yet aware that he was different from most men in the juggernaut of commerce which was rushing on outside. An exile from his homeland ever since he had come out of jail for suspected terrorism, he had never taken any roots in this country for all the thirty years that he had spent here. People stared at him, turned back to look at his queer gnome-like, dark, heavy figure, swathed in a thick overcoat, with the blue turban on his head and pince-nez on his nose. The children whispered to each other about whether he was an African or a Red Indian and cheeked him by asking him the time.

But though he seemed a fool to others, he was a dreamer imbued with the precariousness of life. For throughout his life there had come to him certain impulses and visions, vague and fleeting at first, but which had lingered in him with a subtle sense of beauty, nobility and grandeur, like a melody that moved him strongly at odd moments and then evaporated.

And he knew certain kindred souls whose life had been disturbed in the same way but who had later accepted some kind of compensatory faith. There was Miss Richardson, for instance, a lady of seventy, an ardent Christian prohibitionist, who worshipped the memory of Pussyfoot Johnson, read Dr Mathew's rendering of the Bible in the Reading Room, and fed pigeons in the compound.

'Come and see my little ones,' she said in a squeaky voice as the professor strolled up today.

Professor Cheeta made a noise with his lips in the cooing language of pigeons and then broke out into human speech, 'Come, my sons, come, you flutter like my heart.'

'They are not afraid,' said Miss Richardson with a laugh which knit her shrivelled, lined face with a queer, innocent beauty, the aura of the devoted, of those who believe.

'Hello, Miss Richardson,' said Professor Cheeta almost flirtatiously.

'The pets—they are so hungry!' said the old woman, blushing a little.

'They are happy as the air,' said Professor Cheeta, conventionally. But in his heart there was a tense emptiness, as though he felt the need for wings, but realized that he hadn't even a face, or a tongue to speak with, nor could he even move or look at anyone. And there came a faraway look in his eyes, a kind of fixed stare at the nothingness about him.

'Why so sad, Professor?' Miss Richardson asked as she threw more crumbs onto the palm of her hand.

Professor Cheeta sighed an almost inaudible sigh and, swallowing a choking breath, said in a doleful voice, 'I was born in India, you know, Miss Richardson, in the country of dreams, the fountain of fables, the source of much knowledge and wisdom—and tears . . .'

'How many Christians are there in India, altogether?' asked Miss Richardson. 'I have always wanted to ask you that, Professor?'

'As a young man,' went on Professor Cheeta, without heeding her question, and almost as if he were talking to himself, 'I felt I had a dream. Brighter than all dreams, a glorious vision of myself—I wanted to write a poem in which I could infuse the spirit of fire, which would embody light, which would, if you see what I mean, be radiant, glowing and bright, which would put some meaning into things.'

'I am quite sure if you believe in Jesus . . .' began Miss Richardson.

But Professor Cheeta did not let her finish her sentence, which he knew was the beginning of a quite mechanical speech to convert him that she always delivered in season and out of season. He was too restless and felt as if even his instinct for words was betraying him, as though he were losing his grasp on life altogether. 'Time went on,' he said, 'and the vision still persisted, flashing and sparkling in my brain, flowing like the music of rushing waters, shimmering like the sunshine and bathing me in the aroma of roses, if you see what I mean, a fire consumed me—'

'And then?' Miss Richardson said, now interested.

'Oh lady,' replied Professor Cheeta, moving his head about dolefully till the pigeons took fright and fluttered, 'I was let down, betrayed, put in jail. And since then I have been too preoccupied with mundane struggles. Too pulled about, torn by the strain of it all to believe ever in poetry.'

'Didn't Krishna say, "Live in action"?' asked Miss Richardson.

'He was speaking in another time,' said Professor Cheeta. 'Nowadays, what with atom bombs and the rest, I feel—' And he waved his short arm in a gesture of despair.

'To work then on your dream!' exhorted Miss Richardson, so that the pigeons fluttered with the echo of her voice. 'You have no time to lose.'

Professor Cheeta was affected by the peremptory note in her voice and looked at her for a moment. Then he withdrew his gaze inwards as if he felt the will to have vision anew and was trying to hold fast to a glimpse of it. Taking leave of Miss Richardson with a bow, he fairly ran towards the Reading Room, two steps at a time, hurrying through the swing doors and the hall amid the babble of sightseers' voices. He did not even halt to return the 'good afternoon' of the porter at the doors of the Reading Room, but scrambled towards the North Library, panting for breath. His thoughts seemed to go askew as though the dome had pressed them out and his eyes moved furtively outwards and inwards, as if to keep the vision in control.

'Is this seat taken, Mr Southern?' he asked an old man with the beard of Havelock Ellis and the eyes of Bertrand Russell.

'Sh, sh!' shushed Mr Southern who, though a friend of Professor Cheeta's, was compiling the history of Egypt in thirty volumes and had no time to answer irrelevant questions.

Professor Cheeta's face fell a little and he drifted away, groping for a seat and assuring himself in his mind that if only he could get hold of a seat and a pen he could cause the ink to run into gold and hold the glimpse of the beauty and the tragedy he had lived, captive forever . . . Therefore, he did not acknowledge Mr Davis who was writing a treatise to blow the cancer research racket sky-high, or Father Talbot who was writing up the Spanish Inquisition. But he noticed Professor Palmer, the orientalist, and his heart congealed, for Palmer had written a most vicious introduction to a translation of the Gita and was now doing a commentary to damn the Vedas. Professor Cheeta's eyes quivered with fear and he changed his direction. The Reading Room was full at this time. One of the friendly old assistants, Evans, seeing the professor in distress, came up to him and said, 'You are late today, aren't you? There is only ten minutes to closing time!'

'Yes,' Professor Cheeta said, apologetically. 'Can you get me a seat, Mr Evans? I have something important to write.'

'Wait, then,' Evans said, 'I shall look around at the other end.'

'Thank you,' Professor Cheeta said, and moved towards the corners of hope. Looking up at the clock he felt as if the years were rolling by with every tick of the minute hand. And the urge of the poem in his heart beat louder and louder as he saw the pens of the readers running faster and faster before closing time. Afraid of losing the rhythm of his song, as well as to test its ring on the tympanum of his ears, he paced up and down impatiently, and, losing sight of Evans, stood talking to himself as if he were in a delirium. 'I am no mere bookworm . . . like that Mr Southern there. Buried beneath dusty volumes. I am no mere chronicler of the dead; I have something in me. My love for my country. I am stirred like the waves of the sea, Mr Palmer, ghost of dead ideas that you are! I am possessed by the Sun.'

'Please don't talk so loudly,' a reader said.

But Professor Cheeta was absorbed in himself and went on burr-burring, 'I am the son of the Sun . . . I . . .'

'Please don't disturb me,' the reader said.

'Young man!' the professor said, surprised at the student's lack of consideration. 'I want to sit down.'

'Oh all right, go away from here!' the young reader stammered impatiently.

Now the other readers were disturbed too and there came suppressed whispers of concern, brief injunctions, suppressed threats, silent angry looks, more potent than any words.

'What is all this noise?' a minor official said coming up to SS2.

'Oh, my head aches,' Professor Cheeta was saying to himself.

'Throw him out! . . . Sh . . . Chuck him out!' the readers said, bursting from beneath a hitherto suppressed hysteria which seemed to have been waiting to explode in the silence.

'I shall fetch the superintendent,' said the official.

Possessed by tremors of hate and frustration, Professor Cheeta turned towards the exit. His whole frame quivered with the fear that all the Englishmen in the Museum were following him and that they were going to lynch him. Above these delusions, the smoke of chagrin covered his thoughts, his head hung down and there was a light in his eyes which was too furtive to stare ahead. As he raced along, the turbulent music of anguish in his body blinded him completely and he fell headlong across the steps, by a bookshelf, with a giant thud.

'Oh, the poor old man!' someone said.

'Give him a hand!' another said.

'Now, now, what have you done, Professor!' Evans said, rushing up after him.

The Assistant Keeper of Printed Books came down from his perch at this uproar, a tall, towering, bald-headed man. He scowled at the people who had gathered round the old man, whispered something to himself and went away. He knew that Cheeta, like several other people, regarded the library as a social club, and disliked him for making himself a nuisance.

'And I found you a seat, too!' Evans was saying consolingly to the professor as he lifted him . . . 'And you go and fall down like that! Come!'

At that instant, the closing bell of the Reading Room rang.

'There you are, you couldn't have written much today, anyhow,' said Evans, seeing him to the door. 'Now steady as you go . . .'

'Thank you, Mr Evans, thank you for your trouble,' Professor Cheeta said as he hobbled along.

Then he felt for his turban which had come undone. He did not stop to re-tie it, however, and went along, clutching his old portfolio securely in his left hand and mumbling, 'Oh my head! Oh my head!'

'Hello, Professor! Hello!' someone called to him by the cloakroom.

But he did not want to meet anyone now and hurried out.

'He seems very restless today!' the porter said to the policeman, as he saw him rushing away without the familiar, long drawn-out conferences with Professor Carlo, the Professor of Languages, and Mr Matthews, who came to the Reading Room to pick up newspapers from the wastepaper baskets, and the various Indian students.

The next day he received an official, brief, curt letter from the Keeper of Books informing him that his Reading Room ticket was cancelled. After he had lain in bed the whole morning, recovering from this shock, he tried to get up and proceed to the Museum as usual. But as he was dressing, he fell with a thud on the floor and was laid out for months and confined to bed with an undiagnosible malaise.

When he recovered slightly, he begged his wife to wheel him to the compound of the Reading Room. But the doctor disallowed any such exercise.

After that he was bedridden and kept losing weight as if something inside him was gnawing at him and corroding his strength.

Miss Richardson came to see him twice or thrice and tried to give him faith. But he seemed inconsolable. Having lingered, for some months, with failing powers of physique, he passed away one afternoon, at almost the time he used to go to the Reading Room, mumbling to himself the while,

'I am the son of the Sun,
I am the Sun,
The Sun . . .'

The Tractor and the Corn Goddess

My uncle Chajju it was who really caused most of the trouble about the tractor. Of course, not being a devout person he was not the person who raised the slogans 'Religion in Danger', 'The Corn Goddess Has Been Insulted', 'No Truck With This Tractor', 'The Invention of the Devil', and so forth. In fact, as soon as the affair began to assume the form of a Hindu–Muslim issue, he literally put his foot down on the machine and very proudly had himself photographed, as a sahib has himself photographed with his foot upon the back of a tiger which a shikari has actually shot. Nevertheless, it was a phrase of his which was responsible for the whole rumpus, or rather a great deal of it.

The facts of the case, which has assumed the significance of a legendary happening in our parts, were these. When the big landlord of our village, the Nawab Sahib of Bhagira, died, his only son, Nawabzada Mumtaz Ali Khan, who was reputed to be a worthless, irresponsible fool, addicted to such European habits as bad company and drink, came home from abroad and started to behave in a manner which most people thought was quite mad, or, to say the least, somewhat strange. For, in the old days when a zamindar died, his son and heir generally levied a tax for the funeral expenses on the peasants and followed it up by levying another tax still for the motors and the horses he had brought and generally made the peasants aware of the advent of a new order. But, on his arrival, Nawabzada Mumtaz Ali Khan issued a proclamation that the sum of seven lakhs, which had accrued through the illegal dues of the previous year would be distributed equally to all the peasants of his seven villages and that anyone who came to see him and put token money at his feet before making his plea, would not be listened to at all, and that Uncle Chajju, who was the ringleader of the goondas of our parts and had been exiled, was to be allowed to come back.

Most of the peasants, whose fathers, grandfathers and great grandfathers had been known to pay nazrana, though secretly happy at being relieved of illegal exactions, still thought that it was bad form on the part of the new Nawab and a breach of the old custom, for, they said, 'After all, the zamindar is in the position of a mai–bap to us.' And Uncle Chajju came back thumping his chest like Goonga, the famous wrestler, the Rustum of Hind, and declared that the new landlord was simply yellow and frightened of him.

When Mumtaz announced his next set of reforms, that he intended, by deed poll, to renounce all rights to his land and form a co-op in which all the tenants had equal shares, there came various deputations from the elders of the villages, relations and friends to restrain him from his insanity before the papers finally went through. The Deputy Commissioner of the area called the errant boy to him and reprimanded him severely for betraying the trust reposed in him by his forefathers, the community and the Sarkar. And, needless to say, the papers were annulled and the reforms were not executed.

Of course, Mumtaz was nothing if he was not a stubborn mule, once he had got hold of a notion in his head. And he began a long series of debates with the Sarkar about his right to divest himself of the land and yet avoid a court-of-wards being imposed on him. But while this matter was still dragging on and all kinds of opinions, good and bad, were being expressed by people about the Nawab's strange behaviour, he brought in that tractor which caused the biggest crisis of all.

Certainly Mumtaz had chosen the wrong moment to introduce this gadget on his estate. For, the months of talk about the new-fangled ideas which he had brought from Europe, and adverse comments on the long-haired, unkempt, dishevelled men and women, called, 'comrades', who went in and out of the 'big house', day and night, his reputation was in that 'state of chassis' when one more error would lead to a final showdown. Perhaps he forgot about the fate of Amir Amanullah of Afghanistan. Or, maybe, he modelled himself on Mustapha Kemal. At any rate, he only escaped by the skin of his teeth and he ought to be grateful that he is alive today.

The actual incident happened under the banyan tree just outside the big house one morning. The giant tractor had been fetched at about eleven o'clock from the railway station by Comrade Abdul Hamid, the engineer. Abdul Hamid brought the monster engine not across the main road, which is mostly empty except for straggling pedestrians, but through the fields of the estate when the peasants were busy ploughing for the rabi harvest, and, as the machine furrowed the earth deeply before it came to rest at Mumtaz's door, the peasants gathered from all sides, chased the tractor, some shouting, some just staring, some whispering to each other, all aghast with wonder or fear at this new monstrosity which had appeared in their lives and which threatened to do something to them, they knew not what.

It was at that juncture that Uncle Chajju took the lead in the crisis. By one expletive he crystallized the feelings of all of them.

'Rape-mother,' he said caustically, even as he sat smoking the hubble-bubble under the banyan tree.

'That's right,' old Phagu chimed in. 'I hear it tore up the earth as it came along.'

'The earth then has been desecrated!' said Shambhu Nath, the Brahmin priest.

'Han, the Corn Goddess, the mother, the giver of all food, has been raped!' said his devotee, Dhunni Bhagat, running up behind him.

'Toba! Toba!' said the maulvi of the mosque, rolling his eyeballs and touching his ears under his green turban.

'Rape-mother!' repeated Uncle Chajju. 'Why doesn't this boy Mumtaz come out and tell us what is in his mind, the secretive one. What is his game?' And he wore a quizzical expression on his frank face, which was more the index of a hurt pride than anything else, almost as though being an open-minded, hearty, old rogue he resented the fact that Mumtaz had not taken him into his confidence.

'I hear,' said Jodha, the oldest peasant of the village, 'that as the White race has never possessed the Shiva-Shakti which was in the sinews of our people, they have been inventing all kind of artificial medicines to make themselves potent. If it is true what Dhunni Bhagat says, that the Corn Goddess has been raped, then this instrument ought to be sent back across the seas to the perverts who have invented it . . . Why, our religion, our shame is involved! Darkness has descended over the earth. What are things coming to? That our boys should be supposed to be so weak that they can't plough the land with the good old wooden plough! That I should have lived to see this insult to our race!'

'Ohe chup kar, Baba!' said Chajju. 'It is not your voice we want to hear, but that of this young landlord of ours.'

'Toba! Toba!' whispered the maulvi, rolling his eyes and touching his ears.

'Why are you touching your ears and whispering because we have spoken the truth!' said devotee Dhunni Bhagat. 'You are very shocked at our language but seem not to care that our mother earth, the Corn Goddess, has been desecrated . . .'

'To be sure, it is a question of religion,' said Shambu Nath. 'No Hindu landlord would have brought an artificial instrument like this to tear up the earth of a Muhammadan village.'

'To be sure!' said Tirath, a crochetty, old shopkeeper, 'Our religion has been despoiled.'

'Ohe chup. Stop this kind of foolish talk and call that young fellow to come and explain to us what he has inflicted on us,' counselled Uncle Chajju.

'To be sure! To be sure!' said one of the young peasants. 'It is probably an electric machine, with power stored in its belly,' said another.

'Uncle Chajju is right—we must know what it is for?' opined yet another and tried to touch the tractor ever so gingerly.

'Ohe careful, ohe careful, it is the magic of Shiva-Shakti in a new form,' speculated Jodha. 'The invention of the Ferungis, who have weakened our race. You might die of the touch as the crows on the electric wire die every day.'

'Our Mahatma had already warned us against such machines,' said

Dhunni Bhagat. 'We will not stand for the rape of the Corn Goddess, specially under Congress Raj.'

At that instant, Abdul Hamid, the engineer, emerged from the big house.

'Now then, come and tell us your meaning in bringing this here,' challenged Uncle Chajju.

'Get away, get away, don't crowd round the tractor,' said Hamid arrogantly, 'Nawab sahib is coming.'

'Ohe look, folks, our religion has been despoiled!' shouted Dhunni. 'And he talks like this. Our Corn Goddess . . .'

'Yes, there is leather on it, I am sure, somewhere,' added Shambu.

'Go, go, lentil eaters,' shouted Hamid.

'Don't you insult the priest of the Goddess after you have trampled upon her body!' said Dhunni.

'Don't you bark,' said Hamid, measuring himself up against the devotee, with his torso stretched tight.

'Toba! Toba!' sighed the Maulvi and wagged his beard.

'Come, come, boys,' counselled Uncle Chajju. 'There is no talk of religion or the Corn Goddess or anything like that. All we want to know is what is this machine, how it is going to be used and what it is made of . . .'

'To be sure, to be sure, Uncle Chajju is right, that is what we want,' said the boys of the village.

'I can settle that easily,' said the Nawab, craning his head behind the knot of men who had gathered round Hamid, the engineer. 'It is a tractor—that is what it is called.'

'So it is the rape-mother tractor!' said Chajju partially satisfied.

'It has despoiled the body of our mother, the Corn Goddess!' shouted Dhunni.

'It has ruined our religion,' said Shambu.

'We will have no truck with this tractor,' said Jodha.

'Toba! Toba!' said the Maulvi.

'Ohe, stop this loose talk,' said Uncle Chajju. 'Let him explain now, let him talk since he has broken his vow of silence, the shy boy.'

'Well, it is a machine which can do the work of a hundred bullocks in one hour. It will till the land of all our seven villages in a fraction of the time that it now takes us to plough it.'

'Are you sure it is not a gari with hidden guns in it?' asked Chajju. 'You haven't brought it to shoot us down with, have you?'

'There is probably imprisoned here all the Shiva-Shakti which the White race has robbed us of during their rule here,' said old Jodha.

'There is magic power in it!' said Phagu.

'Jinns,' said another peasant.

'Bhuts?' said yet another.

'Don't be so suspicious, brothers,' said the Nawab. 'It is for your good that I have brought it. It is only iron and steel, so tempered as to plough the land quickly.'

'I would like it to be taken to pieces before I can believe that there is no magic in it,' said Phagu. 'And jinns and bhuts?'

'Ohe it is the Shiva-Shakti, fools,' assured Jodha.

'It is all right so long as there is not a gun concealed in it,' said Chajju. 'That is all I am concerned with, for I am a man of peace!'

At that there was loud laughter, for my uncle Chajju is too well known as a cantankerous, quarrelsome creature to be altogether accepted at his own valuation as a man of peace.

'Well,' said the landlord after the amusement had subsided, but before the atmosphere of goodwill built up at the expense of Chajju had altogether evaporated, 'the tractor is yours and you can take it to the fields.'

'I suspect it is like the decoy wooden horse that was used by the soldiers in the story of the land across the seas!' said Phagu, shaking his head sceptically.

'I think, Baba,' said Uncle Chajju, 'you are right in suspecting this engine. And I agree with you when you ask for it to be taken to pieces before our eyes. We will only be content if it is reassembled before our own eyes. Because, then, we can learn to master all the jinns and bhuts in it!'

'Uncle Chajju,' said the landlord, 'I can see your meaning. It is right that you should be able to contact the jinns and bhuts in it. I nominate you to be the foreman under whose supervision the Engineer sahib will take it to pieces. And then you shall learn to drive it, so that all the demons in it do the rough work of the village and give us more time to sleep under the shade of this banyan in the afternoons.'

'It is a great shock to my sensibility to learn to harness a steel plough,' said Uncle Chajju, 'especially as I have never got over my love for my two bullocks who died in the drought, but I don't mind putting myself out a little if all of us can really have a longer siesta. In the hot weather there is no place like the shade of this banyan.'

Uncle Chajju is one of those funny men who has only to open his mouth to say a word to make people laugh. Perhaps it is his manner more than his method. Certainly, it is the tonal quality of his theth Punjabi accent that gets the villagers like a contagion. The amusement created by his speech reconciled all the recalcitrants to the tractor, though not until after it had really been pulled to pieces and each peasant had touched its several bolts and knobs and felt the motive power of its dynamo next to their ears. After the terror of jinns and bhuts had been appeased and curiosity satisfied, it remained for honour to have its due share. The Nawab photographed all the villagers with the tractor in their midst. And, of course, Uncle Chajiu, in the role of the new driver, stood like a colossus right in the foreground of the picture, as a sahib stands with his foot upon the back of a tiger which a shikari has actually shot.

The Man Whose Name Did Not Appear in the Census

The thumping on the door was so peremptory that Ramji stopped blowing at the coals in the chillum of his hookah and waited open-mouthed for the worst to happen.

But nothing happened. Only, there was more thumping on the door. And Ramji just could not put his mouth to the base of the coconut hookah, which he held in his left hand. He merely stared into nothingness and cocked his ears to listen intently.

There was more knocking.

Ramji's wife, Luxmi, said, 'Why don't you get up and open the door?'

The words seemed to fall on deaf ears, for Ramji's ears were full, not only of the scum which usually gathered in them so thickly for months until the ear-cleaning barber came to the village, but also of the sound of various kinds of knocks on the door he had heard and learnt to distinguish. He remembered, for instance, the gentle tapping on the door when his father-in-law came, quite unlike this heavy thumping now. Then, the dangling of the latch chain by his wife's impetuous female friends, basically different from this thumping and more like the knocking of the key on the frame of the drum which the women practised on marriages and betrothals in the village. Again, there was the knocking on the threshold of the house by Moti, the family cow, when she came back from pasture. No, this thumping was unlike any of these usual knocks on the door. It was like another kind of sound which Ramji had heard, a knell which sounded every quarter when one of the landlord's henchmen, or the policias came to call him, which had driven the fear of the stave and the shoe into his bones, and which had rendered him dumb and helpless till he was prostrate at the remotest echo of it.

The thumping became impatient, angry and loud, and it was accompanied by an abusive, gong-like voice calling, 'Ohe khol, ohe khol—open the door!'

Ramji sat there on the charpai in the one-roomed barn, which was his storeroom, sitting room, sleeping room, kitchen and bathroom, and he looked almost as though he were a rabbit fascinated by the danger that threatened him.

'Get up and open the door!' said Luxmi shrilly. 'What kind of a man are you that you sit there doing nothing while I am garnishing the spinach!'

'Ooon, hoon . . .' he answered as though he had suddenly come back from some remote country into which he had wandered away. And, thrusting his hookah towards her, he said, 'Fill me another chillum.'

'Hain—what has happened to you?' called his wife. 'Have you suddenly been struck by palsy or something?' And, gathering her dhoti about her, covering her bare breasts and head modestly, she ran towards the door.

Ramji leapt from the bed, still holding the nariyal hookah in his left hand and stood barring her way.

'Don't be crazy,' he whispered. 'I haven't paid the last three-quarters of rent. Do you want me to get a shoe-beating from the landlord's men.'

'Let me go,' Luxmi cried. 'Whoever it is at the door has already heard us, and look, they are peering through the chinks of the door.'

'Oh wait till Shibu comes home,' Ramji said. 'I need my son by me if there is going to be any reckoning of accounts . . . And it may be the policias . . .'

'So you suddenly need your "son",' said Luxmi. 'Why, you were not very proud of him this morning when he asked you for a little money to go to the fair with. Then you called him "illegally" begotten and disclaimed him—'

'Stop your cain-cain, woman, I am not feeling well,' said Ramji, trembling with anger from under the layers of fear. 'How can you be so cruel to me when you know I have no money? Haven't I treated Shibu as my own son all these years in spite of the fact that you . . .'

The knocking at the door, which had ceased for a moment at the sound of stirring feet and hushed voices in the house, started again. And Ramji collapsed weakly on the charpai, panting for breath and with the pallor of death on his face.

Meanwhile, Luxmi hurried towards the door with an abusive impatience that outmatched the impatience of the man at the door, 'May you die! Wait! I am not a machine that I can run to the door and knead the dough at the same time. And who are you, anyhow, making this "khat-khat" at my door?'

'Mother, open the door,' said a voice meekly. 'I am on sarkari business.'

'Now I am undone,' sighed Ramji. And he shook as though he suddenly had an epileptic fit.

Luxmi unhooked the inner chain and fairly spat in the face of the visitor as she said, 'You people never let a person rest—now what do you want?'

'I am a census officer,' the visitor answered briefly but firmly. He was a short, bony babu whose only strong points were the points of his neatly trimmed moustache, with the additional qualification that he knew he had these strong points.

'What officer?' Luxmi queried.

'Census officer!' answered the babu and began to twirl the strong points of his moustache.

Luxmi referred the visitor to her husband with a casual gesture of her head and withdrew to the kitchen.

The visitor called to his attendants and entered.

'Your name?' he said without looking at his victim, and lifting the pencil which stood uncannily balanced on the top of his right ear, he got ready to scribble on the file in his hand.

Ramji got up and, laying the coconut hookah on one side, began to smooth the charpai. Then with both hands outstretched, he invited the babu to be seated. All the sinews and fibres in his feeble body, every particle of his craven soul, was strained to make the sarkari official welcome, so that he would not inflict any punishment on him. And he sat down on the floor, with his hands joined abjectly before him, his quivering dumb face raised towards the officer while his eyes glanced furtively this side and that.

'What is your name?' the official repeated his question.

Ramji only lifted his joined hands higher by way of an appeal.

'Speak, what is your name!' shouted the two attendants of the babu almost in a chorus.

'Oh forgive, please forgive me,' was all that Ramji said by way of an answer.

'Son of forgiveness, tell me your name, your father's name, your caste,' said the babu impatiently.

'Huzoor, mai–bap, forgive,' wept Ramji. And, touching the babu's feet with his right hand, he took the dust from his fingertip to his forehead.

The babu seemed flattered by this servility on the part of Ramji and stood twirling his moustache even as he beamed at the stupidity of the peasant.

'Tell the sahib your name as he has to go to other houses,' said the attendants.

'Huzoor,' said Ramji, 'you sahibs are all-powerful sarkari officials. Surely you can forgive. I have only defaulted on the payment of my dues for three months, because the rabi harvest has been bad. Now, if you forgive me and don't send me to jail this time, I shall make up the arrears and always pay in time. You are like God, all-merciful and just, so forgive me this time . . . The Thanedar sahib has beaten me so hard with his shoe that my body is still aching and my head has gone bald. Take pity on me for the sake of my age . . .'

'Is the man mad?' the babu asked his attendants.

'Apparently he is one of the goondas of the peasant union who got a shoe-beating at the police chowki last month.'

'You officers of the Secret Police know everything, of course, huzoor,' said Ramji, 'but I can assure you that I was quite innocent.'

'But we are not officers of the Secret Police,' said the babu. 'I am a census officer, see—the Sarkar is compiling a list of all the citizens of Hindustan and I have to take down the names of all the people in this village.'

Ramji could not make out what a census officer meant and why he should be making a list of all the villagers. Rumour had it that the Sarkar was soon going to arrest all members of the Kisan Sabha and therefore wanted the names of all the villagers. He would surely be in for it if he gave his name because he had, at the instance of young Shibu, foolishly put his thumb down on the list of the members of the Kisan Sabha and had had to suffer the shoe-beating at the kotwali. Now if the babu and his attendants were not one kind of Secret Police official then they were some other kind of policemen, and he would surely be doomed if he gave his name to them.

'Huzoor, mai–bap,' he said, 'please forgive.'

'Give your name, fool, or I shall really lose my patience with you,' shouted the babu.

Ramji fell away, shrieking as though ten thousand policemen had begun to beat him.

'Come to your senses, answer them, coward,' Luxmi called from the kitchen. 'Why do you weep even before they have begun to beat you?'

'What is his name, Mai?' the babu said turning to her since he saw that she had shown more initiative.

At this Luxmi modestly drew the end of her dhoti on her forehead and relapsed into the dutiful demure Hindu wife who is not supposed to mention the name of her husband.

'Are they quite mad?' the babu said, turning to his attendants.

'Sir, she being his wife will not, according to custom, mention his name,' answered the attendants.

'And he being frightened of the police will not mention his own name?' the babu exclaimed. 'Well, I know a solution to this difficulty— his name will not appear in the census. What is the use of mentioning the name of a half-dead old man on the record anyhow. He just doesn't exist.'

With those words he turned imperiously towards the door and walked away, presuming that he had deprived Ramji of the greatest honour which the Sarkar could bestow on him.

The old peasant lifted his eyes surreptitiously from where he lay, but kept still until the officials were out of sight. Then he got up with some alacrity and, picking up his coconut hookah, cocked an eye at Luxmi.

'The light of heaven has suddenly come into your eyes, coward!' his wife said. 'Look at you winking at me!'

'Crazy woman, you don't know how we have just managed to escape. I tell you, the best thing these days is to remain as far out of the reach of the Sarkar as possible . . .'

And he began to blow at the dead coals and cinders in his chillum to revive the hookah.

'Coward! You crawl with fear at the sight of any man who comes your way in the village,' said Luxmi.

'My father taught me,' answered Ramji, 'work more and make fewer friends.' And he tried to look profound above the yellow pupils of his eyes.

'Oh you make me ill,' remonstrated Luxmi, 'always trying to hide behind my skirt, as though you were a little child frightened of bogeymen.'

'Woman,' Ramji counselled, 'if rulers be tyrants, throw up your land, burn your plough and scatter with the wind—to come back like a whirlwind later.' And, after delivering this homily, he puffed at his hookah and looked smug. Only, the live coal in the chillum had become dead cinders and he thrust the hookah towards his wife.

'Coward! Coward!' shouted Luxmi. 'Coward.' And she came and spat upon him.

At this Ramji was stung to the quick. And he got up and caught hold of his wife by the bun of hair at the back of her head, for if anger once comes on the weak it comes more suddenly than on the strong.

Luxmi retaliated by getting hold of a broom in the classic manner of the peasant wife, and she dusted him hard with it wherever her short arms could reach out against the resilient pressure of his wiry hands.

And they had a good set-to and would have hurt each other if their son hadn't come at that instant and protectively shielded his mother against the father.

Ramji was mad at the favouritism the boy showed towards Luxmi. And he delivered himself of a maxim which expressed the whole essence of his outlook upon human destiny, 'A ruler who is hard upon his subjects as a spider on the flies, a woman who abuses her husband, and a son who is more his mother's son than his father's—these three are utterly bad and ought to be shunned like the plague.'

Only, he loved his land, and the hookah which his wife or his son were constantly filling for him, too much to renounce life altogether.

A Village Idyll

Splashes of red and orange mingle into an aura of burning gold and, in a flash, the sun rises over the rim of the village pond, resplendent.

Gauri comes treading on the pearls of dew on the tufts of grass by the ditch to fetch water, with a pitcher under her arm.

'Oh, the fair one.
Oh, ripe like the juice of a sugarcane . . .'

Govind sighs, as he sits rubbing his clothes with soap on a slab of stone. The glow produced on his face by the brisk movement ripens into crimson and his breath almost fails.

Gauri shyly draws the end of her dupatta over her head and dips her pitcher in the water, but, as she leans forward, the tips of her brave breasts are silhouetted against the skyline.

'May I be your sacrifice!' Govind whispers the familiar ejaculation of heart-squanderers in the streets of Verka. And, as though the words are potent like a magic spell, blood rushes down from his head to his heart and loins, the centres of storm in his peasant soul. 'Oh, the fair one!' he hisses. And the hisses splutter into an embarrassed cough.

At that Gauri laughs even as her pitcher gurgles with a series of hysterical reverberations.

And with that their love started. For, in the tickling of her throat and the saliva on his tongue was the meeting of long distances, of uneasy colloquies, of thumping hearts and reckless yearning.

She stood before him, her breasts heaving towards the morning, her senses sinuously touching the edge of demure restraint, her blood warming and melting and leaping like flames towards a ceiling in a conflagration.

He stared at the wonder of her, his body taut, his breath swelling and unswelling to the tune of his now frightened heart, his soul reaching out to some expression from the groin of endless silences. She seemed like some shimmering cloud image, veiled in sheaths of innocence. 'Ha!' . . . the exclamation escaped from his throat involuntarily. And he leapt towards her like a tiger towards a young doe.

With a shrill shriek she ran, leaving her pitcher where it stood at the edge of the pond. And, as she raced up the steep bank, her torso straining forward but her legs far behind, she knew she was defeated and burst into a smile.

Govind caught her and flung her onto a dune. She fought him back, digging her nails into him and kicking him with upraised knees. He swung her from side to side and pinned her arms to the earth and lay down on her.

'Oh let me go,' she said with tears in her eyes and laughter in her mouth. The colour on his face called to the radiance on her cheeks. And, giddy-eyed, she relaxed, till his lips touched hers. And now she swayed as though her soul was in a delirium of giving.

'Someone will see us,' she whispered.

But, storm-tossed, scampering, wriggling hard, twitching with the concentration of nerves outstretched for months in desire for her, in a fierce felicity, he was intent on the dissolution of her energies, the melting of the snows of her virginity . . .

A little distance away, on the track leading to the rivulet, Lehna, the son of the landlord, went twisting the tails of his bullocks, goading them to drag the manure cart quicker. Govind flapped his arms like a protective male bird covering his mate under his wings, for Lehna was his rival. Gauri snuggled up to him like a cooing female bird. And thus they lay in the heat and the sweat, their voices rustling like the silks of Lahore and their faces glowing above the dune sands like two luminous wild flowers jutting out of the earth. The sun shone above their heads.

The sun shines, and the moon takes light from it, as also the stars. And on the earth, going round the sun, through the eternal movements, we possess in our spines all the planets, as well as a thirsty love and the desire to die in order to be reborn . . . And from the dying, and through the rebirth, there grow lotuses among the reeds, the flaming smiling pinks, pushed up in the quagmire by the vital spark that keeps things alive. In the fruits, flowers, foliages, among the birds, beasts and humans, the same glorious urge prospers. And there is creation.

Gauri smiles like the demure morning. Govind laughs like the temple drum. There is the voice of Shiva in their curly throats. And in their bodies is the sinuous disunion of a broken moment between the lord of storms and his consort, Parvati. And in their touching is the burning of several planets, the extinction of worlds, the smothering of heavens, the dissolution of hells, and the springing of a serene pleasure, muted like a prayer in which we rest, sometimes as before a new miracle and sometimes, as before the juxtaposition of legs intertwined in a ridiculous posture.

And thus begins a cycle.

Govind met Gauri in the lentil field on the first full moon night of autumn when everyone was awake and merry. He lay with her in a hay barn on the eighth day of the new moon before winter, when people were feasting at night after fasting the whole day. And he took her on every moonlit night in the winter. For, after the first flush of raw passion had expended itself under the sun, they began more and more to lend themselves to the mellow light of the moon. Govind wore clean clothes and Gauri always had flowers in her hair.

As Gauri went to meet Govind in the fields by the river on one eclipse night, however, her mother saw her. 'Ah!' she shrieked at the boy. 'If you have spoiled my daughter, you must marry her—you wretch.' And she shrieked at Govind's mother for letting her son roam round like a bull. And Govind's mother shrieked at Govind's father for begetting a seducer. And Govind's father shouted at Govind. To which the boy returned the simple answer, 'Marry me to the girl.'

And then there was much toing and froing among the elders.

And, at last, on an auspicious day, discovered in the scrolls of their fate, for a good commission by Pandit Badri Nath, the Brahmin priest, Govind and Gauri were married . . .

The Hangman's Strike

Our country has been passing through the biggest strike-wave in history—bigger than the biggest we have ever had. Certainly the strike-wave through which we have passed was the most gigantic in living memory, affecting all kinds of workers, the textile workers, the municipal workers, the press workers, the railway workers, the engineering workers, the jute workers, the biri workers, the taxi-cab drivers, the rickshaw-pullers, the black-coated workers and even policemen and naval ratings and soldiers of the foot.

Of course, as long as the profit system lasts, strikes there will be . . .

But no strike caused such a furore in our country as that of the heroic trade-unionist, the only member of his party, Buta, hangman of our mofussil Madhopur jail, who refused to go to work suddenly one day and, battling against the toughest opposition, oppression and ill-treatment from the authorities, at least won a great moral victory if he did not quite succeed in winning his demands.

Actually, Buta went on strike because of his great sympathy for the hangmen in America who, he heard, had been thrown out of employment after the electric chair was brought in to deal with suspected communists and criminals. But even though this distant cause did not stir the public conscience to any extent specially because the hangmen in America were thrown out of employment a long time ago, still Buta's strike aroused a tremendous amount of feeling in our country and is reported even to have led to jubilation among hangmen all over the world. For, the implications of Buta's strike were really worldwide, insofar as he reflected the resentment of all members of his profession, not only against a mere machine, the electric chair, but against all the millions of amateurs who have been qualifying for the hangman's job during the course of the two World Wars. What annoyed Buta particularly in this context was that almost all the potential and actual hangmen who were engaged in killing in these wars had got medals for merely being in on it, and the more skilful of them had even been rewarded with money and land, while he, a professional hangman, had not been given a raise in pay for thirty years and not one word had ever been mentioned to him by the Head Jailor, Sheikh Siraj-ud-Din, about the dearness allowance which had been conceded to almost everyone in India to keep pace with the rising cost of living. Besides, Buta had sensed (and he is a very sensitive man, indeed, as everyone knows who knows anything about hanging) that while all the butchers and marauders had been exalted during the world conflict, he, a more subtle artist than most, had always been looked down upon both because he was a hangman and because he was originally a sweeper by caste. The rudeness of jailors and warders apart, the insults and humiliation he had to suffer at the hands of the banias in the shops, and even from the tongues of little children, had increasingly oppressed him and made him sore. And, as he heard a great deal about democracy from the politicians who had, during the last generation, been confined in the prison cells, or who had gone to their deaths shouting slogans, Buta had been developing an incipient sense of democracy and freedom like most of the great men of our age. Naturally, therefore, when he felt that he had had about enough of the old order, the old status and the old scales of pay etcetera, he struck work.

Equally, naturally, this strike came as a great surprise to all and sundry. For the laws of our society, as well as its conventions, are made by ordinary men, and everyone is rather shocked when he comes across the extraordinary man, the genius, who discovers new aspects of the well-worn and accepted rules of the game. 'How dare this pig, hangman Buta, go on strike?' said Sheikh Siraj-ud-Din, the Head Jailor. 'But why shouldn't I go on strike?' said Buta. 'After all, I too can claim the appellation of Sheikh before my name, for though I am considered an untouchable, I too left the fold of Hinduism and was converted to Islam exactly as Sheikh Siraj-ud-Din was converted . . . Besides, while the meats broil in the pots on the chulhas of the Head Jailor's house and the sauces brew on the angithis and the delicate smoke of birianis and pilaos goes up to high heaven, and he dyes his beard with henna and goes inspecting the jail with a dignity which bespeaks violence, wiles and the radiance of authority, I go about wearing a crown studded with the jewels of my own sweat, and can only sniff at the odours of meats cooked in other people's houses . . . It is not fair, either in the eyes of God or man!'

All such denunciations, however, ended in silence, a silence compelled by the noise that the strong can make to drown the voices of the weak. And Buta found himself opposed not only by the Head Jailor, but by all decent members of society who considered it to be the most outrageous, absurd phenomena that a mere sweeper should 'raise his head to the skies', that a mere messenger of the angel of death should assume the airs and graces of a decent citizen and set himself on the same pedestal as other human beings. Surely, it was said, such scum of the earth, with the blood of so many mortals on his hands, should be tried in a court of law and summarily condemned to be hung for near-murder. Not all the resolutions passed by the various sympathizers could win support for Buta against the middle-class eloquence derived from the schools. And at the best the whole thing came to be a kind of joke. 'Ha-ha,' people said, 'a hangman gone on strike! The fellow must be mad!'

For days the news of Buta's strike figured in the world press, first as a news item, then as a comment by columnists and again as a 'Twilight Twitter' or as a 'Crackling Thorn'. And, then, it became part of the gossip of the bazaars and lanes where the goondas gathered, because those badmashes thought it may be a fairly good strategy to commit all the murders they wanted to commit at the time when Buta was on strike, for surely there would be no one to hang them in case they were found guilty and condemned to be hung. But the more decent members of the public deprecated discussion about Buta's strike, saying that the very foundations of law and order were being undermined, though some people, whose sense of chivalry was aroused at the sight of seeing a man surrounded by so many enemies, opined that all this prating about law and order was conditioned by the way the hangman had, by his courageous action, held up the mirror to all the smug and self-complacent members of the judiciary, the military, the gentry, the nobility, the bureaucracy, and other such interested parties. And it seemed that there was a semblance of truth in this analysis, at least, from the violent frothings on the mouths of all the respectable citizens as soon as the subject of Buta's unprecedented and historic strike was mentioned.

Actually, there was ample cause for the Head Jailor, Sheikh Siraj-ud-Din, to be disturbed. For, Buta had struck in the middle of the execution of Jhanda Singh, the murderer. After the prisoner had been led to the platform of the well and made to stand there, after his neck had been put into the noose suspended from the bracket, and after the hour of eight had tolled on the bell, Buta, who was at that instant to move the lever, did not move the lever which parted the wooden platform in two portions and let the condemned man drop with a sudden jerk into the well.

As Buta refused to do anything, all the jail officials and the warder's squad had to stand there in an unbearable suspense for three minutes.

Then, at last, Buta declared his intentions and put forward his demands. Upon this, Havildar Sher Jung, the Gurkha Head Warder, misunderstanding the whole thing as a trick played by the condemned man, ordered the warders to open fire. The sepoys obeyed the orders and the deed was done, the murderer was shot dead instead of being hung. And no one could do anything about it.

Buta showed remarkable presence of mind. Not only did he not stir from the handle of the lever, though he thought the Head Warder had really opened fire on him, but he repeated his demands.

Now the jail staff, from the superintendent to the warders, knew that there had been an infringement of the law in shooting the condemned man when he had really been ordered to be hung. And, of course, Buta knew this too. Hence arose the inability of the jail staff to hush up the matter of Buta's strike, for they had already had to conceal the manner in which the condemned man, Jhanda Singh, had been disposed off. And hence the difficulty of persuading Buta to call off the strike.

In a panic of fear, lest the Government authorities should get to know what had happened, the jail staff approached Buta, one by one. At first Col. A.K. Kaul, I.M.S., the Superintendent of the Jail, spoke to him, but as Buta had contempt for the Angrezi tongue, the colonel failed to convince him. Then the Head Jailor, Sheikh Siraj-ud-Din, tried his polished Hindustani speech, accompanied by a few quotations from Ghalib, with a due performance of all the flourishes and elegant courtesies. But Buta was a tough Punjabi, who had often heard his own language being insulted by the southerners, and he seemed blind to all the sheikh's blandishments. Later, the two Assistant Jailors had tried the rough stuff with him. Even this had failed, because the hangman knew how much conscience money they took from each convict for granting special favours like tobacco or sugar and for writing their letters and for enabling them to interview their relatives. And, when the rumour of Buta's sit-down strike spread, there was no going back on the irrevocable fight on which the hangman had entered.

Everyone knows the story of the way aunty cat bluffed her nephew, the tiger. The tiger had approached his aunt, the cat, and asked her to teach him how to hunt, which the cat had obligingly done. Whereupon the tiger, immediately he learnt all the tricks, made a dead-set on aunty herself. But, of course, aunty cat was not all that naive, for she had not taught her nephew how to scramble up the tree when in danger, and she escaped the greedy grip of the tiger.

The Head Jailor too knew this parable. And he acted upon it. He locked up Buta in a cell and put him on bread and water.

The hangman was hard put to it to know what to do next. For the jail staff, fearing the consequences of any partiality they might show to their colleague, were loyal to the authorities and would not take any message of Buta to the outside world. And, not knowing how the campaign on behalf of his sensational strike was going in the world press, Buta languished and grew thin.

After a few days, the deprivations he suffered in not receiving the special rations of the rump steak which was generally allowed him, he decided to compromise. He had been thinking out various improvements in the craft of hanging and craved a special audience with Sheikh Siraj-ud-Din. And he let it be known that if only his pay was raised, he would yield better results in the very next hanging. 'For,' he said, 'I can guarantee that death could be prolonged for quite a few moments if need be, by a special jerk on the lever.'

But Sheikh Siraj-ud-Din sensed in Buta's weakening an added strength in his own sinews. And he demanded complete surrender. He abused Buta in the most filthy manner and told him that he would square him properly for nearly ruining his, the Sheikh's, career, and for causing such an uproar.

And, what was more, Sheikh Siraj-ud-Din succeeded in having Buta tried for his sit-down strike by a friendly magistrate and had him sentenced to six months' rigorous imprisonment. As the Head Jailor had taken all the precautions to see that nothing about the illegality of the last execution should leak out, Buta was silently brought back to the very jail where he had wielded power over life and death, and kept in solitary confinement. The arms of the law had certainly proved to be stronger than the will of the hangman.

It so happened, however, that the cell in which Buta was confined was in an obscure part of the jail where some nationalist prisoners were kept. And, in spite of the vigilant guard kept on him, he could see them and hear a great deal of what they said to each other. As they said a great deal to each other and Buta heard all, his head became chockfull of all the subtleties and intricacies of the doctrine of non-violence.

And when he put two and two together, that is to say, when he looked at all the ideas upside down, and downside up, and saw them in every light, the doctrine of non-violence, of the non-hurting of man or beast or bird or even insect, began to appeal to him. But it was so much opposed to what he had himself done as a hangman all his life that he merely repeated the phrases which the Congressites used, like a parrot, and amused himself in that way. As, however, he was a prisoner in solitary confinement, who felt hateful impulses against the cruelties heaped on him by the authorities, he felt anything but non-violent.

But, one day, he heard an old Congressite narrate the history of the various non-cooperation movements which Gandhi had launched against the Ferungis. And some young man said that there was no difference between non-cooperation and a sit-down strike.

This made Buta open his eyes and apply the doctrine of ahimsa to his own action in refusing to pull the lever, and it percolated into his thick wisdom that he himself had only recently been acting in the great Gandhian tradition. And he made several overtures to his neighbours to come and talk to him.

But those worthies had heard all about the tyrant Buta, the hangman, and were scared stiff of him. Death is an extraordinary thing, and everyone connected with it is tainted with its strange odours, so far as the nostrils of the living are concerned.

None of them even dared to come anywhere near the cell where Buta was confined. And Buta, who beneath his thick wisdom had a soul as deep as the hangman's well, realized that perhaps in their eyes he was associated with the uncanny dread that attaches to the murderer as well as to the murderer of murderers. He waited patiently for the days when his solitary confinement would be over and he would be released from jail.

By one of those accidents which often lead to the salvation of us wretched humans, the day of Buta's release coincided with the date on which the bunch of nationalist prisoners were set free.

The jail authorities realized this only when Buta was brought up into the hall and given his old clothes back. And all their designs to rearrest him, by trumping up another charge against him, were foiled by the fact that the hundreds of people who crowded outside the hall to receive the Congressites, saw Buta there. Of course, the Congressites were making desperate efforts not to remain too contiguous to the hangman. But the hall of the jail is a comparatively small place and does not allow much room for manoeuvres.

And, as the door opened, and the eager crowd greeted their

emerging friends and garlanded them, they, spontaneously and unknowingly, included Buta also in the joy and warmth of their cordiality and garlanded him. And, before Buta knew where he was, he was on the shoulders of the crowd, being acclaimed a hero of the Gandhian revolution.

The Congressites in jail sought, after the procession had reached its destination, to disillusion the people about Buta, the hangman, in furtive whispers, explaining his origin and character. But there was a fervent Gandhian who seized upon Buta's abjuration of his post as a hangman, as one of the greatest victories for the doctrine of ahimsa. And thus Buta secured a niche in the gallery of heroes who have given their all to make our country what it is today.

The Signature

There is something sacred about a signature; it makes everything valid, puts the seal upon all undertakings, makes bonds real, guarantees securities, cements pacts of friendship and alliance between states, provides the ultimate proofs of integrity in the highest courts of law. The signature is all in all. Even poets, when they publish new poems, often call them 'New Signatures'. And the radio uses a signature tune as its patent or hallmark. But especially do banks honour the signature; certainly they will not honour anything which does not bear a signature—to them the signature is almost omnipotent, omniscient, omnipresent, supreme!

Now, though everyone who draws a cheque knows the importance of the signature to the bank, through bitter experience of cheques coming back with the usual slip if they do not bear the signature, or if the signature is slightly wanky or blurred, there are still two kinds of peoples who have not yet realized the value of the signature. These are respectively some of the feudal gentry who live in the 'Indian India' or the mofussil or on large estates in the country, and the very poor, who have no bank account to their credit at all.

Of course, it may be said in extenuation of the last class of people, that the reason why they dishonour the signature is because they have been left illiterate. For they do make every attempt to come to scratch when a document is presented to them by putting their thumb forward for the blacking and imprint the very image of their soul, the mark of that stumpy, reliable finger on the page, thus honouring the unwritten convention that a mark of some kind is necessary in order to prove a person's integrity. But the conspicuous disregard of this convention by the former class of people, the feudal gentry, is rather surprising, to say the least, and betokens an attitude which, though rather charming,

causes serious difficulties, particularly to the business of banking—
so the bankers say.

The banks, nowadays, are trying very hard to interest the feudal
gentry to convert their gold into cash and let it flow so that money
should not remain buried in the earth in the classic tradition of our
country and make a Midas of every grandee. But, as the nobility is
incorrigibly lazy in appreciating the values of modernity, there is a
polite war going on between the nobility of the old world and the
nobility of the new order.

Perhaps one cannot call the tension that prevails between these
brothers a polite war so much as a war of politeness, for there is no ill
will in this struggle or hatred or even contempt; there is only a certain
impatience or irritation which is so often followed by laughter that it
is more amusement than disdain.

One of the most amusing illustrations of this little war was provided
the other day by the goings on between Nawab Luqman Ali Khan
Bahadur, nobleman and dignitary of Aliabad State, a Director of the
India and Commonwealth Bank Ltd and Mr C. Subramaniam, Assistant
Manager of this bank.

The India and Commonwealth Bank Ltd is a small but steady bank
founded about ten years ago, which has, with the coming of freedom,
been seeking to increase its business to contribute something to the
making of the new India. In pursuance of this very laudable desire,
they had recently promised a big loan on good interest to a new
optical industry which was being set up by an enterprising young
entrepreneur, against the most unquestionably sound guarantees. The
papers were ready and had been duly signed by all the directors, save
Nawab Luqman Ali Khan Bahadur. That was the situation and there
was nothing very complicated or controversial about it. But Nawab
Luqman Ali Khan, who had been sent the papers several weeks ago,
had not just taken the trouble to sign them and return them.
Meanwhile, the enterprising entrepreneur felt that the people of India
were fast going blind for want of good eyeglasses, and the bank's
normal business was held up.

The manager of the bank, Mr Hormusji Pestonji Captain, wrote many letters, reminding Nawab Sahib Bahadur about his signature on the documents, but there was no reply.

As on all those occasions, when there is no answer to a letter and people begin to worry and postulate the most extraordinary fears and establish the strangest hypothesis, Mr Captain began to think all kinds of things and got into a panic. The documents may have been looted on the way to Aliabad, he felt, for quite a few trains had been held up by armed gangs recently and ransacked; or the Nawab may have fallen prey to a stray bullet in a riot, or he may have gone away to Pakistan. Anything was possible. And, as he waited day after day, the whole business became very nerve-wracking, for the other directors might soon get to know that this loan was still pending and may feel he was inefficient.

So, after much worrying, he thought of a desperate strategem: he would send the assistant manager, Mr Subramaniam, to see Nawab Luqman Ali Khan at Aliabad and get his signature on all the documents. Subramaniam had won his way to assistant managership of the bank by dint of his command of figures, as well as his fingers, and a certain sullen efficiency which, though not exactly American, was typical of the new Indian pioneers. Therefore Mr Captain sent Mr Subramaniam to Aliabad, not by rail, as that was not quick enough now after the Nawab's delays, but by air.

To the hard-working Subramaniam, who had, during twenty year's grind, got into a certain exact and unvaried relationship with the office-table and chair, this air trip was an extraordmary adventure and not altogether pleasant. For one thing, he was told by friends that it would be very cold in the air, and he went to the airline office loaded with a holdall full of blankets which made his luggage so heavy that he had to pay excess from his own pocket. Then, his digestion, trained on 'sambhar' and 'rasam', revolted at the very first bite on the biscuits served by the air-hostess, and he felt, and looked, like a shrivelled up procupine all the way. A further affliction was that at the midway station, where breakfast was served, he had to eat with implements other than those with which he had been used to eat in his orthodox life before. And, he made a fool of himself in the eyes of a couple of Indian dandies who were meticulous with their knives and forks and snobbishly contemptuous of those who were not so adroit. And, when at last he alighted from the bus at the airline office in the main street of Aliabad, he found himself in an incredibly native atmosphere where everyone was dressed in flowing Indian robes and he felt like a monkey in his badly tailored suit.

He tried to look for a taxi, but though some lovely Buicks glided by, there was no motor vehicle available for hire. Perforce, he had to jump on to a strange horse carriage called yekka, from which his legs dangled like the legs of a scarecrow which was being transported to the fields. And all he could see being sold in the shops were colourful bangles and velvet shoes and 'pan-biri'. Subramaniam, who had gone halfway to modernity, thought that he had come to the backwoods and felt very depressed about it all, added to which was the usual panic at going to a strange place.

When he got to Zeenat Mahal, the palace of the Nawab Sahib Bahadur, he was further confused. For all the servants, sitting around the hubble-bubble in the hall, gave him the once-over, cocked their eyes at each other and remained immobile. Apparently, they had been trained only to bow and scrape to the other noblemen of Aliabad, and a mere Madrasi, with pince-nez, arriving in an yekka was not persona grata.

Mr Subramaniam produced his card and asked to see Nawab Luqman Ali Khan Sahib.

This time it was the servants and retainers who were confused, for no one had, within living memory, produced a white ticket of that kind with the request that it be transported to the Nawab sahib.

The jemadar took it with gingerly fingers, and as Mr Subramaniam added a staccato phrase in Angrezi speech, this dignitary ran towards the inner sanctums like a lame duck. Meanwhile, the other servants dispersed like wizened cocks fluttering away from the rubbish heap at the approach of a human being.

Mr Subramaniam began to settle the yekka-driver, who unlike the Bombay gari-wallahs, immediately accepted what he was given, salaamed and went off.

The jemadar emerged after protracted confabulations inside the sanctums of the palace and led Mr Subramaniam towards a little guest house beyond the garden in the courtyard of the palace.

Mr Subramaniam waited for a word of explanation which would provide the clue to what was happening to him, but the jemadar was silent, only being most polite and accommodating, bowing and salaaming now in a manner that seemed more than obsequious. And then he left Mr Subramaniam with the words: 'Please rest and wait.'

Mr Subramaniam took off his jacket and his shoes and lay back in the armchair in, the veranda. In a little while, a servant came and apprised him of the fact that the bath was ready. This made Mr Subramaniam feel that things were moving after all. But, when he had finished his bath, changed into a new suit and come to rest in the armchair with a tea tray in front of him, and nothing happened again, except the passage of time on his wristwatch, he began to feel anxious. The laws of politeness in a Muhammadan household did not permit him to probe into any corner, even of the garden, lest there should be someone in purdah whose chastity might be outraged by the glance of a stranger's eye. The servants seemed to have disappeared. And Mr Subramanaim's hold on Hindustani speech was too precarious to permit him to shout and call the jemadar.

As the afternoon advanced towards the evening, Mr Subramaniam's anxiety became a little more akin to irritation. And he began to pace up and down the veranda almost as though he was a prisoner of time. But this parade was not of much avail, and after he had walked to and fro for a quarter of an hour he sat down again and began to write a letter to the Nawab sahib.

When he was halfway through the letter, Nawab Luqman Ali Khan Sahib appeared, a jolly, rotund figure, dressed in a spotless-white silk uchkin, tight trousers and a strange Aliabad-style round turban, with no parting in front. And he was the very soul of affability, charm, grace and good humour. For he greeted Mr Subramaniam almost as though the assistant manager was a long-lost friend.

'I hope you had a nice journey. And have my servants been looking after you?. . . . Of course, you can't expect the comfort of such a modern city as Bombay in my humble abode. But we have a few modern places, you know . . . For instance, there is the Aliabad Club. I am just going there and you must come and meet my friends . . .'

'Sir, I would like to discuss those papers with you,' Mr Subramaniam interrupted. 'You see, sir, I have specially come to get your signature . . .'

'Oh come, come, my dear fellow, you take work too seriously. After all you have just arrived and you must see a bit of life. To be sure, we are not as advanced as you in Bombay, but . . . And we shall see about business matters tomorrow morning. After all it doesn't take long to put my signature on a paper . . . Come, don't worry. I want you particularly to meet Nawab Haider Ali, the Home Minister, and Nawab Wajid Mahmud, the Education Minister, and Prof. Ram Ratan Gupta—Mr Gupta is our Finance Minister here. He is a wizard. He can count anything at a moment's notice . . . Come along now . . .' And he slapped Subramaniam's back with such cordiality that the poor south Indian nearly broke into two.

Soon, however, Mr Subramaniam found himself seated in a beautiful Dodge and being dodged away across intricate bazaars towards the cantonment and then through the magnificent portals of the Aliabad Club into the monumental palace which housed this august institution.

But, while the drive was fairly diverting, because the Nawab sahib kept up a running commentary on the wonders of Aliabad, Mr Subramaniam's small soul, brought up on an occasional shivering visit to the C.C.I., shuddered with the fear of the unknown on his entry into the hall and shrank into nothingness in the face of the grandees who were assembled here in silk robes and golden turbans and velvet shoes. And, when he was introduced to the various dignitaries, and they rose to shake hands with him, the forefingers of his right hand, with which he usually touched other people's hands, simply wilted like the falling petals of a dirty flower. One dignitary, Nawab Wajid Mahmud, took it upon himself to instruct Mr Subramaniam in the art of shaking hands, 'You know, my friend,' this nobleman began, 'the handshake is the symbol of affection and goodwill. Let this love show itself with some warmth. When a person's hand clasps yours, give your full hand, with its real grip and not the four miserable fingers . . .'

This overwhelmed Mr Subramaniam, until he blushed, flushed and began to perspire profusely. And, all he wanted was to be able to come to scratch, for there was no denying that this was life, brimming over, as it were, with warmth and hospitality. But his eyeglasses were blurred with the smoke of confusion and he was intensely relieved when he could sink back into a chair and contract into the littlest and most insignificant being on earth.

Nawab Luqman Ali Khan Sahib was much in demand. And for a while he went about meeting his friends. Meanwhile, the waiter who looked like a nawab himself, brought a bottle of whisky and some tumblers and began to pour out the liquor.

Soon Nawab Luqman Ali brought the Home Minister and the Finance Minister around.

Mr Subramaniam had tasted whisky twice or thrice and liked it, but his wife had smelt his breath and had given him a long lecture about how he was going to the dogs. Since then he had found it easier to resist the temptation, but the pursuasive tongue of the Nawab sahib, his host, moved him, especially as the other noblemen added their 'please' to his, in a most gracious Hindustani speech. And then the samosas and pakoras arrived, with lashings of podina pickle, and the southerner in Mr Subramaniam felt the call of chillies and forgot all about his wife and Morarji Desai.

Soon he was happy, happier than he had been for years, and those delicate negotiations for which he had been sent here were obliterated by the fumes of alcohol and the seven-course dinner to which Nawab Wajib Mahmud, the Education Minister, insisted on taking the company in the club Dining Room after the appetizers.

Mr Subramaniam slept soundly that night and was as good as dead to the world.

The next morning he felt the existence of a slight hangover.

When he had sufficiently recovered his senses, it was about noon. He finished his previous day's letter to the Nawab sahib and sent that in, requesting him to sign the documents.

There was no answer. Only the jemadar duly returned to the hall and sat smoking the hubble-bubble.

And when Mr Subramaniam made so bold as to inquire about the papers, the jemadar replied that the Nawab sahib was still asleep, but that he was due to wake up soon, for there was to be a midday meal in honour of Mr Subramaniam, to which various friends of the Nawab sahib were coming.

Mr Subramaniam felt more frustrated than flattered on hearing this announcement. And then, there was the residue of guilt in his callow soul about his fall the previous evening. So he began to pace up and down the veranda of the guest house again and, fatigued by this useless occupation, he sat back in the armchair and tried to cultivate patience.

The warmth of the morning conduced to a light slumber and he only awoke when the jemadar shook him and told him the meal was ready and the guests had arrived.

If the dinner at the club had been a comparatively mild seven-course meal, the lunch at the Nawab sahib's house was hospitality in the proper sense of that word, as it is understood in Aliabad. There were saffron tinted 'pilaos' and rich 'kormas', tasty 'kababs' and fish, and fowl, cooked in the most luscious gravies. And even though Mr Subramaniam took a little of everything, his stomach, which was about the size of his fist or less, took in more than was good for him. And he found himself feeling drowsier and drowsier and could not even cope with the polite conversation about finance which Mr Ram Ratan Gupta had started, far less bring the Nawab sahib, his host, to talk of anything so concrete as those documents.

Nawab Luqman Ali Khan himself took the initiative to remind him during lunch that after siesta that afternoon, he would bring out the papers to the guest house and go over them if Allah so willed it.

But Allah did not will it so. For though Mr Subramaniam kept a vigil against all the seductions of sleep that afternoon, the Nawab was deep in slumber till the evening. And then he came like a whirlwind to ask Mr Subramaniam to get dressed to go to the dinner to which Mr Ram Ratan Gupta had graciously invited them. 'Don't worry about the papers,' he added. 'I have got them out and they are lying on my bedside table to sign first thing tomorrow morning.'

So vociferously persuasive was the Nawab sahib in imparting this information that Mr Subramaniam could not put a word in edgeways. And, perforce, he went in and began to dress for dinner.

The dinner in Mr Subramaniam's honour, given by Mr Gupta, was as rich and sumptuous as the lunch given by Nawab Luqman Ali Khan; only, the number of vegetable dishes exceeded the meat dishes. But the general nature of hospitality was the same till Mr Subramaniam began to recognize the unmistakable pattern of grace in Aliabad. There even followed the 'chain effect'; Nawab Haider Ali suggested that it was his turn to invite Mr Subramaniam now and that he would be happy if the honoured guest, and the rest of the company, would come to the hunting lodge of his estate that very evening, for he had received a message from his shikaris that a tiger had eaten the goat tied near the machan and was likely to repeat its visit. The laws of Aliabad hospitality demanded an acceptance of this noble suggestion and the company got into cars and was off into the depths of the night, illumined by a million stars.

The food and drink had broken the defences in Mr Subramaniam's soul enough for him to lend himself to the seductions of this drive. Never before in his life had he tasted the delights of so novel an adventure as a tiger hunt. And though he felt a slight hazard in this game, the fresh air, and the impact of the dense forests through which they were passing, made him forget everything and yield to a 'no care' attitude. As for those documents, how could one think anything so obscene in the midst of this vast anonymity where nature seemed to cancel out all questions, especially banking?

And later, the exhaustion of the tense wait for the tiger to appear, as they sat on top of the 'machan', blotted out even his sense of individuality.

The tiger did not oblige the hunters by appearing. And after a hearty breakfast, served in Nawab Haidar Ali's hunting lodge, the party returned home, only to go to bed when the rest of mankind had begun to resume its hold on work.

Mr Subramaniam slept the clock round.

And when he woke up, he suddenly found himself in a panic. It was strange how this confusion had come on him. But he sensed disaster. And, true to his prognostications, disaster it was that overtook him. For the jemadar came and told him that the Nawab sahib had been urgently called away to his estates in Madhopur and had left a message that Mr Subramaniam sahib was to wait till his return.

'But when will he return?' asked Subramaniam.

'Nawab sahib did not say,' answered the jemadar.

'How long does he go for when he does go to his estate?'

'Maybe a month, may be a week, huzoor.'

Mr Subramaniam let out an involuntary shriek of horror, which he later tried to disguise as the belchings of an over-taxed stomach. His whole body was warm with the heat of anger, resentment, fear and forced ingratitude.

'Go and fetch the papers from the Nawab's bedside table,' he said to the jemadar.

The jemadar paused for a moment and looked askance at him.

Mr Subramaniam understood. He took a ten-rupee note from his pocket and gave it to the servant.

'Fetch the papers and get my luggage ready,' he said. 'And hurry up for God's sake, hurry up! . . .'

The jemadar obeyed the commands of the honoured guest implicitly. What was more, he put the documents, Mr Subramaniam, and the luggage, into the Ford which was waiting outside the hall and bade him a most respectful farewell.

Mr Subramaniam took the night train back to Bombay, having to sleep on the floor of the second-class carriage because he had not booked his berth in advance.

He was shivering with the ague of a terrible fear when he arrived at Victoria Terminus the next morning, for he was sure that he would be sacked as soon as he appeared at the bank.

But Mr Hormusji Pestonji Captain understood all as soon as the papers were put before him without the signature of the Nawab on them. He only asked Mr Subramaniam to look for the documents on which the first and only signature of Nawab Luqman Ali Khan appeared. And he had a rubber stamp made of this precious mark, impression or whatever you would like to call it. And he soon had the necessary papers ready to sanction the loan to the entrepreneur who had set his heart on preventing the people of India from going blind. And he cursed himself for not having thought of this simple expedient earlier.

'What is there so wonderful in a sala signature!' he said like an efficient Parsi.

Mr Subramaniam lifted his eyes from the desk and signified agreement with a terrific forward movement of his abject little head and torso.

The Parrot in the Cage

'Rukmaniai ni Rukmaniai,' the parrot in the cage called in the way Rukmani's friends used to call her when they entered the alleyway of Kucha Chabuk Swaran in Lahore. And he repeated the call even before she could answer him as she was wont to do when she wanted to humour the bird. She did not answer but sat crouching on the fringe of the road about half a furlong away from the Amritsar court.

'Rukmaniai ni Rukmaniai!' the parrot called again.

She was peering through the little clouds of dust raised by the passing motors and tongas and yekkas in the direction from which, she had been told by the roasted gram stall-keeper, the Dipty Collator was to come and she remained heedless to the parrot's cry.

'Rukmaniai ni Rukmaniai!' the parrot called shrilly and went on repeating the cry with the sure mocking bird's instinct that if he kept on calling her she would answer.

'Han, my son, han . . .' the old woman said, after all, wearily. There had been a dull ache behind the small knot of hair on the back of her head and, now, with the mounting heat of the September morning, it seemed to her like the rumblings of the dreadful night when murder and fire had raged in her lane.

Little rivulets of sweat trickled through the deep fissures of old age which lined her face and she shaded her eyes with the inverted palm of her hand to probe the sunlight more surely for the vision of the Deputy Commissioner. Her contracted, toothless mouth was open and a couple of flies came from the direction in which she looked and settled on the corners of her lips.

She waved her left hand gingerly to scatter the flies. But they persisted and set up an irritation in her soul through which she felt a panic sieze her belly.

'Ni tu kithe hain?' the parrot cried another cry which he had learnt from the old woman's friends, who invariably asked on entering the lane, 'Where are you?', for she used to be away earning her living as a maid of all work, cleaning utensils for the people in the bigger houses in the lane or was mostly hidden from view in the inner sanctums of the dark ground-floor room by the well in the gulley.

'Son, I don't know where I am . . .' she said listlessly, in the effort to keep the parrot quiet by assuring him she was taking notice of him. 'I only know that if Fato had not given me her burqah to escape with, I should not be here . . .'

'Ni tu ki karni hain?' the parrot persisted with the third call which Rukmani's friends used to call.

'Nothing, son, I am doing nothing . . . only waiting . . .' the old woman said tiredly, as though now she was holding a metaphorical conversation with her pet to keep her mind occupied. For, from her entrails arose a confusion which was like the panic she had felt at the mad throats bursting with shouts of 'Allah ho Akbar!', 'Har har Mahadev!', 'Sat Sri Akal!', on the night of terror when she had fled from the lane.

There had been flashes of blazing light; cracking of burning housebeams; smoke, smoke, choking smoke. And she had thought that her last days had come, that the earth itself was troubled through the misdeeds of the Kaliyug and that soon the dharti would open up and swallow everything . . . And then Fato had come and told her she would be murdered if she did not leave.

'Ni tu ki karni hain?' the parrot repeated. 'Ni tu kithe hain? . . .'

'Nothing, son, nothing,' Rukmani answered. 'And I don't know where I am . . .' And as she looked steadily towards the junction of the Mall Road and Kutchery Road and saw no sign of the Deputy Commissioner, her last phrase seemed to get meaning.

'Rukmaniai ni Rukmaniai!' the parrot called again.

Her answers to his shrill, metallic nasal cries did not irritate her any more, but relieved the heavy pressure of the demons of the dreadful night on her head and her chest and her bowels.

'Ni tu ki karni hain?' the parrot persisted.

'Son, I am waiting for the sahib, so that he can give me some money to buy bread with . . . They say that the Congress Sarkar will give back what we have lost, son, they say—I heard at the tation, son, at the satation! . . . Are you hungry, my son—you must be hungry. I shall buy you some gram from that stall-keeper when the sahib gives me money . . .'

'Mai, you are dreaming! You have gone mad!' the gram stall-keeper said. 'Go, go your way to the town, you may get some food at the Durbar Sahib temple. You won't get anything from the Dipty Collator . . .'

'Vay jaja, eater of your masters!' she shouted bitterly. Such common sense as that of the complacent gram-seller seemed to break the pitcher of her hopes. And she mooed like a cow in defiance at the end of her speech.

'Acha, don't abuse me. I only said this for your own good,' the stall-keeper answered as he whisked the flies off his stall with the end of a dirty apron.

'Oh, why did I leave home to wander like this from door to door!' old Rukmani whined almost under her breath. 'Oh, why did you have to turn me out of my room in my old age, God . . . Oh why . . . why didn't I tie the rupees I had earned in a knot on my dupatta! . . . Hai Rabba! . . .'

She moaned to herself, and tremors of tenderness went swirling through her flesh. And tears filled her eyes. And in the hazy dust before her, the violent rhythms of the terrors of falling houses and dying, groaning men and heavy, shouting men, danced in macabre trembling waves of sunlight, dim and unsubstantial like the ghosts on a cremation ground before whom she had always cowered every time she had attended a funeral.

'Rukmaniai ni Rukmaniai!' the parrot called and brought her to herself.

Crackling flames of heat now assailed her. And she sweated more profusely. And yet she crouched where she was, only shuffling like a hen sitting over her eggs.

'At least go and sit under the shade of the tree,' the gram-seller said.

The pupils of her eyes were blistering with the glare. She wiped her face with the end of her dupatta and heaved as though she was lifting the weight of a century's miseries up with her. Then she took the handle of the iron cage in which her pet parrot sat, and bent-backed but staring ahead, ambled up to a spot where the precarious shadow of a kikar tree lay on the rutted earth.

'Ni tu kithe hain? Ni . . .' the parrot's monologue continued. So did her self-communings, aroused by the anonymous, meaningless, repetitive calls, 'Nowhere, son, nothing, nothing . . .'

She had hardly settled down when suddenly a motor whirred past, with a motor cyclist ahead and some policemen in a jeep behind, scattering much dust on the fringe of the roadside.

'There goes your "Dipty Collator",' said the gram stall-keeper.

'Hai, hai! Come, my son!' she screamed as she shot up with great alacrity and picked up the cage in her hand. 'Come, I will join my hands to the sahib and fall at his feet.'

'Mad woman!' the gram-seller said cynically.

She heeded him not, but penetrated the clouds of dust.

Behind her, and on all sides, she could hear the sound of rushing feet storming towards the gloomy gates of the kutchery. And their cries whirled in the air, 'Huzoor, mai–bap, hear us! Sarkar! Dipty sahib! . . . We have come on foot all the way from Lahore . . . You . . .' She nearly fell as the more powerful men among the crowd brushed past her and their own women.

'Rukmaniai! Tu kithe hain?' the parrot in the cage cried even as he fluttered his wings in a panic at the voices and the hurtling feet.

The old woman did not answer but sped grimly on. Only, in a moment, the dust storm which was proceeding towards the court was turned back by a furious whirlwind from the opposite direction. A posse of policemen charged the refugees with lathis and angry shouts which drowned the chorus of voices of which Rukmani's sighs and her parrot's cries had been a part.

In the delirium of motion which was set afoot by the lathi charge of the police, all valour was held at bay and turned back.

Rukmani was brushed aside by some desperate arm until she reeled and fell not far from where she had sat waiting for the sahib. But she clung to the handle of the cage in which her parrot sat as she lay moaning in suppressed, helpless whispers.

The parrot was fluttering furiously as though he was being strangled and called out shrilly, 'Rukmaniai ni Rukmaniai! Ni tu kithe hain? . . . Ni tu ki karni hain?'

But the old woman, though concerned for him, had turned in upon herself with a sudden dimness that seemed to be creeping upon her.

After the crowd had been cleared, and the dust settled, the gram-seller was irritated by the parrot's constant cries into stirring from his perch. He was afraid that the old woman had expired. But as he came near her, the parrot called her more shrilly and she answered faintly, 'Han, han, son, han,' and the man knew that she was still alive. He lifted her up and found that her hands and arms were slightly grazed.

'Come and sit in the shade, mother,' he said.

'Acha, son, acha!' she moaned. And she lifted the cage and proceeded towards the shade.

The parrot was a little reassured as he saw the gram-seller helping his mistress and he shrieked less shrilly.

'Come, my little winged one, I shall give you some gram to eat,' the gram-seller said to him.

'May you live long, son!' the old woman blessed the gram-seller in a feeble, strained moanful voice.

'Rukmaniai ni Rukmaniai! Tu kithe hain? Tu ki karni hain? . . .' the parrot called now in a slow measured voice.

'Han, han, son, han, my son . . . I don't know where I am! I don't know . . .'

The Man Who Loved Monkeys More Than Human Beings

Like many noblemen of our country, Raja Rajeshwar Rao, the landlord of Hanumanpur in central India, was very proud of his ancient lineage. But whereas most of our aristocrats are content to trace their ancestry to the Sun, the Moon, to one of the thirty-three crores of Hindu gods and goddesses, or to the kings and heroes of olden times, the zamindar of Hanumanpur brought a touch of modernity to the definition of his pedigree. The fact that he was the first citizen of Hanumanpur and descended from the oldest family of this township had, of course, long ago established the claim of his family that they were descended from the monkey-god Hanuman, who had helped the god-king Ram to defeat Ravan, the demon-king of Lanka, the abductor of Ram's consort, Sita. But Raja Rajeshwar Rao had been to a science college in Bangalore and, there, come strongly under the influence of Darwin and Spencer. So, on ascending his ancestral gaddi, as he came of age (for his father had died when he was seven years old and he had been brought up under a court of wards), he made an historic proclamation, which will go down as a very important dictum in the annals of our time. He said that since, according to Darwin, all men were descended from apes, and since his was the only family which claimed direct descent from the monkey-god Hanuman, therefore his family was the oldest in the world and supplied the missing link that had been lost in the process of evolution.

The audience in the court, where the young Raja was installed on the throne, was composed of the members of his brotherhood, the feudal lords, the managers and officials of the estate, the representative of His Exalted Highness the Nizam, who was overlord of Hanumanpur, and the people of the small kingdom. And, needless to say, they all clapped and shouted 'long live Raja Rajeshwar Rao' at the end of almost every sentence that he pronounced. And they were even fascinated by the prolonged exposition of Darwinism that he gave. And their sense of wonderment at the miracles achieved by science, and their admiration for their master's wisdom, knew no bounds when he told them further that the anthropoid apes could be brought down from the trees and taught to stand upright. Stupendously miraculous, indeed, was the further information which Raja Rajeshwar Rao imparted—that it would be possible in the future to train chimpanzees at military academies to imitate soldiers and stand upright! In this way, more blood would go to their craniums and they would develop more effective nervous systems. Thus, with larger brains and more refined sensibilities, the apes would attain the mental abilities of the average soldier or the peasant, and could be good substitutes for the recalcitrant sepoy and the farmer.

In the general applause which followed the dispensation of such information, the people assembled at the coronation durbar did not realize the full implications of the posture theory of human intelligence. But towards the end of the Raja sahib's speech came a pronouncement of which the meaning was quite clear. Raja Rajeshwar Rao was heard to say that he was henceforward going to make over half of his estate to the monkeys in his kingdom, so that they could be treated as on a par with other men, fed well on grain and slowly trained to cross the borderline which yet divides them from humanity, even as in the remote past his own ancestors had jumped one stage in the history of evolution and become men.

No claps or shouts followed this proclamation. For the vista opened up before the peasants, assembled for the celebrations, was depressingly ominous in days when rack-renting and the other burdens of the landlord–tenant relationship had already brought them to the verge of collapse. The farmers had really come expecting to hear that the new master, who was said to have learnt upto the BA class, and was a follower of Jawaharlal Nehru, would announce the cancellation of arrears of rent and interest on debt, and would distribute the unfilled fields among the needy. Instead, what they had got was the reservation of half the estate for the welfare of the monkeys.

But everyone thought that it was a practical joke played by the young Raja on all and sundry since, they said, he did not like making pompous speeches, full of promises that he could not keep.

Unfortunately, however, Raja Rajeshwar Rao's words were followed by certain acts which left no doubt in the minds of the people that he meant what he said.

He actually had half the kharif crop for the year stored in granaries reserved for the monkeys, who were all lured from miles around to come and settle in a nearby deserted palace by the riverside which was said to be haunted by Goddess Kali. As the monsoon had behaved like a temperamental girl, keeping away from the earth and then falling passionately about its neck in a mad fury like that of Amrapali when young, all the tenants began to starve, specially those whose crops were confiscated.

The respect for his ancestors offered by Raja Rajeshwar Rao, and the posture theory of human intelligence that he had propounded, certainly spelled the doom of the peasantry. They saw before their dazzled eyes the vision of hundreds of monkeys eating good grain, and prodigally scattering it to the birds, while their own womenfolk cursed the Raja or sighed bitterly. Though traditionally soft-spoken, the peasants also consider the monkeys sacred as the ancestors of these animals formed the holy army of Sri Ram Chander ji Maharaj in his war against the rakshasa-king, Ravan. Thus they remained deplorably docile even as some of them began to die of hunger.

Not long, the strange situation was reached when the monkeys were seen to be seated almost upright, their shoulders well back and their chins pulled in, almost as though, by feeding well, if not because of the privileged position accorded to them, they had already achieved intellectual maturity, while the human beings, the peasants, who used to shoo them away from their fields and habitations, crouched with their heads in their hands or slumped over the ground, exhausted in the brain-destroying posture of the apes.

During the stalemate that prevailed, the prospects seemed to be clear that the apes were evolving and the humans were dissolving. For, more than the upright postures increasingly adopted by the monkeys, the ownership of the means of production, the seeds for the sowing of the next harvest, had passed on through the intervention of Raja Rajeshwar Rao to the monkeys.

At this stage, however, an incident happened which was ultimately to settle who was going to adopt what posture and help the processes of evolution and dissolution.

While a young lad Gopal, son of the peasant Thakur, was sweeping up some scattered grain from the courtyard of the royal granary to take home, a ferocious monkey bit at his right hand and drew out blood.

With that the respect for the monkeys of the younger part of the population of Hanumanpur evaporated. And, with the evaporation of this reverence, the docility in the face of the monkeys' ravages on grain meant for human consumption, also disappeared. And there was a regular battle between the apes and the humans, in which the enemies hurled stones and bricks at each other.

At first the older people of the estate, still under the influence of their age-old belief in the sanctity of the monkeys, stayed aloof, and even reprimanded their sons for annoying the descendants of the god-king Ram. But then they found the young bloods bleeding at the hands of the vicious monkeys. So they joined and drove the monkeys away from the granary into an adjoining field and into the Raja's palace.

When Raja Rajeshwar Rao heard that his cousins, the monkeys, were having the worst of it at the hands of the villagers, he was very incensed and got the village priest, Pandit Hari Das, to proclaim, by beat of drum, that anyone molesting the monkeys, the sacred descendants of the god Hanuman, who had helped Sri Ram Chander to beat the demon-king Ravan, would be declared a mlecha, an untouchable.

The older peasants withdrew through the fear of excommunication and the monkeys regained control of their granary.

But the taste of victory, and the desperate hunger in their homes, filled the young men of the village with an ardour which was proof against religious sentiment or brute strength. They broke down a whole brick wall and pelted the monkeys with a shower of this ammunition, until half the monkeys ran away and hid in the nearby trees.

Raja Rajeshwar Rao heard of the continuing battle and came with his police, and palace servants, to scatter the young villagers with staves and revolvers.

The fear of the police is ingrained in our peasant folk, and no one could last out against a lathi charge. The monkeys returned to the granary. And the peasants, old and young, were cowed down.

For a few days there was peace in the township, even though it was the peace of the grave, as the oldest men, and the youngest children, kept on dying through the strain of malnutrition.

Some of the peasants met in the panchayat and decided to go to the mad Raja to end the bitterness and despair that had arisen through his strange dictum. But Rajeshwar Rao was absolutely adamant. He said that he had decided to make the monkeys and men live like brothers, according to Mahatma Gandhi's teaching, and that he had passed orders for the confiscation of half the produce of the estate through his belief that in this way he will bring Ram Raj to his kingdom, besides proving a new theory of science, which may be of inestimable benefit to mankind.

After the delegation left, the young Raja felt that he had been carried away by his own words and was therefore somewhat remorseful. In this mood, he even thought of accepting an offer made in the papers by the Americans to buy up monkeys for good dollars. And he nearly sat down to write to the United States government a special memorandum on how monkeys could be trained to imitate the West Point military posture. But his inadequate mastery of the English language got in the way.

At last Gopal, son of the peasant Thakur, who had been the immediate cause of the struggle in Hanumanpur, thought of a story he had read in his schoolbook, the moral of which was that monkeys, though intelligent, were imitative. And he consulted with the village boys to apply the lesson of that story.

They got the barber's son to fetch some razors from his father's bag. One of these was thrown to the monkeys in the courtyard of the granary. With the other, Gopal began to shave himself, giving a special jerky motion at the throat, and then passing the razor on to the boy next to him and asking him to repeat what he had done.

One monkey in the courtyard imitated the operation of Gopal and fell dead. The next monkey repeated the jerky motion of the second boy near the throat and died. And so the next and the next. As the simple formula of pretended suicide was practised by the village lads on a chain and copied by the monkeys with that genius for aping man which had led Raja Rajeshwar Rao to propound his subtle theory, the bulk of the cousins of the young prince fell dead in the courtyard.

Encouraged by the extraordinary vision of the defeat of the monkeys at the hands of their sons, the cowardly elders of Hanumanpur, came and looted the granary and swaggered about as though they had secured the victory.

The remnants of the monkey army retreated to the Raja's palace and went on hunger strike for the restoration to them of their granary.

In the face of the young bloods of the town, Raja Rajeshwar Rao could not do anything for them.

Then the earlier brainwave passed through his crazed cranium again: he must cable America, making the offer for the sale of the monkeys for experimental purposes and earn some dollars, because it seemed certain that the tenants would force him out of his estate now.

Surprisingly enough, his offer was accepted. And, what is more, a physiologist of the University of Virginia found Raja Rajeshwar Rao's theory about teaching monkeys to stand upright coincident with his own prognostications about enabling anthropoid apes to function as houseboys and butlers. And it was not long before a scholarship was found, through which the young landlord and aristocrat was enabled to go to the new world for prosecuting further research on the posture theory of human intelligence.

Reflections on the Golden Bed

The lure of love and the lure of wealth are the two dominating passions of mankind today. They are so absorbing that men will murder other men and will resort to any expedient, even if they have to go out of their heads, to ensure the permanent hold of these obsessions on their hearts, minds and bodies. And, of the two vital impulses, the second is perhaps the older and more insidious. For, from the time that men began to tread the earth, they began to claim possession of it, of as much of it as their horses could walk over without getting tired. Then they began to reckon in terms of the cows they possessed, or the pigs they bred. Later, they summed up everything in the value left over when they traded their own animals for other people's beasts or birds; as, for instance, when the seller of cows bought up buffaloes, with a basket of chickens thrown in as huckster's profit. But, as they could not carry birds and beasts in their pockets to exchange with merchandise in far-off places, they began to carry clam shells and goat skins or metals of copper, silver and gold, stamped with the profiles of their kings. And these tokens began to signify, not only the belief in the value of the token which the buyer and seller shared, but also symbolized wealth itself. In our own time, the weight of copper, nickle, silver and gold began to play havoc with the sartorial dignity which left fewer and fewer pockets to carry wealth about in. So, the thin paper, which is called the bank note, or the thick paper which is called the cheque, began to express the faith of men in themselves, in each other, and in the future of mankind. Money became a more coveted ritualistic form than any practised by the cannibals.

Lalla Ram Narain, the cloth merchant who owned the big market called Ram Bazaar in Amritsar, was possessed of the lure of wealth. But so were the other lallas of his generation, the valiant pioneers who built up the industries in our country on the crest of the Swadeshi movement.

There was nothing very remarkable, therefore, in his mere preoccupation with money. His chief distinction lay in the fact that he wanted to be the biggest, the wealthiest and most powerful of all the wealthy men, not only in the provincial town where he had begun business, but in the whole of India. And though the spectacular ways in which he sought to amass his fortunes have become legendary all over our country, it was these very sensational methods of money-making that began to draw the attention of his rivals in business, of thieves, the income-tax department and of all those other blood-suckers and money-grabbers who were to give him battle in their various ways and bring about his ultimate downfall. The nobility and the assiduity with which he pursued his passion, however, and the devotion that he brought to the actual preservation of his gains from the pursuit of this passion, have almost given him the place of a near saint in the annals of our time. So that it is impossible for any fair-minded person not to dilate his eyes in sheer wonder at the love he gave to money, or to refuse to pay him the tribute of a sigh for the miraculous ways in which he clung to his faith when all seemed lost.

There is no particular mystery attaching to the particular ways in which Lalla Ram Narain sought to make money. From the time when he inherited a retail cloth shop at the Karmon Deorhi end of Bazaar Sabunian, he had believed that money is in the air, just as there are fishes in the water, and that you have only got to cast your net to catch it all up. This was too simple a story for his contemporaries to believe, and, for sheer spite, they were always insinuating that, like everyone else, in the money game, he must have resorted to all kinds of unconventional means to amass his fortune. But the few people who knew him and respected him, in spite of his eccentricities, believed that he was true to his word and as simple and straightforward in his business methods as he was in his other habits. In fact, the tragedy of his life was brought about by his essential simplicity, even as the comic phases of his experience were due to this ingrained quality.

If we bring that pity to the understanding of his career which is akin to love, we shall be fascinated to see how the petty tradesman in him prospered on the strength of an elementary hypothesis, and how he went down merely through the weakness of this elementary hypothesis.

For instance, it is wonderful to see the bare logic with which he captured the northern Indian textile trade before the war. He argued that there were nearly four hundred million people in India, men, women and children, who needed at least one new loincloth or dhoti every year, as the barest minimum covering to hide their nudity; and that if he could supply even one thousandth part of the demand for covering the private parts of Indian humanity, he would not only do service to the country, which Mahatma Gandhi was insisting upon, but he would make a modest fortune for himself. Surprisingly enough, this approach to the problem of supply and demand had not occurred to anybody else. And soon, Lalla Ram Narain's mills, as well as the various handloom industries he initiated in the villages of Punjab, were flooding the countryside with loincloths and dhotis. Neither Lancashire, with its high priced textiles, nor Japan, with its low priced cotton goods, could compete with him. For he was a model to the workmen engaged in his factories: he himself wore only a simple loincloth and a roughly-cut tunic, with indigenous, rough puthwar shoes, and a small turban on his pin head, in spite of his enormous gains as an industrialist. The labourers emulated his example and believed that each one of them could become like him if only they worked hard enough. And their hard work brought him higher dividends. And these dividends helped him to buy up a whole acre of built-up area in the most thickly populated part of the cloth market in Amritsar, which was named after him, Ram Bazaar.

The other businessmen, specially in the textile trade of this city, who saw Lalla Ram Narain's meteoric rise as an entrepreneur, were dumbfounded and rather angry. The more so, because this magnate kept to his old habits, not only in his habiliments, but also in the simple food he ate, mainly lentil curry with two vegetables and three chapatis per meal, and a tumbler of whey to gulp it all down with. He even practised, with a rigid discipline, the routine of his daily constitutional, going for a walk and a bath at the canal at dawn, and for a ride in his closed Victoria to the Ram Bagh gardens every evening. And, as the public institution which was Lalla Ram Narain, began to assume the form of a legend, the anger of the other lallas turned to bitter resentment and malice. 'He is a miser,' they would say. 'Look at his broken shoes!' Unfortunately for them, he remained unaffected by their jealousy, even when the first gossip campaign became loud-mouthed attack on the occasion of his buying up ten of the fourteen cotton and textile mills in the Punjab. And not content with abusive words, his competitors resorted to direct action: they hired an incendiary and set fire to the whole of Ram Bazaar, where Lallaji had invested his money in real estate and kept his immense stocks of textiles stored up. The frequency of the strikes in the new mills he had bought, with the loss of working days, was another blow dealt to him by his rivals, until his finances nearly collapsed, and he had to sell out half his mills in order to keep afloat in the sea of existence. The remaining mills were not long in his hand, for the income tax department was persuaded to examine his books and, finding discrepancies, penalized him adequately.

Ostensibly, he remained unaffected by the misfortunes that came to him. He would see the gleeful smiles with which the people in the cloth market gloated over his failure, and he knew how they mimicked his walk and his talk behind his back, and spread all kinds of stories about his meanness in the bazaars; but he seemed calm. His outer calm was, however, no index of the pain that pervaded his spirit and sometimes reached to his tingling heart and created perspiration on the top of his head, near his tuft knot, and in the soles of his feet, almost like the fear of death that sprang from somewhere in his eyes, and became an unshed tear, the instinctive recoil of his body against the thought of passing away. And this chemical process created a new kind of metabolism in him, making his taste in food simpler still, and the outlook of his pale face more demure and placid than it had been ever before. And, whereas, he sometimes used to order a four-anna worth of sugar candy from the confectioner's shop by the entrance to the tank of Santokh Sar, as well as an occasional afternoon treat of white flour puris with mango pickle, he dropped all these luxuries and saved his pocket money in the iron safe by which he leaned as he sat in his old shop near the Darshan Deorhi.

The sparks of energy from which had risen the urge to make his first fortunes still smouldered in him, however, and the sinister men, who surrounded him on all sides, only roused the blood in his veins, till he was energy and energy only, working day and night with plans to rehabilitate himself. And through the perennial flow that welled up in him, he was able to conjure up many visions, which became more and more refulgent, especially when he remembered God, and which gave him a single-minded obsession to get back as much as he had lost in the textile venture and a million times more. And, one day, the inspiration came to him that in order to satisfy himself, at the core of his being, he initiate some business where he could actually handle coins, if not to touch them, at least to see them in great, big heaps, or wads of notes; for only the sensations of actual contiguity with money could satisfy him and give the necessary faith in himself and in his ability to go on working and living. Immediately it occurred to him to found a bank in which he could keep all his own money, as well as other people's money, in vaults which he could enter every day and where he could bathe his eyes in the light of cash to his heart's content. So he forthwith started the Ram Narain Banking Corporation, with an authorized capital of ten crores and subscribed capital of two crores.

Lalla Ram Narain brought to this venture the same genius for simplicity that he had used to achieve his magnificent triumphs in the textile trade. 'If you lend money on interest,' he argued, 'your initial investment will swell ultimately by itself.' Fortunately for him, the opening of his bank coincided with a money famine, and soon he was able to do so well with the banking corporation as to increase the subscribed capital, most of which came from the excess money that accrued to him. As this business flourished, he forgot all about his childlike dream of going to see piles of gold coins and wads of notes for the sheer pleasure of looking at them, but he even felt a little ashamed of this foolish idea which he had practised in the beginning of the venture, specially when somebody deliberately told him the story of King Midas and of the sorry fate of this king because of his love for money.

About this time, Lalla Ram Narain, with his addiction to the simple life, in the service of his country, and the love of expanding its influence, came under the spell of Mahatma Gandhi's ideas rather more intensely than before, though he had toyed with these ideas ever since the first Swadeshi movement. He adventured into a satyagraha campaign and went to jail for three months. And he fell foul of the British Raj. And, in the uncanny way in which things used to happen in those days, Lalla Ram Narain came out of jail and found himself on the verge of bankruptcy through the failure of his bank: his enemies had done mischievous propaganda, which had led the depositors to pull out their money suddenly and leave Lalla Ram Narain with nothing in the vaults to look at and caress with that light in his eyes which hungered for the flashing beauty of silver and gold. His wife, Premi, who had encouraged him to follow Gandhi, died suddenly of pneumonia and he was left alone to face the awful world.

The spiritual change which occurred in the tormented soul of Lalla Ram Narain, after the failure of his bank, was more serious than the transformation which had been brought by the failure of his textile venture. He was getting on in life, having attained the age of sixty. And he felt he just could not go on without Premi by his side. And he would sit for long hours recalling to his mind the first flush of enthusiasm which had inspired him to his early successes; and he would remember the favourites among his mills, as also the summits of gold coins piled in the vaults of his bank, smiling like the pollen of the sunflowers; and he would see brief glimpses of the marble corridors, stairways and huge counters of the enormous building which had housed his bank.

One day, however, as he sat absorbed in reverie, his mind went back to the heaps of jewellery which he and his wife had hidden in the earth in the old house of his forefathers. He recalled that, through the shock of her death, and the bitter memories of the disillusionment that had followed the failure of his bank, he had forgotten all about these lovely, rich ornaments, which were worth nearly ten lakhs of rupees. His spirit revived suddenly and he seemed to become young again.

This vision was vouchsafed to Lalla Ram Narain while he was dozing against the dirty cow-tailed cushion of his old shop. He literally ran home and, locking the back room from which the wooden ladder led into the basement, went down to the underground cellar. With pickaxe and shovel, he dug furiously in the corner where the main pitcher, containing the jewellery, had been buried by his wife. He found it difficult going, and he had to persist almost till midnight over the hard gravel and brick, before reaching the mouth of the pitcher. He did not quite remember whether his wife had been so careful as to have a mixture of cement and sand put in on the top layers, and he felt somewhat apprehensive. As he put his hand in the pitcher, however, the apprehension turned into fear. And the deeper the hand went, the more the fear turned into panic, until the tips of his fingers touched the bottom of the pitcher through the vacuum and he sat back, sweating and with palpitating heart, in utter confusion at the mysterious disappearance of the jewellery. The thought struck him that, before her death, his wife may have emptied the contents of the big pitcher and put the jewellery away in other pitchers. So he began to dig up the various corners of the room one by one. When the second corner refused to yield up anything more than a vacuum, and the experience was repeated in the third corner, he knew that there had been foul play. The emptiness of the pitcher in the fourth corner confirmed his prognostications. And he crawled up and lay down prostrate on his bed with a fever which did not leave him for months afterwards.

During his long illness, he realized that his wife's relations had somehow come to know of the secret places in which the jewellery had been buried and had taken it away during the time when he went to Hardwar to throw her ashes into the Ganges.

The kind attention of his old doctors had just enabled him slowly to get rid of his fever, when the Second World War broke out. Most people thought he would have a relapse and never recover again from his seemingly mortal illness. But the war seemed to bring in him an added zest for living, probably because he immediately saw the possibilities of gain arising from it. Before long he was toing and froing between Delhi and Simla, and had secured a contract to make uniforms for the army. And, during the six years of the bloody world struggle, he not only recaptured the riches and power of the days of his first adventure in the textile industry, but also earned some glory, being knighted for his services to the British Empire.

Somehow or the other, things were never the same as they had been when he had entered business in the pristine purity of his Punjabi simplicity. For the moral guilt of having once been a follower of Gandhi, a supporter of the Swadeshi movement and non-violence, and ultimately making money through the war effort, corroded the deeper foundations of his will. On the other hand, there was a compensation in the fact that, towards the end of his life, he had pulled himself together and regained the fortune he had lost. And he continued to enjoy the simple routine of his life, fairly unperturbed by his conflicts. Especially, as during the past war years, he began to donate large sums of money which had accrued in his ledger without being accounted for, to religious causes of various kinds.

But the surface emotions which arise from the donation of money to temples and charities do not seem to have much effect on the fundamental values of a man of such calibre as was Lalla Ram Narain. From somewhere deep in his nature, there would arise tremendous depressions, which held him prisoner for days and cast a gloom on everything around him. And then he would wake up in hot sweats at night and find himself surrounded by his servants, who asked about his welfare with great concern; for, they said, he had been talking in his sleep.

He consulted a fortune-teller of repute, to whom he had always turned for succour in his moments of adversity, and found him very inspiring. The astrologer, Shri Bandophadayaya, told him accurately the cause of his distress: It was the fear of losing money, said he, that disturbed him so gravely. And the only way to compose himself was to put this money in some safe security, where neither the malice of his rivals, nor the wrath of the government, nor the dacoits' skill, could deprive him of his possessions.

After the ups and downs of his long career as a businessman, Lalla Ram Narain was unable to think of any way in which he could secure his fortune. Everything seemed to evaporate suddenly, the breath came and went, and soon one day he might hear that all his enormous wealth had just disappeared through some unforseen calamity. The money market was facing inflation, and country after country was going communist; and though India was now a free country, there was no knowing when the government would nationalize all the industries. The future was precarious indeed! . . .

The fear that gnawed at his vitals made life taste very bitter. And during the turbid afternoons, which melted into the evenings, he could see hallucinations of a violence, the after-taste of which left him no serenity whatever.

One day Shri Bandophadayaya returned and told Lalla Ram Narain that, according to the stars, money would only be safe, if he could have a golden bed made, studded with diamonds, rubies and jewels, so that he could see all his fortune at one glance and keep it within his vigilant care.

This prophecy met the inner curve of Lalla Ram Narain's forebodings and his inmost hopes for security. He decided to have a golden bed made, onto which would be embossed precious stones of the costliest variety. In this way, he thought, he would really be able to put all his money in one place. And as he would be sleeping on this bed, ten hours out of twenty four, at least during that time there would be no danger of his losing any part of his fortune.

The golden bed was duly constructed. It proved to be the most beautiful, throne-like bed that has ever been made in the world, outdoing, some said, the beauty and grandeur of the Peacock Throne on which the Emperor Shah Jahan, the Great Moghul, had emptied his treasury.

And thus, in the wearisome jungle of life, where nothing was safe, all of a sudden there arose the ineffable haven of security and poise, the golden bed, on which Lalla Ram Narain could lie back in comfort and forget the cares of the world as well as emancipate himself from the morbid fear of losing his property. The jewels glistened, the diamonds shone, and the rubies filled his heart with new red corpuscles of blood. There was an incomprehensible change for the better in his whole orientation towards human existence.

But this assurance was not to last too long. For one day, when he came back from his routine walk to the canal bank in the morning, he found a red ruby, costing nearly a lakh of rupees, missing from the side of the bed where he used to lay his head. It was not enough, he realized, with bitter chagrin, to lie on the bed ten hours a day, and to lock the room during the time he was away, because the thieves could always break in and rob him . . . What was he to do? Was there no way by which he could ensure the safety of this indescribably beautiful monument to his industry and pain, this golden bed in which all his wealth lay concentrated? . . . Surely, it could be kept safe in the vaults of a bank! . . . But what if the bank failed, or an atom bomb fell, heralding the new war that was threatened? . . . It could, of course, be insured; but which insurance company in the world would take the risk involved, and how large would the premium be! No, it was impossible. The only thing to do was to keep it under stricter control, to be more vigilant, not depending on the Gurkha watchman whom he had already engaged to look after the house and who had probably stolen the ruby.

So he began to spend longer hours in bed. This suited him, because, in old age, the need for a siesta had become paramount. And, for a while, having reconciled himself to the loss of the big ruby, he was content with the considerable fortune which was still left within his grasp.

A few days later, on his arrival back from his evening ride in the closed Victoria, he noticed that a large chunk of gold had been hewn off one of the posts. He was angry and trembled and shook with the fury of ultimate frustration. All the hopes he had of escaping from fear of loss and deprivation seemed to be dashed to the ground. And there was no growth of any other sentiment in his heart possible from which he could look with assurance towards the future.

In his desperation, he decided to forgo his routine walks in the morning and evening and to do business and conduct all his other affairs from the golden bed. This comforted him, because the terror of his presence made all possible thieves refrain even from looking towards the bed. And, at last, he seemed to have realized the calm that betokens oneness between the body and the soul.

The balance of forces which had been so artificially contrived, however, was to break down by the revolt of the body against the soul. Lalla Ram Narain's physique had been sustained, to a large extent, on the routine of the morning walk and the evening drive, and by the moderate activity involved in sitting at the counter of his old shop. This exercise had made the meagre quota of food he ate palatable. But after the imposition, through insecurity, of another routine, which made him incline on his left elbow or his right elbow, as he lay recumbent on the golden bed, there was no desire left for food, and this made for insomania. He reflected a great deal and murmured gently to God to give him strength. But no prayers could avail him. All that he could do, with the slow ebbing away of his strength from his bone and fibre, was to burr-burr in the midst of certain hallucinations and phantasmagoric dreams in which a great many ugly humans and many more spirits seemed to be fighting and struggling against each other for the possession of his conscience, while that conscience lay choking with the fear of losing even one tola off his precious golden bed.

At last the dwindling resources of his life spent themselves in sighs of despair and, gently, gently, the breath that had survived on the hope of security, escaped one black night, from his lips, never to come back again. The twisted smile of anxiety had screwed his mouth into such a frightening grin that even the hearts of his hearse-bearers congealed in lifting him up from his golden bed to bathe his dead body before taking it to the cremation ground outside Lohgarh gate.

As he had refused to be brought down from the bed, according to Hindu custom, to the earth when he had been gasping for his last breath, they say, in Amritsar, that his soul never rose to heaven but is like a homeless ghost, suspended on top of the bed. So no one ever goes near the golden bed. In death, therefore, more than in life, he has succeeded in possessing his wealth without any fear of losing even a particle of it. But the curses of his heirs have dragged his name through the murky hell of contempt, till the golden bed has only become a bad—a very bad joke.

'Things Have a Way of Working Out'

'How many did you get? How many?' asked Krishan.

'Five,' answered Gopal.

'Ja, liar of somewhere! There are not even three Cadillacs in the whole of Bombay!'

'Arré ja, what do you know? I counted at least four. I was not sure about one—that may have been a Buick—'

'Oh, brother-in-law, you don't even know the difference between a Cadillac and a Buick! The difference between an elephant and a cow! . . .'

'I can count all the Cadillacs I saw—the first one of the Governor, with his grandson and a chaprasi seated in it—'

'How do you know it was the Governor's grandson? Braggart! As though you have been appointed the Governor's chauffeur!'

'I could be if I learnt to drive! What is there in that? Did not Sabu become a film star though he was an elephant boy? And many seths—'

'Arré ja, seth! Sinews of an owl! Don't forget you are cock-eyed! You with the Dilip haircut! . . .'

'Dilip Kumar gave me four annas once for minding his car. I heard him say to Saroj babu that I could be a good actor because I am cock-eyed! . . .'

'Who is that Saroj babu? The man who goes about sometimes in Dilip's car?'

'Han, he is Dilip's tail!'

'Salé, he would beat you if he heard you call him that!'

'Arré nahin, he is a good boy—a Bengali babu! He gave me eight-annas tip for doing nothing—'

'Acha, "do-nothing"! . . . Look there! . . . That may be our chance!

Dugdu is shifting from the threshold. Now is our chance to go and get a foothold—'

'What if he beats us off his perch? He is a bad tempered brute! . . .'

'That he is—we must move cautiously.'

'Perhaps we can wait till it begins to rain. Then he might take pity on us.' Gopal paused for breath, then sighed and said, 'Sometimes I feel I want to go home, away from this big city . . .'

'Salé! You were always a coward and a coward you will remain in spite of your bragging! . . . You know that nothing can get done here without difficulties. But we should forget about our villages and towns, with their narrow lanes and wretched little hovels, full of rats. Why, we have electricity here, and filums and shops and motors and aeroplanes . . . Nor we shall die of cold if we don't move . . .'

'What is all this big city of Bombay if we cannot get sleeping room?' protested Gopal. 'I would like to set fire to it so that we can be warm in the glow . . .'

'Coward! Coward! Coward!' Krishan shouted.

After accusing Gopal of being cowardly, Krishan shot up and began to survey the position of Dugdu to see what chances there were of securing enough sleeping room under the porch before the monsoon showers should pour down. He saw that Dugdu had, indeed, shifted away a little. But how to approach him until he had gone off to sleep, because, as chowkidar of Bhiwandiwala and Sons, he was known to be a well-paid watchdog, and, moreover, one who was ferocious as though he was mad. And unfortunately, all the places which could provide good shelter against the rain had been taken already because tonight they had been held over till nine o'clock at Churchgate station, after the Eros Cinema hours, by a torrential downpour. As his concentrated gaze confirmed the fact that Dugdu had shifted, Krishan said, in the usual bullying tone he assumed in speaking to Gopal, 'Go and see if there is room under the projection for both of us.'

Little Gopal obeyed Krishan's behest, not because he was frightened of his older companion, but because, being younger, he always took on the small jobs which juniors traditionally have to accept among dead-end kids in our country.

About fourteen years old, slight but wiry, Gopal moved like quicksilver, with that extraordinarily uncanny gift he had for spotting the gentleman or lady who wanted a taxi or sought to park a car. He was always ahead of every other boy at Churchgate in accosting the privileged with 'Sahib, taxi?' or 'Memsahib, taxi?' and 'Sahib, car sambhalenga?' And as there was a mischievous twinkle, especially in his left eye, and the bloom of youth on his soft, black, rather plain, triangular face, his appeal was irresistible. The success he enjoyed in this profession of fetching taxis and looking after motor cars had made him more agile, even if a trifle cheeky, but he retained the essential goodness of the orphan bhaiya from Gorakhpur district, Uttar Pradesh, who had come down after the famine and begun, like so many others, to live on his wits. Krishan, on the other hand, was a Punjabi lad, who had run away from his home in Amritsar and bullied Gopal every now and then because of his two year's seniority in age and superior physical frame. But they both got along fairly well and were fast friends, sticking to each other against the vicious aspersions cast against them by the other boys, sharing the one name of the God Krishna between themselves: Krishan Gopal—Gopal Krishan.

Gopal affected a gait as though he was going up unconcernedly towards the pan-biri shop by Elphinston Circle as he passed by the coveted porch; and, taking advantage of the strange angle of his left eye, he reconnoitred the position and found that there was, indeed, room for both of them to curl up on the second and third steps. So he came back and reported, 'There is room enough there, if Dugdu will let us—'

'Acha, then we will go and lie down. It is not his father's property that he can prevent us!'

And with this brave declaration, Krishan got up and led the way, Gopal soon catching up with him, after he had picked up a small sack containing their clothes.

Dugdu was snoring in a low, even key as he lay on his back, on the top step of the threshold of the office building, and Krishan and Gopal tiptoed upto the lower steps.

Krishan hushed Gopal by taking his fingers to his mouth and then sat down carefully on the second step.

Gopal came forward cautiously enough, but, with the unconscious innocence of youth, forgot the warning which Krishan had given him not to utter a word, and asked in his natural voice, 'Shall I open the sack?'

The even key of Dugdu's snoring was disturbed by a gasp as though he had missed a heartbeat.

'Chup! Salé!' Krishan rebuked Gopal.

Gopal was unnerved and stood transfixed for a moment, guilty at the mistake he had made. Then he unburdened the sack on his back onto the step on which Krishan sat.

The soft thud of the falling sack coincided with the turning of Dugdu's body.

The two boys held their breaths as though their doom had come.

Dugdu coughed slightly, breathed a deep breath, moaned and lay on his side, his face tilted towards the street, even as it rested on the broad palm of his hand.

Krishan felt as though he was right in the lion's mouth, because Dugdu's visage was only one foot above his head. In order to recover his equanimity, he made a comic gesture indicating Dugdu's full moustache.

Gopal smiled and then sat down nimbly on the lower step.

Suddenly, the sleeping Dugdu seemed to have an apperception of the presence of intruders on his preserve, with that sixth sense of the chowkidar. And, with a start, he lifted his head, open-mouthed and shouted, 'Kaun? Who is that? . . . What are you doing here?'

'Krishan and Gopal—it is us boys, Dugdu,' Gopal ventured.

'Go away from here!' Dugdu snarled.

'But the door of your office is closed and there is an iron gate behind you!' protested Krishan.

'Go! Go!' shouted the watchman.

'But we have slept here before when the Pathan Lalla was chowkidar!'

'The Lalla has been sacked! And now I am here! Go, go away—do you need the talk of the stick!'

The boys got up gingerly and drifted away towards the threshold of another door, seven yards away, which had a brief canvas awning over it.

'Sala!' commented Gopal.

'Han, sala!' agreed Krishan.

They were silent for a while, as they crouched on the hard stone of one step of the new threshold, with the silence of defeat. They did not even look at each other, but merely sat 'taking their own faces'. The darkness of the street was accentuated by the gathering of menacing black clouds, like a horde of elephants who might soon trumpet out thunderous noises if a cool breeze struck them, like the premonition of disaster.

At last Gopal bent his head on the sack and seemed to be overcome with slumber, while Krishan tenderly caressed Gopal's crouching body and allowed his companion's legs to stretch out.

As sweetly as Krishan showed this favour to his friend, as bitterly did he think of Dugdu's behaviour. And his feelings bordered upon the hopelessness of securing a perch for one's body if one was late earning a few extra annas anywhere. And he muttered a curse against the rainy weather, 'Rape-mother rain!' which was responsible for his discomfort, because, in the ordinary weather, there was any amount of room on the pavements of Bombay for one to stretch oneself. And he recalled, with a certain nostalgia, those hot nights of May, only a month ago, when the whole gang of boys from Churchgate had congregated together, stretching side by side in a small street off Phiroze Shah Mehta Road, which they had captured and where they had played cards and gossiped and told smutty stories to each other before going off to sleep. Even then, of course, Gopal had gone to sleep early, because, being young, he got tired and lost consciousness quickly. The little one felt hungry the same way, suddenly, and then he must have food. Krishan felt protective towards him, and also a trifle guilty, because he took advantage of his seniority and bullied him or pretended to do so. For, actually, no one could say much to Gopal or take advantage of him. He was that smart!

Krishan's glance indulgently surveyed Gopal's curled up body, but could not distinguish the features because the darkness had now enveloped everything. A gust of cool breeze coursed down the street. The boy looked up instinctively and saw the dark clouds low enough to touch the roofs of the tall buildings in the street. And hardly had his eyes withdrawn when a streak of lightning tore through the hordes of black elephants and scattered them with its whip of fury. The elephants groaned in a reverberating thunder and ran in a hot sweat, which soon began to pour down on the earth.

Gopal was not disturbed by the thunder or the rain, in such a deep sleep was he. And, even though Krishan shouted at him before getting up to stand glued to the doorway behind, under the scanty shade of the cloth awning, the little boy did not come to. Only when the many drops of rainwater fell upon his face and legs did he wake up, rubbing the sweat on his neck and looking about him with half-open eyes, as though he was in a state of derangement.

'Arré, uth!' Krishan goaded him. 'The sack will get wet and then we will nave no dry clothes!'

Gopal got up with tremendous alacrity now at this reminder of the disaster that might follow if the sack became wet. His eyes dilated with the cool of the rain. And, as Krishan hauled the sack up from him to hold it against his stomach, the little boy emerged into the state of ennui and torpor bordering upon wakefulness, until, in a few moments, he could see the water pour down before him.

'Like a pitcher breaking upon our heads, this sali Bombay rain!' he said somnambulistically, forgetting that he had always made this comment on seeing the monsoon showers come down. And, as always, he repeated the further wisdom he was wont to give forth from the depths of his nostalgia for Uttar Pradesh, 'In our parts, the rain comes softly, like a shy girl with tinkling bells!'

'Oh, shut up, you and your shy girl, ohe!' shouted Krishan, irritated by the squalls of water which were brushing past the lower parts of their bodies and threatened to drench them completely.

Gopal accepted the rebuke silently and was dozing off, till a strong shower douched his entire body.

'Oh Ishwar!' he cried, automatically remembering the name of God.

Seeing Gopal's despair, Krishan sought to amuse him, 'Look, I am pregnant with wealth like a seth!'

But Gopal did not look at his friend; nor was he amused. For the sheets of rain were now sweeping past them in continuous waves and already they were wet from head to foot. And, what was more, there were exciting sounds from Dugdu's perch as though the fellow was asking them now to come over to take shelter there.

'I am going to that perch of Dugdu's whether you come or not!' the little one said emphatically. And, without more ado, he ran forward.

Krishan saw his companion run. Then he heard Dugdu shouting at the top of his voice.

Without thinking any more about it, Krishan followed him, the sack of clothes on his back.

As they got near the steps under the wooden porch, which was Dugdu's domain, they heard, above the swish of rain, heavy, abusive words and threats ensuing from the upper step. They dared not advance any further beyond the lowest step because Dugdu was locked in a furious grip with another figure whom the boys could not recognize. The muttered curses of the two wrestling bodies lit up the atmosphere like sparks of lightning. And as they hit each other, they seemed to echo the thunder blows.

'Is this . . . your father's estate?' the stranger struggling with Dugdu was saying, grinding his words in the clenched teeth.

'Wait till the morning!' Dugdu was saying. 'I shall show you!'

In a tense moment, sudden as the oncoming of the disastrous rain from the grim clouds, the two bodies hurtled to the last step, scattering Gopal and Krishan, and rolled over each other, with the stranger on top.

Gopal instinctively called out aloud, 'Police! Police!'

'It is Ali, cook from the George Restaurant!' Krishan said, recognizing the stranger. 'Look, he is on top . . .' And like a bloodthirsty spectator of a wrestling match, he turned from Gopal and encouraged Ali, 'Mar! Mar! . . . Hit the brother-in-law Dugdu hard! Hit him! He fancies he is Homi Wadia's jungle hero Zimbo!'

Gopal was trembling with the fury of the quarrel before him and was a little frightened. Dugdu's groans could be heard from below the oppression which the little young body of Ali cast on him, while the conqueror strained to keep his grip, even as he heard the encouraging words of Krishan.

Perhaps, however, those words distracted him a little. Because, in a flash, Dugdu had heaved himself from below, turned and felled Ali. The cook kicked him desperately from below. But Dugdu had whipped out his knife and sat threateningly on Ali's stomach.

'Don't do it! Don't!' shouted Gopal.

'Let him dare!' challenged Ali as he held Dugdu's hand with the knife away from his shoulder and kicked him in a sore spot. 'The sala drank the liquor and then threatens to tell the police about where I make it!'

Dugdu seemed to get the courage of pain and pushed the knife down, grazing Ali's shoulder, by the neck, till warm blood oozed like spurts from the fountain of his victim's body.

Ali let loose a shriek and a wierd howl, 'Ya Allah!'

A host of people had run up by now, including a policeman at their head, and they loomed like shadows in the darkness washed by the rainstorm, agitated, shouting, insinuating, highly excited.

The arm of the law got hold of Dugdu's hand, with the knife still in its grip, and detached him from Ali's body.

'He is bleeding from the neck,' shouted Gopal impetuously.

Krishan restrained him with his uplifted arm and, cynically pointing to the first step on which Dugdu had slept, whispered to his companion, 'Go and take the place before anyone else gets it.'

'To the police station—both of you!' the policeman said to Dugdu and Ali.

'Arré, Sarkar, not the fellow who is bleeding!' protested someone from the crowd. 'It is the murderer who should be taken.'

Dugdu raised his head to look for a moment at the man who had called him a murderer, so that he could recognize him and settle scores afterwards.

'Come, come, don't hang around here!' the policeman ordered him.

'Can I get my wallet from my bed?' Dugdu asked.

'Han, but I will come with you,' said the policeman, indulgently now because the accused might have thought of greasing the palm of the law with some money. The sepoy had the inborn cunning of the downtrodden who sides with authority in order to survive if only as the best among all the defeated.

As Dugdu took the wallet from under his pillow on the first step, he saw Gopal sitting on his bedspread. He contemplated the boy's figure silently for a moment. And Krishan, apprehensive that there may be trouble, came and sat down by Gopal to shield him in case Dugdu should hit out. But the watchman only looked at the two boys, first hard, then soft, and again, with a twisted smile and said, 'So you got here after all, boys!—Things have a way of working out!'

The Gold Watch

There was something about the smile of Mr Acton, when he came over to Srijut Sudarshan Sharma's table, which betokened disaster. But as the sahib had only said, 'Mr Sharma, I have brought something for you specially from London—you must come into my office on Monday and take it . . .' the poor old despatch clerk could not surmise the real meaning of the General Manager's remark. The fact that Mr Acton should come over to his table at all, fawn upon him and say what he had said was, of course, most flattering. For, very rarely did the head of the firm condescend to move down the corridor where the Indian staff of the distribution department of the great Marmalade Empire of Henry King & Co. worked. But that smile on Mr Acton's face!—specially as Mr Acton was not known to smile too much, being a morose, old sahib, hard working, conscientious and a slave-driver, famous as a shrewd businessman, so devoted to the job of spreading the monopoly of King's Marmalade, and sundry other products, that his wife had left him after a three month's spell of marriage and never returned to India, though no one quite knew whether she was separated or divorced from him or merely preferred to stay away. So the fact that Acton sahib should smile was enough to give Srijut Sharma cause for thought. But then Srijut Sharma was, in spite of his nobility of soul and fundamental innocence, experienced enough in his study of the vague, detached race of the White sahibs by now and clearly noticed the slight awkward curl of the upper lip, behind which the determinded, tobacco-stained long teeth showed, for the briefest moment, a snarl suppressed by the deliberation which Acton sahib had brought to the whole operation of coming over and pronouncing those kind words. And what could be the reason for his having being singled out, from amongst the twenty-five odd members of the distribution department? In the usual way, he, the despatch clerk, only received an occasional greeting, 'Hello, Sharma—how you getting on?' from the head of his own department, Mr West; and twice or thrice a year he was called into the cubicle by West sahib for a reprimand, because some letters or packets had gone astray; otherwise, he himself, being the incarnation of clockwork efficiency, and well-versed in the routine of his job, there was no occasion for any break in the monotony of that anonymous, smooth working Empire, so far at least as he was concerned. To be sure, there was the continual gossip of the clerks and the accountants, the bickerings and jealousies of the people above him, for grades and promotions and pay, but he, Sharma, had been employed twenty years ago, as a special favour, was not even a matriculate, but had picked up the work somehow, and though unwanted and constantly reprimanded by West sahib in the first few years, had been retained because of the general legend of saintliness which he had acquired . . . He had five more years of service to do, because then he would be fifty-five, and the family raising—grihasta—portion of his life in the fourfold scheme, prescribed by religion, finished, he hoped to retire to his home town Jullunder, where his father still ran the confectioner's shop off the Mall Road.

'And what did Acton sahib have to say to you, Mr Sharma?' asked Miss Violet Dixon, the plain snub-nosed Anglo-Indian typist in her sing-song voice.

Being an old family man of fifty, who had grayed prematurely, she considered herself safe enough with this 'gentleman' and freely conversed with him, specially during the lunch hour, while she considered almost everyone else as having only one goal in life—to sleep with her.

'Han,' he said, 'he has brought something for me from England,' Srijut Sharma answered.

'There are such pretty things in UK,' she said. My! I wish I could go there! My sister is there, you know! Married! . . .'

She had told Sharma all these things before. So he was not interested. Specially today, because all his thoughts were concentrated on the inner meaning of Mr Acton's sudden visitation and the ambivalent smile.

'Well, half day today, I am off,' said Violet and moved away with the peculiar snobbish agility of the memsahib she affected to be.

Srijut Sharma stared at her blankly, though taking in her regular form into his subconscious with more than the old uncle's interest he had always pretended to take in her. It was only her snub nose, like that of Sarupnaka, the sister of the demon-king Ravan, that stood in the way of her being married, he felt sure, for otherwise she had a tolerable figure. But he lowered his eyes as soon as the thought of Miss Dixon's body began to simmer in the cauldron of his inner life, because, as a good Hindu, every woman, apart from the wife, was to him a mother or a sister. And his obsession about the meaning of Acton sahib's words returned, from the pent-up curiosity, with greater force now that he realized the vastness of the space of time during which he would have to wait in suspense before knowing what the boss had brought for him and why.

He took up his faded sola topee, which was, apart from the bush-shirt and trousers, one of the few concessions to modernity which he had made throughout his life as a good Brahmin, got up from his chair, beckoned Dugdu sepoy from the veranda on his way out and asked, 'Has Acton sahib gone, do you know?'

'Abhi—Sahib in lift going down,' Dugdu said.

Srijut Sharma made quickly for the stairs and, throwing all caution about slipping on the polished marble steps to the winds, hurtled down. There were three floors below him and he began to sweat, both through fear of missing the sahib and the heat of mid-April.

As he got to the ground floor, he saw Acton sahib already going out of the door.

It was now or never.

Srijut Sharma rushed out. But he was conscious that quite a few employees of the firm would be coming out of the two lifts and he might be seen talking to the sahib. And that was not done—outside the office. The sahibs belonged to their private worlds, where no intrusion was tolerated, for they refused to listen to pleas of advancement through improper channels.

Mr Acton's uniformed driver opened the door of the polished Buick and the sahib sat down, spreading the shadow of grimness all around him.

Srijut Sharma hesitated, for the demeanour of the Goanese chauffeur was frightening.

By now the driver had smartly shut the back door of the car and was proceeding to his seat.

That was his only chance.

Taking off his hat, he rushed up to the window of the car, and rudely thrust his head into the presence of Mr Acton.

Luckily for him, the sahib did not brush him aside, but smiled a broader smile than that of a few minutes ago and said, 'You want to know what I have brought for you? Well, it is a gold watch with an inscription on it . . . See me Monday morning . . .' The sahib's initiative in anticipating his question threw Srijut Sharma further off balance. The sweat poured down from his forehead, even as he mumbled, 'Thank you, sir, thank you . . .'

'Chalo, driver!' the sahib ordered.

And the chauffeur turned and looked hard at Srijut Sharma.

The despatch clerk withdrew with a sheepish, abject smile on his face and stood, hat in left hand, the right hand raised to his forehead in the attitude of a nearly military salute.

The motor car moved off.

But Srijut Sharma still stood, as though he had been struck dumb. He was neither happy nor sad at this moment. Only numbed by the shock of surprise. Why should he be singled out from the whole distribution department of Henry King & Co., for the privilege of the gift of a gold watch! He had done nothing brave that he could remember. 'A gold watch, with an inscription on it!' Oh, he knew, now: the intuitive truth rose inside him—the sahib wanted him to retire . . .

The revelation rose to the surface of his awareness from the deep obsessive fear, which had possessed him for nearly half an hour, and his heart began to palpitate against his will, and the sweat sozzled his body.

He reeled a little, then adjusted himself and got onto the pavement, looking after the car, which had already turned the corner into Nicol Road.

He turned and began to walk towards Victoria Terminus station. From there he had to take his train to Thana, thirty miles out where he had resided, for cheapness, almost all the years he had been in Bombay. His steps were heavy, for he was reasonably sure now that he would get notice of retirement on Monday. He tried to think of some other possible reason why the sahib may have decided to give him the gift of a gold watch with an inscription. There was no other explanation. His doom was sealed. What would he say to his wife? And his son had still not passed his matric. How would he support the family? The provident fund would not amount to very much, specially in these days of rising prices . . .

He felt a pull at his heart. He paused for breath and tried to call himself. The blood pressure! Or was it merely wind? He must not get into a panic at any cost. He steadied his gait and walked along, muttering to himself, 'Shanti! Shanti! Shanti!' as though the very incantation of the formula of peace would restore his calm and equanimity.

During the weekend, Srijut Sharma was able to conceal his panic and confusion behind the facade of an exaggerated bonhomie with the skill of an accomplished natural actor. On Saturday night he went with his wife and son to see Professor Ram's Circus, which was performing opposite the Portuguese Church; he got up later than usual on Sunday morning; and spent a little longer on his prayers, but seemed normal enough on the surface.

Only, he ate very little of the gala meal of the rice-kichri put before him by his wife and seemed lost in thought for a few moments at a time. His illiterate but shrewd wife noticed that there was something on his mind.

'You have not eaten at all today,' she said, as he had left the tasty papadum and the mango pickle untouched. 'Look at Hari! He has left nothing in his thali!'

'Hoon,' he answered abstractedly. And, then, realizing he might be found out for the worried, unhappy man he was, he tried to bluff her. 'As a matter of fact, I was thinking of some happy news that the sahib gave me yesterday. He said he brought a gold watch as a gift for me from Vilayat . . .'

'Then, Papaji, give me the silver watch, which you are using now,' said Hari, his young son, impetuously. 'I have no watch at all and I am always late everywhere.'

'Not so impatient, son!' counselled Hari's mother. 'Let your father get the gold watch first and then—he will surely give you his silver watch.'

In the ordinary way, Srijut Sudarshan Sharma would have endorsed his wife's sentiments. But today he felt that, on the face of it, his son's demand was justified. How should Hari know that the silver watch, and the gold watch, and a gold ring, would be all the jewellery he, the father, would have for security against hard days if the gold watch was, as he prognosticated, only a token being offered by the firm to sugarcoat the bitter pill they would ask him to swallow—retirement five years before the appointed time. He hesitated, then lifted his head, smiled at his son and said, 'Acha, you can have my silver watch . . .'

'Can I have it, really, Papaji? Hurray!' the boy shouted, rushing away to fetch the watch from his father's pocket. 'Give it to me now, today!'

'Vay, son, you are so selfish!' his mother exclaimed. For, with the peculiar sensitiveness of the woman she had surmised from the manner in which her husband had hung his head down and then tried to smile as he lifted his face to his son, that the father of Hari was upset inside him, or at least not in his usual mood of accepting life evenly, accompanying this acceptance with the pious invocation—'Shanti! Shanti!'

Hari brought the silver watch, adjusted it to his left ear to see if it ticked, and, happy in the possession of it, capered a little caper.

Srijut Sharma did not say anything, but, pushing his thali away, got up to wash his hands.

The next day it happened as Srijut Sharma had anticipated.

He went in to see Mr Acton as soon as the sahib came in, for the suspense of the weekend had mounted to a crescendo by Monday morning and he had been trembling with trepidation, pale and completely unsure of himself. The General Manager called him in immediately the peon Dugdu presented the little slip with the despatch cleric's name on it.

'Please sit down,' said Mr Acton, lifting his grey-haired head from the papers before him. And then, pulling his keys from his trousers' pocket by the gold chain to which they were adjusted, he opened a drawer and fetched out what Sharma thought was a beautiful red case.

'Mr Sharma, you have been a loyal friend of this firm for many years—and—you know, your loyalty has been your greatest asset here—because . . . er . . . otherwise, we could have got someone, with better qualifications, to do your work! . . . Now . . . we are thinking of increasing the efficiency of the business all round! . . . And, well, we feel that you would also like, at your age, to retire to your native Punjab . . . So, as a token of our appreciation for your loyalty to Henry King & Co., we are presenting you this gold watch . . .' And he pushed the red case towards him.

Srijut Sharma began to speak, but though his mouth opened, he could not go on. 'I am fifty years old,' he wanted to say, 'and I still have five years to go.' His facial muscles seemed to contract, his eyes were dimmed with the fumes of frustration and bitterness, his forehead was covered with sweat. At least they might have made a little ceremony of the presentation; he could not even utter the words, 'Thank you, sir!'

'Of course, you will also have your provident fund and one month's leave with pay before you retire . . .' Again, Srijut Sharma tried to voice his inner protest in words which would convey his meaning without seeming to be disloyal, for he did not want to obliterate the one concession the sahib had made to the whole record of his service with his firm. It was just likely that Mr Acton may remind him of his failings as a despatch clerk if he should so much as indicate that he was unamenable to the suggestion made by the sahib on behalf of Henry King & Co.

'Look at the watch—it has an inscription on it which will please you,' said Mr Acton, to get over the embarrassment of the tension created by the silence of the despatch clerk.

These words hypnotized Sharma and, stretching his hands across the large table, he reached out for the gift.

Mr Acton noticed the unsureness of his hand and pushed it gently forward.

Srijut Sharma picked up the red box, but, in his eagerness to follow the sahib's behests, dropped it, even as he had held it aloft and tried to open it.

The sahib's face was livid as he picked up the box and hurriedly opened it. Then, lifting the watch from its socket, he wound it and applied it to his ear. It was ticking. He turned it round and showed the inscription to the despatch clerk.

Srijut Sharma put both his hands out, more steadily this time, and took the gift in the manner in which a beggar receives alms. He brought the glistening object within the orbit of his eyes, but they were dimmed with tears and he could not read anything. He tried to smile, however, and then, with a great heave of his head, which rocked his body from side to side, he pronounced the words, 'Thank you, sir . . .'

Mr Acton got up, took the gold watch from Srijut Sharma's hands and put it back in the socket of the red case. Then he stretched his right hand towards the despatch clerk with a brisk shake-hand gesture, and offered the case to him with his left hand.

Srijut Sharma instinctively took the sahib's right hand gratefully in his two sweating hands and opened the palms out to receive the case.

'Good luck, Sharma,' Mr Acton said. 'Come and see me after your leave is over. And when your son matriculates, let me know if I can do something for him . . .'

Dumb, and with bent head, the fumes of his violent emotions rising above the mouth which could have expressed them, he withdrew in the abject manner of his ancestors going out of the presence of feudal lords.

Mr Acton saw the danger to the watch and went ahead to open the door, so that the clerk could go out without knocking his head against the door or fall down.

As Srijut Sharma emerged from the General Manager's office, involuntary tears flowed from his eyes and his lower lip fell in a pout that somehow controlled him from breaking down completely.

The eyes of the whole office staff were on him.

In a moment, a few of the men clustered around his person.

One of them took the case from his hands, opened it and read the inscription out aloud:

'In appreciation of the loyal service of Mr Sharma to Henry King & Co., on his retirement . . .'

The curiosity of his colleagues became a little less enthusiastic as the watch passed from hand to hand.

Unable to stand, because of the wave of dizziness that swirled in his head, Srijut Sudarshan Sharma sat down on his chair with his head hidden in his hands and allowed the tears to roll down. One of his colleagues, Mr Banaji, the accountant, patted his back understandingly. But the pity was too much for him.

'To be sure, Seth Makhanji, the new partner has a relation to fill Sharma's position,' said one.

'No, no,' another refuted him. 'No one is required to kill himself with work in our big concern . . . We are given the Sunday off! And a fat pension years before it is due. The bosses are full of love for us! . . .'

'Damn fine gold watch, but it does not go!' said Sriraman, the typist.

Mr Banaji took the watch from Sriraman and, putting it in the case, placed it before Srijut Sharma. He then signalled to the others to move away.

As Srijut Sharma realized that his colleagues had drifted away, he lifted his morose head, took the case, as well as his hat, and began to walk away.

Mr Banaji saw him off to the door, his hand on Sharma's back.

'Sahibji,' the Parsi accountant said, as the lift came up and the liftman took Srijut Sharma in.

On the way home, Srijut Sharma found that the gold watch only went when it was shaken. Obviously, some delicate part had broken when he had dropped it on Mr Acton's table. He would get it mended, but he must save all the cash he could get hold of and not go spending it on the luxury of having a watch repaired now. He shouldn't have been weak with his son and given him his old silver watch. But as there would be no office to go to any more, he would not need to look at the time very much, specially in Jullunder, where time just stood still and no one bothered about keeping appointments.

Old Bapu

They say, in our parts, that, at the solemn moment of death, even when death is sudden, every man sees the whole of his past underneath his skull.

Old Bapu fancied, as he walked along towards the Gurgaon bazaar, that his end had come. And, as though by the power of this suggestion, the various worlds rose behind his head, way back in the distance of time, rather like balls of heat wrapped in mist, projections of the omnipotent sun that shone overhead, veiled and blurred by the haze of memory . . .

The city was still a mile away, and the flesh of his feet burnt where it touched the new, hot metalled road through the holes in the shoes. And the sweat poured down across the furrows on his face, specially through the two sharp channels which stretched from the nose towards the chin, like rivulets flooding a fallow field . . . A bluish shimmer flickered across his vision of the houses ahead.

As though compelled by the discomfort of slogging on foot and the weakness in his joints after the seven miles tread from Shikohpur, he felt his body evaporating, and his soul in the state of that lightness which disclosed the saga of his past life, going round and round in his cranium. And as he felt near enough to exhaustion and death, and yet did not want to die ('May Ishwar banish such a thought from my head,' he prayed), the agitation of his nerves produced the aberration of a phantasma, like the red stars over a toothache . . .

'I am not old,' he said to himself in the silent colloquy of his soul with his body. 'The boys call me "old Bapu" because I am older than them . . . The caste Hindu urchins have no respect for the untouchable elders anyhow. And their fathers want to throw everyone of us into the garbage pit to use as manure for better harvests . . . But I do not want to die . . . Hey Ishwar!'

The saga of his life forced itself into his head, in spite of his protests, in several minute details, bits of memories entangled with the awkward drone of heat overhead, drumming into his ears.

He was a child, sitting by the revolving spinning wheel of his mother, disturbing the iron needle, because she would not get up and give him the stale bread and pickle . . . Little specks of wool arose from the cotton in her hand, soft as the sighs which she uttered in despair at his mischief—or was it because there was no roti in the basket inside? . . . And then she awoke from the trance of her eyes, rivetted on the thread of the takla and said, 'Acha, wait, tiny, I will go and borrow some food for you from the mother of Ram Dutt . . .' And while she was gone, and he played about with the spinning wheel, against her strict injunctions, a rat gnawing in his belly . . .

Lighter than air, his body proceeded on the way to Gurgaon bazaar, flitting into a cloud of unknowing. He walked almost with his eyes closed, seeing himself as a small boy singing a song, against the counterpoint of the wheel of the well, as he drove the bullocks round and round . . . And the big boys came and pulled his slight frame from the seat and began to take a ride on the shaft. And, as he sought, with his tiny hands, to grip them, they thrust him away and threw him into the well, where he shrieked in panic, holding on to the chain of earthen vessels, while they all ran away, and he slowly climbed up, exhausted and dying . . .

Drifting from that early death into life, he felt he could ward off the present feeling of weakness in his limbs, and perhaps, he would be lucky with at least half a day's work.

'Stay with me, son; when you go from me, I shall die!' he heard his mother's words beckon from the mythical memories of his adolescence. 'Your father went soon after you were born, and you will have no one after I am gone . . .' And he recalled that in his eagerness to work in the fields, and to become a tall man and not remain the small creature he was, he had gone away that afternoon, and then he had come home to find his mother dead . . . His spirit tried to fly away from the ugly thought of his betrayal of her, but its wings were rooted in his coarse little body, and in spite of a violent cough, which he excited in his throat, even as he spat on the dust a globule of phlegm, the soul held the vision of his mother's dead face, eyes dilated and the teeth showing in the terror-dark of their hut . . .

'May Ishwar keep her soul in heaven!' he prayed. And, as though by magic, his treason was forgotten in the next few footsteps . . .

But even as he mopped the sweat off his face with the forepaws of his right hand, the scales seemed to lift from his eyes, and his soul was face to face with the forepaws of his right hand, and then with a monster, his uncle Dandu Ram, who shouted, 'I am tired of you! Good for nothing scoundrel! Everyone is tired of you! Inauspicious bastard! You cannot plough the fields well! Nor can you look after the cattle! Go and eat dung elsewhere—there is no food for you in my house.'

The bushes on the roadside exuded the same smell in the parched heat, which had come from the clumps of grass amid the mounds and hollows of Shikohpur where he had wandered, half crazy with hunger and the beatings which the boys gave him, like birds of prey falling upon a weaker member of the flock . . . Oh the cruelty of it! And the laceration of abuse and bitter words! . . . And Dandu had taken his half bigha of land saying, 'You are an idiot, incapable of looking after it!'

The lavamist of heat pressed down over his eyes and half shut them through the glare. The mood of his soul became more and more seraphic, accepting the vision of the crusts of black bread and lentils which he loved so much, after the work when he was engaged as a field labourer by some prosperous Hindu farmer of the upper caste.

Only the anxiety of not getting work today began to gnaw into his being as the houses of Gurgaon loomed up fifty hands away.

A man mounted on a bicycle brushed past him from ahead after tinkling his bell furiously. And Bapu realized that he must be careful in town if he wanted to escape death . . .

The city was a labyrinth of jagged shops, tall houses and rutted roads. And waves of men coursed along the edges of the streets, receding, returning towards the hawkers, who sat with condiments and fruits and vegetables before them.

The broken asphalt attracted him. He had worked on road-making. Fetching stones and breaking them. So much cement was put down on certain roads that they never broke. But here, the contractors were paid to make pavements hard, and to fill the ruts every season, for after every rainy season the ruts reappeared.

That was the work he had come to ask for.

Suddenly, he turned in the direction of Model Town, where the Sikh contractor, Ram Singh, lived.

In his heart there was an old cry of fear at the potential temper of this man, which had always cowed him down. His glance fell at his fingertips which had been blunted through hammering stones. The congealed flesh of corns at the ends of the fingers gave the effect of toughness and he felt strong to see them, knowing that he was capable of the hardest work . . . Distant, more distant seemed to grow the contractor's house with the courtyard, even though he had entered Model Town, but his feet marched more briskly.

Sardar Ram Singh was sitting on a charpai under the neem tree, the bun of his hair a little loose from sleep.

Bapu joined his hands and stood looking at him.

'Aoji, Bapu!' the contractor said surlily, breaking the edge of his taciturnity.

The vibration of each part of Ram Singh's face made Bapu's soul shudder and he could not speak.

'Ohe speak—what do you want?' Ram Singh asked, fanning himself the while with a hand fan.

The voice surged up in Bapu even as he breathed deeply to sigh. But the sound would not come out.

Ram Singh stared at him for a prolonged moment.

Bapu made a sign with his hands and opened his mouth to say, 'Work.'

'Ohe ja ja, oldie! You can't work, with that frame of yours!' admonished Ram Singh. 'Doing half work for full pay! . . . Besides the rains have not yet abated. Don't be deceived by this sunshine . . . The big rains have yet to come! . . .'

A low and horrible sound was in Bapu's belly, and he felt that his throat was being strangled by the serpent of sweat that flowed down to his neck from the face. His lips twitched, and the tone of the contractor's words sounded like the news of doom in his ears. 'How old are you?' Ram Singh asked, eyeing him with seemingly cynical indifference.

'The earthquake in Kangra—when it came, I was born!'

The contractor was startled. He smiled, and, surveying Bapu's frame, said, 'About fifty years ago—but you look seventy. Life in our country is ebbing away. The workmen seem to have no strength left. Look at you, two-legged donkey that you are! One of your legs seems to be shrivelled, while the other feeble one seems to be waiting to drag it on . . . All of us have become lame and go hopping, tottering and falling, wishing for the Sarkar to carry us forward. Comic and undignified and shameless! . . .'

'No land, no harvests!' Bapu said desperately. 'And—' And he stretched out his hands.

'Acha, take this and go!' the contractor ground the words and looked away. 'Let me rest. Take this . . .' He took a nickel piece and threw it at Bapu.

The labourer bent his eyes over his hands, joined them in supplication and gratitude and still stood.

'Ja, don't stand on my head!' Ram Singh shouted. 'The work on the roads will begin when the rains are over!'

Bapu was more frightened of his agony of frustration than of the contractor's words. He controlled the tears in his eyes and slid away on ambling feet.

The prolonged burbling of a beetle from the slime in a drain stirred a feeling of terrible self-pity in him. He wanted to drink some water to avoid breaking down. And, seeing a lone pan-biri stall, tucked away between the walls of the two different houses, a little further away, he headed towards it.

His eyes were almost closed. His lips twitched against his will.

And he was like a somnambulist, walking blindly towards some unknown goal. The fact that he had a nickel piece in his hands warded off the feeling of death that had pre-occupied him on the approach towards Gurgaon. Now, he only felt the precariousness of the dim future, in which his good or bad deeds would rotate in the inexorable rhythm of work and no work.

'Pani!' he said to the shopkeeper, joining his hands, first in greeting, then unfolding them as a cup.

The pan-biri wallah eyed him suspiciously, then relaxed in the face of the sun's merciless stare, and began to pour water into the stranger's cupped hands from a brass jug.

Bapu drank and belched his fill. Then he caressed his face with his moist hands and touched his eyes with the water on his fingertips. The cool touch of liquid seemed to revive him.

And, as though from some instinct for seeking reassurance, he looked into the mottled mirror that hung down from the pan-biri shop. He had not looked at himself in such a glass for years. He saw that his face was shrivelled up, lined with the wrinkles which had been sharpened by hard work in his youth, and many small lines crisscrossed the corners of his eyes, his forehead, his jowl and neck. And a greyish pallor covered the visage, more than the abject anxiety to please the contractor, rather like the colour of death which he had apprehended as he had walked along the road. The shock of the old face disturbed him and he turned away from the mirror. 'About seventy years!' Ram Singh said. So he turned towards the mirror again.

'Oh ja, ja, ahead,' said the pan-biri wallah. 'Don't break my glass by showing it your ugly old face!'

Old Bapu ambled along ahead, hoping to buy four annas worth of corn to sustain himself in the illusion of youth.

The Tamarind Tree

Ochre-red was the colour of the ripe tamarind fruit, bursting out of the green-brown shells on the branches of the shady tree in Aunt Kesaro's courtyard. And Roopa stared at the bud almost as she had contemplated her own juicy lips in the broken mirror before she became pregnant. She did not know why the saliva filled her mouth. But she felt an irresistible longing for the taste of the sharp, sweet fruit . . .

She withdrew from where she had sat scrubbing brass utensils with ashes in the open-air kitchen of her mother-in-law, and went towards the alcove where her husband kept the mirror. The stolen glance from under the projection of her headcloth showed her the reflection of her pale lips, dried by sighs and the muffled breaths in which she uttered words in answer to others . . . Perhaps she had wanted to put on the rich ripe colour of the tamarind fruit on her lips and cover the pallid hue. She blushed at the thought, waved her head and turned away . . . She knew that it was the turmoil in her belly that was creating the wild swirling waves of desire. And the flavour of the tamarind alone could appease her yearning.

Demurely, she covered her face against possible stares, though her mother-in-law was out washing clothes on the well. Perhaps 'they' would come home from the office and tease her. This husband of hers was clever, both with words and the way he could steal back home when father and mother were not there, and hug her or bite her lips.

The warm spring air swept the head-apron aside with a strong whiff, like that of the first wave of a dust storm. And, again, she found her eyes uplifted to the ripe rich fruit of the tamarind tree.

The branches of the tree swayed a little. The young mother-to-be also moved on her haunches towards the earthen pitcher, as though the rhythm of work was the same as the swaying of the tree, with the uprush of energy in its waving branches.

The craving for the tamarind in her mouth was renewed.

'But you have just eaten the midday meal, mad one!' she told herself. 'You are not hungry—it is true mother-in-law gives you just enough and no more, but you are not hungry . . .

She felt that she was a child again, the way she was longing for the tamarind and talking to herself. Only she could not now venture out into the courtyard of Aunt Kesaro, as she had broken all bounds as a girl, jumped, capered, run and climbed trees. Oh, for the innocence of girlhood and its abandon! Oh, for those afternoons filled with games! And, hai, those companions with whom one quarrelled, only to make up by linking finger to finger . . .

Oh, if only she could now go and get the tamarind cloves which had already fallen on the ground.

As her eyes traced the curve of her longing, she saw Aunt Kesaro sitting up from the cot where she had lain under the shade of the tamarind tree. The range of the old woman's vision had been dimmed long ago. And she seemed to blink at the glare of the sun of the afternoon. But her wrinkled face was a dry brown-black with the anxiety to preserve the fruit of the precious tree against all poachers.

One day Roopa had ventured to pick up a clove of tamarind from the courtyard of Kesaro and the old woman had just let go a torrent of abuse. The sweat had bathed her body, even as she had run home to avoid being caught, and for fear her mother-in-law may have seen her poaching, because Kesaro and her husband's mother were of like mind about the way the young were going down the drain.

The young woman raised her eyes and contemplated the gnarled face of the hag. The old woman now seemed to be counting coins from her little string purse. No, that could not be, for Kesaro depended on her son and had no money. Perhaps, she was scratching her waist because of the lice in the pleats of her skirt.

For a moment, Roopa had a terrible premonition which bedewed her nose with jewels of perspiration. She too would some day become old and wretched like this hag, with an obsession that all the young were stealing the fruit from her tree.

And would her strong young husband, with the clipped moustache, become like her father-in-law, a crochety old man, uttering foul words to make his wife generous to her—Roopa?

Just then there was a swirling movement in her belly. Perhaps the little one was kicking to get out . . . Let us hope it will be a girl, because then she could dress her in satin, with its lovely sheen. But never mind if it is a boy, because he would bring home a beautiful moon-faced birde . . .

'Give me a glass of water!' the gruff voice of her husband came.

Did her thoughts bring him home so suddenly? Why? . . . How? . . . But oh why? . . . Why?

She pulled the edge of her head-apron quickly over her eyes.

'Come, hurry, not so many blandishment!' 'They' were saying.

The sweat covered her face. And her heart drummed for fear. For a moment she was shivering with the shock.

And then there were swirling movements in her tummy. And, somehow, the thought came to her of the moments of the night when he wanted her blandishments. She had become pregnant, when, on that hot night of end summer, half out of fear and half out of coquettishness, she had evaded him on the top terrace of the house and he had chased her, caught her in his arms and crumpled her on the bed. Oh that night! All the shame had disappeared from her face and she had looked at his strong face, with the hard jaw, relieved by the big black eyes. All the impulses of her youth had flared up into the fire which consumed her and filled her with the insouciance of dreams, and before she knew she had gone off to sleep. Oh that night! . . .

She quivered with trepidation in case 'they' should ask her to come inside. And yet she felt the pang of remorse that she had resisted him always. Why, even now she felt the gnawing desire to be with him . . .

'I would like some tamarind from Aunt Kesaro's tree,' she breathed the only words which she could mention to evade the longing to be touched by him.

'And I heard you singing with the girls the other day: "Where have you gone, oh gone away?"' he said to her, restraining his voice almost into a whisper.

'I cannot reach the branches,' she said ignoring his meaning. 'And anyhow, the old woman is vigilantly guarding her tree.'

'Come, come inside,' he coaxed her.

Only, at that moment, her father-in-law coughed a wheezy cough, ground the phlegm in his throat, and spat out the weight of age in the direction of the tree. And he called, 'The wife of my son—what about my hookah?'

Roopa sighed.

Her husband wheeled on his feet, stamped the earth with the harsh resentment of defeat, twisted his mouth into unuttered speech and went towards his bicycle.

She sat open mouthed, holding the tumbler of water she was going to offer him. And in her upraised right hand there was also a resentment, a spite against the whole world that her inner impulses always remained where they were, incommunicable even to her man.

She felt she wanted to cry. And she covered her face so as not to be seen in her weakness.

She strangled the cry in her belly.

Then she got up and began to prepare the hubble-bubble for her father-in-law.

As she blew at the smouldering coal covered by the ashes in the oven, the smoke drew tears from her eyes. And she was gratified that she could pass off her sorrow under cover of the smoke. And her pallid face glowed with the agitation of effort to go towards her father-in-law.

Quickly, she recovered her equanimity after she had placed the hookah before the old man and came back.

At that moment, however, she heard Kesaro shouting, 'That is you? Daughter-in-law of Rakha? . . . And what ails you, young woman—that you cannot even produce the child you have been carrying in your belly all these months? . . . And, in spite of all the tamarind you have stolen and eaten from my tree . . .'

Roopa wished she could run away—far, far away from these cruel harsh words.

But these sentiments were reinforced by the voice of her mother-in-law, who had just then returned from the well.

'Sister, these girls look at the mirror all day! Or they sit about longing for their husbands to come back! They don't want to bear children . . .'

The young woman reeled as she stood by the kitchen. She felt she might faint. So she rushed towards the inner sanctum of the barn and lay down on the bridal bed that had come in her dowry.

The body with which she had borne the aggravated state of her pregnancy flowered into shooting stars of pain. Almost as though her belly was being churned up . . . And she tried to think of the softer things which she felt for the forthcoming offspring.

'Moon-faced one—will it be? Or rough? Certainly, it was the creature of violent loving? But she had not eaten enough of the good things which made a child's bones strong! The scanty money of her husband's pay as a peon hardly provided bare bread and lentils . . . The terrible thought occurred to her: Will the lack of enough nourishment turn the boy into a robber. It may know somehow that it never had enough as a child, and it may wish to revenge itself on others. But, perhaps, if it was a robber it may be like Jagga, the bandit, who robbed the rich to feed the poor and sang in the loveliest words.

Roopa lay prostrate on her bed. The pains now gripped her.

And she tore the ceiling with her shrieks.

The mother-in-law came to her and held her hand, smoothened her straying hair and wiped the sweat from her face. And then she went and called Kesaro who had been midwife at the birth of Roopa's husband.

The shrill cries of the little boy soon tore the quiet of the courtyard.

Groups of neighbouring women from beyond the tamarind tree came over to greet the newly born.

'May he live long!' old Kesaro said. 'He will give me a tunic of velvet and a silk headcloth.'

'May he not have to beg for food,' the mother-in-law of Roopa said to avert the evil eye.

'May he survive!' a neighbour said grudgingly. 'And may my own daughter-in-law become green! . . .'

Spring turned into early summer. And that year the tamarind tree bore more fruit than ever. Only Roopa never tasted a clove of this fruit which she had desired—the neighbouring children having looted everything in spite of old Aunt Kesaro's vigilance.

But the lips of the young bride were ripe and blood-red as she put her mouth to her babe—even though her face was sallow like the leaves of the tamarind tree . . .

Lajwanti

The loo of May flew into Lajwanti's face like flames from the hearth of heaven. The sun from whose mouth the fiery breeze came seemed to be standing relentlessly behind her, even as her heavy-jowled brother-in-law, Jaswant, often stood, apparently to goad her on to work but really to draw her attention to himself. And, as the sweat moistened her hands, she tightened her grip on the handle of the cage in which her maina bird sat, docile and dumb, under the oppression of the heat. But she persisted in her determination to trudge along to Gurgaon, where she hoped to catch the bus to her father's house in Pataudi.

'Talk to me, Maina—say something!'

The maina fluttered in the cage, perhaps to indicate to Lajwanti that she was alive.

'I will give you water as soon as I get to the bus stop.'

And, urged by the heat spots on her feet where the torn soles of her chappals exposed her flesh, she hurried towards the shade of a solitary mango which stood a little way away from the Mehrauli–Gurgaon road.

Once in the cool, she phewed several hot breaths, wiped the nape of her neck with the end of her headcloth, then forgetfully smudged her face with the soiled dupatta, licked her palate with her tongue, put down the cage of the maina, and looked in the direction of Gurgaon.

The dense heat-mist enveloped everything. But, beyond the green grove of mangoes half a mile ahead, she could see the outline of the old caravanserai.

Quickly she lifted the cage and went forward. She had the echo augury that Jaswant would be hot on her trail, as soon as her mother-in-law realized that she, Lajwanti, had not returned from the well for more than two hours. And he had a bicycle.

'Come then, my little maina, we shall soon be there . . .'

The exalted bungalows of the police lines of Gurgaon, sequestered behind hedges, under tall trees, quenched the thirst of her eyes. The green leaves of neem trees were like cool sherbet to her spirit. And there seemed to be a confectioner's shop where she might be able to drink a tumbler of whey and give the maina a little feed and water.

Somehow, the last lap of a foot journey is always the most arduous. Her legs seemed to drag along. And the burning on the exposed parts of her soles became unbearable. And the echo augury about Jaswant catching up on her enveloped her mind. And she was nearly at the end of her tether. And yet she pushed forward, as though she was possessed by the demon of flight.

There was a moment of weakening as the maina became utterly still; and, without looking to see, she felt that the bird might have fainted with the heat and died.

And in the panic of this premonition, she felt the chords of guilt choke her dry throat. She might have borne the humiliation. She might have given in to Jaswant. She could have closed her eyes. Her husband Balwant was away at college. Her benevolent father-in-law would not have known. And the mother-in-law, who wanted her son's son, more than anything else, would not have worried even if she had come to know, because she favoured Jaswant, who worked on the land and not Balwant who wanted to be a clerk.

'Talk to me, Maina. Don't go away from me . . . If you go, I too will be finished . . .'

As the bird did not even flutter, her heart seemed to sink, and the sweat just poured down her body.

'Maybe I am being superstitious,' she said to herself. 'I should have done a magic ceremony on the crossroads of Hauz Khas to ensure my safe arrival in Pataudi. And then God would have kept my enemies dispersed . . .'

Destiny spread the length of dumb distance before her, however.

And, facing the emptiness, she felt as though the whole earth was opposed to her. And she wanted to kneel down before the Almighty for all the sins for which she was being punished.

'Oh gently, gently, show me the path!' she cried out in her soul.

At that juncture, she heard the sinister shout of Jaswant, 'Stop, madwoman, or I shall kill you!'

She did not look back, because she knew the authentic accent of her brother-in-law's voice. She merely ran, with the instinct to fly, to get away, out of his reach, to the group of men who were resting by the confectioner's shop.

The maina fluttered its wings wildly. And now that it apprehended disaster, it shrieked and cried.

'Stop . . .' The voice of doom repeated itself.

Descending into the pit of confusion, Lajwanti was lost in the primal jungle of turmoil. The tortures of hell awaited her. But perhaps she could make it.

'Lajwanti,' Jaswant called in a more mellow voice.

This startled her, weakened her, and made her regret she had not given in.

She fairly ran, about twenty yards before the confectioner's shop. Jaswant passed by her on his bicycle. Then he descended and, putting the machine athwart, barred her way.

Lajwanti conjured up in her downcast eyes the smile of horror that beamed on his heavy, pock-marked face.

She swerved away and outflanked him by diving into the ditch and making for the confectioner's shop from the side of the depression.

He dragged the bicycle and raced upto her.

After he had reached the confectioner's shop, he dropped the machine and ran towards her with an enveloping movement.

Lajwanti fell into his outstretched arms almost like a willing victim.

But once she became aware of the hard embrace of the wild beast, she recoiled back, to free herself.

Again she ran.

Startled, he turned and chased her, catching her by the headcloth before she could sit down on the wooden bench by the confectioner's shop.

'Why did you run away?' he asked. 'Have you no shame? Look, folks . . .'

The straggling peasants looked nonchalantly at the scene, without coming any nearer. And three schoolboys came and stared.

'Let me go—I want to go to my father's house,' Lajwanti said, without lifting her gaze to Jaswant.

The maina fluttered in the cage.

'No, you are returning to your husband's home!' Jaswant ground the words. And he twisted her wrist as she tried to get out of his grasp.

'Brute!' she cried. And, without shedding any tears, she began to sob. 'Leave me alone! . . . Let me give the maina some water to drink . . .'

The throttling grasp of Jaswant's bestiality gripped her young body and he shouted hoarsely, 'Prostitute! Bad woman! Running away! . . . What will our brotherhood think? You disgracing us like this!'

Lajwanti collapsed in a huddle at his feet.

The brother-in-law hit her with his right foot.

At this the confectioner half got up from his greasy cushion and appealed, 'Ohe, do not hit her. Persuade her to go back with you.'

But as the woman sat mutely like a bundle, the tangled undergrowth of Jaswant's emotions became concentrated into the fury of his stubborn, frustrated will. He slapped her on the head with his loose right hand.

Lajwanti gave herself to the torment and sat dumbly, suppressing even her sobs.

And now a crowd of passers-by gathered to see the fun, but no one intervened.

Grating of brakes and the dragging of wheels brought Engineer Din Dayal's jeep to a sudden halt, twenty yards ahead of the confectioner's shop.

'Go quickly,' Shrimati Shushila Dayal ordered her husband. 'I saw him slapping the woman.'

'Let us find out what's what before getting excited,' said the dour, taciturn engineer. And he turned to the confectioner, 'What has happened? Who are they?'

'Sir, it seems the girl has run away from her father-in-law's house and wants to go to her father's house. But her brother-in-law came and caught her . . .'

Shrimati Dayal jumped out of the jeep and ran ahead of her husband.

'Cowards! Get aside! Looking on! As though this is a funfair!'

The crowd scattered and revealed Jaswant holding Lajwanti by the headcloth, which he had twisted into his hand with the plait of her hair.

'Leave her alone!' Shrimati Dayal ordered.

'Sister, she has ran away from her husband's house,' appealed Jaswant. 'And our good name is at stake!'

'She must have come away for a good reason,' Shrimati Dayal said. 'Where has she come from?'

'From near Hauz Khas,' Jaswant said.

'Hai—on foot? . . . Ten miles? She has walked.'

Jaswant nodded his head.

'Poor child!' Shrimati Dayal said turning to her husband. 'I will not allow the girl to die of a heatstroke. Put her in the jeep and let us take her home.'

'I will not let her go now that I have caught her,' Jaswant said, timid but frontal.

'I will call the police and hand you over!' threatened Shrimati Dayal.

'Anyhow,' Engineer Din Dayal counselled Jaswant, 'come and talk things over at my house . . . Persuade her to go back with you. Don't force her . . .'

'Come along,' said Shrimati Dayal, lifting Lajwanti even as she brusquely extricated the twisted plait of the girl's hair out of Jaswant's grip.

'Give me the maina to hold,' Jaswant bullied his sister-in-law.

Lajwanti merely her nodded head in negation and proceeded.

In the cool shade of the veranda of Engineer Dayal's bungalow, Lajwanti removed the hood of her headcloth and revealed her tender, tear-stricken eyes and said, 'Give me some water for the maina, mother.'

'Gurkha,' Shrimati Dayal called her servant. 'Give some cool water to all of us. Make it lime and water . . . Plain water for the bird . . .'

The servile Gurkha, more taciturn than the engineer, took in everything at a glance and went towards the kitchen.

'Why did you beat the girl?' Shrimati Dayal asked Jaswant.

'Time after time we have told her,' said Jaswant, 'that her husband has only one year more to do at college before he finishes his BA. But she wishes to be with him or go to her father's house.'

'Mother, he is a liar!' Lajwanti shrieked.

'You must have oppressed her very much to make her say this of you!' said Engineer Dayal.

'Sir, we have been good to her,' pleaded Jaswant. 'She comes from a poor home. My father is Chaudhri Ganga Ram, sarpanch of the whole village . . . I have a wife too, but she is a gentlewoman from a big house . . .'

'Like a cow,' Lajwanti flared up. 'And you want many more wives—'

'Don't bark! Shameless one! Or I will hit you!' Jaswant said.

At this Shrimati Dayal got up with a cool deliberation of her torso and delivered a clean slap on Jaswant's face and said, 'How do you like this?—If someone else hits you?'

The man was taken completely unawares. He sat with his mouth open but speechless.

'That is what I should have done when he tried to approach me!' said Lajwanti, her head turned demurely away from the engineer.

'Clearly, this girl is not happy with your family,' said the engineer. 'Let her go back to her father's house till her husband has finished his studies. And then she can come back to your family.'

'That is right!' added Shrimati Dayal. 'I will not allow the child to be in your grip. You can have one wife and not two . . .'

In the quivering scale pans of balance, created by the voices of injustice, Lajwanti felt the first moment of calm which had come to her during two long years. But immediately she felt the fear of Jaswant's revenge for the slap he had received on the face. She looked at the maina and said in speechless speech, 'Angel, suppose there is a cool place somewhere in the world where we two can rest . . .'

'Ask her to decide,' Jaswant said. 'If she goes to her father's house, she can never come back to us. If she comes back with me, we might consider sending her for a little while to her father's house.'

'Tell him what you feel, girl?' said Shrimati Dayal.

'I want to go to my father's house and never want to set foot on their threshold again,' answered Lajwanti.

'There!' said Shrimati Dayal. 'That is her answer for you. And if you are a decent man, go back to your home. I will see the girl to the bus which takes her to Pataudi . . .' And, she turned to her husband for confirmation of her decision.

'That's right!' the engineer said.

'Gurkha!' Shrimati Dayal called.

'Coming, bibiji,' the servant answered. And he appeared with lime water for all and a little plain water and cumin seed for the maina.

Lajwanti arrived with the cage of the maina in her hand, at her father's house, when the old man was just going out to bathe his buffalo at the well. He stood open-eyed and open-mouthed, asking himself whether what he saw was his daughter or her ghost. When she bent down to take the dust off his feet, he could smell the acrid summer sweat of her clothes and knew that it was Lajwanti. He dared not look at her face, because a daughter coming back home without due ceremony was inauspicious. Gentle as he was, however, he did not ask any questions. Only, he called to his young son, who was chopping up fodder for the buffalo.

'Indu, your eldest sister has come. Wake up your little sister, Moti . . .'

Lajwanti was sad for her father. She knew that a man who had borne the grinding pressures of years of survival on one bigha and a buffalo, and whose wife had died leaving him with three small children, was in no condition to receive a grown-up married daughter, who had returned without even the proverbial bundle of clothes to change into.

Indu left the chopper and rushed towards her, clinging to her legs as though he saw the ghost of his mother standing by the door. To be sure, Lajwanti looked the spit image of her mother. Only mother had become sallow with lungs, while Lajo's colouring was pucca brown, and gave richness to the small even face, with the fine nose, flawed by a big tattoo mark on her chin.

Tears welled up in Lajwanti's eyes at the warmth of the boy's embrace.

'Look at this poor maina,' she said. 'She has come all the way with me from New Delhi.'

The young boy grabbed the cage from his sister's hand and soon forgot about Lajwanti in the effort to make the bird talk.

'I should give her some lentils to eat and a little water,' Lajwanti said, sitting on the threshold of the veranda. 'Then she might talk to you . . . Though, I hope she does not say too much . . . The neighbours will know everything . . .'

For now that she was here, she wanted her return, somehow, to remain a private occurrence. She knew, of course, that everyone in a small place knew everyone else's business. And she had no hope of escaping censure from the tongues which had wagged when, before her marriage, she had played openly with boys of her own age, and seldom cared to cover her head with her dupatta because she did not want to look like a ghost. All the elders called her 'Mad Lajo', while the boys called her 'Meena Kumari' after the film heroine she resembled. She wanted, as she sat there, to know what was in her father's heart—whether he had understood her mysterious will, and the instinct which had inspired her always to do the odd things. He had always told her that he was sorry he had named her Lajwanti, which means sensitive plant, because she had lived up to her name. Indu pushed a cup of water into the bird's cage. And lo! the maina began to talk.

'Lajo, what does she say?' the boy asked. Lajwanti smiled, even as she looked at the torrid sky.

After her father returned from the well, he tied the buffalo and put what cattle food Indu had chopped up, before the animal. As the boy had not cut enough, he took the chopper and began to prepare more. He was not the kind to scold anyone, and least of all did he want to blame his son for getting excited about his elder sister.

When the buffalo had been looked after, he proceeded to soak the lentils for the evening meal and to light the fire.

'I will do all that, Bapu,' Lajwanti said.

'Daughter, it does not matter,' he answered and stubbornly went on with the chores. And, turning to his son, he said, 'Give your sister a mat to sit on.'

Imperceptible as were his feelings behind the mask of his calm wrinkled face, she saw a pallor on his lips as he said this, and she knew that she was not wanted. That mat was only given to guests.

The courtyard was filled with shadows long before the fire in the sky became ashes. Lajwanti could see the clouds tinted red as though the world had witnessed some gruesome murder.

And, frightened of her own self, she tried to hold her breath.

'Sister, I have brought you a pitcher of water to bath with,' Indu said.

Before Lajwanti could answer, Moti had been disturbed by her brother's voice and awakened, whining.

Lajwanti leaped forward to her and embraced the child, consoling her.

'Lajo,' her father said, 'the children want a mother. And I would have kept you here and not given you away if people had not begun to talk about you . . .' He paused after this statement for a long time, and then after blowing at the hearth fire, he continued, 'Now, I am both father and mother to them . . . And, as for you, I will take you back to your parents-in-law's house. I shall fall at their feet and ask them to forgive you. The disgrace of your widowhood without your becoming a widow is unbearable . . . They will only call you ugly names here. They do not know that you are "sensitive plant" . . .'

Two days later, a postcard came addressed to Shri Hari Ram, father of Lajwanti, written by Jaswant, on behalf of his father, saying, that as Lajwanti had run away, without permission from her husband or her parents-in-law, the clothes she had brought on her wedding were being returned and that no one in Delhi was now willing to see her 'black face'.

Old Hari had already been trying to arrange for someone to look after his buffalo, his son and his daughter, so that he could take Lajwanti back to her parents-in-law. He had sent for the midwife, who had delivered all these children, from Pataudi proper, because he did not know anyone in the small village who would oblige without the payment of some cash.

Fortunately, the midwife Champa arrived on the same morning after the postcard was received. And she was more than willing to take on the job of looking after the household.

'Why,' she said, 'I had hoped to see our Lajo with belly. And I had waited to be called to her bedside to deliver her of a son. And, now, my loved one, you are here, without a sign in your eyes of the coming of the happy event . . . If only for the sake of the soul of your dear mother, go, hurry back. And come soon with your lap full of a child.

'I am putting my turban at your feet,' said old Hari Ram to Chaudhri Ganga Ram, literally removing his enormous crown of cloth from his head and placing it on the shoes of his daughter's father-in-law.

'Oh, come and sit here with me,' answered Chaudhri Ganga Ram, brushing the bedstead with his left hand as he smoked the hookah under the shade of a neem tree.

Lajwanti crouched a little way away, with her face covered by her headcloth and averted her gaze from her father-in-law towards the torrid fields. Her heart was in her mouth, lest her brother-in-law, Jaswant, might suddenly appear from the barn, or even her mother-in-law, come on the scene suddenly before the father-in-law had forgiven her. At the same time, she knew that there would be no forgiveness, but only a reluctant nod to indicate that she could stay.

The nod of approval was, however, long in coming. For Chaudhri Ganga Ram kept silent, after having lifted Hari Ram to sit by him, and only his hookah spoke a little agitatedly.

Meanwhile, Lajwanti felt the sweat gathering on the nape of her head and flowing down her spine. And she looked at her blessed Maina in the cage to see if the bird was not dead. The journey had been easier this time, because they had come by bus from Pataudi to Gurgaon and then caught the connection from Gurgaon to the bus stop half a mile away from the little village of her father-in-law. And as the bird seemed still, she spoke to her in wordless words, 'My Maina, tell me what will happen now? My heart flutters, as you often do when you are frightened of the cat coming to eat you. And I do not know if Jaswant will relent and not pursue me any more. But perhaps now that my father has brought me back, I will allow myself to be eaten. Only the humiliation will be complete now. Oh, if only I had warmed to him and not thought of my own man who would never have known! . . . I am really defeated. And words are of no use . . . And yet within me there is desire, and there is life—a river of feelings like the ancient Saraswati river which has gone underground and disappeared from the surface . . . How shall I control those feelings, those prisoners, trying to burst out . . .'

She opened her eyes to make sure.

The vision was real.

Involuntarily, her eyes closed and a sigh got muffled into the folds of her headcloth. Sparks like stars shot out of the darkness of her head, and the agitation of nerves pushed up a copious sweat all over her. She knew that the constellations in the sky above her were ominous.

'So the dead one has turned up!' the mother-in-law's voice came, as the old woman returned from the well with one pitcher on her head and another one on her left arm. The heavy breathing of the woman, forced to fetch and carry and do all the chores in the absence of Lajwanti, accented her voice with bitterness.

'She is your daughter,' said old Hari Ram to appease the woman. In his innocence he imagined that the proverbial mother-in-law had become the cause of his daughter's flight. 'I have brought her back . . . The midwife, Champa, said that the girl has made a mistake . . .'

'To be sure,' answered the mother-in-law. 'There was no question, since Balwant has not been back from kalej for more than a few days at a time . . . Unless she has cast the spell of her grey eyes on someone else. Jaswant says he has seen her winking at the visitors on the roadside . . .'

'We are respectable people,' said Chaudhri Ganga Ram to reinforce his wife's speech.

'I . . . what shall I say, Chaudhriji,' answered Hari Ram meekly. 'I wish fate had made her not so good-looking . . . But, now, I have brought her back. And you can kill her if she looks at another . . . Here is a ring for my son Balwant. I could not give much dowry. Now I will make up a little for what the boys did not get . . .'

From the wearisome acceptance of her fate, there swirled up incomprehensible violent urges of truth in Lajwanti, so that she shook a little and was on the point of telling them the horrible facts. And she was mad at her father for effacing himself and bowing before her in-laws. But the tremors in her entrails ended in choking her throat. And the lofty flights of anger only befogged her brain.

'Jaswant! Jaswant! . . . Come over here . . .' the mother-in-law called her eldest son.

The scarecrow in the field turned round. Then he lifted the palm of his hand to see. He understood. And he began to walk back.

In the silence of doom, Lajwanti quivered as though the demons of hell had let loose snakes and scorpions on her body. And, in a fit of crazy abandon, she felt herself borne from the underworld, on a bed, by her heroic husband, his arms wrapped around her . . . Actually, beneath the trembling flesh, she knew Balwant to be a coward, who dare not even raise his head to look at his elder brother.

'She has come back!' Jaswant ground the words in his mouth, throwing the white radishes away on the ground near the outdoor kitchen.

'She could not tell you that she wanted to see the midwife,' old Hari Ram said. 'It was a false alarm.'

'There are midwives here also!' Jaswant answered pat. 'Why, there is the Safdarjung Hospital! . . .' Do not be taken in by her stories, uncle. She has looked at more than one before her marriage. She is just a bad girl! . . . The way she insulted me when I went to fetch her back. She sat there, answering back! And allowed that afsar's wife to slap me on the face! Prostitute!'

'Bus! Bus! Son!' Chaudhri Ganga Ram said to restrain the boy.

'Take that for having me beaten!' Jaswant said and kicked Lajwanti on her behind.

'Jaswant!' his mother shouted.

Lajwanti quivered, then veered round, almost doubled over, and uttered a shrill cry before beginning to sob.

'You deserve a shoe-beating!' shouted Jaswant, towering over the girl like an eagle in a malevolent glee of power, his arms outstretched as though he was going to hit her again.

'Come away!' shouted his father.

'Let him punish her if he thinks she has done wrong,' said Hari Ram. 'And let her fall at his feet. My daughter is pure.'

After saying this he felt pangs of remorse at his own cowardice and he was caught in the paroxysm of a dry throated cough, and water filled his eyes.

'Maina, my Maina,' Lajwanti said under her breath. I cannot bear this . . .'

'Deceitful cunning witch!' Jaswant said and he turned towards her father. 'Take her away. We have no use for her here! After she has disgraced us before the whole brotherhood . . .'

'Not so many angry words, son!' Chaudhri Ganga Ram said. 'You have punished her enough!'

'Son, let her get up and work!' mother-in-law said.

'Bless your words of wisdom!' said Hari Ram. 'I knew you would be merciful . . . And now I leave her in your care. Kill her if you like. But don't let her come to me without her lap full of a son. I shall not be able to survive the disgrace if she comes again.'

'Maina, my Maina, who will talk to you if I go away forever?' Lajwanti asked the bird in the cage even as she washed her with palmsful of water from the bucket.

The bird fluttered wildly evading the shower.

'Will you shriek if I drown you in the water, my little one?' Lajwanti asked.

The bird edged away as though in answer.

And she sat down on the ledge of the well, away from the surging waters which were all around her dizzy brain.

If she stopped to think, she felt she would never do it . . . It was now or never, when there was no one on the well except herself and the maina. The village women had finished fetching the water for the evening. And soon it would be dark—

From where she sat, a tilt—that would do it.

But no. She must not wait any more.

And with a jerk of her torso, interrupted by her indecision, she forced herself into a heave.

The fall was ugly. Her left shoulder hit the stone on the side before she fell sideways into the well. She sank to the bottom.

But, in a second, she felt her body rising up as though from its own momentum. Unfortunately for her, she was a swimmer. She could not decide to let go of her breath. And now, her hand pushed up above the water. And she found herself using her arms to keep afloat.

Still there was a chance.

Rising from the torso, she ducked down, with her nose tweaked between her fingers.

She stayed under the water for a minute and then tried to drown herself by letting go of her hand from the tweaked nose.

The head rose above the water, panting for breath.

'Lajwanti! Lajwanti! Bad one—come out!' her mother-in-law's voice came in a shrill appeal. 'This is not the way of respectable people . . .'

There was no way by which Lajwanti could put her head into the water. Perhaps she really did not want to die. How had the old woman turned up? Because, left to herself, she would have gone under with a second or third try. Not even in the darkness was there an escape . . . Above the well, life would be a worse hell than ever before . . .

Gently, she let go. And then water began to fill her nostrils and her mouth. And she was submerged.

Before she had lost consciousness, however, she felt herself lying down in the slush near the well.

They were pressing her belly. Someone was sitting on her. And the spurts of water oozed from her nostrils and mouth. The rancid taste of stale air was on her palate—the taste of life's breath.

And as she lay dissolving under her heavy eyelids, the bitterness of her breath seemed to lapse, and sleep shaped her eyes into a fixed stare.

And yet, within a moment, more water had come up through her nose and mouth.

And, within her, she could hear her foolish, tormented heart pounding away.

And then the drowsy eyelids opened. And she could see the maina in the cage by her.

'Alas,' she said in wordless words, above the ache of the head and the thumping of the heart, 'there is no way for me. I am condemned to live . . .'

A Dog's Life

On the edge of the road, under the shadow of one branch of a pipal tree, in range of the smell of food in the free kitchen run by Bhendi Bazaar of Bombay, sat a mangy dog, spotted black and white, but with his hair eaten away here and there by the itch, so that one could not look at him without disgust.

I had passed by several times, with almost averted eyes, which are partially guilty of looking and partially ashamed not to look and see.

One day, as I met an acquaintance and had to stop under the shade of the pipal tree to talk to him, I noticed that Spotty, as I instinctively called him, wagged his long tail at me gracefully, upturned his eyes with a most pathetic appeal, and waited to see if I would take notice of him. In spite of my revulsion against his nearly leprous skin, I smiled, bent away from my acquaintance, and whistled to the dog.

Spotty did not need any encouragement to arise from where he lay and come near me. But, seeing that I had reverted to my original stance of conversation, he lay down again, brushing the earth with another sweep of his tail, maybe to attract my eyes.

At that juncture, a stall-keeper, who was selling beads ten yards away to possible tourists, shouted, 'Hat, sala!'

And Spotty got up, looked at me for help, and then slunk away to his first position.

Unfortunately for him, a young boy on a cycle drove past and, out of a sheer sense of mischief, loosened a kick at Spotty with his left foot, which did not hurt the dog but sent him yelping for the fear of being hurt. And now he stood desolately on the road, looking this side and that.

The shout of a riksha-wallah bearing a fat man and a lean woman on his vehicle again sent Spotty back to his original location.

I dislocated myself from my acquaintance and began proceeding towards the temple. Sensing a streak of sympathy in the second look that I had given him, Spotty followed, a safe distance away.

A beggar who sat at the gateway of the shrine saw in the dog a possible rival and lifted his staff to the accompaniment of the foulest abuse.

I did not enter the temple, but thought that I would go to my room, get a few biscuits and appease my conscience. As I about-turned, Spotty seemed to understand that I was inclined to be kind to him and waited a few yards away for me to note the direction of my advance.

Actually, I was undecided. I had really intended to go and see the manager of the free kitchen about securing a ration card for an old man who did not belong to Bodh Gaya, but had come to work here and then lost his job as he was not a local. And I had begun to think of fetching biscuits for Spotty.

With duty to humans first, I changed my direction and made towards the free kitchen, condescending to smile at Spotty as a gesture of ultimate practical goodwill.

The dog followed me devotedly at some distance, wagging his tail the while, almost as though he understood my noble intentions.

As I got to the door of the tent of the free kitchen, I regretted my decision to come here first, because Spotty would never be allowed to enter it.

I turned around and could not see him.

I felt a fool to be engaged in these irrelevant, indecisive thoughts and acts. And yet I persisted in tracing him.

Before long I heard a yelp, a howl, and a protracted series of 'choon choon' from the directions of the tent, and then saw the Gurkha watchman chasing Spotty with his uplifted lathi.

Before I could stop the man from clubbing the dog, the watchman dealt a free blow and caught Spotty on his behind.

The dog ran with more yelps and frantic cries. 'Don't,' I shouted at the watchman.

The Gurkha turned back, swaggering, sweating and pleased at the successful hit on the target.

I went towards Spotty and saw that he was making an effort to wag his tail at me, but could not because the spine of his hind part was broken. With large, painshot eyes, and twisted body, he lay down, choon-chooning, then raising his voice again to shriek and later subsided with a moan.

I conquered my disgust and pushed him away with my right foot into the relative shade of a hedge. Then I thought of those biscuits which I had meant to fetch for him—and now water. Obviously, Spotty's instinctive greed for the free kitchen food he had smelt had taken him from behind me towards the tent and the Gurkha had spotted him and swooped down on him. It had all happened in a split second.

I paid a rupee to the beggar at the gate of the temple and borrowed his bowl, which I filled at the temple pump. And I brought it to Spotty's mouth.

The dog lapped up the water hastily.

I then returned the bowl to the beggar, afraid that he might suspect I had put it to a dog's mouth, and quickly went to my room to fetch some biscuits.

On the way home, I wondered what I could do for the incapacitated dog. There was no veterinary surgeon in Bodh Gaya. And I was in rented quarters, where a pariah dog would hardly be accepted. I was beginning to know myself as a vascillating, do-gooding, vague man of sentiment, with no real capacity for suffering in the service of my fellowmen, not to speak of dogs.

I brought the biscuit carton and emptied it before Spotty.

Although he was badly hurt and exhausted by the pain, he had been hungry for days and greedily assailed the biscuits. I left in order to avoid seeing the dog gorging on them.

The next day I found that Spotty had dragged himself to his location under the pipal tree and sat there almost as though he was waiting for me. He could not wag his tail, but stirred it and moaned, moving his eyeballs in a manner which showed both gratitude and expectation.

I had hardly reached him to scrutinize his wound, when the beggar from the temple door, who was sitting on the plinth of the pipal tree, shouted, 'You have spoiled my religion by giving the dog water in my bowl—I was told so by the stall-keeper that you—'

'That is true!' I said guiltily. 'I will pay you for a new bowl.'

And I walked up to Spotty and threw some biscuits before him.

As soon as the beggar saw me offer food to the dog, he raced up from the plinth and kicked Spotty.

The blow fell exactly on the spot where the Gurkha's staff had broken the dog's back.

'Hat, sala!' the beggar shouted and dealt one final blow with his staff on Spotty's head. The tender eyes of the dog smiled their last look of horror and were covered with the blood of the broken skull.

Somehow the sight of the blood of the dog inspired the beggar to greater fury against his rival and he belaboured Spotty with more blows.

My head reeled at the bloodshed and my neck was sweating from the confusion of helplessness, chagrin and anger.

Overpowering as was the interest which bound me to the animal, I turned away, unable to look at the mess that poured out of his cranium.

I tried to rationalize my turning away by thinking that, through the cruelty of the beggar, I had myself been freed from the unbearable responsibility of looking after the dog, of my hope for its life, which I had half wanted to save, if only I could find some ways and means to do so, and which I did not want to save because, at the best, he would drag his hind legs about for the rest of his sordid existence.

As I passed by the pipal tree in the late afternoon of the same day, my eyes awakened from the after-effects of the siesta to a new and strange vision. A great big vulture, looking like the high priest of the nearby temple, was sitting on the corpse of the dog, as though presiding on the death ceremony of Spotty, after it had eaten up all the flesh and entrails, leaving the skeleton intact.

I saw that the tail of the dog was almost intact, and lay in the curve in which it had first wagged at me.

I pillaged, with a sort of cold rage, the wreckage of my soft feelings for the curve of that tail, as it had swayed when the pariah first greeted me.

Fear of Fear

Grovelling in the dust, the corners of his mouth dribbling a mixture of saliva and earth, his cheeks swollen with sobs, his tunic and pyjama sodden with sweat, Dev lay near the doorstep of the hut in the lane, almost as though he was doing 'Dharna' against his parents.

As soon as he heard some footsteps, he would move from sobs into loud weeping, so as to draw attention and gain sympathy. Otherwise, he dozed in between the sobs and sobbed in between the dozing.

'Son,' his mother said, as she came for the fifth time to reconcile him, 'come and eat—I have garnished the dal with oil and onions . . . Come, my son . . .'

He shook his head and whined, 'Go away—I don't want that dal— always, every day, you give me dal! . . . Go, burn it! . . . Hai . . . I don't want that dal!'

His father, the schoolmaster passed by, and, seeing him recalcitrant, in spite of the mother's appeals, kicked him, saying, 'I will fetch the cane from the school and skin you, if you don't get up and eat the food. It is difficult enough to buy dal and rice nowadays on my pay. Swine, you want—ambrosia!'

At midday, the drama repeated itself. Dev still sobbed and slept amid his sulks. His mother spoke soft words every hour. His father promised dire consequences.

In the evening, in between the sulks, Dev writhed as though the rats of hunger were gnawing inside him; he wailed every now and then a hiccupy wail against 'Beastly father!'—'Bullock!' 'Tyrant!' And he pronounced shrill shrieks against 'Widow—mother!' And he sisked in strange murmurs, his breath uttering ejaculations as though he was going to utter the last breath rattle. His clothes were now soiled with the grains of the nearby drain.

As the hour of cow-dust came and the neighbours who wanted to bring their cattle home advised him to get up lest he might be crushed by the beasts, he was possessed by a trembling fit as he lay and rolled in the lane.

The fear possessed him so that he became silent. And, in the silence, he felt more frightened of the father's cane. And, in the grip of the obsession, he felt mysterious murderous impulses rise in his sides, dangerous swirls of wrath against his father, which combined hatred and revenge, till he burst now and then into hysterical loud shrieks which brought the villagers to the scene.

Lying there like that, stubborn, full of wild impulses, of which he did not know the cause, he prayed, 'Hai Ma, save me!'

And yet, when the mother came to lift him, he refused to get up. He was feeling what he had never felt before, sensing things he had never touched, possessed by a brain fever that overwhelmed him. There was no more liquid in his eyes for tears, no breath for sisking or wailing or shrieking, no energy even to change his position.

At last, he heard his father approach. He imagined there was the swish of the cane. Certainly, there were cruel words of abuse, 'Wretched! Get up, or I will skin you!'

Clenching his teeth, breathing sharply from the echo of deep rumblings in his belly, the back of his head athrob, he got up and sprang upon his father, digging his nails into the old man's face, thrusting his head into the hollows of his progenitor's chest, like a wild goat.

'Oh! Oh! . . . Oh swine!' the father shouted.

The neighbours tore the son away from the father.

Convulsed, astonished at himself kicking everyone, furiously fisticuffing the interventionists, Dev was carried to the feet of his embarrassed mother.

She took him in her lap as she had done when he was a child.

Weeping, he fell asleep there.

A Select Glossary

Abhi	Right now
Acha	All right
Amrapali	A classical heroine of India
Angithi	Portable clay vessel for lighting fire for cooking
Aoji	Come
Ayaji	Coming
Bahin-chod	A swear word. Literally, rape-sister
Beti-chod	A swear word. Literally rape-daughter
Bhut	Evil spirit, ghost
Bonnee	First auspicious sale of the day
Bus	That's enough, stop
Cain-cain	Idle chatter, noise
Chalo	Let's go
Chowki	Police station
Chulha	Fireplace for cooking
Chup kar	Keep quiet
Dharti	Earth
Dholki	Musical drum
Dhup	Incense
Dohai	An exclamation demanding 'justice'
Durbar Sahib	The Sikh Golden Temple
Ferungi	European; literally foreigner
Gandu	A swear word. Literally, homosexual
Gari	Vehicle

Gora	A person belonging to the White race
Grihasta	Second stage of life dealing with social and family obligations
Hai	Exclamation indicating despair, surprise
Hain	A surprise query, meaning 'really?'
Han	Yes
Hat	Move, get out
Hosh kar	Attention, beware
Ja	Go
Jagirdar	The holder of a hereditary assignment of land
Jemadar	Head servant; generally subaltern officer in the Indian Army
Kaka	A child, a young boy
Kalej	College
Kaliyug	The present age; according to Hindus, the age before the end of the world
Kanjus	Miserly
Kisan Sabha	A peasant movement which gained political status
Kutchery	Courthouse
Lakhpati	One who has a hundred thousand rupees
Lalla	Hindu gentleman, generally of the merchant class
Loo	Hot winds preceding the monsoons
Madar-chod	A swear word. Literally, rape-mother
Mai–bap	Mother–father
Nahin	No
Narsinghas	Large horns
Nazarana	A ceremonial gift, a votive offering

Paltan	Army
Poorbia	Person from upper India
Rabba	God
Rais	Indian gentleman holding high position, a chief
Sahukar	Moneylender, banker
Sala/salé	Brother-in-law, used sometimes as a term of abuse
Sali	Sister-in-law, used sometimes as a term of abuse
Sambhalenga	Will look after
Shiva-Shakti	All-pervading divine energy
Subedar	A local chief officer; a junior army officer
Sur ka bacha	Son of a pig
Takla	Small spindle
Tehmet	Loincloth
Tehsildar	A revenue officer of a sub-division of a district
Thanedar	Sub-inspector of police
Toba! Toba!	Shame! Shame!
Tola	An Indian weight measurement
Uth	Get up
Vakil	Lawyer
Vay	Punjabi form of address for a male
Vilayat	Foreign country, usually designates British Isles
Yekka	A two-wheel horse carriage, inferior to a tonga